ON THE ROPES

KATHRYN NOLAN

That's What She Said Publishing, Inc.

Copyright © 2021 Kathryn Nolan

All Rights Reserved

This is a work of fiction. Names, characters, places, and incidents either are the products of the author's imagination or are used fictitiously. Any resemblance to actual persons, living or dead, businesses, companies, events, or locales is entirely coincidental.

Editing by Faith N. Erline
and Jessica Snyder
Cover by Kari March
Photo: ©Regina Wamba

ISBN: 978-1-945631-80-1 (ebook)
ISBN: 978-1-945631-81-8 (paperback)

093021

For those who take up space, demanding attention and justice in the face of larger forces trying to make them silent or invisible. Here's to loving loudly and proudly.

And for Philly. This jawn's for you.

A QUICK NOTE FROM KATHRYN

ON THE ROPES is a friends-to-lovers romance. It's flirty, steamy, and extra adorable. However, I did want to mention that this story touches on a few topics that may be sensitive to some readers, including healing from a concussion, racism toward a family member and homophobia/biphobia. It occurs mostly off the page (and is not graphic).

ONE

DEAN

I leaned back against the wall outside my neighborhood bar and called the same damn number for the tenth time this week. I knew the recorded message by heart now: *Thank you for calling the City of Philadelphia's after-hours hotline. Please listen to the following menu of options.*

I tipped my head back and hit 5. It was supposed to send me to a cheerful operator who would help with my "property emergency." All I'd ever gotten was an endless phone tree maze. I scowled, turned my head as the automated music filled my ear.

It was a hot July night in South Philly. People were either drinking beer on their front stoops or drinking beer in the bar behind me. The sound of the baseball game filtered out onto the block.

Thank you for your patience. We are experiencing longer than usual wait times.

I caught the attention of two guys walking across the street, still in their suits from whatever job they had uptown. What they were doing in this neighborhood, I had no fucking clue. Their watches flashed, their suits looked tailored. Even their teeth looked too white. I probed the back right of my jaw where two of my own were missing. A consequence of going nine rounds with Ricky Hernandez when I was nineteen years old.

I pressed the phone hard against my ear as they whispered to each other. Their wariness was obvious, even from here. People gave me a wide berth in this neighborhood. It didn't matter if I was just on the phone, standing on a street corner.

I was still Dean the Machine even if I was a quitter.

A rough-sounding voice suddenly came through. "Yeah, this is Fred. What's the emergency with your city property?"

I shifted on my feet, startled someone had finally picked up. "Uh...sorry. I've been calling about a vacant lot on my block. The one at Tenth and Emily. City tore down my neighbor's house a year ago. It's just been sittin' there."

Fred coughed. "Okay. And?"

"And...I want to know what the city plans on doing with it. 'Cause right now everyone on my street has to live with an abandoned lot that's turning into a neighborhood dump."

There was grumbling. Some clicking noises. "I don't know what to tell ya, pal. Based on what I'm seeing here, there's no movement. And no interest."

"No interest in what?"

"Doin' anything about it."

I raked a hand through my hair. "So, the city wants...what? A trash heap filled with rats on a block with kids running around?"

Fred made a frustrated sound. "I don't know what this city wants, okay? I'm just the guy who reads the reports, and this report right in front of me, on my computer, is saying they wanna let it sit there."

My shoulders twitched. My right hand curled into a fist. Uncurled, slowly. "What do we do in the meantime?"

There was a beeping sound and a few rustling papers. "I don't really know, and it's not really my problem. No offense."

"Okay," I said through gritted teeth. I'd spent the past week glaring at the empty space on our street. Being in a boxing ring was awful on a good day and absolutely brutal on a bad. But at least I knew how to handle my opponent. How to get what I wanted from him.

Now I couldn't even get some underpaid city employee to listen to me.

"Hey," Fred said. "The zip code for this lot. It's where I grew up too." His voice dropped. "I'm only saying this because I'm guessing you and me went to the same school. But I ain't ever seen this city move fast to clean up anything in that zip code. Have you?"

I looked down at my running shoes. The sidewalk was cracked. Uneven. "No."

"What's your name, by the way?"

I hesitated. I wasn't in the mood. "Dean," I said. "Dean Knox-Morelli."

He barked out a laugh. "Are you shittin' me?"

"I am not."

"Me and the guys used to watch you down at Snyder's Tavern, off Oregon Ave. You know it, right?"

It was one of the bars in the city with a dedicated following of boxing fans. Place was packed for every match. It used to be I could walk in there any night of the week and drink for free. I wasn't welcome there anymore.

"Used to know it, yeah," I said.

"How long has it been since you quit?" he asked.

My shoulder muscles twitched again. "I retired three years ago."

"Huh," Fred said. "Time flies. You were really somethin' else in that ring. But I guess you already know that."

"Yeah, thanks," I mumbled.

I got all kinds of responses from fans who had opinions on my early retirement from professional boxing. Sometimes fans like Fred were the hardest. The wistful ones. Like I was already a has-been, and they were sad *for* me about it.

"Listen." His voice dropped even lower. "Take this from a, uh, friend from around the way. But with what this city is facing in terms of fixing up vacant lots, they're not in a rush. I don't think they'll care at all what you do with it. Clean it up, put it to good use? If they come knocking five years from now and you've basically done their job for them, for *free*, they won't be complaining. You get what I'm saying?"

I spotted Rowan on the corner. I raised a hand in greeting. "You think we should fix it ourselves?"

"Exactly. I gotta go take the next call, but it was a real honor chatting with one of the greats. My buddies aren't gonna believe it."

I winced as my best friend reached me. "Thank you for your...advice."

"God bless, and go Birds," he said and then hung up.

Rowan cocked a lopsided grin my way before clapping me twice on the shoulder. "Are you about to punch something, big guy?"

I slipped my phone back into my pocket. Shoved open the door. "I'll tell you at the bar."

It was darker inside. Cooler. Two giant TVs displayed the bottom fifth inning of the Phillies game. Benny's Bar hadn't allowed smoking in years, but there was still a whiff of it in the air. An angry slew of curse words went up—directed at the pitcher on the screen—as Rowan and I moved through the tables to the stools.

The bartender gave me a nod of recognition. I held up two fingers, and he sent Yuenglings our way. Rowan perched on the edge of his stool, legs spread, elbow propped up as he took a swig. Rowan O'Callaghan had been my friend since we were four years old. He'd grown up next door to me, living with his grandmother Alice. Like so many others, her family had moved from Ireland to this part of Philadelphia when she was a little girl. Her accent was as strong as ever. Even Rowan picked it up a bit when he was around her.

Rowan and I had grown up together, gone to school together. Were brothers more than anything else. While I got pulled into boxing, he was a baseball player who'd gotten drafted into the minor leagues right out of high school. He'd even been called up to the majors before he blew out his shoulder. If anyone understood the pain and frustration of a career-ending injury, it was him. He was almost as tall as I was, rangy and too confident, with dark red hair and pale skin.

I narrowed my eyes at him. "What's that smile for?"

"I'm in a good mood 'cause I had a great date."

I glanced at the clock on the wall. It was past 8:00. "Did you leave her somewhere?"

He smirked. "The date started at eight *last* night. And that's why I'm smiling."

My eyebrows shot up. "You like her?"

He lifted a shoulder. "I liked having fun with her. She was looking for the same kind of thing, so it worked out."

I sipped my beer and sniffed. Dating was always easy for Rowan.

He tapped my knee. "Who was on the phone?"

"The city," I said. "Finally got through to someone about Annie's old place. The guy said the city doesn't have any plans for it. He told me on the sly that we should fix the damn thing ourselves."

He scoffed into his beer. "Figures."

Out of the corner of my eye, I saw a loud table of local guys sharing a pitcher. I thought I heard my name.

"You could do it though."

I tapped the side of my beer and looked at the TV instead of Rowan. "What do you mean?"

"You've got some extra time on your hands," he said. "If you started cleaning it out yourself, you don't think everyone on that block wouldn't come help?"

My hackles wanted to go up at the mention of my extra free time right now. But it was Rowan. He was only saying a nicer version of the words I heard in my head every day: *You retired from pro boxing three years ago. You haven't moved on, and news flash? You're not doing shit.*

Didn't mean I was ready to carry the weight of people's expectations again. No matter how minor.

"I don't think so," I said.

"What if I helped you?"

"You've got a lot going on right now. You don't need one more project."

Rowan was one of the coordinators at the rec center in our neighborhood. He was trying to get a food delivery program for seniors off the ground. It was hard work. Long hours.

But now he was shrugging again. "So we organize a few cleanup days? Come up with a plan for what would replace the mound of stinking trash? Doesn't seem so bad to me."

"What would we replace it with?" I asked, curious.

"I don't know. A fucking tree? It'd be nice to have one of those around."

I rubbed my jaw. He wasn't wrong. Our neighborhood wasn't known for its *green space* or whatever. I'd only been thinking about getting rid of what was there. Not what would come after.

I shook my head. "I know what you're doing. I'm still a *no*."

He stretched his arms out wide. "And what am I doing?"

I shot him a look. He chuckled, sipped his beer. I wasn't a kid who looked for trouble growing up. Especially not after finding boxing at thirteen. Except I had a best friend with *Trouble* as his middle name. This whole song-and-dance routine was as familiar to me as the squeaky sixth step on my old staircase. The one I'd had to avoid when Rowan would convince me to sneak out.

He nudged me with his elbow. "Will you think about it?"

He knew I'd do more than think. I'd overthink. "Maybe. I still want to push the city to do its job though."

"I'll take it."

There was a burst of noise from behind us. The rowdy table with the pitcher. They definitely said my name this time, loud enough for half the bar to hush.

"Ignore 'em," Rowan said. He waved the bartender over for a second beer. "Besides, this very pretty lady at the end of the bar has been trying to get your attention the entire time."

My gut twisted. Throw me in the ring with some bare-knuckled brawler and I didn't bat an eye. Because I could study fight tapes for hours. Train until I could barely stand after. Mental preparedness was how I won, every single time.

Dating was the mystery to me. And Rowan was basically a walking version of a fight tape but for women. He'd done his best since we were teenagers to impart his knowledge, and every time it was like he was speaking a different language.

I waved off what he said. "Are you sure she's not trying to get your attention?"

"Nope. Believe me, she's gunning for Dean the Machine over here. Do you want me to head home so you can go say hi?"

I felt my face go hot. "Um...no. It's okay."

Only Rowan and my parents could get away with using

that old nickname with affection. The papers used to say a glare from Dean the Machine could strip paint from the walls—and that my hits were so precise they weren't human. Like I was a robot.

"It's the middle of summer," he said. "The perfect time to have some casual fun. And just to be clear, I'm talking about fucking. Easy, casual fucking."

I snorted. "Say it a little louder. I don't think Father O'Sullivan heard you across the way."

Rowan's smile was devious. "Father O'Sullivan would be very disappointed with some of my actions recently."

It was true. And Rowan was the king of whatever easy, casual fun was. To me, that sounded like a minefield of miscommunication and hurt feelings. I had never been in love before, but it seemed like being serious was kind of the point.

At the height of my pro boxing career, there was a lot of interest in me from women when I went out. I'd had my fair share of one-night stands, where things like talking or being nervous didn't come up in the dark with a stranger you weren't gonna see again.

It scratched an itch. I didn't always feel that good about it afterward though.

"I'm still fine." I pushed my empty beer away from me. "And not interested."

The rowdy table at the back finally decided to start shit. We could hear them, drunkenly trying to get my attention. Benny's was small and crowded. As Rowan cursed beneath his breath, I tossed cash onto the table and knocked my knuckles against the bar top.

"Let's go," I said, clapping Rowan on the back. We weaved past crowds and out into the muggy summer night. The group followed, hot on our heels. This wasn't our first rodeo, so we hung a sharp left to cut across the street.

"Hey, Dean," a slurred voice called out. "Dean the Machine—that's you, isn't it?"

"Don't they know your fists are literally lethal weapons?" Rowan whispered.

He meant it as a joke. The potential for harm, however, was real. I'd worked hard the last three years to control my body's instincts to use my hands instead of walking away. Because guys like that—die-hard sports fans who believed I was the scourge of the earth because I'd let them down—only wanted to poke the bear and see what happened.

"*Deeeaaaaaaan*," the guy taunted. The block we walked down was free of kids, thankfully. But full of folks on their stoops or lawn chairs on the sidewalk, gossiping with their neighbors like they did every night.

If I hit this asshole, the whole neighborhood would know by dawn.

Rowan and I nodded as we passed houses, greeted a few people we knew. They were very aware of the tiny mob behind us, their eyes wide. I kept my body language loose. Comfortable. The second we turned onto 11th Street, in front of an old, boarded-up deli, a hand grabbed the back of my shirt and pulled.

I stopped. Rowan spun and said, "Come on, *man*."

I waited for the guy to release me. He didn't. His fingers tightened in the fabric. "My friends said I couldn't take *Dean the Machine himself*." I felt him wobbling. "But I said...*I said*... that piece of shit quit three *fucking years ago*. Pretty sure I could beat his ass."

"Chad, let him go."

"Yeah, Chad," Rowan said. "Listen to your friends over there. They seem smarter than you."

Chad yanked, but it was pointless. Being steady on my feet had been a requirement in my fighting days. As gently as I could, I reached behind and gripped his wrist. Squeezed, just a little. His fingers popped open.

"Hey, *watch it*—"

I turned on my heel. Chad was red faced, swaying, and about a foot shorter than I was. Drunken bravado had his right fist sailing sloppily toward the middle of my chest. I caught it midair and stepped into his space. He audibly gulped.

"I don't fight anymore," I said firmly. "I won't be fighting you either. Now go home."

"You scared?"

Behind me, Rowan started laughing. Even Chad's friends were starting to shift uncomfortably on their feet.

"Not at all," I said.

"Then let's do this."

I released his fist with a grunt of frustration and stepped away. It was an almost monthly occurrence, the way guys like this felt the need to show me up after one too many beers. Turns out prioritizing your own health over winning a championship belt was never gonna sit well with this city I'd disappointed.

Chad huffed a half-laugh, half-hiccupping sound and charged me. My hand shot out, connected with his chest, and then I shoved him back against the brick wall of the deli. I didn't do it as hard as I could. I did it as softly as I could. He still flinched, and I felt bad about it.

Real fear flickered across his face.

Sometimes I had to meet their stupid intimidation tactics with my own to avoid an actual fight. I didn't like it. It wasn't in a ring. It wasn't regulated. There wasn't a ref or pads or gear. My body was a road map of injuries that never healed right, making my muscles and joints ache like I was forty-five and not twenty-five. I was overly cautious of inflicting that onto others. Even if Chad's boozy, smug face had me questioning my ethics.

"Knock it off," I snapped. I took a step closer. He gulped again. A *zap* of power shot up my spine. It was only a taste of how I used to feel. But it was enough to be confusing. I didn't want to feel that when I was being a bully. Problem was I didn't know how to feel it now that I couldn't fight. And I sure as hell hadn't found another way.

I let him go and rejoined Rowan. We didn't turn back around to engage. Didn't say a thing when Chad shouted, "*Next time, you asshole.*"

We walked in silence for a minute. Then Rowan said, "I know it sucks every fucking time."

"I'm used to it by now," I said. "It doesn't bother me."

That was a lie. And he knew it.

We hit the turn toward Emily Street, toward the giant trash heap I couldn't stop being mad about. As we passed people on stoops and kids running in packs, I tried to carry myself like I was still Dean the Machine, the pride of this city. A man to be revered and respected.

But the only stray glances our way I saw were full of sympathy.

And not the nice kind.

TWO

TABITHA

As the taxi pulled away, I hefted my bag onto my shoulders and faced the busy brightness of the Italian Market.

I stepped around people haggling over the prices of produce, iced trays of fish and clams, giant racks of beef hanging in windows. I dodged honking cars and trash cans lit with fires. I walked past clumps of tourists waiting in line for cheesesteaks, past locals speaking Italian, Spanish, and Mandarin. Tortillerias and taquerias sat cozy against shops selling pasta made fresh in the window.

Curving around Seventh Street, I turned down the block where my big sister lived. Kids raced past on the narrow streets on bikes. I waved to a few neighbors hosing down their front stoops and watering window boxes.

I hadn't been home for any real amount of time in more than nine years.

My phone buzzed with a text from my dad: *Are we a go, or what?*

I stopped on the sidewalk and grinned. *Almost there,* I sent back. *Hold your freaking horses.*

My sister's row home was red brick with light blue shutters and Juliet's chalk drawings decorating the sidewalk like a painted garden. I paused to study the green tendrils and rainbow-colored hearts spilling out across the pavement. Dropping my pack to the ground with a sigh of gratitude for my aching shoulders, I smiled again when I realized how much Juliet's drawings looked like Alexis's when we were little.

My smile faltered. Alexis had stopped coloring our stoop when our mom told her they were ugly. That it made our house look *trashy*.

"Pssst."

I looked up and immediately disregarded the memory. My dad was peeking through the front window looking like he'd just won the lottery.

"Go inside," I whispered, trying not to laugh. "You'll ruin it."

"I'm too excited," he whispered back.

Rolling my eyes, I wiped chalk from my knees and dragged my pack to prop it against the side of the house. As I crept up the stairs, I could hear an old Smokey Robinson song that was a family favorite, my stepmother Kathleen singing along. I didn't want to risk checking my appearance in the reflection of the window—besides, I knew I looked unwashed, rumpled, and sleep deprived after my red-eye from California.

I knocked three times. Stepped back with my hands to my mouth, hiding the squeal trying to get out.

I could hear Alexis as she approached. "...know who it is? Could be a package, I guess."

She pulled open the door. There was a dishrag over her shoulder and Cheerios in her short blond hair. And the moment she saw me, she screamed and jumped into my arms.

I threw my head back and cheered. I'd prepared for her to

do what she'd done since we were kids—leap onto her much taller little sister like a baby koala bear.

Alexis was shrieking, "What are you doing here, *what are you doing here?*" as I spun her around. Half the block came out to investigate, of course.

"Surprise," I said, hugging her tight. She slid down my body and took a step back, grabbing my arms like I was a mirage she worried might vanish.

"But we video chatted last night," she said.

"I *know*."

"You were at the airport and told me you were flying to Miami."

I winked. "I was *lying* to you the whole time."

Her eyes widened. "Because you were coming *here?*"

"You got it." I propped my hands on my hips. "I took a red-eye all the way from Sacramento. Dad and Kathleen helped me plan it."

I nodded at the man standing behind her in the doorway. He and I shared the same auburn hair, freckles, and dark brown eyes.

"Dad, you *sneak*," she said.

"Did you tell her the best part yet?" he asked.

We were interrupted by my stepmother, Kathleen, pushing past my dad and sweeping me into her arms.

"Hi, babe," I said, coughing a little at the strength of her hug. She and my father had remarried when I was in my early twenties. She was a *fierce* defender of her stepdaughters, my biggest champion, and my most ardent social media follower.

"I sent your last video to *everyone* in my book club, you know," she said in her low, expressive voice. "They loved it. They love you. They want you to come to our next meeting because they've never met a real live *internet celebrity* before."

Alexis and I shared an amused look. "Oh yeah? Sign me up. I'll give them all the hot gossip as long as they provide the alcoholic beverages. And don't care that I'm not actually an internet celebrity."

"Oh, the girls will be *so* excited. And we've been drinking something called *adult water ice* at book club, which is mostly tequila," she said, squeezing my hands with a happy smile. Kathleen was my father's age and came from a mixed Italian and Polish family. She had big, curly black hair; an addiction to hot-red lipstick; and glasses she wore on a chain around her neck.

And then she was turning and pushing me up the stairs while ordering my dad to make me a plate of breakfast and a cup of coffee. I pulled Alexis against my side for another hug. For sisters, we looked almost nothing alike—she'd inherited our mother's blond hair and blue eyes and had not a single freckle to her name.

"I'm so glad you're here," she said, sighing. "I miss you so much."

"How is that possible?" I said with a laugh. "We talk *every* single day."

"I know we do," she said with a sheepish smile. "But it's different when you're home. Don't you think?"

I kept the breezy grin on my face. The people in this house comprised the biggest fans of my scrappy career as a freelance videographer, always on the road. And we were in almost constant communication, from phone calls to video chats and a continual stream of text messages. When they wished I was home more—or home *permanently*—I didn't let it bother me. Because it didn't. And because they knew staying here wasn't my destiny.

"I think I love being around my family in all different

ways," I said lightly. "And that includes video calling you from the Las Vegas strip or showing you the sunset in the Grand Canyon."

Alexis wrinkled her nose. "Okay, that *is* pretty fun."

I squeezed her close. "But I hear you, and that's actually why I'm—"

"*Aunty Tabby is here.*"

The tiny force of nature that was my niece, Juliet, barreled into my midsection. I stooped down, hefted her up as she laughed.

"Is this my favorite person in the whole wide world?" I asked, kissing her cheek.

She pointed at her chest with a serious look. "It's me."

"It is you," I said with a wink. "And who taught you to call me Tabby? This is new."

My brother-in-law, Eric, stepped out of the kitchen. "Aren't you a sight for sore eyes." He grinned. "Aunty Tabby."

"*Ha*, so it *was* you."

"Kids these days," he said. "Who knows where they pick up annoying yet cherished nicknames for their aunts?"

"Mm-hmm," I smirked. I shifted Juliet higher on my hip as she began telling me a story from the day before and walked into their brightly lit kitchen. Their fridge hadn't changed much since my last micro visit except that even more of their daughter's art hung from an assortment of mismatched magnets. There were a few faded pictures of Alexis and Eric when they were younger; a few random postcards I still loved to send from the road; a happy picture from my graduation from UCLA, which was my dad's first time on an airplane.

Eric and Alexis had been together since their senior year of college at Temple University, and over the years he'd become more of a close friend than an in-law. He was a tall, broad-shouldered Black man with a shaved head and a perpetually kind expression. He and Alexis were both teachers at the public elementary school nearby—he taught kindergarten and Alexis taught third grade.

Juliet had a smile like Eric's and a laugh that sounded just like my sister's. She had thick, curly hair; light brown skin; and, at five years old, already loved dressing herself in mismatched patterns.

"Here, I'll take Juliet and you sit," Alexis said, indicating the small patio out back. "We can eat breakfast and catch up on your glamorous life."

I peeked at my jet-lagged appearance in the reflection of the toaster. "I don't know about the glamour part. But I can tell you all about the fun part."

Dad hauled my pack against the wall and brushed his hands together. "Is this all you got? No suitcases coming, right?"

We all trooped out to the patio. I sank back into a chair, tipped my head up toward the sun, and let out a huge, *I've been traveling for twelve hours straight* sigh of relief. "That's literally *all* that I've got. I still have that little storage unit in LA with some of my furniture and gear. But I only need my camera, my microphone, and my laptop." I nodded at the bulging pack. "And a whole lot of dirty laundry."

I was twenty-seven and knew from various social media accounts that my friends were pursuing the exact opposite path from the one I was wandering along—moving in with romantic partners, getting married, putting down roots in a million different ways.

At some point I'd have to get my shit together and stop living out of a backpack. Except just *thinking* about white picket fences and two-car garages tied my stomach into knots I wasn't sure how to unravel.

My sister plopped a giant plate of French toast, oozing

with syrup, directly in front of me. "I don't deserve you," I said and immediately shoved a giant bite into my mouth. "Oh my God, this is amazing."

"Well, it's your dad's recipe," Eric said, sitting down with his own plate. "I've just subtly perfected it over time."

My dad grinned. "You'll be comin' by the diner while you're home, right, Tab?"

"Long as you're cooking up chicken cheesesteaks," I said, taking another giant bite.

Alexis nudged me from under the table. "What's the deal? Are you only home for the weekend, or what? I thought after California you were supposed to be spending a few months in Key West."

Juliet handed me a piece of her breakfast.

"Why *thank you*," I said. To my sister, I waggled my eyebrows with every bit of dramatic flair I possessed. "How would you feel about me being back home for two whole weeks?

Dad and Kathleen shared a secretive smile. Alexis caught it.

"Wait, what?" She poked my dad in the arm. "You knew all about this, didn't you?"

"Your old man's still got a few tricks up his sleeve." His eyes were twinkling when they met mine. "Your sister told me some things with her next trip weren't gonna work out. And I happened to be dropping off some extra food from the restaurant at your aunt Linda's house when she called. You know Lin's down the shore every July no matter what."

"She offered me her place while she was gone," I added. "And I thought, why the hell not? I need something a little stable for a bit anyway while I hustle up my next few contracts and story ideas." I leaned over to kiss the top of Juliet's head.

"Now I get to spend the next two weeks with my favorite people."

"What happened with the Key West gig?" Eric asked.

I leaned back in the chair and sipped my coffee. "They got hit bad with early hurricanes, and the hotel I'd contracted with to produce their new tourism video is closed while they get things fixed up again. But that means for the first time in a while I'm kinda...in limbo."

And broke—but I was always broke. We didn't have a ton of money growing up so living on a frugal budget didn't bother me much. It was nice to have a free place to crash—especially since I didn't have anything lined up yet.

Freelancing paid my basic living expenses while I was traveling around the country, moving contract to contract. Tourism videos like the one I'd had lined up in Key West paid the best. And I worked with restaurants and small businesses and bigger corporations. But my *real* passion was filming stories about neighborhood activists or local nonprofits. Mural artists, street fairs, community gardens. All the fascinating ways people took care of one another, finding hope in even the darkest places.

"You know, you could make movies about *right here*." Kathleen tapped the table twice as she said this. "Take your camera down the street, and you'd have something interesting by dinner time."

"I don't doubt it," I said.

Alexis propped her chin in her hands. "If you're here for a while..."

"Yeah, maybe," I hedged but followed it with a wide grin. "Or *maybe* I just hang around you all day, annoying the hell out of you until you beg me to get back on the road."

Kathleen grabbed my hand. The sincerity on her face tightened my throat. "Honey, that is not possible."

"It's good to know that when Alexis can no longer stand me, I'll have safe harbor with you, the book club, and that adult water ice."

My sister gasped. "You're such a little liar. We only ever annoyed each other that one year, right, Dad?"

He looked up from his plate. "The year you two were twelve and fifteen is a year that will haunt me to an early grave."

Eric chuckled as he sipped his coffee. "Oh, this is a year that lives in infamy, to hear Alexis tell it."

"Because they were a nightmare," Dad said, though his words lacked heat.

"Oh my God, *so dramatic*," Alexis said with an eye roll. "We weren't that horrible."

Dad's eyebrows shot up in response.

I smirked. "There were nights when you and I were arguing so much, you would take your dinner upstairs and eat it away from me because you couldn't *freaking stand looking at my freaking face*. A direct quote."

Alexis dropped her head into her hands with a groan. "Okay, *yes*, I was a slightly dramatic teenager. But *you*, dear sister, were doing things like reading my journal, listening to my phone calls. You stole my curling iron and hid it, and that was my prized possession that year."

"You did love that curling iron," Dad mused with a sigh. "I sent your mother out late on a Friday night to buy you a new one because I asked Tabitha where she'd hid it." His lips twitched. "And she'd forgotten."

Eric threw his head back and laughed. "That makes this story even better."

I pressed my fingers to my lips. "I think it might be buried in the alley next to Mrs. Kozlowski's house."

"That thing was my one true love before this guy came

along," Alexis said, nodding at her husband. "But by the next year, it was as if it had never happened. And we've been inseparable ever since."

I smiled at my niece and wiped syrup from her cheek. "Even when we're far away."

Alexis squeezed my hand under the table three times, the sister code we developed the year after our sibling arguments ended and the simmering unhappiness between our parents erupted. The burst of high-pitched sounds, the never-ending back-and-forth, the anger and grief evident in every vowel and consonant. In a tiny row home, with almost no privacy, we had a front row seat to the end of our parents' marriage, even as Dad tried to protect us from it.

He wasn't the problem though. And it became obvious to Alexis and me that a united sisterly front made our days a lot easier to get through.

The far-off look in my dad's eyes had me changing the subject. "But enough about curling irons and whether or not they're still buried somewhere." I tapped the watch on my wrist. "I'm home for exactly seventeen days, which is when Aunt Linda said she's coming back from the shore and kicking me out. And I'll need to be hitting the road again anyway. You better enjoy me while ya have me."

"You're the *fun* aunt, Aunty Tabby," Juliet said wisely.

"I'm also your only aunt, sweetheart," I said with a wink. "And we can do all the things your mom and I liked to do as kids."

"Except with more tequila," Kathleen stage-whispered.

Eric reached behind him to the little speaker, turning up the music as we got back to our summer morning breakfast. I was already picking up on the sounds and smells of the neighborhood—radios turning on, kiddie pools filling up, barbecues getting lit.

Always pack light had been my motto since UCLA, and it had served me well until now. Of course, South Philly had an extra charm in the summer. There was charm in every city I traveled to.

I didn't get too attached to those places either.

THREE

DEAN

I shifted the carton of oranges in my arms and nodded at the group of white-haired veterans sitting in lawn chairs on the sidewalk, telling the same old stories while they sipped coffee from Styrofoam cups. Bells rang out from the nearby Catholic church as I walked past the Cambodian temple, with its Buddhist statues and bright red tiled roof. When I rounded the corner onto Tenth, two little kids with dark hair ran past me, backpacks bouncing.

"Buenos días, Dean," Marco yelled as he and his little sister, Lía, ran for the 47 bus about to stop at the corner.

"Buenos días," I said. I spotted their mother, Natalia, leaning outside her storm door with a smile. She and her husband, Martín, had moved here from Mexico City about ten years ago. Marco, Lía, and a big group of other kids played on these streets late on summer nights until various adults called them home. It was what Rowan and I had done—and the kids before us and the kids before them. Of all the neighborhood traditions, it was the strongest one.

"Did they make the bus?" she called out. "They're late to summer camp every morning."

I glanced over my shoulder. "Looks like they did."

"And tell your parents I'm bringing by some of my cherry tomatoes for them."

"Thanks," I said. "It's appreciated. If you have any extra..."

I trailed off, but Natalia understood. "It's no problem. I hear Eddie loves tomatoes too."

"Yeah, he does," I said, starting to walk again.

She cleared her throat. "I hate to say this, but...it's, well, it's starting to smell."

I paused mid-step, my teeth grinding together. She didn't need to explain what *it* was.

"It's probably the heat," I said. I shifted the oranges to my other arm and glared at the eyesore I was avoiding.

I'd grown up on a typical South Philly block with connected, two-story brick row homes; front stoops; and a street narrow enough for neighbors to yell out their windows at each other if they wanted to know the score of the ball game.

My house was third from the end. Next to it was Linda Tyler's place. And next to *that* was the abandoned lot now knee-high with trash and busted up furniture. Weeds grew ragged around it. A vine covered the rusted metal fence. We could hear raccoons and possums rustling around in there at night.

It had been two days since that call with the city. Since Rowan had hinted at what we could do. It bothered me nonstop, like the constant whine of a mosquito buzzing around my ear.

"It's only going to get worse," Natalia said, echoing my thoughts. "I know you told Maria and Midge you were going to handle it. But maybe it's something we can do together. That's a lot of pressure on you."

I rolled my shoulders back. "It's okay. I'm gonna get the city to fix it."

If the city fixed it, like they were supposed to, then I could pass the buck to them and avoid the spotlight. I wanted it taken care of *yesterday*. What I didn't want was people looking to me to organize a cleanup effort I could only fail at.

"Let the rest of the block know if you need help though," she said. "I'm serious, Dean."

"Okay, I will." I avoided her eyes and kept walking down the cracked, uneven sidewalk. It was barely 9:00 am and the morning was already hot and sticky with humidity. The air smelled like water on asphalt. Folks moved to their stoops and benches to escape the heat inside hundred-year-old houses without central air. Beneath that was the buzz of window units, the roar of the bus, and a neighbor blaring the local classic rock station.

At the end of the block, Alice O'Callaghan, who was eighty years old, hosed down her stoop, the steam rising around her. One of my mothers sat on the bench in front of our house, drinking coffee and listening as Alice recited whatever gossip had cropped up from the night before. My other mother, who I'd called Midge since I first learned to talk, was dancing along to the radio and watering the flowers that grew in large pots lining their sidewalk.

I bent down to kiss Midge on the cheek. "Good morning. Plants look nice today."

"They better," she said out the side of her mouth. "Eddie's been strutting around over there like he *knows* his petunias will be nicer than mine. But we'll see about that, won't we?"

I made a sound of agreement but remained silent. It was the only way to survive the vicious wars that sprung up around front stoop conditions and decor. Midge practically had an urban jungle growing out the front of our house, while Eddie kept two tidy planter boxes he was very proud of.

Alice's house, however, was still covered top to bottom in her giant, plastic Christmas decorations which she refused to take down or change.

"Natalia's bringing you tomatoes, by the way," I said, hefting the carton of oranges down onto the stoop. I grabbed a handful and then kissed Mom on the cheek.

"Hi, Mom," I said.

"Hello, darling," she replied. Mom was as short and quiet as Midge was tall and loud, always the life of the party. Both of their families had arrived in the city from small towns in Italy. When I was growing up my parents spoke a rapid blend of Italian and English to each other, and my own Italian was still pretty good.

"Are those oranges from Diego's stand at the market?" Alice asked.

I nodded, handing them to Alice as I gently pried the hose from her papery fingers. "Go sit with Mom. Remember, you're letting me do shit like this for you now."

The sun bounced off her white hair. "My, my, such *language* from such a sweet boy."

I hid a smile. "Stuff like this," I corrected. For an Irish woman who'd been strict as hell about the *language* Rowan and I used growing up, she cursed a goddamn blue streak whenever she felt like it.

A drop of sweat rolled down my back as I worked the hose, squinting up at the sun from under my hand.

"Dean, baby, can you stay for breakfast?" Midge asked.

"Can't," I said. I turned off the spigot. Shook water from my hands. "Edna Kozlowski hired me to fix her fridge this morning. I've gotta go in a minute."

"Oh, Edna, off Cantrell?"

I nodded again as I wrapped the hose around my arm. I'd been killing time the past few years as a handyman, doing odd repair jobs for neighbors. It was easy. I was good at it. And if I was lucky, the person would ignore me and let me work quietly in peace. That wasn't the case with Edna, so I had to conserve my limited conversational energy.

"We know her from church, don't we, Alice?" Midge said.

"Oh yes, that we do," she answered. "She used to babysit the Tyler girls when their parents were going through their"—Alice dropped her voice—"*terrible divorce.*"

"Hush, Alice," Midge said. "Their father is a sweet, *sweet* man, and he makes one heck of a pork roll at that diner of his. He didn't deserve an ounce of what that woman did to him and his daughters."

I froze as I was bending down to drop the hose. Turned my head. "The Tyler girls? You mean Linda's nieces?"

"The very same," Alice said, indifferent to my mother's mild scolding. "Tabitha was in school with you and Rowan. You remember, right? Was she older than you or younger?"

"Older," I said, then wished I hadn't spoken so quickly. "Let me bring the oranges in. I'll be right back."

I lifted the carton and stepped inside the house I'd grown up in. The decor hadn't changed in thirty years. As I walked to the tiny kitchen, I ignored the framed photographs of my boxing matches and magazine covers.

Every conversation in South Philly was some iteration of *you remember, right?* But Tabitha Tyler wasn't a person you could easily forget. She'd been two grades above me. And in high school, I had a crush on her that rivaled the size of the fucking sun.

She was a cheerleader. She wrote for the school paper. She was friendly, popular, never without a giant smile. And she was pretty in a way that had tied my tongue every time we talked. Tabitha grew up just three streets away. For two years, until she graduated, we walked to school together every Wednesday and Thursday morning, Tabitha chatting away while I nervously tried not to trip and fall.

But she was nice to everyone. And there wasn't anything that original about the shy kid having a crush on the beautiful, popular girl.

I pushed open the storm door and shook off the memory. I hadn't seen her since she graduated. Tabitha had gotten out of this neighborhood in a way most people didn't, going to college in LA. I assumed she spent her days driving a convertible down a street lined with palm trees, now even more out of my league.

"Have you seen Eddie?" I asked everyone. "I got oranges for him too."

"Speak of the devil," Midge said, pointing over her shoulder with her gardening gloves. "He must have seen me over here with my plants and decided to show me up."

I flashed her a warning look. She shrugged. "What? You don't think it's true? Natalia told me he buys organic soil and sneaks it into his pots when he thinks we're not looking. Organic, can you believe it? Like he's so fancy over there?"

I rolled my eyes as I crossed the street. My parents, Alice, and Eddie were the old-timers on this block. Had lived here for most—or all of—their lives. Midge and Eddie's flower wars were competitive but lacked any real heat. If he ever saw my parents facing any kind of insults or discrimination, he was always the first to step in and protect them if they needed it.

Eddie stepped onto his Astroturf-lined porch and lit a cigarette, still in his bathrobe. He was Italian American, like my parents, and a decade older. He spent most of his days spying on people and trading intel with Alice.

"Hey, how ya doin', Dean," he grumbled, then brightened when he saw the fruit. "Did you bring those for me?"

"Yeah, I did." I handed him a handful of oranges. "You've got tomatoes coming your way from Natalia's garden too."

He ducked his head vigorously but avoided looking at me. "Yeah, yeah. That sounds real good. Nice to have a little extra if I need it, you know?"

I raked my hand through my hair as he took the food inside. When he came back out, I said, "We all need a little extra. It's no big deal."

"Sure, yeah." He patted my arm, cigarette dangling from his mouth. I frowned, unsure of what else to say. Like a lot of folks in this area, he'd worked at the same oil refinery outside the city his entire life. Eddie had also been the neighborhood handyman for as long as I could remember. Until I needed a way to stay busy after retirement. And then he'd been nice enough to show me the ropes.

He never asked for help. And now that his pension couldn't pay all his bills, he definitely didn't ask. But Midge couldn't cook a dinner only for two to save her life, so her leftovers came his way. And the rest of us dropped off a few groceries on his stoop when we could.

Everyone in this city had neighbors going hungry. Eddie was one of them. But not the only. I just didn't know what the hell to say to a stubborn old man with a lot of pride.

"Yo, Dean," he said, catching my attention. "You meet my new cat?"

I raised an eyebrow. "What new cat?"

He waved me over to the small bench in front of his house. He'd installed a red umbrella, a small bed, and a row of tiny bowls. I peeked around the umbrella to find a white cat napping in the sun.

"There she is," he said, affection in his voice. "She ain't

nothin' but a stray, but I started feeding her a few weeks ago. Made this little setup so we could sit on the bench together. She likes it under the umbrella when it gets too hot or if it rains."

"What's her name?" I asked.

He smiled and managed to keep the cigarette in his mouth. "Pam."

"Pam?"

"Yeah. I named her myself."

I looked back down at the sleeping cat. "Isn't that a person's name?"

He scratched her ears. "I don't fucking know. She looks like a Pam, so I named her Pam."

"And it's a lovely name at that," Alice called from across the street, clearly listening to our conversation.

"Thank you, Alice," he yelled back. "We want her to feel comfortable here on the block. The kids have been helping me feed her, and Alice knitted her a blanket for if she gets cold."

I scratched Pam behind her ears. "She's, uh...she's very cute, Eddie."

"I already spoil her. I know it's too early, but Alice said she'd knit a stocking for her at Christmas."

He tied his robe closed, stubbed out his cigarette in the ashtray on his stoop. Then he grabbed his coffee and made his way over with a lawn chair to sit on the street facing Mom and Alice. On the hottest nights, the four of them filled a kiddie pool with water and sat with their feet in it, drinking beer.

I glanced at my watch while Eddie got settled. "I'm headin' out to the job now. You need anything before I go?"

Midge gave me a playful smile. "Just for you to stay for breakfast. We never see you enough."

"I'm here every day and also live on the same street as you."

"It's never enough," she said, throwing up her hands. Potting soil went flying. "But say hello to Edna from all of us. If this weather holds, it's gonna be a kiddie pool night."

"Damn straight," Eddie said, lighting another cigarette.

I went to leave but got distracted by the metaphorical mosquito buzz in my ear. I glanced uneasily at the lot. My neighbor Linda was down the shore this whole month, and her house was the one that butted right up to it. A month from now, when she returned, would it only be harder to live next to?

"So I uh..." I cleared my throat, rubbed the back of my neck. "I finally got through to someone at the city two nights ago. The guy told me they don't have any plans to fix it up. He said it was our problem to deal with."

Eddie growled into his coffee. Midge muttered something in Italian that I didn't hear.

"It's always going to be there," Mom said softly. "I can't believe they're abandoning it."

"I can believe it," Eddie said.

"Me too," Midge added.

I went to tell them what else the guy said—that we should fix it ourselves—but held back. "I'm going to keep trying. Someone uptown will know who we need to put pressure on to take care of it."

"Are you going to keep doing that thing where you glare at the trash while standing in front of it?" Midge asked.

I looked at her over my shoulder. "I don't do that."

"Every night you try to glare that lot *to death*," she said. "The whole neighborhood sees you do it. We've been talking all about it around the kiddie pool."

I swallowed a frustrated sound. "I know it's pointless to ask you not to gossip about me."

"It's not gossip. It's sharing. We've been *sharing* about you, is all."

Sighing, I shifted on my feet. "I'll remind all of you that, back in the day, I was kinda known for scaring people with my facial expressions."

Mom sniffed daintily. "Do you think your mothers have forgotten the way you used to stomp and scowl around this house as a teenager every time we asked you to clean your room?"

I hesitated. Debated my choices. "No, ma'am. I know you haven't forgotten."

"That's what I thought," she replied.

I fought the urge to make the face they were all referring to. The look that newspapers claimed was harsh enough to strip paint from your walls had no effect on the women who'd raised me.

"Besides, Dean is just a teddy bear," Alice added, unhelpfully. "He's as cuddly as a kitten. He only likes to act scary—we all know that."

I raised my eyes to the sky. "I am very tough and scary," I said beneath my breath. To the group of senior citizens smirking at me, I said, "Whether or not I'm glaring at it, I'll force the city to follow through. Then it'll be out of our hands."

Mom walked over. I bent low so she could kiss my cheek. "You're a good son, Dean. You know we trust you, right?"

My throat went tight. I nodded, said, "Uh-huh."

And then I spun on my heel and headed toward my next job. An odd job. Because the thing I loved the most, my whole identity and all of my passion, had been boxing. But even boxers much older than me understood the short expiration date on our dreams.

And the night I'd fought Bobby McKee—the night that changed everything—had sped up that expiration date before I was able to process that had been my last fight, my last time stepping through those ropes, feeling the heat and pressure of those spotlights.

The last time enjoying the electric lightning bolt of power zapping through my body.

You remember, right? This neighborhood's memory was long and permanent. I'd always be known as the local boy who'd quit pro boxing just as he was about to be a champion. And who'd been drifting about ever since, with no sense of direction.

It was hard to escape the clutches of that permanent memory.

Most folks around here would say it was damn near impossible.

FOUR

TABITHA

"Okay, *three*."

"Wait."

"We can't wait. We're doing a shot countdown. We've got *momentum* to keep up."

"Half of mine just spilled down my hand." My sister—pink cheeked and a little extra giggly—mopped up drops of tequila from the side of her wrist. "Okay, okay. Now I'm ready."

"Two," I said.

Alexis burst out laughing. I kicked her under the table. "You're as bad as Kathleen when she makes us go drinking with her boozy book club friends."

My sister leaned in, shot glass raised by her face. "After they finally read *Eat Pray Love*, she dragged me out *club hopping* with her and that book club. Eric had to come pick me up because I lost my keys, wallet, and cell phone because I was that drunk and a kindly bartender had to call him for me." She pursed her lips. "Later, all of those things were found in the trunk of Kathleen's car."

"How the hell did they get there?"

"*Who knows?*"

I laughed. "Okay, *come on*. One more shot before you head home. You wanted me to bring my trademark spontaneous fun." I indicated the beer bottles and shot glasses on the table. "I brought it, bitch."

She nodded somberly, like she was the pitcher and I was the coach, sending her in when the bases were loaded. "I love you."

"Love you." I winked. "*And one.*"

We licked the salt on our hands, threw back the tequila, and bit down hard on our limes. I shook my head, hair flying, nose scrunched up. Then I *whooped* and clapped my hands together.

"Oh my God, that one tasted like regret," she said. "Of the tomorrow variety."

"Then that's tomorrow's problem, babe." I pushed a tall glass of ice water her way. "Drink up."

My sister and I were at Benny's, the local bar down the street from Aunt Linda's house. After a lovely day with my family yesterday—plus a shower and some vigorous laundry—I'd moved myself and my backpack into Lin's house this afternoon. There was a bed, a coffee pot, and more embarrassing pictures of my and Alexis's preteen years than I knew what to do with.

We'd been posted up outside at a table on the sidewalk for the past few hours—people watching, idly chatting, doing shots when the mood hit us. It was still hot, the sky slipping from a rosy sunset to a lavender twilight. It seemed like half the neighborhood was out, strolling on by, while the other half was cheering for the baseball game inside.

Plus, our server was extremely adorable, and my sister and I agreed he was *definitely* flirting with me.

Alexis sipped the last drop of water, then fell back against her chair. "Twenty more minutes, then I'm leaving you to be with my daughter and cuddle with my sexy husband."

"Get it, girl."

She tracked the movements of said adorable server. "You think you'll stick around?"

I fluffed out my hair. "I don't know. How do I look?"

"Drop-dead gorgeous, as always."

"Then definitely *yes*." I scanned the rest of the sidewalk crowd. "Or I'll chill at the bar inside. There's a one hundred percent chance we went to school with at least six people in there."

I don't think you'll ever leave this place. Do you?

I blinked and scrubbed my hand down my face. That was twice now my mother's voice had slithered back into my thoughts, when usually I was able to mute her. But I was twenty-seven years old. I was not a *child*. And I was completely capable of being back home and not having her ruin it.

"Are you okay?"

"Oh yeah," I said, beaming up at Alexis. "I'm awesome. I'm excited. Happy to be back, doing shots we'll regret with my favorite person in the whole world."

She propped her chin in her palm. "I'm a little drunk."

I squeezed her arm. "You'll always be the cutest little lightweight."

A groove formed between her eyebrows. "Hey, you didn't tell me what happened with you and Shelby. She's back in California still, isn't she? Are you two doing a long-distance thing now or...?"

I twisted my water glass back and forth on the table. "Shelby and I broke up."

Alexis cocked her head with sympathy in her eyes. "I'm so sorry, Tab. What happened? You two were so sweet together."

I dropped my elbows onto the table. My sister was always

more upset over my breakups than I was. "I liked Shelby a lot. But I was upfront with her when we started hanging out. Told her I was only there for three months, max, before my next travel gig and that I wasn't emotionally available for anything...serious." I swallowed hard around the word. It must have been our family reminiscing yesterday that had me feeling more sensitive than usual.

My sister frowned. "I thought she was so great for you."

"She *is* great," I said. "I have no doubt she'll end up being with a person who's just as great. She just wanted more. More of me, more investment, more time. I didn't have it to give. She took our breakup really hard. I haven't said too much about it because, honestly, I feel kinda shitty."

I chewed on the end of my thumbnail to keep from wincing. My sister and I had seen the way two people in a relationship could hurt each other. It was always my intention to avoid that outcome every time, but I'd missed the warning signs that Shelby was growing more attached than I was. Breaking up with her, seeing her anger and her hurt had shaken me more than I wanted to admit.

But now I was more concerned with the trepidation on Alexis's face, her shoulders hunching up toward her ears.

"Hey, hey," I said, soothing. "You've got your worried-big-sister face on. I promise I'm totally, *totally* fine. And not all of my relationships end like that. There are plenty of people I've dated who are into the casual thing and when I ultimately pack up and leave, we're both fine with it."

She narrowed her eyes for a few seconds before a silly grin spread across her face. "Okay. I'm less worried about your nonexistent broken heart now. You can tell me *all* about your hot flings if you want."

The handsome server caught my eye again. "Seeing as how I just got back into town, I don't have one." I matched her grin.

"Yet. But the situation I'm currently in is the *perfect* setup for a sexy summer fling, don'cha think?"

"But how do you do that though?" she asked.

"Do what?" I leaned back in my chair, recrossed my legs. The still, humid air caressed my bare skin.

"Keep your emotions out of it. Keep it light without getting invested." Her cheeks got pinker. "Sorry, I'm your slightly drunk older sister whose been with the same person since college. I don't know how to *handle* what you do."

I laughed. "You make me sound like a robot."

"That's the thing," she said emphatically. "You're such an affectionate and loving person. How do *you* not get too attached?"

A stray breeze cooled the back of my neck. I tossed my hair again as the server smiled at me. I returned it. Then I leaned in close to my adorably drunk sister. "It's all about the *crush*. I love that heady, flirtatious feeling. When you're making out in movie theaters and texting each other constantly and you get butterflies when they say your name. That's exciting to me."

Having a crush was delicious. Addictive. Compelling in a sexy, primal way. That fleeting pull of lust and fascination felt safer to me than anything a steady relationship could provide.

"It's not hard to stay casual if you keep your conversations surface level. If you don't share too many secrets or personal stories. Or make romantic future plans. It's very much in-the-moment. Fully present. The second the other person starts dragging me toward something more intense, I can feel it."

My sister's smile was sweet and dreamy. "When you're falling in love, you mean."

I hesitated but kept smiling through it. "I guess? I don't really know what that feels like."

I *almost* said more but finished my beer instead, swaying to the music before setting the glass back down. I didn't want to bring our mom into this conversation, but our parents' divorce was like a far-off storm cloud on a beautiful day. Even when it wasn't over our heads, it hovered in the distance, a presence even in its absence. Alexis had found a soul-mate kind of love in Eric. And held tight to it.

I wasn't ashamed to say our experiences growing up made me want to run from anything that might hurt me or the person I was—casually—spending time with.

My sister's eyebrows were still raised, waiting for me to continue. "You got something to say?"

She gave a huge shrug. "*You guess you don't really know?* That's your response to falling head over heels in love with another person?"

"I sleep with people I already know I won't fall in love with," I said airily. "It's pure lust and sex appeal. It lessens the risk that I'll do something stupid like open my heart and—" I stopped.

"Open your heart and what?" She touched my wrist. "Maybe get hurt?"

I waved off the concern in her eyes. "I was *going* to say complicate my personal life and career all at the same time." I wasn't going to say that, but I charged ahead anyway. "Right now, all I want is to hop on airplanes with my camera and go where the stories are. I don't have a grander vision than that, but I'm really, *really* happy with this tumbleweed life. On the road, on the move. No roots just yet."

Alexis sank back in her chair and scrutinized me closely. She was swaying, just a little bit.

"You okay there?" I teased.

"Totally," she said, drawing out every syllable. Then she cocked her head with a giant big-sister smirk. "I'm sitting here, thinking it's *real* clever that Tabitha Tyler believes she can control once-in-a-lifetime, stars-in-your-eyes, soul-mate love."

I mimicked her expression, trying not to laugh. "Oh yeah? Watch me."

She started to giggle but then reached for my hand again. "I'm sorry, I'm being a brat. I want you to know that you can talk to me about messy love stuff. Or heart stuff. Or getting hurt stuff. Not 'cause I'm desperate to shove you into a relationship. But those feelings..." She swallowed hard, and my own throat started to tighten. "I understand why you might have them. I have them too."

This was the closest I'd ever come to blurting out all the things I never shared. The secrets, the shame, the locked-away memories that lurked like that storm cloud on sunny days.

"I want you to feel safe and comfortable and *happy*. Not just for dating but for your own heart, which is the most important. Although if you ever get married, I'm prepared to be the best maid of honor the world has ever known."

I covered her hand with mine. "Thank you for saying that. I'm deliriously happy with my life right now. With my career and traveling and having flings with sexy people. But five years from now? I hope I'm married and having a ton of kiddos."

Alexis brightened. "Cousins for Juliet?"

"Tons. Hundreds, even."

She leaned across the table and gave me a sloppy kiss on the cheek. "That sounds pretty awesome to me."

"I got it all figured out up here," I said, tapping my temple. "You don't have to worry. I *do* feel like I need to worry about you. That's why I texted Eric ten minutes ago to walk you home."

My brother-in-law appeared just then, strolling up to us with his usual charming smile. "Good evening, ladies. I'm looking for my soul mate—have you seen her? About this tall and so pretty I still get nervous around her?"

I yearned for my camera. I never filmed stories about Philly, my family, or anything too personal. Because moments like this—witnessing the unfiltered, joyful affection on my sister's face as she admired her husband—were the moments I wanted to document and keep only for myself. A bright spark to tuck away inside my heart, to gaze at when I needed a reminder that true love did exist.

Alexis reached forward and grabbed his hands. "Eric, Tabitha made me do shots. I swear it."

My jaw dropped. I tossed a napkin at her face. "*Made you?* You little sneak."

Her smile changed from simper to mischief. "Okay, it was at least half my idea."

"Everyone thinks I'm the fun one, but Alexis Tyler is the original real deal."

"Oh yeah," Eric said. "We were wild in college, staying up late in the library, getting wasted on coffee and microwave popcorn, working on mock lesson plans."

He helped my sister stand and tucked her against his side.

"Where's our brilliant daughter?" she asked.

"Valerie was still up and was happy to keep an eye on her for a few minutes so I could come collect my delightfully inebriated wife," he said.

"Smart thinking," she said. Then she blew me a kiss.

"I love you forever," I said.

"Hard same, sis." She ducked under Eric's arm, then turned back to me. "*And have fun with whoever you take home.*"

I laughed. "Do you think you're whispering right now?"

She held a finger up to her lips with bright eyes and red cheeks. I watched them walk back down the street with a soft tug in my sternum I had no business having. My time here was set. And homesickness was an old friend of mine while on the road, but I fought it with my family's nonstop communication. If I was missing my dad, he and Kathleen would hop on a video chat to have virtual dinner with me at a moment's notice—even if that meant it was late in the evening here.

I had no room to complain. And no reason to ache for this place. Like hot flings and casual sex, it was best not to let myself get in too deep.

Alexis and Eric finally disappeared from my view, and the tug in my chest loosened a little. I opened the camera on my phone and covertly checked my appearance. My eyeliner was smudged from the heat, my cheeks as flushed as my sister's had been. But my dress was short and I didn't smell too sweaty, so it would have to do.

I was very briefly home. Newly single. And *very much* ready to mingle. Talk about the ingredients for a perfect summer fling.

I'd been fifteen when I came out to my sister and told her I was bisexual. A week later, with my permission, she threw me a little coming out party in our backyard, with pizza and cupcakes, for friends and family who wanted to celebrate with me.

When I told my dad—right after my sister—he'd been heading off to work, apron in hand, and I'd blurted out, "Hey, Dad, guess what? I'm bisexual."

He'd paused at the front door. "I don't know what bisexual means yet, but if that's what you are it must mean I love it, right?"

I'd flashed him a watery smile. "It means I'm attracted to genders like mine and genders that are different than mine. It's who I am, on the inside."

He hugged me then, smelling of kitchen grease and the aftershave he still used. "I love you, Tabitha. I love who you are on the inside. And I can't wait to see who you fall in love with."

Unfortunately, my mom and new stepfamily hadn't been as accepting.

I ran a hand through my hair as I stood up, taking my beer with me. The night was young and I was on the happy side of tipsy. I brushed past a group of excited baseball fans and one extremely loud older dude who was flailing his arms at the TV, yelling about the score. He was blocking the cramped space between the bar and a tiny table, where another man sat with his back facing me. While I waited for Flailing Guy to calm down, my eyes skated over to the man.

I admired the elegant lines of his broad back and the lean muscles of his arms. The hand gripping the glass in front of him was large, the fingers thick, the knuckles a little swollen. I could see the veins in his forearm flexing every time Flailing Guy bellowed. His head turned slightly, revealing a crooked nose, a heavy brow, and a strong jaw clenched tight.

My brain said *huh* with a flicker of recognition.

A rowdy cheer went up from the people I was sandwiched between, and the man at the table twisted around in response, dark eyes flitting up to the TV screen. His heavy brow knit together, a ghost of a smile on his lips. He was white with dark brown hair, short at the sides and curly at the top, including one curl that flopped adorably over his forehead. His five o'clock shadow was subtle and sexy against his plain white T-shirt.

That flicker burst into a tiny flame. *Oh,* my brain said. Followed shortly by *wowza*. The recognition propelled me forward, my smile already growing.

"Hey...hey...*hey, excuse me*," I half yelled at Flailing Guy, trying unsuccessfully to duck again. He was like a tank. Then the sports fans behind me all stumbled at the same time, shoving me hard.

"Wait, *whoa*," I started to say, just as the tank in front of me stepped to the side. The momentum spun me forward, and I dropped, not very gracefully, right into the lap of the sexy, stubbly, broad-shouldered hottie at the table.

"*Oof,*" I gasped, happily stunned at the warmth of his body, the muscular arms boxing me in, his thighs like steel beneath me. When our eyes met, my tentative smile transformed into a full-on, cheesy grin. His cheeks flushed immediately.

"Of all the laps in this damn city, I had to fall into yours," I said.

"Tabitha?" he croaked out.

"The one and only," I said with a wink. "Nice to see ya, Dean Knox-Morelli."

FIVE

DEAN

When I was eighteen years old, I took a surprise right hook to the jaw during an amateur match that sent me sprawling to the ground. Every boxer takes a bad one early in their career and learns something from it. I learned that I didn't like having my goddamn head snapped back without warning.

But before that hook? I didn't think you could take a punch that had you seeing stars.

That one made me a believer. I laid flat on my back that night in a world of pain, and the entire fucking solar system spun around my face.

Tabitha Tyler falling into my lap at Benny's Bar had me believing again.

One minute I was studying the screen, pissed off at the loud asshole next to me. The next? A gorgeous redhead toppled into my arms. And even though I hadn't seen her in *years*, the very second she aimed that shiny smile my way, I was nothing but a dazed teenager again.

"Of all the laps in this damn city, I had to fall into yours," she said in her low, melodic voice.

I blinked at her. Blinked again. My mouth went dry as a desert. My body shivered with jittery nerves. I didn't want to stare, could only take in quick glimpses of her—pale white skin, freckles and delicate tattoos, dark red hair, those big brown eyes.

"Tabitha?" My voice came out strangled, like she was an illusion I couldn't trust.

She winked at me. Tabitha Tyler, former head cheerleader and popular senior girl, the source of my long, hopeless crush, *winked* at me.

Stars exploded across my eyes. So did the planets, the moon, the sun. I wasn't prepared to take a hit like this. Could only try not to let my jaw hang open at the shock.

"The one and only," she said, still smiling. "Nice to see ya, Dean Knox-Morelli." Her body shifted in my lap, wiggled around, and I learned the true meaning of the word *willpower*. "Although word on the street is you go by Dean the Machine now, and I have to say, that nickname is *bad ass*. Is that what I should call you? Or something more formal like Mr. Machine?"

I was speechless. Though my brain was saying *what the actual fuck is happening?*

"So...Mr. Machine it is, then?" She brushed her hair over her shoulder. I did *not* stare at the curve of her throat. "I like it. It's formal. Respectful. Commands a certain amount of authority. Though I've known you for, like, a million years so maybe it's a little weird. But this is South Philly. Who haven't we known for our entire lives?"

An embarrassing memory floated up—a dozen exchanges like this one, in school hallways or walking down the street or after the support group we'd attended together. Tabitha talking to me as if she had no idea who she was—and no understanding of how I wasn't deserving.

"Hi," I managed to say. It was the one word I could rescue from the chaos of my thoughts.

She bit her lip, looking almost shy for a second. "Hi."

A beat of silence passed between us. One where the door of a bizarre reality opened and I was a regular guy at the local bar, sitting with his very pretty girlfriend in his lap. A girlfriend with bare skin warm against mine, the tips of my fingers grazing the top of her thigh, her smell of sweet oranges all around us.

"Not that I don't appreciate you catching me, but uh...you can...you know..." Her eyebrow was lifted, teasing, and then her fingers pressed against my arms. The arms locked tight around her waist.

I cleared my throat and quickly released her. "I'm...so sorry. I don't—"

She slid easily from my legs to the chair right next to me, her bare knees pressed against me in the crowded space. "One of my dreams has always been to fall into the lap of a famous athlete. I should be thanking you for making a girl's dream come true."

The solar system drifted across my face again. I felt like a fried circuit breaker.

Next to me, the very drunk, very loud guy spun around and directed his attention toward the two of us. "Oh shit, did I trip you, doll?" he slurred. "You wanna let me buy you a drink or—"

I turned my face slowly toward his with the energy I once brought into the ring. I didn't say a word. Only stared. He flinched, face ruddy, stepping back and then farther away.

"Uh, you know what, I'm gonna go over here. Sorry about that, uh, Dean. And Dean's...lady."

I waited until he disappeared before turning around to find Tabitha with a bemused smirk on her face. "My dad told me you were a pro boxer. He didn't mention that you could literally scare a man with a *scowl*." She sat up straighter and raised her chin. "It's an honor to now be known as *Dean's Lady*. Do you know what the requirements are to be your lady? Do I appear at all your matches and wave my hand like a queen? I'm not super into wearing a crown, but obviously I've rocked a tiara before and I'd be more than willing to wear one for you."

My lips wanted to tug into a smile. Tabitha always had that effect on me.

"It's nice to see you," I said.

She dropped her chin into her hand. "You too. I guess it's been, what...since I graduated, right? So nine years or so? *Fuck me*. I missed you. How are you? What's new? Everything, I'm assuming."

My fingers gripped my beer bottle tightly enough to shatter it. It was the shape of her lips saying *fuck me* followed by a phrase I never thought I'd hear her say: *I missed you*. But she was always like that in school and around the neighborhood. Friendly. Warm. Hell, I'd clocked five other former classmates here in the bar tonight. She would probably say *I missed you* to them too.

"I'm okay," I finally said. "What are you doing here? Home for a visit?"

She nodded and ran her fingers through her red hair. It was shoulder-length and wavy. She had a ring in her nose and flowers tattooed down her left arm. She had the same cluster of freckles across the bridge of her nose. But more freckles now, on the tops of her shoulders.

"I'm back for a little longer than my usual whirlwind weekend. A whole two weeks this time," she said, eyes searching mine like she really had missed me. "Before this I was out in Sacramento, working on a video series about a nonprofit that helps middle school students publish their stories and poetry. They hold these glamorous publishing events where the students read their work in front of an audience. There were photo shoots and autographed signings. It was maybe the cutest thing I'd ever seen, and I once spent a week in St. Louis where I literally filmed rescue puppies all day."

I was having a hard time keeping up. Tabitha was making movies about...puppies? Not in LA? And, most importantly, back home for a bit.

Chris, the bartender, walked past and grabbed my empty bottle. "You want another one of these?" he asked.

I made eye contact with Tabitha. I'd already had one drink. Two would be a mistake with the grueling workout I had planned at dawn the next morning. She was chewing on her lip, flushed.

"I'm down to stay for another if you are? We could always share a cocktail."

"Share? A...drink?"

"A bold concept, I know," she said. "Is there a delicious cocktail that you like?"

My lips twitched. "Yuengling."

She laughed. "Philly's most famous beer is your favorite cocktail, huh?"

I lifted a shoulder. "I like what I like."

Her eyes narrowed playfully. "Only twenty-five and already firmly set in your ways. Such a curmudgeon, Mr. Machine."

Chris sighed. "I don't got all fucking night for you two to flirt. Are you having anything or not?"

Only the fact that I'd known Chris for years kept me from doing some version of the scowl. Besides, Tabitha was from this neighborhood and could hold her own against an asshole bartender.

"I've already been drinking tequila, so I think a margarita is the one true path forward," she said. "Can you make one with salt on the rim for the two of us to share while flirting all fucking night?"

Chris scoffed but then relented. "Yeah, sure. Is the cheap stuff okay with you?"

"Oh, *definitely*."

The second he was out of earshot, she turned back to me. "What a charmer."

"Want me to scowl at him for you?"

She touched the center of her chest. "I am Dean's Lady, after all. And you can have half of my margarita if you want it."

I shifted in my chair. "I don't usually have more than I should."

"Ah," she said. "Are you still on that strict regimen because of your training?"

Chris returned and placed a margarita on the table, then left without a word.

Tabitha brightened, her tongue darting out to taste the salt. Her eyes closed with satisfaction. I was grateful she was no longer sitting in my lap.

"Yeah, something like that," I said.

Once I knew I was going pro, I gave in to the structure and restrictions that came with elite-level training six days a week. As a teenager, I adopted a classic boxer's diet: meat, vegetables, carbs. No sugar, no soda, *very* little alcohol. I didn't indulge because I knew how it would make my body feel later, and that wasn't a risk I enjoyed taking. And when I was near the height of my career, wasn't a risk I even wanted. There was too much riding on each victory—money, reputation, and the weight of the fans sharpening my focus.

The fight nights might have stopped but my diet and workouts hadn't, a weird vestige I hadn't been able to give up.

Tabitha held the cocktail across the table. "Do you do cheat days?"

I shook my head.

"*Never?*"

"Never," I said.

She studied me over the salted rim of her glass. My shoulder blades rippled with restrained motion. Having Tabitha Tyler across the table from me, legs touching mine, tempting me into drinking alcohol with her, was urging me toward actions I'd never have the courage to take. To place my lips and tongue where hers had been. To enjoy the tart lime, the burn of tequila, to overindulge because it didn't always have to *mean* anything.

"Mr. Machine?"

I blinked, muscles flexing in response to the husky tone of her voice. "You go ahead and have the whole thing. Thank you for the offer though."

She held my gaze. "No getting a little wild for you, then?"

I cut my attention to my phone. "It's now thirty minutes past my bedtime. You're seeing me at my most spontaneous."

She reached for my wrist. "It's truly an honor to witness this debauchery. I only hope being seen with you while you're so clearly out of control doesn't besmirch my innocent and angelic reputation around here."

I chuckled softly and looked away, sure she was a fever dream. But when I let my eyes rise back up, there she was—beautiful, happy, and very real.

"Tabitha," I said.

She was knocking her drink back. "What's up?"

"I'm not a boxer anymore." I scratched the back of my

head. "My workouts are grueling, but I'm not...training. I retired three years ago. I'm just Dean now."

She placed her glass down gently. Licked her lips. "When we were in school, I thought *just Dean* was pretty awesome. Did you retire for good reasons or hard reasons?"

My knee jumped up and down beneath the table. No one ever asked me that. "Hard reasons."

"Well, that sucks."

Her candor startled a smile from me. "You're from here. You can imagine..." I waved my hand around me.

"The city of brotherly love does not, in fact, love any of its athletes," she said. "Maybe I should be going around scowling on *your* behalf instead. Or I can use the pepper spray I carry. That works just as well, if not better."

I turned my attention to the giant TV to give my brain a second to catch up. In school, the nicer Tabitha was to me, the more nervous I got, stammering through one-word answers to her friendly questions. But while she was off filming movies or whatever, I was stuck in a fucking rut, hanging around the neighborhood bar with nothin' to show for it.

I wasn't embarrassed by my injury or my decision to retire. I was embarrassed because I wasn't doing shit and I knew it.

"It's all fine though," I said, hoping I sounded casual and not like I was totally lying. "It was a great career while it lasted. I'm happy."

"Good," she said. "I'm so glad to hear it. Am I embarrassing myself if I admit that I've never seen you compete before? Like seen any of your videos or anything?"

I kept my face impassive. "Wait. You're not my biggest fan?"

"*Biggest fan?*"

"That's what I heard around the block."

She went still. "How is that possible? I don't...really... even...watch sports?"

I sniffed. "Your dad told me you never missed a match. Used to make me feel proud, knowin' you were out there, watching me. That I had a hometown fan who believed in me."

Those gorgeous eyes went wide as saucers. "My dad said *what*?"

I stayed silent.

Her mouth scrunched up to the side. "I'm so sorry, there must be some mistake. Are you mad? Please don't be mad. I'll go home and watch them all on YouTube. I don't know what my dad was talking about. You know, he's over the grill all day at the diner and there's, like, a lot of fumes and stuff. Maybe it's affecting his memory? *Oh my God* this is next-level awkward."

I managed not to smile at her rambling, but just barely. She was adorable. A word I never used. But I did maintain eye contact until she realized what I was doing. Dropping her face into her hands, she laughed, the sound muffled. Then she fluttered her fingers to her red cheeks.

"You're joking, aren't you?"

"Should I tell your dad you're concerned about those grill fumes?"

She tipped her head back on another laugh loud enough to garner a few stares. But those same stares saw me and immediately dipped away. I didn't care. This golden feeling of making Tabitha Tyler laugh was brand new. And wouldn't last. I knew not to put much faith in it beyond the present moment.

"You really had me going there for a minute," she admitted, brushing the hair from her forehead. "I will watch your fights soon. Because you've got my interest piqued, and I'm sure you are amazing to see in action."

Pride warmed the center of my chest. I hadn't experienced that in a while.

The side door opened and three more groups of noisy fans streamed in. The volume level grew louder. Tabitha leaned all the way across the table and placed her mouth at my ear. My heart stuttered to a stop. My mind exploded with sensory details, and not of the solar-system variety. Soft skin, oranges in her hair, the dent in her bottom lip, the swell of her breasts—although I tore my eyes away to stare up at the ceiling.

"It's getting too loud in here," she whisper-yelled. "Want to walk me home?"

I must have grunted out an answer, too stunned for real words. She motioned for me to follow her. The bar patrons parted for her easily—less because of my presence, more because there was confidence in every step she took.

There always had been.

And as I followed close behind, I hoped I didn't look as eager and hopeless as she always made me feel. Because those few classmates I'd spotted shot me discreet looks as Tabitha swayed past. It didn't take much effort to interpret them.

Maybe if things were different. Maybe if I was still in the ring, taking what I wanted, winning all the damn time, being around a high school crush wouldn't have even registered.

But things weren't different. And Tabitha wasn't any old crush. She was *the* crush. And only home for a minute before chasing those dreams of hers far from South Philly.

It didn't matter if tonight she'd tumbled into my lap or laughed at a rare joke. This was all temporary for her.

And she was permanently out of my league.

SIX
TABITHA

Once outside the bar, my body greeted the wisp of a breeze with open arms. From the second I'd landed in Dean's lap, I'd been blushing from the ends of my hair to the tips of my toes. I *had* been on the prowl for a summer-fling candidate. I just wasn't expecting to be pressed against Dean's powerful legs or stunned stupid by his brooding, dark-and-stormy good looks.

And that deep voice of his was carved from granite, with the kind of low, rough edges that turned romantic words, dirty and sweet promises into filthy acts. Dean was as tall as he'd been in school, but all that rangy, teenaged-boy energy had transformed into a big man with a thrum of intensity beneath dense boxer muscle.

We had a two-grade age difference, but I was always friendly with Dean. Like everything here, we'd been connected in a myriad of ways—my aunt lived on his block, and Alexis and I grew up three streets over. Our parents went to the same church. Midge and Maria ate at my dad's diner every Saturday morning. I walked to school with Dean and his friend Rowan a couple times a week. We'd cross paths at whatever teenage hangout was cool over the summer—FDR Park, the public pool, the Wawa parking lot.

But of all those many connections, the strongest one was the monthly support groups we'd attended together at a nonprofit called the Lavender Center—a group for LGBTQ teens, families, and their allies.

"I thought you were in Los Angeles," Dean said. "Working with movie stars."

It took me a moment to surface from my memories. "Sorry...what did you say?"

"All this time," he continued. "We all heard you went to UCLA to pursue film. I always thought you were, like, a producer or someone kinda famous."

"Oh, nope, not me," I said, stepping over a jagged crack in the sidewalk. "I did go to UCLA but became pretty disenchanted with the Hollywood scene almost immediately. I knew I wanted to tell stories about people, about communities and art and all the things that make us feel human. I'm a freelance videographer and photographer now, and I go wherever the business takes me. I can usually piece together enough corporate or tourism contracts to pay my living expenses. But I use social media and my website to share videos I make that are more like passion projects."

"About what?" he asked, brow furrowed.

"Neighbors helping neighbors," I explained. His lips quirked up at that. As we waited for a car to pass before crossing the street, I toed a cluster of purple violets that had sprung up through a fracture in the cement. "I like to tell stories about wildflowers growing through sidewalks, basically. All the things that take up space, demanding attention and justice in the face of larger forces trying to make them silent or invisible."

Dean was watching me closely, that dark gaze of his

causing all the hair to stand up on the back of my neck. Given his success in a sport I thought of as being violent, I hadn't expected him to be the same person I'd grown up with—a little shy and a lot serious, thoughtful and deliberate, like he knew his words mattered. Though I'd glimpsed the look he'd given Flailing Guy, noticed the clench of his thick fingers and how his body's movements seemed restrained in some way. Like he was holding back from doing what he really wanted.

"So yeah..." I continued, laughing. "I'm not working with movie stars."

"And you're always on the move?" he asked.

"Pretty much. It depends on who I'm working for. I've stayed in cities for as long as six months sometimes if I'm getting interesting stories or acquiring contracts that pay well. But mostly?" I grinned. "I go where the stories are. And the slightly cheesy tourism videos. What about you? Is there anything calling you away from here? Traveling or exploring or taking spontaneous road trips with no destination in mind?"

He shook his head. "Maybe when I was pro, fighting matches in different cities. But I always came home. Always wanted to come home in the end." We turned down Emily Street. "Don't you miss Philly?"

Now it was my turn to scoff. "There's too much to see, too many people to meet. Besides, my job requires it, and that makes me a very lucky lady indeed. It's only me, my pack, my camera and mic, and the editing software on my laptop. I travel light, but it lets me go pretty far."

"But do you miss it?" he repeated.

I swept the hair from my neck and contemplated blowing off his question. But I was surrounded with sounds that pulsed with nostalgia—the neighbors to our left laughing on their stoop, the buzz of people passing by, the window units humming, the distant jingle of the same ice cream truck we had as kids. And then there was Dean, surprising me with something like tenderness in his expression.

My throat squeezed shut. "Of course I miss Philly and my family. I love it here."

It also holds all my very worst and most confusing memories.

I lightly tapped his arm and decided to change the subject. "Do you remember our support group at the Lavender Center? I was thinking about them the other day."

His shoulders relaxed. "I kept going after you graduated. Rowan came with me a lot. And you know Mom and Midge still talk to some of the other gay parents they met there."

There was a pinch in my chest. It wasn't often that Dean spoke up in our group. When he did, he talked about what it was like growing up with two moms. The homophobic things said to him and his parents in school and out in public.

"I remember how scary it was, sharing in that giant chair circle with a whole bunch of people staring at you," I said. "I always felt so nervous and sweaty afterward."

"It made my sparring matches seem like a fucking picnic in comparison."

I laughed softly. "That's an apt description. I appreciated every time you shared. I didn't have any queer friends when I started going, and I looked up to your parents so much. Looked up to you. It was like glimpsing a future I wasn't sure was possible. No matter how awful or challenging things got, your mothers seemed so in love."

He nodded. "They are very happy together." He paused, cleared his throat. "I, uh…didn't see many families in South Philly that looked like mine. After you came out, I felt like my world expanded. If that makes sense."

"It makes total sense," I said firmly. "We all want to be seen. But we also want to know there are others like us out there. Sitting in those support groups on those creaky chairs, it was the first time I ever saw my *own* story."

Those nights taught me a lot about the connected threads of storytelling. I saw how my story was both wildly different and incredibly similar to others. It was such a powerful feeling of coming *alive*. And I noticed the spinning of those same threads whenever I was behind a camera.

I slowed to a stop, nearing the turn onto Tenth. "I'm glad I fell into your lap, by the way," I said. He smothered a cough. "We could even hang out again, if you wanted."

Dean's response to that was to stare at me like I was the toughest question on a math test.

"You know..." I continued, "paint the town red. Go a little wild. Have *two* margaritas, or even stay out till midnight."

I was rewarded with a half smile. Gone in an instant, like a shooting star. "That sounds like a job for Rowan, not me. You know I'm not the wild type."

Our eyes connected and held. For a person who claimed not to be *wild*, the naked lust that flared briefly in his gaze felt untamed to me.

I cocked my head to the side. "What about dancing?"

He looked down at the ground, then back up at me. Shy. Adorable. That spark of passion had vanished, and I wanted to tempt it back.

"You do not want to see me dance, Tabitha."

"I thought your physical prowess was well documented, Mr. Machine?"

His lips curved up again. "A boxing ring is different than a dance floor. You wouldn't enjoy it."

I had a strong hunch there were a lot of things I'd enjoy doing with Dean.

"Maybe some other time, then," I said. "You know where I live." I glanced around where we were standing. "Which is here, believe it or not—at least temporarily. How'd you know where to walk me home? Are you staying at your parents' house tonight?"

He shoved his hands into the back pockets of his jeans. "I didn't know. I moved out a few years ago. Bought that house over there."

I followed where he was pointing. "You live next to my aunt? She never *told me*, and we're constantly texting about *The Real Housewives*."

"The real...what? Wait, are you staying in Linda's house this month?"

I spun back to face him with a wide smile. "That is exactly where I'm staying. Dean, we're about to become *neighbors*." I dug Linda's keys from my purse and walked toward her stoop, sniffing a little at the smell of the trash in the empty lot. "I meant to tell you at the bar that I was staying on your old street. I had no idea you lived here too."

I peered up at his row home, which was near identical to Linda's. Red brick and slightly run down like everyone else's. White trim, white door, curtains slightly parted. He had a tiny chair and table next to his stoop.

"I like your house," I said. "I'm guessing it doesn't contain as many embarrassing photos of me and Alexis during our teen years. That's really the whole vibe Aunt Linda was going for, decor-wise, in this place. Plus a lot of photos of both Bruce Springsteen *and* Jon Bon Jovi. Right over her TV is a framed copy of the *Inquirer* the day after the Eagles won the Super Bowl. I think she and my uncle have the final score tattooed on their arms. They wouldn't be the only people on the block with *41–33* inked somewhere on their body."

My old friend—and new neighbor—studied me apprehensively. "You and me...we're neighbors."

"Yep."

"We'll definitely be seeing each other, then."

"If by *seeing* you mean dancing all night in bars uptown, then yeah. We sure will."

He looked at me. Looked at Linda's house. Back and forth for a few seconds. Then he said, "I don't have any embarrassing pictures of you. I do have that same article framed on my wall. And I listen to more Springsteen than most people would guess."

"And that Super Bowl tattoo?"

He hesitated. "Not yet."

I leaned against my front door. "See? That's pretty wild. Call me up when you go through with it. I'll come with. And I'm a good neighbor, I swear. Quiet. Respectful. I sing loudly in the shower, so you might hear that, but feel free to bang on the wall and I'll shut up."

"Um. Okay." His voice was rough.

I slid the keys into the front door and cracked it open an inch. "Do you know the story about this lot? Linda mentioned when I was moving in that it might be a bit of a problem, though you know our street growing up had plenty of empty lots, so I'm used to it." I scrunched up my nose. "Funny that she made sure to bring up the possibility of possums running rampant next door but *not* that her neighbor was Philly's most famous boxer."

We all loved our aunt Linda to the moon and back, but she was the epitome of *quirky relative* and nosy as hell with a devotion to dating shows. It made me wonder if this was some kind of sneaky setup—not that I was complaining. But I'd thrown out a few flirtatious signals to the dark-and-stormy hunk standing in front of me, and I couldn't read his reactions.

Except when he turned toward the lot, revealing his crooked-nose profile. *That* reaction I could read just fine. He glowered at it, the look not unlike the scary scowl he'd unleashed on Flailing Guy at the bar.

"Yeah, I know the story," he said tightly. "After the city tore that house down last year, they've left it there. I spoke to a guy a few days ago; he said we were on our own with it. I'm trying to figure out what to do, but..." He trailed off, hand on the back of his head.

"Huh." I tilted forward, craned my neck, and winced at how wrecked it looked. "I bet you could fix it up. In fact, I bet folks on this street would help. I would help you too."

He grunted and shrugged. I was curious about the last few years since his retirement, about the depth of emotion buried beneath the surface of his words. How the sentence *It's all fine though* made it obvious that everything was not, in fact, fine. I was an expert in bullshitting my way through questions that required a vulnerable answer, and I was pretty sure Dean was bullshitting me.

"For what it's worth, I've been lucky to meet a lot of neighborhoods across the country facing abandoned structures like this, in cities with a lot of blight and a lot of people willing to fix it themselves if no one else will."

Dean cut his eyes toward me but didn't respond.

"It's something beautiful to behold." I held his gaze. "A block coming together to do some good. Just an idea to chew on, neighbor to neighbor."

He nodded. "Thank you. And, uh...thanks for..." He trailed off again, and I *almost* thought he was blushing under the streetlight.

"Literally falling into your lap?" I suggested.

There was that ghost of a smile again. *Swoop* went my insides. "It was nice. Seeing you, I mean. Not...the lap part. That wasn't not nice though."

I grinned as I stepped inside. "I agree. It wasn't not nice." I winked at him before closing the door behind me. "Good night, neighbor. I'll see you on the stoop tomorrow."

As soon as the door shut, I fell back against it and let out a long, happy sigh.

The next two weeks just got a whole lot more interesting.

SEVEN
DEAN

I slowed to a stop before turning the corner onto Tenth Street. Hands on my head, I tipped my face back. Breathed heavily for a full minute. It was barely 7:30 in the morning and the air was sticky, the sky bright blue. I didn't need to run home after my workout. But I wanted to. Anything to burn through the excess energy buzzing through my limbs.

My trainer was a neighborhood institution everyone always called Sly—in his seventies now, he was tough as an old tire, brusque, and constantly under-impressed. He'd worked with me from the first day Mom and Midge had taken me to his gym. And he understood, more than most, what my career-ending concussion had cost me. He'd been around long enough to know how to keep me in fighting shape without the damaging side effects of real fighting.

Sly's workout this morning had kicked my ass from one side of the gym to the other. Everything hurt, but the way it used to. The normal kind of hurt. Not the daily pain that came with competing in the ring—the broken teeth, the cracked ribs, the migraines. I'd been out for three years and I still hadn't healed right in some places. I didn't miss the scars that came from having my cheek split open or the constant ringing in my ears.

I did miss the power. I had more of that than I knew what to do with.

Wiping my forehead with the end of my shirt, I fished my keys out from the pocket of my running shorts. Refused to notice Linda's house. *Tabitha Tyler's* house, at least for the rest of the month. Halfway through the door, my phone beeped with a message. I scooped it up from the table but got distracted by the sounds of laughter down the street. The kind I recognized.

Standing in the open doorway, I read the message from Rowan on my phone: *The kitchen sink at the center is busted again. You got some time this morning to fix it?*

The South Philly Rec Center on 8th and Federal was housed in a falling-down building the same way most rec centers in the city were. I did as much work for Rowan as he requested. Anything to help.

Yeah, give me fifteen, I sent back. Then I ditched my phone back on the table and glanced toward the sounds of laughter. I scrubbed a hand down my face, sure I was seeing things.

Nope.

It was Tabitha, lounging in a lawn chair next to Eddie like she'd never left home at all. They were drinking coffee with my parents while Alice swept the sidewalk.

Give me thirty instead, I texted Rowan.

I shut the door tight behind me, giving Natalia a wave as she walked with Marco and Lía to the bus stop. As soon as I was in full view of Tabitha, I rolled my shoulders back. Stretched my neck from side to side. I didn't linger on her long, smooth legs or the tank top she wore, one strap sliding down her shoulder. Her red hair looked messy, and her black eyeliner was smudged.

She raised her large coffee mug, brown eyes flicking to mine. Her pink lips curved into a smile that slammed into me like a goddamn upper cut.

I blinked. Stars, again.

That fiery energy snapped through my veins, every muscle going rigid with anticipation. Last night's sleep had not been restful. I usually had time to mentally prepare before matches, to scrutinize attacks, counterattacks. To memorize every physical quirk and surprise jab. Instead, I had Tabitha sharing a wall with me. She'd woken up in a warm bed right next door, with wild hair and sleepy eyes, looking like every dirty fantasy I'd ever had.

"Now there's my favorite son," Midge called out. Up went a chorus of greetings from the usual crowd. As Eddie stubbed out his cigarette, I noticed that his cat, Pam, was asleep on Tabitha's lap. "Did you know Tabitha was home for the month and staying at Linda's place? We were so surprised to see her walking up the street looking pretty as a picture."

"And she brought us bear claws from her dad's diner," Eddie said with a crooked smile of appreciation.

"She's famous now, you know," Alice mused. "Did you know there are so many videos of her on the internet, Dean? And on all kinds of websites."

Tabitha was staring down at Pam, smoothing her hand over her fur. But I spied her shoulders shaking with silent laughter.

I gently took the broom from Alice so she could sit down on the bench. As I swept along the sidewalk, I said, "Is that true? So many websites?"

"You're making me sound quite salacious, Mrs. O'Callaghan," Tabitha said, tossing a wink at me. "But I'm not famous, I promise."

"Just don't get too fucking fancy for this place," Eddie

grumbled, slurping his coffee. "Pam might not recognize you when you come back."

"We can't have that now, can we?" Tabitha said, tapping Pam on the nose. "I'm happy to trade homemade diner fare for hot block gossip any morning that you'd like while I'm home."

"Deal," Alice and Eddie said in unison.

"*Or* secrets about my new neighbor Dean."

My mothers laughed innocently, but I didn't take my eyes off that pair of troublemakers. "Secrets, baby pictures, old report cards," Midge said. "We'd do a lot for a fresh bear claw."

I leaned the broom against the brick. "You're selling out your only son's secrets for donuts?"

Midge shrugged. "Am I proud of it? No. Am I still gonna do it? Yeah."

Mom hugged my ribs, too short to reach any higher. "She's only teasing, sweetheart. Unless Drew Tyler starts baking those lemon squares I love, and then all bets are off."

Tabitha was smirking over the rim of her cup. We shared an amused look, but I tore my eyes away before I could read too much into my comfort level around her.

"How did you sleep last night?" Midge asked. "Do you need food? Do you want some leftovers, or will we see you for dinner?"

I let her kiss me on the cheek. "I can come by for dinner, yeah. I need to swing by the rec center to help Rowan, but after I'll hang that wallpaper in the upstairs bathroom for you."

"And bring my grandson along. The one I haven't seen in three days and who's basically abandoned me," Alice added.

"I can pass along that message."

"*Bless you*, Dean. What would we do without you?" Alice said.

I nodded at her but didn't respond. I rolled my shoulders

back again, muscles sore. Tight from punching drills this morning. Tight from dozing last night with one ear listening for Tabitha in case she needed anything. I was so jumpy that someone had laid on their horn around midnight and I'd almost had a fucking heart attack.

"I should go help Rowan, but I'll drag him back here for dinner." I walked backward down the street. "And no secrets for lemon bars."

"I make no promises," Midge said. I spun forward so I wasn't tempted to look at Tabitha or smile at her or fret over what to say. I was a former pro boxer suddenly reduced to the shy kid not fitting in at school again. It was the reason my parents had signed me up for boxing lessons in the first place. Not because they wanted me to fight in the hallways. Because they thought it might give me a place where I felt comfortable. And it had, in more ways than I could say.

Having Tabitha see me now—as a disappointment, and not during my glory days—had me itchy and anxious, like my skin didn't fit right. Here I was, blushing and nervous around my new neighbor, who was now a grown woman, gorgeous and confident, worldly and ambitious.

Not a damn thing about me had changed.

EIGHT

DEAN

I took a fast shower and grabbed my toolbox, walking to the rec center beneath a sun only getting hotter. Sweat clung to my shirt as I moved down the narrow streets I'd been traveling my entire life. I passed tiny corner shops and delis, butchers, panaderías, and pho restaurants. The air smelled like sweet cannoli. But once I hit the block right before the rec center, the sugar scent was replaced by incense, burning outside a large Buddhist temple, which sat next to a program that worked with refugees settling in our neighborhood.

The rec center's basketball court was always full of kids playing ball. There was a playground, a library, a computer lab staffed with social workers and literacy volunteers. Various food programs operated from inside, but the new priority was helping the large number of older folks going hungry.

I walked through the small lobby and down the hall toward Rowan's office. It was more of a busted-up desk in a room that faced the playground. The two of us had used this place all the time, a couple of kids with too much energy in a city without real backyards.

He nodded at me as I walked in, his feet kicked up on the table. "Thanks for comin'. I don't know what the hell is up with that sink."

"It's no problem." I indicated all the boxes on the floor. "What's up with all this food?"

He gave me a wry look. "We need a coordinator for the senior program and haven't found the right person yet. Speaking of, I wanna get Eddie signed up to start receiving one of these food boxes every week."

I crossed my arms over my chest. "I think it's a smart idea. But also, good fucking luck."

"Yeah. He's a tough old bird." He let his feet drop back to the floor. "So what's going on with your shit? Any ideas for the vacant lot?"

I cut my eyes to the ground. I had thought about it during last night's tossing and turning. *It's something beautiful to behold,* Tabitha had said. The words had spun on repeat through my brain, tugging me toward ideas I wanted to do but wasn't sure I could make happen.

"I have thought about it," I finally said.

"Yeah?" Rowan looked impressed. And surprised. "Anything specific?"

I knocked my knuckles against the wall. "Not really. I'm back to getting nowhere every time I call the hotline. Maybe..." I trailed off. "Maybe taking it on ourselves is our only real option."

He dropped his hands on top of his head. Pointed to the window. "This lot situation makes me think about Miss Mekenney's class."

"You mean sixth grade social studies?"

"Uh-huh," he said. "She always talked to us about community, right? That we lived in a place where people looked out for one another."

He waited, and I filled in the rest. "She said every day was your chance to make your city better."

She didn't only say it. There was a mural with those words painted on the hallway in front of her door. I never gave it much thought. Of course, we all looked out for one another. I didn't know there was another way.

Rowan indicated the view out the window again. "These kids out here grew up just like us. What would you tell them to do if they had this same problem?"

I knew what he was doing, but he also wasn't wrong. Our neighborhoods had been half-abandoned by a city because of our zip code and funding problems and budgets that went to rich people over working-class families.

I sighed. "I'd tell them...*hell*, if no one's coming to save us, then we have to make it right. So I guess that means I'll do it. I'll figure out how to clean out Annie's lot and turn it into...whatever."

He grinned, rubbing his palms together. "You know I'll help and the neighbors will pitch in. I wouldn't worry too much about coming up with ideas. It'll be great no matter what."

"We'll see," I grunted.

His expression grew serious. "I know it's easier to retreat. You know I've been there before. And the feeling fucking *sucks*. But I think this is the kind of work you were born to do."

My muscles loosened a little. Rowan understood how it felt to be an athlete with a whole identity and persona controlled by other people. Whether you were good or bad, working hard or phoning it in, loyal to your city or a traitor. Since making the choice to retire, I'd found it damn near impossible to expose myself like that again, to feel like a raw nerve all the time.

Hiding was safety. Retreating was at least an action I could take, even if I wasn't doing shit with my life. I knew it was only a vacant, trash-filled lot. But it shoved me back into a spotlight, no matter how small. And *that* made me shrink away.

"Yeah, it is easier to retreat. I hate...letting people down again," I finally said. "I know you get it. And we'll figure it out. I'm just extra distracted right now."

"Oh, you mean because the girl you were into when we were in school is living next door to you now?"

I opened my mouth. Shut it. Scowled out the window. "It's been less than twenty-four hours."

Rowan held up his phone with a smirk. "Alice O'Callaghan has been texting me nonstop since the break of dawn. She's no amateur."

"Your grandmother is a menace to society."

"That's for goddamn sure," he said. He handed me his phone. "She hasn't learned how to text not in all caps, so it always seems like she's yelling at me."

I studied the screen. Pinched the bridge of my nose. "Jesus Christ."

"I know, dude."

Starting at 4:45 in the morning, Rowan had received a dozen messages—*DID YOU KNOW TABITHA TYLER IS BACK HOME SHE IS FAMOUS ON THE INTERNET NOW* and *I JUST SAW DEAN FOR COFFEE. WHY ARE YOU ABANDONING ME?*

"I'm supposed to bring you by for dinner, by the way."

"I should know better than to let two or more days go by without seeing her." He dropped his phone back onto the desk. "But seriously. Tabitha's *living* next to you?"

I shifted on my feet. "Isn't there a gushing leak that you need me to fix right away?"

"Nah, it can wait," he said, eyes darting to the clock on the wall. "Though I do have a meeting in ten minutes, so we'll have to do the real deep dive before dinner tonight."

I hesitated, felt my neck seize up again. I needed to calm down before I gave myself a migraine.

"Tabitha is back home until the end of the month and staying at Linda's place. We bumped into each other at Benny's. She's a videographer now, but freelance. She moves around constantly."

"Ah," Rowan said. "That's why my grandmother is convinced Tabitha is an internet celebrity."

"Something like that, yeah."

His lips quirked up. "This is a very exciting situation you currently find yourself in."

I lifted a shoulder. "Nothin' exciting about it to me."

He pinned me with a discerning look. "It was always easy for you to talk to Tabitha."

"Easy? She scared me shitless."

"But you still *talked* to her," he pointed out. "Because unless she's changed a ton, she was one of the nicest people we knew. Nice in a real way. She always liked you."

"She likes everyone," I said. "She was out this morning with Eddie's cat on her lap like no time had passed at all. And what's your point anyway?"

He raised his palms up. "Don't come for me, big guy. I just want to know what you and Tabitha could get up to while being neighborly for the next few weeks. The kind of no-strings-attached situation I think would do you some good."

I frowned. "What the hell does that mean?"

"It means please, for the love of God, *go get yourself laid this summer.*"

I rolled my eyes. "Sorry I've been inconveniencing you with my dry spell."

"You're only inconveniencing yourself," he shot back.

I tried not to laugh but couldn't. "You're such a pain in my ass."

Rowan picked up a clipboard and a mug that said *Philly Underdogs*. "You should go for it, dude."

"She's way out of my league."

"Based on my grandmother's all-caps messages, Tabitha only had eyes for you this morning."

I scoffed. "No offense but Alice is full of shit."

"Tabitha is single," he replied. "My grandmother confirmed it."

I balked a little. "She is? Never mind. That's none of my business, and so what?"

He elbowed me as he walked past. "I'm saying now's your chance to ask her out, ten years later."

"That's a big *no* on going for it."

"Give me one good reason."

My nostrils flared. "Willie Kaminski."

His eyes narrowed. "Wasn't he a kid you boxed against in high school?"

My cheekbones tingled with past pain. "When I sparred with Kaminski, I knew to watch his right hook every time. If you took one to the cheek it was like being hit with a fucking sledgehammer. I wouldn't step into a ring with Willie and *lean into* a hook. I'd avoid it. Sleeping with a woman like Tabitha, whose gonna leave any day now and probably not come back for another ten years, might end fine for her." There was a sharp pinch in the center of my chest. "It doesn't end fine for me."

Rowan looked ready to argue this point—like he always did—but one of the other staff members called his name from down the hallway. "You got saved by a staff meeting. But maybe I see your point. Although my two cents is—"

"I don't think I need it."

"—you might be overthinking things."

I scooped up my toolbox and followed him down the hallway. "You wanna come keep lecturing me while I fix the sink for you?"

He laughed at that. "Yo, I call it like I see it."

My phone buzzed with an alert. A text message from an unknown number.

I swear this is a coincidence, but my dad just told me he's baking lemon squares for the diner tomorrow. Guess this means I'm getting all of your secrets and/or baby photos!!

A slow smile spread across my face. *I'm assuming this is Tabitha*, I sent back. *And I have no secrets.*

That wasn't true at all. And one of my biggest ones involved her.

It is Tabitha, your new neighbor and local gossip instigator here on Tenth Street.

There was a beat, then: *And we all have secrets, Mr. Machine. I'll just need to tempt them out of you.*

The warmth that spread through me didn't feel like a right hook, but I wasn't stupid. Nor could I pretend that Tabitha's friendly encouragement about fixing the lot didn't have an impact on why I was now deciding to do it.

And that was an even bigger problem.

It was a good thing I now had another problem to focus on and fix. It would make it a lot easier to avoid my beautiful neighbor and all the ways she might tempt me.

NINE
TABITHA

I woke to the sounds of rustling and a shovel striking concrete. Blinking one eye open, I groaned at the bright sun streaming through the bedroom curtains, which were flimsy and Phillies-themed.

I covered my eyes with my hand, briefly disoriented. That dizzy, *where the hell am I* sensation was as familiar as the homesickness I battled on the road. Just a consequence of my perpetual motion.

I inhaled slowly, stretching my arms overhead. I was in South Philly, in Aunt Linda's house. And Dean Knox-Morelli was my neighbor.

My disorientation shifted to curiosity. After seeing him yesterday morning, I'd distracted myself with work all afternoon, following up on potential leads, editing my last few videos, answering stray emails. Even still, I'd spent an awful lot of time gazing dreamily out the window, thinking about the breadth of those shoulders of his. Those intense eyes and that quicksilver smile that transformed his face from ruggedly handsome to charming.

He'd been like that in school too—a little shy, cards close

to his chest. But whenever I could get Dean to smile, it would make my day.

The staccato *rap-rap-rap* of that shovel came again. Then a rough voice yelled out a "*Hey, how ya doin', Dean.*"

Yawning, I crawled out from under the covers and glanced in the gaudy, gold-plated mirror to pull my snarled hair into a bun on top of my head. I was bra-less, in a tank top, but you couldn't see my nipples and my teeth were food-free, which felt like a win to me. I walked to the window without the air-conditioning unit and peeled back the curtain, searching for the source of that sound. I shoved open the window and pushed the screen wide, propping my elbows on the ledge.

"Good morning, Mr. Machine," I called down.

Dean looked up from the middle of the abandoned lot, squinting against the sun. He wore a sleeveless black shirt and running shorts, revealing every inch of his boxer arms and thick thighs, muscles rippling and flexing.

"Did I wake you?" he asked. My toes curled against the shag carpeting. That *voice*.

"Not at all," I lied. "Are you doing what I think you're doing?"

He appeared slightly sheepish. "I don't really have a plan. But between my pain-in-the-ass best friend and you—"

"A proud pain in the ass, thank you," I said.

His lips twitched. "Thought I'd see what we're working with, at least."

I arched an eyebrow. "And what's the verdict?"

He indicated the mountain of garbage behind him. "Not great."

I had a fuller view from up here, so I could agree with his initial assessment. "I know I've been gone a bit, but I'm guessing the city *isn't* investing in sanitation and trash collection, right?"

He nodded. "Or street maintenance."

I sighed, dropping more heavily onto my elbows. My hometown had a reputation for being, literally, *trashy*. It was unfair, horribly untrue, and painted whole communities of people as not caring about their surroundings. But having an accumulation of trash happened all the time in a city with an underfunded sanitation department and narrow, three-hundred-year-old streets that complicated pickups and sweepings. People dumped their trash illegally because there was often no place—and no one—to take it.

"Well," I called down, "if there's any common refrain I hear when I interview folks doing community work like this, it's that you've got to start with the first small step even if you don't know what you're doing."

Dean picked up an old Wawa hoagie wrapper with a wry expression and dropped it neatly into a trash bag. "Like this?"

I grinned. "Smart-ass. Have you had coffee yet, neighbor?"

He shook his head.

"Give me a sec." I slammed the window closed, tossed on a bra, and brushed my teeth, skipping down the stairs to turn on Linda's ancient coffee pot. While it hissed and brewed, I pulled on a newly-clean tank top and a pair of shorts from the pile of laundry I'd left folded on the couch. My aunt's house was disorienting for a couple of reasons. I was used to long-term hotel stays or short-term rentals, places where the majority of items I lived around I had only a shallow connection to.

This wasn't the house I grew up in, but we were a tight-knit family so everything here *felt* personal—old pictures, dusty Christmas wreaths, faded towels that Alexis and I would wrap around ourselves after running through sprinklers as kids.

For the first time, my beloved hiker's pack looked sad and lonely, propped against Linda's bookshelf. But owning too many things made me feel as burdened and uncomfortable as the concept of *settling down*. Alexis and I spent our teenage years witnessing my mother's transformation into a manipulative, image-obsessed social climber. Less than six months after divorcing my father, she married the man she'd been seeing behind my dad's back for a very long time.

She'd been eager to leave us for the life she wanted but complained our dad had never given her: a giant, ostentatious house in the wealthy suburbs outside the city; a husband with multiple degrees and a private practice; two children—my stepbrothers—whom she loved and doted on in a way she never did with me and my sister.

I grabbed two chipped white mugs from the cabinet and filled them with fresh coffee, cream, and sugar. Balancing them both in one arm, I pushed open the door and stepped barefoot into the humid air. The stoop was warm beneath my bare skin as I settled down on the top step and carefully placed the mugs below me.

Dean was currently occupied with two of the kids who lived across the street excitedly showing him something on their phones. They stared up at him with sheer glee while his brow was pinched, body stiff and a little awkward. I propped my chin in my hand and smiled when our eyes met, the connection fleeting.

He was almost *too* cute.

I waved to a few folks sweeping the sidewalk in front of their stoops. Tipping my face up toward the sun, I inhaled the smell of asphalt, coffee, and the bacon one of our neighbors must have been cooking. I closed my eyes, heard the spray of hoses; the sparrows perched on telephone poles; conversations in multiple languages; the steady, colorful rhythm of a neighborhood waking up.

My heart lodged in my throat, an unexpected emotion and

one I couldn't encourage. After chatting with my too-cute neighbor, I needed to spend the day focusing on where I was going next. The clock was ticking, after all.

When I opened my eyes, Dean was strolling toward the stoop, one hand raking through his hair. I offered him a mug and indicated the spot next to me, but he stayed standing.

"I thought I'd find you with your feet in the kiddie pool down at the other end of the block," he said.

I grinned and glanced approvingly in that direction. "They sure know how to have a good time. I stopped by the kiddie pool for less than an hour last night and still *stumbled* back here. Is it just me or can Midge convince a person to do literally anything? Like take shots of Crown Royal even when it's barely past five o'clock?"

He raised his mug to his lips. "People think I'm the dangerous one in the family. But it's Midge you need to watch out for."

"A warning I plan on heeding," I said, trying not to get too distracted by the veins in his forearms or the coarse texture of his voice this early in the morning. "What's the deal with you shoveling up beer bottles all by yourself?"

He looked down at the sidewalk then back up at me. "I want to fix the lot and turn it into...well, I don't know, to be honest. The guy from the city that I talked to said if it looked nice and the city finally got its act together to come out and look at it, they'd probably leave it be if we were putting it to good use."

I tapped my nails on my mug. "He's probably right. Are you worried an investor will snatch it up? Although that's not always a bad thing, depending on what they're planning to build."

A muscle ticked in his jaw. "Unless it's the kind of investing that'll make it too expensive for folks *from* here to keep living here."

"I hear you," I said, stifling a worried sigh. "And let's hope not. I think the best plan of action is to do exactly what you're doing. Two years ago, I spent a lot of time in Baltimore with a neighborhood group that created these 'pocket parks.' A tiny splash of green space that made use of vacant sites in the city. The one I was filming was turned into a sunflower garden, no bigger than this lot, I'd say. There were benches and string lights. The whole neighborhood got behind it."

I felt, more than heard, the notes of curiosity in my voice. The same notes I got when a new story idea appeared in my inbox or a random conversation sparked inspiration.

His heavy brow knit together. "A pocket park?"

"Pretty cool concept, right? I might have done a little research in my spare time yesterday. Just out of pure interest," I said quickly. And *definitely not* because I had already gone down a rabbit hole, digging up some of Dean's old matches and watching them with my mouth slightly open.

The former boxer in front of me grunted a *huh* response and fixated on the empty space in question. Besides the bend to his nose, there were a few jagged scars under his eye and on his cheeks and one indenting his bottom lip. His knuckles were slightly swollen, wrists thick. I had no clue what the announcers were saying during his fights or the calls the ref made or any of the names of what Dean and his opponent were doing.

I did feel like I finally understood the true meaning of raw, unrestrained power. Seeing him in action *was* like watching a finely tuned machine. In the ring, his face remained impassive —except for the snarl on his lips and the knife-sharp glint in his eyes. It had been mesmerizing—all those flexing muscles, the sweat gleaming on his skin, the full reach of his arms.

But it was impossible to ignore the dark underbelly of each fight, how every strike to his body had me wincing in sympathy. And that Dean took hit after hit to his head seemingly without complaint.

"Penny for your thoughts?" I asked.

His gaze darted back to mine. "I like that idea of a small park. I can't see it though. I only see the problem."

I made a sound of agreement. "I think that's pretty normal, don't you? People can't see the change—or make a change—because the problem is so big it blocks out everything else?"

He was quiet for a moment. "Yeah. That's true."

I set my cup down and crept down the steps. Careful to avoid broken glass, I walked to the very edge of the lot, reached in and pulled out a plastic bag filled with napkins. When I turned around, Dean was holding up the trash bag with a half smile playing on his lips as I dropped it in. "One small step at a time," I repeated, then perched back on the stoop. "Have you asked folks what they might want to see here?"

He shook his head.

"I could help with that," I said, my words tumbling out before I could snatch them back. "But only if you wanted the help. Or needed it. I totally, *totally* understand if I'd only be an annoying distraction."

Dean's fingers curled into fists at his side. "You're not... annoying, Tabitha."

I arched my eyebrow. "But am I a *distraction*?"

I was joking, as usual, but the slight flush in his cheeks had my own face heating up. We broke eye contact, me to drink coffee and him to twist the shovel into the sidewalk. I was probably still jet-lagged. Flirting with attractive people didn't generally evoke this kind of fluttery reaction.

"You might be slightly distracting," he finally said, eyes

crinkling at the sides. I smiled at him, surprised and blushing everywhere now. But before I could flirt back, Eddie walked past us with Pam behind him, twitching her tail.

"Morning, how youse doing?" he grumbled, squinting at the shovel.

Dean grumbled back and I said, "*Hello there, Pam.*"

"She follows me now," he said proudly. "Never saw a stray cat do that before, but she must like me."

I crouched down and cooed as Pam rubbed her cheek against my leg. "Would you like some coffee?"

"Nah," he said. "I'm heading to your dad's diner. Meeting a few army buddies. You doing some shit with the lot, or what?"

I shot a bemused look at Dean. "You should ask Mr. Machine over here."

Dean rubbed the back of his neck. "I am doing some shit, yeah. It's time we make it better whether the city wants us to or not."

Eddie nodded once, apparently satisfied. "I'll help you with it."

"Eddie," Dean warned.

"What? I can still do things—or at the very least, me and Alice can cheer everyone on from the benches."

"We can make that work," I said brightly. I stood up and brushed the hair from my face. "If you could have it your way, what would that space look like to you?"

Eddie sniffed, cocked his head. Pam wound between his legs, purring. "That used to be Annie's house. Annabeth was her name, but we all called her Annie. She was old as dirt when I was a kid, honest-to-god lived to one hundred and four all on her own. We all took care of her, of course, but that's what you did for each other, ya know?"

I need to be filming this. I blinked rapidly, surprised again at the burst of inspiration.

"Annie didn't have a lot of family here. Most were all back in Italy. But I know they appreciated us taking care of her. She used to throw parties..." Eddie whistled low under his breath, then grinned. "Man, I ain't ever been so drunk in my life. She gave back though, cooked meals for people, volunteered with her church. Kept us all going when times were tough. We did the same for her."

My stomach went hollow. Yesterday I was very aware of the many tiny ways this block was taking care of Eddie. I recognized the gentle—but forceful—methods his neighbors were using to make sure he had enough to eat. I'd watched my dad do it, had seen Kathleen do it for her siblings. Alexis and Eric had started a food pantry for the parents and guardians of their students that operated out of their classrooms.

And I'd witnessed this kindness on the road, in every town and community, right through my viewfinder.

"Watching that house of hers get so run down just about broke my heart," Eddie continued. "She was so proud of it. Seeing it get bulldozed was pretty bad." He waved at the lot behind us. "This is worse. She would've hated this."

I swallowed hard, all of my complex memories of home zipping around, jumbled and confusing. "What would have made Annie happy?"

Eddie let out a sigh. "You should ask the others, especially Natalia and Martín. They've got kids—little ones—maybe they'd want a swing set or something. Annie would like that. Some trees. A little garden. Would be real nice for people turning onto this block to see a park instead of garbage."

Dean trapped my gaze with his dark-and-mysterious one. My skin prickled with awareness. "That would be nice," he said. "Especially if folks on the block wanted to do it with me."

"This block?" Eddie said. "You wouldn't even have to ask. You'd have more help than you knew what to do with." Then he scooped Pam into his arms and shuffled off in the direction of my dad's diner, tossing a wave goodbye as he did so.

"Tell my dad to bake more lemon squares," I yelled.

Eddie barked out a laugh as he rounded the corner.

When Dean finally turned to me, I raised my eyebrows as in *See? I told you.*

His lips curved into a half smile that had my toes curling. "Still trying to blackmail your elderly neighbors into spilling secrets about me?"

I reached behind my screen door with a smirk and produced a tiny white box. Flipped it open to reveal four lemon squares, nestled in powdered sugar. "I swear it was a coincidence."

His eyes flicked down, and his chest rumbled with soft laughter.

"Want one?"

"I'm good, thanks," he said. "My mothers will take all four off your hands."

He tapped the shovel up and down, striking the sidewalk with a gentle *rap-rap-rap*. His internal struggle was obvious, but I didn't push. Finally, he said, "Would you like a secret?"

I bit my lip. "Sure. But I'm happy to offer up one myself if it'll feel more even."

He tapped the shovel a few more times. "I've taken knockouts that feel better than asking for help or accepting it when it's offered. I hate doing it. But if you're offering—and could help me with this—I could use it. I could use a...friend."

His sincere tone, coupled with his earnest expression, propelled me toward promises without hesitation.

"Absolutely," I said. *Gushed* was more like it. "It's practically in Aunt Linda's backyard, and I can't let you take on such a huge project by yourself. Besides, I'm not only an incredible neighbor. I'm a hard worker, skilled at team building, I *love* working with my hands. I'm sure they're not as skilled as yours, which are quite skilled. Right? I swear I haven't been thinking about your hands, it only sounds like I have."

I trailed off at the very end and knew my face was a unique shade of red my sister Alexis swore made me look like a tomato.

Dean looked equally amused. "Tabitha."

"I feel like if I apologize again for talking about your hands, I'm only going to make it sound creepier."

He was clearly fighting a smile. "You're not wrong. But thank you for helping me."

I swayed on my feet, the motion a warning. I had more than enough on my plate and needed to keep my movements here light and relaxed, untangled and loose. I had a rare break from the grind of video producing and *should* have been using this time like the gift it was. It was a time to assess and re-prioritize my career, to hustle up contracts and meaningful stories. Offering to help Dean, to help this street was already giving me that heart-stuck-in-my-throat feeling, that craving for *home* I had successfully resisted for years now.

But I'd always been able to control my emotions—and entanglements—in the past, so I decided not to worry.

A lopsided grin appeared on his face. "Whatever happens with this space, it'll probably be a beautiful thing to behold," he said, repeating my words from the other night. "Don't you think?"

"I certainly agree. The person who said that sounds super smart and amazing."

He nodded, the heat in his eyes taking my breath away. "And she's definitely a distraction."

TEN

DEAN

Half an hour later, Tabitha returned to the lot, gripping a large trash bag and a pair of heavy gardening gloves. Her dark red hair was in a messy bun. Her sunglasses were giant and hot pink. She wore a massive shirt over running shorts with Bruce Springsteen's face on it.

"I totally stole this from Aunt Linda's closet," she said, pointing at the center of her chest. "What do you think? Is it fashion or what?"

I held my tongue until I could trust the persistent thoughts I'd been having about Tabitha. Fantasies. Late-night ones. I was strict with my training and strict with anything decadent. That applied to sex too. The casual encounters I'd had left me unsatisfied past the basics of pleasure and relief. I had a sneaking suspicion what was missing for me beforehand was connection or conversation. Friendship. Things that I always struggled with.

I never explored what I wanted from sex. Never allowed a deeper discovery because I was too worried I'd never experience it in real life. I'd already lost so much. Could I really stifle any more of my body's desires?

But I'd been helpless to resist Tabitha's charms as a teenager. And as a man, sharing a wall with her had obliterated the mental lock on that door. Last night I'd finally given in, stroking myself to a reel of images I couldn't seem to stop: this gorgeous redhead fisting my shirt in her hand and dragging me inside her house. Demanding me on my knees. Hiking up her skirt so I could bury my face between her luscious, tattooed thighs. I'd serve her eagerly—and often—if only she asked. I'd come with a strangled groan and had to bite my pillow so she wouldn't hear.

"What I'm getting is that you're utterly stunned by my beauty in this Springsteen shirt my aunt definitely got at a concert in Jersey in 1995?" she said.

I cleared my throat. Cleared my head. "How did you guess?"

She smirked. "Sorry it took me a second to get back out here. I checked my inbox and had a few messages from this retro hotel in Austin that's entirely solar powered. I pitched them an idea to do a video on their sustainable design and the future of eco-conscious tourism." She tapped the side of her temple before yanking on her gloves. "I've got a few story sparks about it. Anyway, where should we go first?"

"That's a good question," I said, still catching up to her calmly mentioning moving to Texas. "Maybe start in the back, work our way out? We'll barely put a dent in it today, but it'll be a start."

"Sounds like a plan to me," she sang. Then began gingerly stepping her way through knee-high piles of garbage. "What about this corner right here?"

I followed close behind. The bare nape of her neck was elegant, a few strands of hair falling out.

Talk about a distraction.

Jaw tight, I tied my bag to the top of the metal fence and shoved the edges out, opening it wide. Tabitha pulled up an old VCR tape with the ribbons hanging down. With an amused shrug, she tossed it in.

"What's your secret, then?" I asked.

"Coffee. Mascara. And I always wear sunscreen, of course."

I cocked my head, confused. "What?"

She shoved her sunglasses up into her hair. "You asked me my secret, right?"

I scooped a pile of newspaper. "Yeah. You promised me one."

She clapped her gloved hands together. "*Right.* Right, right. I thought you meant, like, *what's your secret to success?* So I gave you the first bullshit-y, celebrity-sounding answer I could think of."

I slid Midge's gardening shears from my pocket and bent down to tackle a tangle of heavy vines. I ducked my head, hiding a smile. "Mascara though?"

"You can't see, but I'm batting my gorgeous, mascara-ed eyelashes at you as we speak, Mr. Machine."

I snipped a vine. Allowed my gaze to float up to Tabitha's. She was fluttering her eyes at me like a princess. A tattooed princess with a nose ring. "Beautiful," I said, then ducked my head back down again.

That was twice this morning I'd let myself flirt with Tabitha. She somehow made it easy. Both times had given my body a swift jolt of energy instead of my usual awkward restraint. I didn't give it much thought. Ever since leaving the ring, my physical instincts were off, confusing and untrustworthy. And I'd once been known as a boxer with perfect reflexes.

"Thank you for that," she said, with laughter in her voice. "But to answer your actual question...I'm assuming we'll be sharing a lot of secrets with each other while on this vacant-lot journey."

I raised a brow at her, unconvinced.

"I'll save my juiciest ones for later." She rolled her lips together as she balled up some magazines and tossed them into the bag. "I guess...I hated being a cheerleader. And *really* hated being head cheerleader my senior year."

My hands stilled in the vines. I looked up. "Yeah?"

"God, that's kind of a juicy one, huh?" she said, lips pursed. "I don't even think Alexis knows how much I despised it. Absolutely no shade on cheerleading. That sport is *intense*. It just wasn't for me. But I tried out the summer that my mom got remarried and my dad was so worried about us. The day I came home and told him I made the team was the first real smile he'd worn in months." Her voice caught at the end, but she coughed through it. "He thought having a big group of friends, something to focus my attention on would help me get through the tough parts of their divorce. When I would have traded all the terrifying moments of flying through the air for spending more time working on the school paper."

I stood and shoved the vine in the trash bag, the shape of it like the tentacles of some ancient sea monster. "Makes sense to me," I said. "You wanted more time to tell stories."

She tilted her head. "It was all I thought about, even if I was just writing up articles about the yearbook club or new football mascot designs. I managed to grin and bear it through cheerleading for three years and never, ever admitted it to my dad. His heart was very...fragile at that time. I didn't want to put any extra pressure on it."

I watched Tabitha yank weeds and trash with her usual exuberant energy, dancing around like this was a regular morning hangout between friends. And I wondered about a person who seemed so open—about life and her wants and her feelings—but had lied to her family about her own happiness just to keep them smiling.

"Would you ever tell him the truth?" I asked.

She hesitated, mid-motion. Then she shook her head. "Probably not. The guy still has every picture and trophy up in a dusty glass case in our house, right next to the pride flag he's been hanging out the second-story window every June since the year I came out. Seems pointless now, doesn't it?"

I wiped the sweat from my forehead with my arm. "I know what you mean. And I've been there. Sometimes it's harder telling people the truth if they've already got this idea about you in their head."

Some of the tension left her shoulders. "It really is." She hauled a large tangle of weeds into the bag. "Remember how we walked to high school together twice a week?"

"Wednesdays and Thursdays," I said, then turned away, feeling too eager.

"*Yes.* Because Tuesday night, you, me, and Rowan were all in different practices for our various sports. And I have such a strong memory of us comparing weekly injuries as we walked —or limped—in our sweats to class. Didn't you show up to a support group meeting once with a black eye?"

I rubbed the back of my head. "Probably. In my early training days if I didn't work the speed bag right, it'd smack me in the face. It's not even a cool injury."

She laughed good-naturedly. "*Oh my God*, one time I was holding pom poms, doing that clapping motion in front of my face at a football game. And I hit myself in the nose with my own fist so hard I got a nosebleed."

"That's a pretty hardcore injury, Tabitha."

"Clearly"—she indicated her outfit—"I've always been a hardcore person. But I was always grumpy about doing splits and push-ups. You, on the other hand, seemed totally at peace after a grueling workout."

I hooked my fingers into the top of the metal fence. "Boxing did that for me. I'm not very good with words. Moving my body, pushing it to its physical limit made me feel relaxed and comfortable. I like punching the hell out of things, I guess."

Her face filled with more affection than I could handle. "I finally saw some videos of you punching the hell out of things. By *things*, I mean another dude's face."

I turned away from her to tackle a patch of weeds filled with soda bottles. "Oh yeah?"

"*Oh* yeah. You were amazing to watch, as I predicted," she said, giving me another jolt of power. "Of course, you were joking the other night about me being your biggest fan, but now I'm wishing you still sold merch."

I tossed a look over my shoulder. "You're not serious."

"I *am*. You can now refer to me as a Dean the Machine Superfan, thank you very much."

It took every ounce of willpower in my body not to tell her how absurdly pleased it made me, that she'd seen me at my best. I heard a rustling sound behind me. Tabitha's *very pretty* legs suddenly came into view. My hands curled into the weeds, gripping. Those instincts were urging me to do something stupid—lean forward, slide my palms around the back of her thighs, and kiss every inch of her skin until she was trembling for me.

She dropped to her knees, barely a foot away, and pushed those ridiculous glasses back into her hair. Eye contact this close gave me even more stupid ideas. Of slipping my fingers behind her neck. Pressing my mouth to hers. We were in an actual trash heap on a hot summer's day, and she was that tempting.

"Seriously," she said, "you were amazing to watch in that ring. I didn't want you to think I was joking. I'm not." She raised one dark eyebrow. "You're also amazing now. And I like your words, neighbor. Just to be clear." She stood back up before I had a chance to respond.

It was for the best. I was a little speechless.

When I finally hauled out the weeds, she was standing at the trash bag, holding it open for me. "Thanks. For what you said. I'm happy to know I have a—"

"Superfan."

"Yeah. That." I dropped the weeds in and took a step back, tugging off my gloves. "If you want merch, I can see if Rowan still has shirts lying around in the back of his trunk."

"*Ooh.* Classy."

I couldn't help it. A gigantic smile spread across my face. The motion rattled all the locks on all the pieces of myself I kept hidden. She reached forward and squeezed my wrist. A completely friendly gesture. The pressure of her fingers on my skin, though, sent those late-night fantasies surging to the surface. When she turned away, I almost snatched her hand back.

A few seconds later, her face brightened as she was tying up the second bag. I followed her gaze to find Eddie, shuffling back down the block with Pam in his arms.

Tabitha pressed onto her tiptoes and called out over the fence, "Hey, how was the diner, Eddie?"

He responded with a thumbs-up. "Your father makes a biscuit that should be illegal, in my opinion. And he said to tell you to come by tomorrow night for his late shift. Bring your sister and Eric and your niece along."

"I think I can do that," she said. "What do you think of our progress? We've got one bag down, literally billions to go probably."

Eddie gave us that same crooked smile, like he was seconds away from mischief. "I'm impressed, you two. Why don't I round up whoever else is around on a Saturday, see if they wanna help?"

"That would be nice, thank you," I said. As he walked over to Natalia and Martín's house, Tabitha looked giddy.

"It's a beautiful morning for a neighborhood cleanup day," she said. "Oh man, this is so *exciting*, isn't it?" She hurled a ball of trash into the bag with a *swish*. "Is this how you thought you'd be spending your Saturday? Gettin' wild with garbage?"

I leaned on the shovel. "If I wasn't doing this, then probably a baseball game with Rowan and some of his coworkers. Or out for a couple beers. Maybe help my mothers with their pretty demanding house projects." I glued my eyes to the ground as I twisted the tip of the shovel back and forth. "Used to be Saturday nights were fight nights. If not mine, then someone else's. I'm not as welcome in those spaces as I used to be. Not at the bars after either."

Tabitha pressed her lips together. "Because you retired and people are still mad about it?"

"Memories are long here. Tempers are short," I said.

She made a sound of agreement followed by a breathless *oof* sound. When I looked up, she was attempting to lift a heavy, water-logged box. I closed the distance between us and took the box gently from her hands. I hid a grimace, not wanting Tabitha to see. It wasn't that heavy, but the space between my shoulder blades lit up with pain, the echoes of past muscle tears and a rotator cuff injury that had never quite healed right. Whenever I found myself missing boxing the most, my body was more than happy to remind me of all it had endured.

"Oh, thanks so much," she wheezed, blowing the hair from her face. "I swear it looked lighter on the ground before I tried to valiantly lift it. I tend to leap without looking, as my sister always says. Too impulsive."

I hefted the box into the bag. "Rowan would say I overthink everything. That I'm too restrained and never have any fun. I never leap because I look too long."

Tabitha tapped her chin. Stared at me like I'd given her some award-winning idea. "That's an interesting concept."

"What is?"

"Hear me out. What if the two of us had some fun together this summer?"

Her hands in my hair. My mouth, hot and open on her slick skin. No thoughts, only pleasure.

"Sorry, what?" I was glad my voice didn't crack like a middle schooler's.

She stepped right up to me. "You and me. Having some spontaneous, impulsive, *unrestrained* fun. Fuck all the people who took your Saturday nights away from you. They suck, and if you pointed any of them out to me, I'd dump a pitcher of beer all over their heads."

I rubbed the back of my head, torn between amusement and hesitation.

"If you need a friend to help you out with this"—she indicated the hanging row of trash bags—"then I need a friend to enjoy Philly with while I'm home for the next two weeks. Getting water ice at John's. Eating a cheesesteak like a tourist. Running up the Rocky steps at the art museum, something I'm sure you're quite good at, Mr. Machine."

I laughed. Her enthusiasm was contagious. "I'm…sufficient at that, yeah."

"*Sufficient?*" She whistled under her breath. "Okay, I'm amending my statement. You and me? We're racing to the top of the Rocky steps now. And don't think I'm letting you off the hook for dancing."

I gazed around at the garbage nightmare we were standing in. "I do owe you for agreeing to do this with me."

"You don't owe me a thing, and I would help you regardless. *But* if it makes it feel fair to you, we can do a work hard/play hard theme. This will be a worthy endeavor but a hell of a lot of work. I'll make sure you intersperse it with some spontaneous joy."

It was much too late to attempt a strategy of avoidance now. Because I'd underestimated my opponent, had let her sneak past my best defenses with charm and humor and a beauty that made my chest ache. I didn't even need to anticipate the blow.

It had already happened.

She held out her hand. "Whaddya say, neighbor? We got a deal?"

I foolishly shook it.

"Deal," I said.

ELEVEN
TABITHA

The very next night, I was rushing out the front door with my phone in one hand and a photo album in the other. I was late, as usual, for dinner with my sister and Eric at dad's diner. But I also had an email in my inbox, from that hotel in Austin, with the subject line: *Contract Proposal Follow-Up.*

"Now that's interesting," I murmured, eyes on my screen as I scrolled. I flew down the front steps and hit a brick wall that smelled amazing. Strong hands gripped both of my elbows, keeping me steady. They were a fighter's hands, turned gentle. I looked up at Dean Knox-Morelli, and my knees were grateful for the extra stability.

"Hiya, neighbor," I said, breathlessly.

His brow furrowed, dark eyes lingering for a beat too long on my lips. "Are you okay?"

He released me and took a step back, putting a decent amount of space between us.

"Ah, so the brick wall I hit was your chest," I said. "You should keep an eye on those shoulders of yours. They're a real danger to the common person."

His answering smile was a little crooked and a lot adorable.

It was official. I had a crush.

My instant attraction to this handsome boxer had me dreamy-eyed and dazed. Dean the Machine was 100% summer-fling material. And if that swooping feeling in the pit of my stomach felt a little different from all the other times, I sure didn't dwell on it. At some point yesterday, Dean had started openly laughing and smiling at my jokes. Although this glimpse of openness was only muddling my many, *many* sexy thoughts about him.

Luckily for me, one of the only things I *did* own was a high-end vibrator. That thing worked orgasmic wonders on a regular day, but with Dean as erotic inspiration, I'd broken some kind of personal record in orgasms last night.

"Tabitha?"

I blinked, refocused. "I'm a little spacey today. And still a little dazed from being attacked by your chest."

His lips twitched. "Or you could watch where you're going."

"That's *never* going to happen," I said, brushing past him. "I prefer to rely on you to catch me with your shoulders or lap." I hooked my thumb toward the street corner. "I'm meeting my family at dad's diner. Do you want me to pick you up anything to eat?"

He shook his head, then glanced back toward Eddie's house. "If there's any extra..."

I touched his arm. "I got it. And it's no problem."

"Thank you," he said.

I paused, mid-step, in front of the lot. There was significantly less trash in the small quadrant Dean and I had worked through yesterday. "*Whoa*," I said. "It's already looking way better. Who showed up after I left?"

The hint of pride in his face gave me for real butterflies. "Natalia and Martín. My parents, who brought along a few of their friends from church just to help. And Rowan's nonprofit arranged getting a dumpster for us in a couple days so we can get most of it cleared out."

I chewed on my lip, feeling almost absurdly intrigued. My editorial instincts were clamoring for attention now, even if I didn't want to give in.

I *did* allow my brain to frame out a few shots and piece together a tiny arc of narrative. The transformation here was primed to be dramatic. And this street was a mixture of everything South Philly represented—tough older folks and nosy gossips and younger families and new immigrants. A blend of language and food, cultures and traditions, all jammed into brick row homes and front stoops.

"You know what...wait here a sec. Do you mind holding these?" I shoved the photo albums into his very capable arms, raced inside, and snatched my camera from the dining room table.

When I returned, I snapped a few shots of the lot from a couple angles and checked their quality on the digital screen. "We should have evidence of what the space was before. It'll *really* blow people's minds when they see what we do with it."

His brow lifted. "What *are* we going to do with it?"

"We'll figure it out, don't you worry," I said. "But I didn't want this historical moment to go undocumented."

He gave a pointed look at my camera. "Have you ever worked on any film projects about Philly?"

As a rule, I did not. Filming was intimate work. It was much harder to hide the truth. It was much easier to expose every sneaky vulnerability or complicated family secret.

"I haven't, and I don't have an interest in doing so. Part of the appeal of freelancing is that I get to see so many new and different places," I said, lifting the strap over my head. "But I can take a few photos here or there while we're working together on it."

His eyes darted back to the space. "What if I...*we*, mess it up somehow?"

I touched his arm and couldn't ignore the shock of sparks. "We won't, I promise." I cleared my throat and took a step back. "The reason why I ran into you is because I think I snagged a new contract. In Austin. You could be looking at Texas's newest resident."

"Congratulations. They'll be lucky to have you, Tabitha."

There was an uncomfortable flicker in my chest that felt an awful lot like disappointment.

"Thank you, Mr. Machine," I said. I peeked at my phone and balked at the time. "And, holy shit, I'm super late now, so I'm gonna take this photo album of embarrassing pictures and get on my way."

"If I'd known they were embarrassing, I would have peeked while you were inside," he said.

Knowing who he was, that was so *not true*. "You don't have to spy. As one of our adventures, I can take you on a trip down memory lane. Surely you recall all of my fashion disasters as a teenager."

"I wouldn't say no to that," he said. "Will we even have time for that stuff if you're heading to Texas?"

I shook my head, walking backward down the sidewalk. "You're already lookin' to get rid of me, huh? Because of *course* we'll have time. We made a deal."

"Dancing, et cetera," he said in a dry tone, but humor shone in his eyes.

"And I'll come by to help when the dumpster arrives," I said, waving as I turned the corner. "Unless I see you for some spontaneous fun first."

I had to resist taking a picture of Dean surrounded with golden hour light, his strong jaw and smattering of scars, the strength in his stance, and the slow return of confidence when he looked at me now. The image gave me that top-of-the-rollercoaster feeling in the pit of my stomach, but that was purely artistic inspiration.

The deal I made with Dean yesterday was sincere—he was a friend I'd always liked, and I had some extra time on my hands for the first time in years. But the hard truth had more to do with a fierce protectiveness that surprised me. This man had sacrificed his body for a brutal sport only to have fans deny him pleasure or relaxation. He couldn't seem to move through this city without someone sharing their very public opinion about his very private decisions.

I remembered feeling this way after we started attending those groups together. His parents and his experiences looked the most like mine and that made me want to stick together.

So I couldn't give him those Saturday nights back, when he clearly felt pride and kinship with those around him. But I was an expert in impromptu joy of all shapes and sizes. That was the beating heart of storytelling, no matter the medium.

Crush or not, it sure was nice to see Dean Knox-Morelli with a smile on his face again.

TWELVE
TABITHA

I stood outside the Broad Street Diner—open twenty-four hours a day, seven days a week—and prepared to take a new job in Austin, Texas.

"Based on the contract, we're anticipating this to be six months of work," Meghan, the hotel communications director, was saying.

I leaned against the signpost and faced Broad Street, all lit up with cars. "I really appreciate those connections. I've been fascinated with eco-tourism and the way hotels can make climate justice an integral part of the hospitality industry."

"Oh, of course. We believe it's essential," Meghan said. "And as a lifelong Austinite, it's likely you'll come here and simply never leave. I've seen it happen dozens of times."

I tilted my head back against the signpost. That was highly *unlikely* of me.

"I've been getting messages about coming to Austin for years from some of my social media followers. I'm long overdue to explore your lovely city."

"We'll wait for you to sign the contract, and then we'll go

from there with details and setting up the interviews," she added.

"Great," I said cheerfully. "I'll start booking all of my travel arrangements now. And keep an eye out for my contract."

We said goodbye and ended our call. I stood by the sign for a few more seconds, tapping my cell phone against the center of my chest. A few days ago, I would have been thrilled at the possibility of heading to Austin, a city renowned for embracing its quirky weirdness. It was a storyteller's dream. Now I was peering up at the twinkling, amethyst skyline thinking about family dinners and empty lots and Dean's shy smile.

I shook my head, clearing my confusion, and skipped up the stairs into the diner. A bell rang over the door and my dad popped out from around the counter, tossing a rag over his shoulder. It was boisterous in here as usual, the dinnertime rush a steady tradition. If I closed my eyes, I could have been in middle school again, sitting at the counter with Alexis and doing our homework while sharing a plate of french fries.

My dad opened his arms for a hug. "You got a reservation, or what?"

"Nah. I thought I'd barge in and demand you serve me."

I stepped back only to have Juliet barrel into my legs with a squeal. I dropped down and lifted her around my waist. She squeezed my cheeks with her hands.

"Hi, Aunty Tabby," she said.

"Hi, kiddo." To my dad, I said, "I don't know what you're cooking tonight, but I've been thinking about a chicken cheesesteak all day."

He tapped my arm. "You got it. And is that Lin's photo album?"

I held it in my outstretched hand. "Oh, you mean these

pictures of her *Saturday Night Fever*–themed birthday party? Why yes, yes, it is."

He gave a funny shrug. "My memory is that I looked good in those silver bell-bottoms."

Juliet poked my cheeks with her fingers. I made a silly face at her. "I plan to give the best ones to Kathleen so she can put them on your Christmas card this year."

I walked over to Alexis and Eric in their red vinyl booth.

"Gimme, gimme," my sister said, taking the photo album. "We promise not to laugh too hard, Dad."

"I'm unable to make that promise," Eric said.

Dad's response was to flash us a mischievous grin as he tossed the towel back over his shoulder. "You laugh now until you're waiting an hour for your dinner."

He slipped back behind the counter, and Juliet very seriously slid a coloring book my way with one purple and one green crayon. "Will you color with me?"

"Of *course*," I said. "Your mom and I used to come here after school. We'd do our homework while Pop-Pop cooked food for people."

Alexis snorted. "I learned all of my best curse words as a kid from the people who sat next to us at that counter, yelling at whatever was happening on Action News."

I leaned over the table to see what pictures she was looking at. They were slightly faded, some more blurry than others. My dad and his sister, Aunt Linda, looked like they'd walked off the set of the *Stayin' Alive* music video. He had his arm around her shoulders, and they were laughing outrageously at some joke we'd never know.

"She still has those same curtains," I said.

"They were legends, man," Eric said.

I looked affectionately at the picture in front of me. "You're not wrong."

Alexis looked up and shut the album with a dramatic flair. "Did I read your text this morning correctly? Are you really helping Dean Knox-Morelli clean the abandoned lot next to Linda's house?"

"Looks like it," I said. "Although most of the neighbors have been helping, and I think it's likely we'll be done with the trash-removal part in a few days. The harder part is organizing what they want to put in there. Dean said the city doesn't care, so they've got free rein." I propped my chin in my hand as I colored in a unicorn's tail. "I told him about the stories I did on pocket parks in Baltimore. Mini green spaces. And I called Linda, who was sunbathing on the beach in Wildwood. She was relieved to know we were doing something about it, said she loved the idea of flowers or trees that would attract more birds and butterflies."

"It's a great idea," Alexis said. "We could swing by one of these days and talk to Dean about the community gardens at the school."

"It's changed everything for the kids," Eric added. He slid his elbows onto the table. "To be able to go to school and grow things, to watch the transformation, to work together on a project with real results you can touch and see and smell. Or even to eat. And for that part of the parking lot to not just be a hot slab of asphalt filled with Coke bottles and straw wrappers. But something green and alive."

I nodded enthusiastically. "And Dean is, like, the perfect person to tackle this thing. I don't think he notices how much his neighbors look up to him as a leader."

Alexis arched a blond eyebrow my way, clearly amused.

What? I mouthed.

Nothing, she mouthed back, with the slyest grin I'd ever seen.

We let out a rousing cheer as Dad dropped off our delicious-smelling food for us.

"Gimme fifteen minutes, then I'll clock out and come eat with you guys," he said. "Kathleen is rushing over to see the photo album."

I popped a french fry into my mouth. "She will not be disappointed."

Juliet looked up from her grilled cheese. Her curls were in two tiny, poofy pigtails that sat on top of her head. "Are you taking our picture?"

I chewed, swallowed. "What, sweetheart?"

She pointed to the camera I had slung across my shoulder.

"I totally forgot I brought this." I popped off the lens and peered through the viewfinder at Juliet, who was posing for the camera. "Do you want one of just you or with your mom and dad?"

She scrunched up her nose and said, "*With them,* Aunty Tabby."

"You got it, kiddo." I made the universal *scoot in close* gesture. Eric wrapped his arm around my sister and pulled her in. Juliet popped onto his lap, and he rested his chin on top of her head.

"Are you ready?" I asked.

"*Ready,*" Juliet said. "Say cheese."

I laughed. "I say that part."

"*Say cheese!*" she yelled.

The shutter went *click*. I checked the digital screen to see how the first one came out. I'd caught all three of them mid-laugh.

My heart swelled at the image, stirring up my jumbled thoughts from earlier. It was like my brain was now refusing to acknowledge the boundary I'd carefully constructed after I moved away.

Alexis and Eric were definitely a *story*—two people who fell in love in college while bonding over their commitment to public service. Teachers who fought for their students, who listened to their needs and met them without judgment. They marched and protested, did park cleanups, and led voter registrations. And every year, on June first, my sister had rainbow-colored cupcakes delivered to whatever random address I was staying in.

For a person who valued the joy of community so much, I sure was missing a lot of it here.

"How does it look?" Alexis asked.

I grinned through the tight grip on my throat and passed her the camera. She and Eric lit up when they saw it. Juliet was less impressed and eagerly went back to her coloring.

"Pop-Pop says you take pictures as your job," she said, her little face screwed up in concentration.

"That's a pretty good explanation," I said. "I take lots of pictures, but mostly I take videos and make little movies for people to watch."

That got her attention. "Can I make a movie?"

I slid out my phone and turned the video function on. "Anyone can make a movie. I bet your dad can help you. Go for it."

The expression she wore waving my phone around had my sister and me exchanging a look of surprised happiness.

"You might have a little director on your hands," I mock-whispered.

"I'd be okay with that," she replied.

Juliet pointed the phone at me. I waved and blew a kiss for the camera. "If you want, you can ask me questions. That's how I start making my movies."

"Okay," she said, *very* seriously. "Do you miss me when you leave?"

"Every single day."

"Can I still call you when you leave again like we did before?" she asked.

"You can call me anytime," I said. "I promise."

She was zooming all over. I couldn't contain my smile, watching her work, the astonishment radiating from her movements. It was an astonishment that I recognized.

"Do you have friends?" she asked.

I smothered a giggle. "I do have friends. Your mom and dad are my best friends."

"But when you go away and leave us, I mean?"

"Wow," Eric said. "No more softball questions for you, Aunty Tabby."

I snorted and said, "Of *course* I have friends. I meet people everywhere I go."

Which was objectively true. The contact list on my phone was filled with friends I'd made during my travels and random temporary roommates and people I'd dated. But I hadn't spoken to any of them since coming home.

I thought Juliet might want to keep questioning me, but she'd already dropped my phone to go back to enjoying her grilled cheese, which wasn't a decision I could fault her for. It was a Drew Tyler specialty.

I leaned across the table. "I just confirmed my next contract. I'm heading out to Austin at the end of the month."

My sister's eyes went wide. "Can we come visit? We've been wanting to go there for years."

"I'm in," Eric said. "We'll still be off from school for most of August. Could be our summer vacation destination."

"If Dad and Kathleen come, she will leave a trail of tequila and destruction through that city," Alexis said. "And, personally, I can't wait."

The characterization of my wild and raunchy stepmom

was accurate. But my own physical response to what I'd normally consider great news was a little muted. Perhaps it was sitting in this cracked, red-vinyl booth, draped in affection and bittersweet nostalgia, and thinking about everything I had to do only to leave again—the long plane rides, the empty hotel room, the temporary housing, the loneliness of being on your own in a new city.

My headspace was all over the map tonight.

"Austin is probably ripe for a hot summer fling, right?" Alexis asked.

I took a giant bite of my cheesesteak to avoid answering. Dean wouldn't be in Austin, obviously. And that was fine. *Obviously.*

The bell over the door jingled, and I smelled Kathleen's perfume. She slid into our booth just as my dad returned, passing me a Styrofoam container with *Eddie* scrawled in black marker.

"I happened to make extra chicken tonight if he wants some," he said.

Thank you, I mouthed, squeezing his wrist.

"Hi, Grandma," Juliet said, sounding shocked. "What are you doing here?"

"Hi, baby," she said, picking a piece of lint off her leopard-print top. "I'm here because I wanted to see pictures of your Pop-Pop."

Dad was trying to wrestle the photo album out of Alexis's hands.

"The world deserves to see this," she said, swatting him away. "You can't keep the people from the truth of your platform shoes."

Alexis shoved it to me, and Kathleen immediately moved in close. I was squashed at the very end, with Dad and Kathleen next to me, our plates of food and drinks in a colorful array around us. With each flip of the page, she and my dad burst into laughter. My sister and I hadn't been born yet, but the pictures of Aunt Linda's house and the street were essentially the same.

Some houses looked a little nicer now. Some a little worse. But the composition of each image was alive with the vibrations of loud music, sticky summer nights, too many beers and just enough food. The kind of party that couldn't be contained in a row home, spilling out onto a block full of neighbors happy to join in.

On the very last page was a picture jammed into the bottom corner, bent at one end. I narrowed my eyes as I reached for it, wiggling it free.

"Hey, I recognize these party animals." I flipped it around to show my dad. "That's a much younger Eddie, Alice, and Midge and Maria. Dean's parents."

His eyes crinkled at the sides. "They were always up for a block party."

"Still are now," I said, bringing the picture close to my face. Midge had her arm thrown around Maria's shoulders. Their hair was dark, faces unlined, and they wore matching yellow bell-bottom pants.

"Dean and I were just talking about our support groups at the Lavender Center, how hard it was for his parents to be themselves, especially in this city at that time."

"It was extremely hard," Dad said. "They told me that they relied on their neighbors to keep them safe. Stand up for them if they needed it. They welcomed them at holidays if they weren't welcome at their own family's dinner tables."

I placed the picture down. "I didn't know you talked to Dean's parents about their experiences."

He rubbed a hand through his hair. "When you came out to me, I went to go see them."

I don't know why, but I still asked, "With Mom too?"

Kathleen muttered a few unkind words beneath her breath.

He shook his head, and I felt an unexpected wave of disappointment.

"At the time, we hadn't started going to those support groups yet," Dad continued. "I'd always liked Midge and Maria, and they were kind to me when your mom and I got divorced. They didn't gossip about us, even though everyone else we knew did. Told me they weren't saints but knew a bit about what it was like to live under a microscope, you know?"

Under the table, Alexis squeezed my fingers.

"One night, after your sister threw you that Pride party, I brought a six pack over and told them I wanted to know how I could be a good dad to you. Besides loving you—that's always been easy. But they had some insight I just didn't. About listening and not judging. Stuff like that." His smile was bashful. "I'm sure I wasn't perfect, but they helped me a lot."

The pressure in my throat grew. I had to swallow three times before I could speak again. "You were the perfect dad for me."

He beamed at that and ruffled my hair like I was a kid again.

"I see them both now, staying at Aunt Linda's house. I'll make sure to thank them," I said. "Let them know I turned out all right."

"More than all right," Dad said. "And that son of theirs is one of the good ones, I don't care what anybody says."

I shifted back and forth on the vinyl. Dean was most assuredly *one of the good ones.*

Alexis tapped the album with her finger. "There isn't a single picture of Mom in here, oddly enough. Did she turn her nose up at Aunt Linda's disco-themed party?"

Dad looked a little nervous. "Uh, no. Your aunt threw away every picture of your mom after we split up."

Alexis and I exchanged a glance. "I don't know if I'm impressed or terrified," I said.

"Your aunt is a ferocious woman that sticks to her guns." From Kathleen's tone, it was obvious she considered that a compliment.

"Well," Eric said, "maybe the two of you will have to throw your own theme party. I bet you can rummage up some groovy seventies clothes at the thrift stores around town."

Kathleen grabbed my arm, mouth open. "Like maybe before you leave?"

My mouth twisted to the side. "Probably not. I was just telling them about the contract I signed with a hotel in Austin."

This time I was watching closely, caught the split second of sadness on Dad's and Kathleen's faces before they congratulated me.

"I think this calls for hot fudge sundaes to celebrate, yeah?" my dad said. "I can whip some up in the back."

"Absolutely," I chimed in, smile frozen on my face. We went back to eating and making jokes and enjoying too much ice cream with one another. But churning beneath was a tangle of feelings and memories only growing louder with every day I spent back home. I was beyond lucky to have a father and sister—plus a brother-in-law and stepmom—who loved me without question, who were willing to celebrate every part of my identity, every accomplishment and achievement.

My mother, on the other hand, used criticism as a form of control, held Alexis and me up to a level of expected perfection that was never, ever possible. And we'd disappointed her so badly that she'd gone ahead and gotten herself a brand-new family.

She'd involved me in her secrets and lies when I was *much* too young to comprehend what she was having me do—which was help her break my father's heart so deeply that my aunt Linda *threw away* pictures of her.

I kept these secrets close and locked away because the idea of hurting my father and sister again was *the worst thing* I could imagine a person doing. My mother had already hurt them enough. Yet in the face of their honesty and support, lying gave me an icky, turbulent feeling in the pit of my stomach.

This quick layover in Philly was just that and nothing more. The longer I was here, the more grateful I became that I could leave.

THIRTEEN
DEAN

I stepped out of the shower to knocking at my door while my cell phone rang. With a soft curse, I wrapped a towel around my waist and ran a hand through my wet hair. My rib cage ached as I inhaled. Sly had worked me on the pull-up bar at the gym and had me skipping rope between sets. I'd welcomed the burn in my muscles and the diversion from analyzing every interaction I'd had with a certain vivacious redhead.

Nothing seemed to temper my lust for her though.

I snatched my phone from the top of the dresser. "Yeah, what's up?"

"You don't even say hello to your agent anymore?"

I tucked the phone between my ear and my shoulder as I tightened my towel. "Harry?"

"Yeah, how you doing? How's Midge and Maria?"

Harry Fleet had been my agent since my amateur boxing days. I still heard from him a couple times a year, usually about some appearance or re-airing of a classic fight, but it had been more than six months since he'd called me up out of the blue.

"My parents are good. Healthy. And I'm fine." Someone knocked at my door again. A little more persistently this time. "You're not at my house, are you?"

"In South Philly? No, why would I be?"

I walked down the stairs to another round of knocking. "Uh...never mind. Is everything okay?"

He chuckled. "Yeah, everything's okay. Everything is *great*. Are you sitting down?"

I twitched open the front curtain. Tabitha was on the top of my stoop in a cropped black tank top and jean shorts. She turned, ponytail swinging, and smiled at me like I was her best friend in the whole world. In her hands were two small white containers with plastic spoons.

Then we both realized I was naked from the waist up, in only a towel, at the exact same time. Her eyes dipped down my torso. Lingered long enough to have all the blood in my body coursing south. The path her pretty gaze traveled seemed slow on purpose, like she was enjoying the view.

"Dean?" Harry said.

I didn't respond. I was riveted to the goddamn spot, watching Tabitha watch *me*. I felt it like she was right here. Like those hands of hers were trailing down my chest. Like those fingers were hooking into the top of my towel. Like she would eagerly fall to her knees while my own fingers wrapped around that ponytail.

"Dean, are you there?"

"Just a minute," I said roughly, wiping my hand across my mouth. Tabitha finally snapped out of her own daze and covered her eyes with a flirtatious smirk.

"Oh my God, sorry for being such a fucking *perv*," she yelled. "And sorry for yelling that on your front stoop for anyone to hear. I'm definitely making this situation worse and not better. But I randomly picked up mango and lemon water ice from John's and thought it was spontaneous enough to have you join me on the stoop?"

Her fingers separated an inch so she could peek through. Electricity snapped off my nerve endings like heat lightning. I was grateful for the literal brick wall separating us. *This* was fight night power. The unstoppable kind. The addicting kind.

And I hadn't closed the curtains or covered myself up either. I'd let Tabitha check out my body like she was as overcome with temptation as I was.

I cocked my head at the door and let the curtain drop. Then I placed the phone down on the table and cracked my front door open. Her cheeks were pink, lips parted.

"Let me finish this call, and then I'll come eat your...water ice."

Her dark brows shot up. "Okay, now who's the perv?"

I rubbed my jaw. "I'm learning from the best."

She tipped her head back and laughed. And was still laughing as I let the door click shut.

"Sorry, Harry," I mumbled into the phone. "It was my neighbor."

"Yeah, whatever," he said. "But listen...Dean, I'm telling you. I've got *huge* news. The network called, asking about your availability."

"What network?"

"Are you kidding me? *The* network. Game Time. The largest sports entertainment channel in the country isn't ringin' a bell for you?"

I pinched the bridge of my nose. "Of course it is. But why are they calling about me? I'm out and I've been out."

Game Time didn't usually air amateur fights, but they aired the Golden Gloves the year that I won, which was a large part of my popularity once I went pro. Every bar in Philly streamed the weekend fights on the Game Time channel.

"Not to box. As a *commentator*. Their top guy is leaving, and they want to replace him with someone who's retired but on the younger side. You are on an extremely short list. And, look, they know you would be young compared to a lot of the other commentators on their network, but it's the new angle they're looking for. You could grow into a new career."

I fell back heavily against the door. "A...commentator?"

"That's what I'm saying."

"But I can't..." I trailed off. Sports commentators wore fancy clothes and sat behind desks while facing a camera crew. They interviewed athletes and analyzed performances.

Most of all, they weren't people like me. Sure, flirting with Tabitha the past few days was boosting my confidence. That didn't mean I was ready to put on a tie and get beamed into people's households after every match.

"Harry," I started again. "They know what I'm like, right?"

He coughed. "Yeah, they know you're not that into the spotlight. But every person they put in front of that camera gets training and mentoring. You better believe it. If they choose you, they're gonna be putting in years of work and money out the *wazoo*. Even better? It's in Vegas, baby."

My ear caught the sound of Tabitha's voice, talking to someone on the sidewalk. My agent was calling me about a once-in-a-lifetime opportunity, and I was trying to go get water ice. "I'm sorry, what? I'd have to move to Las Vegas?"

"That's where their studio is. It's the epicenter of the sport."

I didn't know how I felt about that. I traveled a bit when I was pro—and obviously to Vegas before. The only thing I remembered was hating every fucking thing about it, but that wasn't the point really. The point was—could I pack up the way Tabitha did all the time and leave?

"I know it's a lot to take in. And they haven't made their

decision yet. But I wanted you to know in case it happened so you would have time to consider it. I don't think I'm stepping out of line here if I tell you that, as your agent, this is the dream. This would mean being back in the business, back doing what you do best, without having to get your ass kicked in a ring. You feel me?"

"Uh-huh," I said, still processing.

There was a pause. Then Harry said, "How have things been since you left?"

"They're fine," I said. My standard response. "I still train with Sly, I just don't—"

"Take any hits to that big head of yours?"

My nostrils flared. There was a reason why Harry annoyed the shit out of me. "Something like that."

"But what are you *doing* with your life?"

What was I *doing*? I was doing odd maintenance jobs around South Philly for family and friends and meticulously training for another fight that would never come. All while bearing the weight of a city that felt either pissed at me or sorry for me.

I walked into the kitchen and poured myself a glass of water. Right by the sink was a framed picture from one of the matches I won. The ref had my left fist in the air while my right arm dangled at my side. I had a cut on my cheek and a swollen lip. Sweat dripped from my hair and down my chest. The look on my face didn't resemble some robotic machine at all. I looked like an animal. I looked *feral.*

"I'm not doing much," I admitted, putting down my glass and picking up the frame. "But I'm not saying I want to get back into it again."

"Not even if this could count as your comeback?"

I went still. I'd never admitted to Harry how conflicted I was about retiring sometimes—those low, late-night thoughts that were impossible to ignore. He'd take that ball and run with it, have me signed up for some exhibition in no time.

"Do I want a comeback?" I asked.

"I don't know. Do you?"

A dull pounding started up at the base of my skull. "Harry."

"What?"

I hesitated, eyes flicking up to the ceiling. "What's the network's stance on concussions and TBIs? Are they doing anything about it?"

This time Harry took a second to respond. "Full disclosure? No. They're not changing the rules. You're gonna see boxers take a lot of punches to the head, just like you did."

"They can't operate from that mindset," I said urgently. "These are injuries that boxers can't just bounce back from. I *still* have side effects, and I was one of the lucky—"

"Dean," he interrupted. "Dean, *Dean*. I get it, okay? Your sport obsession of choice isn't perfect. And which sport is? But if that's a question you'd have for them, I can pass it on to the guy I've been talking to."

I stretched my neck from side to side and contemplated hitting Harry just for fun. "I would appreciate that, thanks."

"Are you at least slightly interested?" he asked.

That picture of me in victory stared at me accusingly. Saying no would be a full lie, even if I didn't want to admit it. "I'm slightly interested."

Harry whistled. "Well, okay then. At least I know we can play a little hardball now. I'll be in touch. It wouldn't hurt to peek at some apartments in Vegas. In a nice neighborhood, if you catch my drift."

He disconnected before I could answer. I held the phone out and stared at it, wondering what the actual hell was happening.

One call from my agent with an opportunity that wasn't even locked down and that rare confidence was filtering back in. *Slowly*, and the texture was different, but I couldn't deny its existence. What would it be like to have Tabitha Tyler flirting with me if I was about to become a big-time sports announcer—and on my way to Vegas? If my time here was suddenly as fleeting as hers?

I rubbed the back of my neck, easing the tight pressure there. What would it be like to work for a network that encouraged—even glamorized—the violence that had left my body with real scars and permanent consequences for my health?

All of that wasn't even the real question though.

The *real* question was if I didn't take this opportunity, what was I going to do instead?

FOURTEEN
DEAN

I took a minute to towel off and throw on a shirt and gym shorts. Then I shouldered open the storm door and stepped out, barefoot, into a muggy night. It was late, the sun was setting. Past Tenth Street came the sounds of a block party and a mix of loud music from open car windows. Lía, Marco, and a handful of kids walked down the street, eating ice cream.

"You're here for water ice, I assume?" Tabitha asked.

She was sitting on the top step of her stoop. She beamed at me, crossed one leg over the other. I had to remind myself that we weren't back in school. That she wasn't about to perform at a pep rally in her white-and-red uniform with pom poms glued to her hands. And I wasn't slouched and surly in the back of the auditorium, wondering why I couldn't have a crush on a regular girl and not *the* girl.

"So I've been told," I managed.

She extended both containers my way, biting her bottom lip. "I'm not sure what Emily Post would say regarding the apology etiquette for what happens when you see your neighbor half-naked in a towel and kind of *spy* on him—

completely by accident, of course—and then call yourself a pervert loud enough for the entire street to hear? So, I'm hoping letting you choose between the lemon and mango flavors will suffice."

Feeling my head spin in Tabitha's presence was par for the course. This time, that feeling was competing with another one. The recognition that mere minutes ago the same woman who made my heart race with every stray glance—not a regular girl but *the* girl—had openly checked me out. That was the only explanation for why I reached for the container on the right. Reached for yet another thing I'd denied myself for so long.

The very tips of our fingers brushed together. "I haven't had lemon water ice in a long time. Used to be my favorite."

She looked pleased by that. "Then it's all yours."

My eyes held hers, a small smile on my lips. "And your apology is accepted."

She arched an eyebrow. "And you won't refer to me as *pervert* from now on?"

"Sure seems like an accurate nickname."

Tabitha pressed her palms to her cheeks. "I can feel myself blushing. But you must know how you look in a towel, right? You're like one of those *Sports Illustrated* calendar models."

"A...calendar model?"

She blew out a breath, looking adorably flustered. "The fact that I'm babbling like an obsessed fan girl should paint a more accurate picture of what I mean."

I had no response to Tabitha referring to herself as an *obsessed fan girl* when the object of that obsession was me.

"If Emily Post saw you, she'd understand my dilemma." She patted the spot next to her. "Come sit. Unless, of course, my very awkwardness has made you want to abandon this friendship permanently."

Swallowing hard, I sat on the top step. It took me a second to get comfortable, stretching my right leg out. Her bare thigh pressed tight to mine, and I could see the chipped pink polish on her toes. Her pale skin was covered in a cluster of freckles near her knee. A few scars. Along the side of her leg was a large tattoo of a compass with leaves and petals.

She handed me one of the spoons. "Spontaneous water ice is a favorite summer activity of mine on the rare occasion that I'm back home. But I know how important your training is to you. I don't want you doing anything you're not comfortable with."

The random dessert wasn't the problem. It was letting go. Giving in. Funny how often every coach and trainer used to comment on the strength of my iron willpower. It was apparently no match for the feel of Tabitha's soft skin against mine or the odd intimacy of seeing her bare feet.

I dipped my spoon into the bowl and took a bite. Flavor burst on my tongue—tart lemon and sweet sugar. It tasted like summer vacation and lightning bugs. Long days and hot city nights. It was only Italian ice—and yeah, I was only a man after all—but my first thought as soon as I swallowed was *what the hell else have I been missing?*

I licked my lips. Let my gaze rise to meet hers. "Goddammit."

She was enjoying her own dessert. "It's good, right?"

I shook my head in disbelief. Took another bite.

She laughed, licking mango water ice from her spoon. "We've already stayed up past your bedtime and cleaned up trash together. What can't we do?" She nudged my arm. "Can I ask who was on the phone? You looked both surprised and pissed at the same time."

"That would be Harry Fleet. My agent. He's usually surprising me with something I'm irritated by."

"Ah, now it makes sense."

"He called with a job offer. In Vegas."

Her mouth opened. "Uh, *what*?"

"There's a primetime sports network called Game Time. They air all the boxing matches, including some amateur ones like the Golden Gloves. Definitely all the different belts and championships. Lightweight, heavyweight. They're considering me for a commentator role. Like an analyst. Instead of boxing, I'd be talking about it."

Tabitha slowly dragged the spoon from between her lips. "This is huge news, Dean."

I nodded, shaking my right knee up and down. I wasn't sure what the nerves in the pit of my stomach were trying to tell me.

"And you'd want to do it? Move to Vegas, get back into boxing?" she asked.

I glanced at her sideways. Paused. "I have no fucking idea. Can't tell if I'm excited or scared shitless."

She grinned around her spoon. "That's a feeling I know well."

I dropped my elbows to my knees. "Would you take it?"

"In a heartbeat," she said. "But, as we've previously established, I'm fond of taking giant leaps without looking. I said yes to that contract in Austin and didn't even take a day to consider it. I'm sure I'll love it there. And wherever I go always ends up being temporary. But still." She shoulder-bumped me. "I wouldn't knock your penchant for *over*thinking. This sounds like more than just the next gig. This sounds like a massive change to your entire life."

I let out a long, low breath. "And a move. To be on TV."

"And Alice thinks *I'm* internet famous. She won't know what to do if she can legitimately watch you on television whenever she wants."

I turned my head to look at her. "Wearing a suit too."

Her eyebrow lifted. "Maybe I'll tune in. For the suit alone."

I forced myself not to release her gaze. I was enjoying this moment with her way too much—her curiosity, the warm laughter in her voice, her goofy flirting. Being on the receiving end of Tabitha's charm caused that fight-night flicker in my chest to spark even more than the job offer. It was a different kind of power. One that had the same muting effect on my tendency to hesitate. To overanalyze every word and action from too many angles.

With my gloves on, I never once wavered when facing an opponent. Because I had instincts I could trust. As my eyes dropped to Tabitha's full lips, I wondered if those same instincts were trustworthy. Or if being around this woman just made me really fucking stupid.

Tabitha dipped her spoon directly into my bowl.

"Used to be I commanded a certain level of respect in this city," I said with a smirk.

She didn't reply. But she ate water ice off that spoon with a self-satisfied smile.

"I thought being Dean's Lady allowed me certain dessert privileges," she said.

I tilted the bowl her way. She handed me her own. We swapped flavors, and I refused to scrutinize how fast my heart was racing.

"When will you find out if you get the job?" she asked.

"Harry didn't say. But I got the impression things were happening fast."

She hummed under her breath. "Wouldn't it be funny if we both ended up at the airport together in a couple weeks?"

I didn't know what it would be. And I hadn't even begun to wrap my mind around what it would mean to leave the only home I'd ever known. My parents. Rowan. Eddie and Alice.

It must have shown on my face. Because Tabitha squeezed my arm and said, "I'm not saying you should definitely take this job or anything. But you should know they'd be making a huge mistake if they didn't select you."

She went back to her food, tapping her foot in time to the song coming from the block party.

"You like being far away from home though, right? Traveling all over?"

I caught a flicker of *something* across her eyes. She blinked and said, "I love it. There's a bold, beautiful world out there. I feel lucky that I've gotten to see so much of it. If you decide to leave Philly, I think it'll still be hard for you." She cut her eyes to the ground. "I never told my family this, but I spent my first week of freshman year at UCLA sobbing into bowls of cereal in my dorm room. It's not—" She paused. "It's not that it's easy to leave. But you have to make the right choice for you over what anyone else might want."

That first night we'd bumped into each other, when I'd asked her if she missed home, there'd been a forced quality to her answer. *I travel light, but it lets me go pretty far.* It was at odds with how happy she seemed here. How comfortable.

"When you move to Austin, if you ever need a...a friend. You can call me, Tabitha."

I was grateful for the dimming twilight. Could feel the heat in my face.

Her reply came in the form of a genuine smile that made me think of stars and planets again. "Thank you. The same goes for you too." She pointed at my water ice with her spoon. "No matter where I'm living, when I see any place selling Italian ice in the summertime, I get horribly homesick. John's is my dad's favorite, of course. After he and my mom got divorced, Alexis and I would make him go there with us every summer weekend. It was a surefire way to get him to laugh a little. Seeing all the families and the kids. Running into old friends. It used to be if we could get dad to laugh at John's, it would be an okay week."

She'd spoken about this the other day. When she admitted she'd secretly hated cheerleading. *His heart was very...fragile at that time. I didn't want to put any extra pressure on it.*

"Was he sad because he still loved your mom?" I asked, a little tentative. I wracked my brain for memories of her sharing about this in our support group. My impression had always been that her mom wasn't in their lives anymore.

"Not at all," she said emphatically. "Now that I'm older, I understand he was mourning the person she'd turned into. She wasn't a loveable person. And she's much too manipulative to love my dad the way he deserves." Her face filled with affection. "Dad refers to Kathleen as his extremely patient soul mate. He took some extra time finding her."

"I think I've only met her a couple times," I said. "My impression is that she's very...protective."

Tabitha snorted. "That's an accurate impression. Having Kathleen as a stepmom is like having six moms."

"I know the feeling," I said, brow raised. "I actually have two moms. Still feels like I have at least double that."

She laughed. I wondered if making Tabitha laugh was something a person could ever get tired of.

She twirled her spoon through the water ice, carving little circles. "You know, those nights at John's? I think deep down Dad was worried about us and we were worried about him and it was like a cyclone of keeping each other happy. But you know my dad. Seeing that guy sad is like watching an otter cry. It's heartbreaking."

A few beats of silence passed. Then I said, "You take good care of your family, Tabitha."

She shot me a wry look. "When I'm home. I'm constantly on the road."

"They must miss you a lot."

There was that flicker again. But I would have missed it if I wasn't paying such close attention to everything about her. The strands of hair around her face, blowing in the warm breeze. The flecks of gold in her brown eyes.

"Yeah, they do. I miss them all the time too," she said. I sensed she wanted to change the subject before she did. Something about the way her spine straightened. I wondered if this was what she meant about *traveling light*. Like revealing vulnerable parts of herself weighed her down.

Thinking about the things we had in common wasn't helping my heart rate. Neither was the current position of our bodies. We'd both shifted on the stoop at the same time, and my right hand was now trapped between my thigh and Tabitha's. We realized it at the same time. I could feel her muscles flexing against the back of my hand. The tips of my fingers grazed the inside of her knee. I froze. Didn't move.

Tabitha did move. Maybe it was coincidence. Or an accident. The pressure against my hand increased, like she was pressing into me.

I didn't dare look up. The sexual desire storming through my brain was a temptation I didn't need. Eating dessert on a summer night was innocent even if she was being cute and teasing. But now I wanted to drag her inside, to splay her out on my couch and let my fingers glide up her thigh. I could work open those shorts, then work my hand inside.

I'd make her come on my fingers over and over. See that satisfied look on her face for a totally different reason.

"I probably should have asked this before I invited you over to...eat my water ice. But you don't have a *Mrs.* Machine hanging out in there, do you?"

It was dangerous to make eye contact. I did it anyway, lured by the soft tremble in her voice.

"Are you asking if I'm single?"

She was staring at my mouth. I got hard. Immediately. "Just being neighborly. A super nosy one."

"I'm single," I said in a raw-sounding voice. "What about you?"

"I'm definitely single," she said with a breezy smile. "I was seeing this woman in Sacramento. Shelby. But I broke things off before I came back home. I travel so much, it's better if I don't get too attached to anyone. Or for anyone to get too attached to me. Right now, I'm more interested in temporary hookups than bouquets of flowers."

A strange sort of jealousy twisted in my stomach. Who the hell were these people who could have sex with Tabitha and not want more?

"But that's good," she continued. "Knowing this block, someone's been watching us chat on this stoop all night, which means by dawn half of South Philly will believe we're engaged in a passionate and torrid love affair. Especially if they think I'm the other woman."

I felt my lips twitch. "My innocent reputation will be ruined."

"*Your* reputation?" She clutched her chest. "Sure, you're a nice guy and all, but you don't seem very innocent to me."

If she only knew.

That heady feeling of adrenaline and confidence wanted me to *act*. If Rowan were here, he'd be begging me to live a little. Fuck each other, have some temporary fun, and then move on.

But Tabitha wasn't an extra dessert or a hangover I'd regret. She was my most challenging opponent yet, and there was no training my way out of this unnecessary complication.

With the last remaining scraps of that willpower, I sat back and pressed my shoulder blades to the storm door. It freed my hand and put a couple inches between us.

Tabitha had had me on the ropes from the second she'd fallen into my lap. I'd had a thing for this woman since high school. She was my neighbor. And I'd just asked her to build a *park* with me.

I was already too attached.

FIFTEEN
TABITHA

Dean slid back on the stoop, away from me. I observed the clench in his jaw and his newly rigid body language. When he cast a tiny self-conscious smile my way, a tidal wave of disappointment swept over me.

"You, um...*we* should be prepared to be talked about around the kiddie pool," he said. "Or at church on Sunday."

I regained my composure and raised an eyebrow. "That's how you know you've really done something scandalous. We're sitting outside together, where anyone can see. Dessert is involved. It's *way* past your early bedtime." I dropped my voice to a dramatic whisper. "And tomorrow? I'll be helping you put a whole lot of trash in a dumpster."

He was a deliberate person. Some part of me understood his pulling away was a gentle *no* to my unspoken question. Though who was I kidding, I hadn't been that unspoken about anything. I wanted to blame seeing Dean Knox-Morelli in a towel and still wet from the shower. I'd watched his fights. Technically, I'd already seen him shirtless.

Up close was different. Up close had—apparently—broken my damn brain.

His shoulders had been wide as a country barn, chest covered in dark hair, every glorious ridge of his abdomen flexing. The towel had slid half an inch past his hips, and drops of water had run down his skin. His muscles had shone like a work of art, highlighting even the hidden scars.

I'd gazed longingly at that man like he was a giant ice cream cone I desperately wanted to lick. At first, I'd been embarrassed to be caught gawking those initial, awkward seconds. Until I realized he was watching me do it with a searing intensity in his eyes. He'd rubbed his hand across his mouth, throat working, and for one heady moment I'd thought he might loop his arm around my waist and drag me inside.

Dean laughed, the sound carrying on the light breeze. "I didn't know you'd be this much trouble when you moved in next door. I think you claimed to be a quiet and respectful neighbor."

"That was a lie," I said, then handed him my container. "Here, I saved the last bite for you."

His gaze slid to the side. "Is it that obvious I want more?"

"It's super obvious, Mr. Machine." I bit the tip of my thumb so I wouldn't blurt out the real answer—that it was making me happy to see him happy and if he wanted a bathtub-sized trough of water ice, I'd haul it here in a flash.

My cell phone reminder alarm jangled, and I was disappointed again. I tugged it from my front pocket and shut it off as I reluctantly stood.

"It's work," I said apologetically. "I planned a late meeting with the marketing team from the hotel in Austin."

He nodded and stood slowly next to me. We were just as close as we'd been sitting down, but peering up at him, feet almost touching, had my stomach flipping again. Until I saw him clearly hide a grimace.

I touched his wrist. "Are you okay?"

He rolled back his shoulders. "Don't ever start boxing. Or train to be one. It makes a lot of things hurt, even years later."

His tone was about as light as was possible for a man like Dean. I didn't buy it. A litany of questions burst in my brain. *How many times did you break your nose? Does your body still hurt every day? Do you really want to take that job in Las Vegas?*

But he put his hand on his front door and pulled it open. "What do you think the next surprise activity will be?"

I had to work awfully hard not to appear *too* delighted by this question. I pinched my fingers together and mimed sealing my lips. His grin made it worth it.

"I liked this one," he said. "A lot. Thank you. I needed it more than I realized."

"Did you like it more than that time I accidentally fell into your lap?"

He shook his head, eyes meeting mine, filled with an alluring heat. "You're the one whose gonna get us gossiped about. Not me."

"But I'm not even a little bit scandalous."

He stepped one foot inside, lips curving into a smile that was almost *rakish*. "I find that very hard to believe, Tabitha."

The door clicked shut behind him. Butterflies began playing a rousing game of badminton in my stomach, and I was literally speechless.

A few seconds passed before I was able to yell out a shaky sounding, "*Good night!*"

I might have gotten a grunt in response, but then I checked the time and let out a stream of curses so filthy I half expected Alice to come by and hush me.

Inside, I threw off my crop top and pulled on the one button-up shirt I owned, wrinkle-free thanks to Linda's ironing board. I opened my laptop at the tiny kitchen table and checked the time. I had five minutes, *thank God*, so I fiddled with my hair and threw on another coat of mascara for good measure.

Notebook in front of me, I sat down and prepared to wait for Meghan and her team to call in. I opened a few extra files where I'd been compiling ideas and research for the promo video we'd be shooting together. I scanned the screen to get reacquainted with my thoughts and had to breathe through a flutter of unease when I realized how uninspired they sounded.

Filming videos about hotels—even ones on the forefront of ecotourism—wasn't always the *most* inspiring. But still, I was usually a *little* bit excited about new projects. Even the boring, corporate ones, where the story I needed to get across was *come visit and give us your money.*

I tapped my pen against the table. Two more minutes to go. I heard the distant sound of a faucet running. Footsteps on a staircase. These were sounds I now associated with Dean heading to bed. Where I assumed he'd be stripping his shirt off. Stretching his long, muscled arms out across soft, cottony sheets. Looking sleepy and adorable when he woke in the morning.

One minute left. I checked my appearance with my laptop's video camera and cringed at my pink cheeks. It was super obvious—to me *and* probably to Dean—that my crush on him was gaining *mega-crush* status. As in, feelings I normally could get my arms around and cinch tight were growing cumbersome.

I didn't think it would be a problem though. Based on his reaction on the stoop, he wasn't a *temporary hookup* guy. That made it highly unlikely I'd ever experience the pleasure of being kissed by Dean...or any of the other filthy acts I'd been dreaming about. This morning I'd woken gasping from the most vivid sex dream I'd ever had—of Dean lifting me onto the kitchen counter, ripping off my clothes, and fucking me with my knees wrapped tight around his waist. I remembered every detail, from his hand covering my mouth to the cups and dishes clattering to the floor.

The real problem was everything I yearned to do that *wasn't* having sex on a kitchen counter. Like making him smile with desserts and sorta-kinda wondering how cute he looked sleeping.

So maybe, due to this *cumbersomeness*, it was smarter to stay friends after all. I never wanted a marriage like the one my parents had at the very end. My mother had yanked her love away like a warm blanket on a cold night, and it took years for the three of us to recover. I preferred *casual* because I never wanted someone to get hurt, never wanted to dive deep into the messy, confusing, turbulent parts of being in love.

But my darkest fear was that my ability to flit from person to person was because I was just like my mother all along.

My laptop trilled with an incoming video call. I blinked rapidly, surprised to find my eyes a little wet. Then I sniffed, cleared my throat, and answered it.

"Hello from Austin," Meghan said as a team of people waved behind her.

I waved back. "Philly says *hey*."

She shifted on the screen, looking slightly pixelated. "Tabitha, I have to tell you how gosh darn excited we are to work with you. The team here has some great ideas, and they're looking forward to getting to know you a little better."

I glanced quickly at my list of lackluster ideas, feeling guilty. "I can't wait to get started."

They launched into a discussion about climate justice and the hotel industry and quirky live concert venues. Over the next hour, they painted a picture of a city on the cusp of real environmental progress, a city of bright lights and good food and music on every street corner.

By all accounts, Austin would be an amazing place to live. But I spent most of the meeting thinking about front stoops and water ice.

SIXTEEN
TABITHA

"Order up."

A hot plate slid across the counter. Two fried eggs with scrapple.

I looked up at the chef. "How'd you know exactly what I wanted for breakfast?"

My dad leaned his elbows on the table. "I know when my daughter needs the healing power of greasy food." He topped off my coffee. "I'm surprised to see you here for the breakfast rush. Last time you were in the diner this early you were probably prepping for a school final."

I picked up my fork and took a giant bite. "Perfect, as usual. I was out of groceries and raiding Linda's pantry was unsuccessful. And *maybe* I just missed my dad. Though don't go gettin' a big head about it."

"Your stepmother will be heartbroken to know I'm your favorite."

I narrowed my eyes at him over my coffee as I slurped extra loudly. He chuckled and tossed a towel over his shoulder. "Let me check in with Tony but I'm sure he can cover me for a few so I can sit with you."

"Oh, Dad, you don't have to do that," I said. "I can sit here and annoy you while you're working just fine."

He waved that statement away like it was a pesky fly before heading to the kitchen. I tapped my fingers against my cup with an ache in my chest. Unconditional love was stopping in the middle of the busiest two hours of your day to sit with your daughter who'd shown up at the most inconvenient time possible. If I wanted to make a movie about all the things he'd done like this for me and my sister over the years, it'd be a thousand hours long.

He returned a few seconds later, rounded the counter, and perched on one of the stools, wearing the same black pants and black rubber work shoes he'd worn my entire childhood. The rest of his wardrobe consisted of Phillies hats, Eagles jerseys, swag from the colleges Alexis and I went to, and a faded shirt he loved that said *Proud Dad of a Bi Daughter*.

I didn't even buy it for him. He bought it *himself*.

I lifted off the stool and wrapped my dad in a fierce hug.

He lightly patted my back. "Either you really missed me or the scrapple is that good."

"Scrapple's real good," I said through a lump in my throat.

When I sat back down, he had a sheepish look on his face.

"You're the coolest dad I know. All the kids are saying it."

"Kathleen says the same thing." He bobbed his head. "I missed you too, Tab. Feels like you just got here and you're already about to leave. How many days till you fly off to Texas?"

"Ten," I said. "Not that I'm counting or anything."

"Still plenty of time for Kathleen to get you to that boozy book club of hers."

I snorted, popped another bite of scrapple in my mouth. My dad's attention landed on the open notebook page I had propped in front of me, full of ideas I'd jotted down.

He tapped the center. "What's this?"

"Story ideas I'm playing around with."

"For that hotel?"

I shook my head. "For Tenth Street, actually."

His eyebrows shot up. "Are you making a movie about South Philly?"

I scoffed into my coffee and took another big sip. It had not been a particularly restful night, between my vague unease when I thought about moving to Texas and then my constant thinking about Dean while pretending I wasn't thinking about him. "I don't know what I'm doing yet, exactly. I'm supposed to be getting prepped for the Austin contract, but I can't stop thinking about that abandoned lot. The folks who live there and love there. The way they've so eagerly taken up this task and supported Dean in the process."

My dad didn't even have to tease me about the fluttery way I said *Dean*. They could probably hear it all the way at City Hall. So I shoved eggs into my mouth and avoided looking at him.

He was paging through my notes with a curious expression. I'd spent the night looking at the emails Eric and Alexis had sent me with the specs of their school community garden. And I'd read about other neighborhoods in Philly turning their own abandoned lots into tiny parks.

I truly wanted to help Dean. But it wasn't like I needed to get *this* involved. Filming was intimate work, especially when I was following some sparkling idea that didn't come from a contract but came from pure inspiration. When I walked past the lot this morning, I spotted bits of scraggly grass and dandelions peeking through the remaining clumps of debris. The miracle of green things, forcing their way to the sun, activated every single storytelling instinct I had.

It was my other instincts, however, that urged me toward

caution. The ones more concerned with self-preservation than creative muses.

"I bet if you made a video about this process, it would inspire a lot of people," Dad said. "And even better, at least they'd have a recorded memory of it. Kinda like the way me and Kathleen have been laughing our asses off over all those old photo albums you keep finding at Lin's place. It's nice to remember something like this. Something good." He shrugged. "Don't you use your Instagram page to raise money for the community stuff you've worked on?"

"And what do you know about my Instagram feed?" I asked with a laugh.

That sheepish grin reappeared. "Kathleen likes to follow different cats online—"

"Makes sense."

"Oh, and famous people who are bisexual."

"Ah," I said warmly. "That's why I get a text from Kathleen every so often about bi celebrities."

My stepmother showed her abundant unconditional love in a dozen different ways that often came in the form of cat videos and celebrity gossip.

"And you know she's obsessed with everything you do, so when you post videos she shows 'em to me." He tapped my notebook again. "I like your park idea. Sounds like people on the block like it too. It's gonna cost money though, right?"

I dropped my chin into my hand. "It *will* cost money."

He pointed to his temple. "I told you your old man's still got some tricks up his sleeve."

Tony yelled my dad's name from the back, and he slipped off his stool to duck his head into the kitchen. I let my gaze wander to the large windows facing Broad Street, lost in thought. Thinking about fundraising videos. Like a lot of freelancers, I used my Instagram feed to show off samples of my videography and photography skills. Dad was right. I had a large enough platform that if the organizations or activists I was filming needed resources, it was easy to shout it out.

I wondered if I could do the same for Dean. I mean, *the park*.

Dad returned and dropped his apron back on, washing his hands in the sink behind the counter. "Tony's gonna need me in the back in a second. Aren't you doing a big cleanup today? I can throw together a few boxes of food if you want."

I pursed my lips. "Lemon bars and bear claws?"

"For Midge and Maria, right?" he said with a grin.

"They've promised secrets about Dean in exchange for delicious pastries."

This time, he did cast me a sly look that I nervously ignored. He dried off his hands, then planted them on the counter. "In case I wasn't clear enough the other night, we're real excited about you going out to Texas. And wherever you go from there. We miss you all the time, but I don't want you to think it doesn't mean how happy we are for you. And proud of you, honey. So damn proud."

I squeezed his arm. "See? Coolest dad around."

"I understand how hard it must be to come home and then leave again," he added. "I know why it feels good. There were times when it was so bad between me and your mom, I used to dream about packing you girls up and hittin' the road too. Just to escape."

My hand froze, a forkful of eggs halfway to my mouth. "You never told me that."

"Yeah, well, some things you don't tell your kids at the time. And the divorce was hard enough—and ugly enough—that I wanted to protect you and Alexis from it as much as I could. Hiding those feelings might not have been the smartest move on my part, but..."

I grabbed his arm again. "Dad. You did the best you could at the time. I completely believe that."

Emotion rippled across his face. Then I watched him perform a maneuver I knew well: smile at me as if I'd mentioned the weather or asked him how work had been. Calm and pleasant.

It was the first time in years—maybe ever—that I seriously wondered if I wasn't the only member of my family holding onto shameful secrets and uncomfortable guilt from those awful years.

"I'll wrap up some food for you, how does that sound?" he said. Another maneuver I'd perfected over the years. A light, rapid subject change to avoid any emotional pitfalls or entanglements.

"That sounds good, Dad," I said. "Thank you. You're too sweet."

He got Styrofoam containers and began filling them with pastries from the glass container near the register.

"Now it's been a while but if I remember correctly, on the rare occasion he ate here, Dean the Machine was a pork roll man." He said this innocently, in a tone devoid of mischief.

I peered up from eating the last of my breakfast, thinking about Dean saying *I needed this more than I realized*. Something as simple as lemon water ice was able to smooth the lines in his forehead and release the tension in his shoulders.

I fiddled with my ponytail. "I guess if you have any lying around, I wouldn't mind bringing Dean some of his favorites."

"You got it," Dad said with a wink.

I knew criticism well. It was always the first choice out of my mother's mouth, and that habit of hers never changed. But that night I'd gone down a Dean Knox-Morelli rabbit hole, I hadn't only seen videos of past bouts and matches. There were articles, written by local sports writers and national commentators alike, ripping Dean's decision to shreds. Every headline used some iteration of *Philly's Greatest* or *South Philly Golden Boy*, raged at an athlete leaving the sport one match before he was favored to become the next light heavyweight boxing champion. I did come to understand that Dean hadn't just pissed off drunk assholes at Benny's Bar but an entire industry that had gotten behind his career.

I hoped another tiny surprise would elicit that same crooked grin on Dean's face. That it would bring a measure of random, just-because joy for a man who seemed unsure of his place in the world.

I shifted on the stool and ignored those badminton-playing butterflies. Because I wasn't getting too involved at all.

Not one bit.

SEVENTEEN
DEAN

I stood in front of the vacant lot holding a cup of coffee. A guy from the rec center had just dropped off the dumpster. It sat behind me, empty, ready for what I hoped was our final cleanup day before whatever we decided to do with it.

Yesterday I'd installed a bench at the spot where Tabitha and I had cleaned that first night. As promised, Eddie and Alice sat there—grumbling around a cigarette and drinking coffee, respectively. Pam was curled up between them.

"You're not even glaring at it, you know," Alice said.

"Yeah," Eddie added. "You look happy or somethin'. Or at least not pissed off."

I sipped my coffee. "I am happy. If today goes well, we won't be staring at this shit anymore."

"And that's the only reason you're happy?" Alice asked.

I narrowed my eyes at her. "Guess the Phillies didn't suck last night."

Eddie stubbed out his cigarette. "It's a fucking miracle."

That seemed to satisfy her curiosity for now. Mentioning the game was a lucky guess. Only one thing—one *person*—

dominated my attention all night long, and it sure as hell wasn't baseball. Or that phone call with Harry. Given my current situation, considering the Game Time opportunity would have been the sensible idea.

Instead, I fell asleep with the taste of lemons on my tongue. And Tabitha's long legs and pretty lips in my dreams. An indulgence if I ever knew one.

A burst of noise drew my attention. Natalia and Martín walked down the street with a small group of their friends, holding shovels and garbage bags. My parents were close behind with folks from their church. I caught snatches of their conversation in Italian, giving a small wave when they made eye contact.

Neighbors from all down the block began trickling toward the dumpster, carrying various tools. I hadn't made a big deal about it. Just knocked on doors and let people know what the plan was for the final clear-out today. It surprised me, since a lot of them had already been helping.

A week had gone by already, and the change was dramatic. Since retiring, I was used to my presence evoking a swift anger or an almost patronizing sympathy. This sense of camaraderie, of working together, seemed totally different.

Boxing was a solitary sport. And for me, a mental game more than a physical one. Brute strength and speed had their limits. But there was no limit to scrutinizing your opponent's weaknesses and then using them against them. No limit to analysis. No limit to honing a precise focus.

The vacant lot in front of me was getting cleaned up. But it was messy and unorganized. The shape of its future was fuzzy and tenuous. Everyone seemed to be having a good time working together though. Working toward something that would improve our community, no matter how small.

Harry's words came back to me.

But what are you doing *with your life?*

I rubbed my hand across my mouth and thought about having to tell my parents about Harry's call. About Vegas and getting back into a sport that could have easily killed me. The pit of my stomach twisted into knots.

I knew exactly how they'd react. And it wouldn't be positive.

There was another burst of noise, this time to the right of me. I knew who it was from the way the hair stood up on the back of my neck. My gaze drifted over to the red-haired ray of sunshine keeping me up at night. She was waving to all the gathered neighbors like Miss America, holding a plastic bag from the Broad Street Diner.

"Be right back," she called out. "I've got breakfast courtesy of one Mr. Drew Tyler."

Mom turned her head. "Lemon bars?" she asked sweetly.

"Of course. How could I forget?"

Tabitha breezed right past them and crooked her finger at me. "I've got an idea," she said as she walked toward Linda's stoop. I followed her, working to keep my posture relaxed and not eager. I was sleep-deprived and running low on restraint.

I was liable to say yes to any ideas she had.

She placed the plastic bag on the top step and began removing containers. I leaned against the brick, took another sip of coffee. She seemed tired.

I wondered if I was keeping her awake too.

"How was your meeting last night?" I asked.

She looked up, pushed the hair from her eyes. "With the hotel in Austin? It was good. Great. It's going great, I mean. I've got to book my plane ticket actually since I leave in ten days."

My fingers squeezed the mug I was holding. I set it down gently and slid that hand into my pocket. "That's...soon."

She opened the last container and perked up. "It's very

soon but will probably be better for you. I don't think Aunt Linda is a saint or anything, but she's probably much less trouble and a *lot* less scandalous." She extended the container out to me. "For you, by the way. You obviously don't have to eat it. But my dad casually mentioned it was your favorite, and I... well, I don't know..."

I opened it. Looked back up at her. "Tabitha, did you bring me a pork roll?"

"I've heard it's the neighborly thing to do."

A smile slid up my face before I could stop it. It matched her own sparkling one.

"Knew I could get you to smile," she said.

"They are my favorite."

She bit her lip, cute as a fucking button. Only the fact that the lot next to us was swarming with people kept me from dropping the container and kissing her.

I sank the right side of my body on the middle step and stretched my left leg out. I picked up the sandwich. It was a classic—the roll, the meat, the melted cheese, egg, and butter. "Are you okay with me wolfing this down?"

"Please, Dean. You've eaten my water ice. There are no more secrets between us now."

I shook my head with a low laugh. "You're working hard to ruin my innocent reputation today, aren't you?"

She winked at me, then opened her own container. I peeked over as I ate, saw piping hot donuts covered in cinnamon and sugar. She broke off a piece. "But seriously. Wolf away while I run through an idea that I had. Well, technically, it was my dad's idea first."

I nodded, eating and listening.

"I know we haven't settled yet on exactly what's going to happen to that space once all the trash gets cleared out today. But no matter what's decided, it's likely you're going to need funds to do it. You're not waiting around for the city to kick in some cash or some special donor at a nonprofit. This is, essentially, a rogue operation."

I swallowed my food and stared out at the neighbors. "I hadn't...fuck, I didn't think about that."

"Well, it's one step at a time," she said in a kind voice. "Pulling everyone together to work on a project like this and to clear a *year's* worth of garbage is, quite honestly, the hardest part. And it's almost done. Now it's on to the step that requires money."

"I don't want to ask people here to fund it," I said.

"I agree." She popped a piece of donut in her mouth and chewed. "I'm not an expert. Not in the least. But I have definitely worked with community groups who did online fundraisers for local projects like this. For simple things, like supplies and seeds."

I put down my now empty container. "You think total strangers online would give money for something like this?"

"I do." She brushed the crumbs from her hands. "I want to make a movie about Tenth Street. About the lot and your neighbors coming together. My idea is to edit them down into short segments I would share on social media with a direct link to a donation portal. Super short videos that are engaging and could maybe rally folks to donate. Especially in Philly itself. We'd need to work on a budget, make things transparent. But I don't think that should be a problem."

I felt my eyebrows raise. "I thought you didn't have an interest in Philly."

Those were the exact words she'd said the other night, and I couldn't forget them. Based on how fiercely she loved her family, loved this city, I would have imagined her art would reflect that.

She looked a little self-conscious. "I did say that. I might be changing my mind a *little* bit."

I rubbed my jaw so I could hide a smile I didn't want her to see. I didn't know why that made me happy. But it did. Not that it mattered long-term. Filming a cleanup wasn't the same as staying here. And she wasn't staying.

I cocked my head back toward the lot. "So what's the story, then?"

"It's a story about Annie. A story about her legacy. It's about taking care of one another even if your city or government won't. Or can't." Her dark eyes stayed glued to mine. "And I believe it's about family. And love. All the different ways that can look."

That last part—about families. That was the kind of stuff we talked about at the Lavender Center.

"Who would you interview?" I asked.

"Only people who were interested and who felt safe and comfortable. Privacy is my main priority."

I looked over my shoulder at my parents, who were laughing with Eddie and Alice. "You won't have a hard time finding subjects. But I wouldn't have to speak, right?"

She shook her head. "Of course not."

I thought about the call with Harry again. He said my hesitancy to be in the spotlight was fine. That I'd get some kind of mentoring. An investment in my career *long-term*. I couldn't dwell too long on how hypocritical that was, given their position on head injuries.

"Maybe..." I hesitated. "Maybe I should consider it. Because of the commentator job. If I got it and accepted it, I'd be in a live studio."

"That's a *much* bigger audience than I have," she said. "I'll be small potatoes to you by then."

"That's not possible, Tabitha," I said.

We were motionless in the middle of so much movement: music, people talking, cars driving by. The air was still charged between us. It kept happening every time we were alone together. It was dangerous, like an accelerant.

A few crystals of cinnamon and sugar lingered on her lower lip. "You have some..." I gestured with my thumb toward my own mouth, and her fingers flew up instantly, brushing the opposite side.

I felt a muscle ticking in my jaw. *What the hell else had I been missing?*

"Can I?" I asked.

"Please do." She tipped her face up. I slid the tips of my fingers around the back of her head and hovered my thumb over her mouth. I swiped it softly once, twice, across her bottom lip. The sugar fell. Our eye contact never wavered. Lust hollowed out my stomach, sent waves of desire surging through my limbs.

"Thank you, Mr. Machine," she said quietly. But didn't pull away. I heard the vague echo of a trip gong in the back of my head, the kind that indicated a boxing match could begin.

I stroked my thumb across her lip a third time.

It wasn't necessary. Or needed.

It was the definition of *indulgence*.

I heard her breathing hitch. Saw the attraction I felt reflected on her face—her fluttering eyelashes, her throat working, the puff of air on my thumb as she finally exhaled. As I reluctantly let go, I dragged my fingers through her tresses.

"Got it," I whispered.

She tucked a strand of hair behind her ear, looking shy in a way I'd never seen before. "So I'll, um..." She whirled around once. Twice. Touched her forehead with her hand. "I'll work on getting people's permission and see who's interested.

And I'll try and get some interviews in before we start all the heavy trash lifting today."

I nodded, unable to trust my voice.

She paused halfway through opening the front door. "You're part of this story too, Dean."

EIGHTEEN
DEAN

Tabitha fluttered between Eddie and Alice, positioning them on the bench in the lot. Behind her was a tripod and a fancy-looking digital camera. An orange microphone was secured on top. Seeing her with the tools of her trade reminded me of pulling on my boxing gloves, the way it boosted my confidence.

In the last hour, we'd made good headway on cleaning. And Tabitha had spoken to every person there, explaining the situation and getting permission. Everyone was on board, even if they were just in the background.

Eddie and Alice, however, had volunteered *themselves* to be interviewed. While Alice had rushed home to "put her face on," Eddie wore his work jeans and had a cigarette dangling from his mouth.

"Now how many people do ya think will watch this?" he asked.

Tabitha wrinkled her nose. "I don't know. I've got over fifty thousand followers on Instagram, but I can't really estimate how many will see it."

Eddie seemed pleased with that answer. "A lot of people have told me I'm real fucking inspiring."

I crossed my arms across my chest. "Eddie taught me how to drive. He was definitely inspiring as a teacher."

Tabitha brightened. "I didn't know that."

Eddie was chuckling. "Yeah, Dean was a good student. Midge and Maria were working those back-to-back shifts, remember? So I told them I'd do it. We used, what, Rowan's big truck, yeah?"

I nodded. "You told me that in South Philly you were legally allowed to park on top of the sidewalk as long as you asked first."

Tabitha shot me a bemused look.

"And, uh..." I cleared my throat. "The rules of the road were sorta, kinda—"

"*Guidelines*," he said emphatically. "Tell me it ain't true if you live in this city."

Tabitha was trying not to laugh. "A true inspiration."

Alice primly placed her hands in her lap. "I, for one, am ready for fame. I texted my grandson to let him know. He'll be so excited. You know, you should put him on the internet too."

"Rowan doesn't need any more attention than he already gets," I said mildly.

Alice pursed her lips. "You could be internet famous, Dean."

"Or even a calendar model," Tabitha said under her breath as she peered through the viewfinder. She tossed a sly grin my way.

I quirked an eyebrow. "What would Emily Post say?"

"Oh, I *love* the way you two flirt with each other," Alice said.

"We're not flirting," I said.

Eddie stubbed out his cigarette and blew smoke from the

corner of his mouth. "Aw, leave the kids alone, Alice. They're just having a little fun."

Tabitha bent down to the viewfinder of her camera again. "We're not kids. But I have definitely been flirting with Dean all day. How can you not? I mean, look at the guy."

I couldn't even pretend to frown. One taste of something sweet. One press of my thumb against Tabitha's soft lips. I was starting to get it now. A similar thing happened when my coach decided I was ready for my first boxing match. I'd knocked out my opponent in the second round. Heard the roaring sound of my name being cheered from the audience.

Once I allowed my most untamed desires to see the light of day, it was a hell of a process to tame them again.

Mom and Midge appeared next to me as Tabitha crouched down in front of the bench, speaking quietly to the two future movie stars. They were holding a garbage bag between them, wearing matching baseball caps and sunglasses.

"Do you think she'll interview me and your mom?" Midge asked.

"I'm sure she'd love to," I said. I studied them both for signs of heat exhaustion. "You're both okay, right? Not too hot?"

"Oh, horseshit," Midge said with an eye roll. "We're not a hundred years old, for Christ's sake."

I ducked between their shoulders, looked straight down and frowned. "And you're okay with snakes, right?"

Midge shrieked and jumped back. And realized almost immediately I was lying. "*Dean Joshua Knox-Morelli.*"

Mom was laughing quietly behind her hand. "It's been a good long while since we got you good, honey."

Midge clicked her tongue at me, the motion dissolving into a smile when I looped an arm around her shoulders. The first year after my concussion had been the hardest of my life.

My parents took it even harder. It was the migraines and the memory issues. My complete loss of identity and the near constant shit we heard about my retirement. In hindsight, I recognized how they rallied our neighbors, closing up ranks to protect me. But I only felt like I'd let everyone down.

Now they were back to being happy and loud and quick to tease. Though I'd never forget waking up in the hospital after my last match and seeing the real fear carved into their faces.

Mom patted my cheek softly. "All of your hard work is coming together so wonderfully."

I indicated the neighbors and friends around us. "They're all doing the hard work."

Midge scoffed. "You're underestimating yourself, Dean. Sometimes certain situations need a leader. We're proud of you for stepping up."

I cast my eyes to the ground, uncomfortable with their praise.

"I always thought Tabitha was special," Mom said quietly. "I used to tell Drew after those groups we went to at the Lavender Center that she would do great things. And I wasn't wrong, was I?"

"You weren't wrong," I said, trying not to think too hard about stars and solar systems and right hooks.

"So I think we're ready," Tabitha said, propping her hands on her hips. Alice perked up like she was about to meet the Queen. "And you don't need to worry about saying the perfect thing. I'll be editing, but people don't like perfect responses anyway. They like recognizing themselves in others. That means flaws and awkward stuff and messiness."

Eddie shrugged and Alice smiled.

"Why don't you start by telling me how Annie took care of this corner of Tenth and Emily Street."

"Well," Eddie started, "Annabeth...Annie, she was a one-of-a-kind lady. She didn't trust nobody to come help us if we needed it. Did trust her neighbors though. She believed we all needed to stick together. That's why I know if she could see what's been happenin' where her house used to be, she'd be mad as an alley cat."

"And what has been happening here?" Tabitha asked gently.

Alice sniffed, raised her chin. "The city condemned Annie's beautiful house. Tore it down without any sensitivity to the fact that a human being once lived there. But I believe turning this place into something that makes our neighbors happy is exactly what she would have wanted."

"Like what?" Tabitha asked.

Eddie looked around. "You've been talking about making it like a park. I like that a lot. Just having all the trash gotten rid of makes me feel proud of what we can do, you know?"

"Oh yes, I agree," Alice said.

"And what were some of your favorite things about Annie?" Tabitha asked.

Alice actually *giggled*. "Do you remember how she used to dress up as Santa Claus on Christmas Eve and make those presents for the kids?"

Eddie chuckled. "Oh yeah, of course I do. It'd be fucking midnight—wait, can I curse?"

Tabitha grinned. "Sure, why not?"

"So it'd be fucking midnight," Eddie continued, "and Annie would come walking down *this* street in some dime-store Santa outfit, trying to drag a bag full of toys while singing."

"She had a truly, *truly* terrible singing voice," Alice said sweetly.

"Like nails on a chalkboard. But the chalkboard was in a

room full of sick pigeons," Eddie said. "We never had the heart to tell her. Not even in church."

"Sometimes, after she'd leave presents for all the houses with kids, she'd leave these tiny flasks of liquor for the parents. She spent Christmas Day at rotating houses, since she didn't live with anyone and her family was so far away," Alice said. "But having to leave the people you love to come to some place new is a common experience in this neighborhood, even today. We all knew what it was like to have your heart in two places at once."

I saw Tabitha blink rapidly.

Eddie leaned closer to the camera. "And let me tell you, that woman could throw a block party like it was her damn job. You never saw so much food in your *life*."

"When was the last really great party you can remember?"

"When Dean won the Golden Gloves," Eddie said.

My mothers went rigid next to me. It was funny how people's opinions of me affected even good memories. Victorious memories. Nights that made me feel alive and like I finally belonged.

Tabitha cast a questioning gaze my way.

"It's okay," I said.

"Ah, shit. Sorry Dean," Eddie said. "Didn't mean to bring you into this."

"It's really fine," I said, then cracked a slight smile. "It was a good night, yeah?"

Eddie whistled under his breath. "A good night is when the Birds win on a Sunday. This was like something out of a movie."

Tabitha stepped back from her camera, propping her hands on her hips. "What are these Golden Gloves? Some totally cool boxing thing, I imagine?"

A whole lot of eyes landed on me.

Not even if this could count as your big comeback? The blinking recording light of Tabitha's camera wouldn't let me stop thinking about that phone call.

I cleared my throat and crooked my finger toward that light. Tabitha's brows shot up. Watching me closely, she slowly turned until the camera was on me.

"It's an amateur boxing competition," I said. "They hold them in a bunch of different cities. But there's also a national one. The year it was held in Philly, I competed." I paused. "And won."

"The whole thing?" Tabitha asked, looking impressed.

"Yes."

"So when you say *block party*, you mean—"

"The whole fucking neighborhood partied till dawn," Eddie said, clapping his hands together.

"And there was the cutest little parade down Passyunk Ave," Alice said.

Tabitha cocked her head. "You don't seem like the parade kind of guy, Mr. Machine."

"I'm not," I said. "I didn't want it. Felt too…" I mulled over the right word. "Flashy."

But then Midge nudged me with her elbow and a look of maternal scrutiny. I rubbed a hand along my jaw before finally relenting. "Okay. I'll admit it. It was one of the best nights of my life. Because people that I cared about showed up for me. People who knew how hard I'd trained. How hard and brutal boxing can be. It was important. And I was grateful in the end."

Tabitha peered over her camera at me. I cleared my throat again, suddenly nervous. I realized how easy it was to share something so intimate with her, even if she was recording it.

"We're as proud of our son now as we were then," Midge chimed in. "His life's passion could be watching paint dry and

I'd tell everyone I knew about it. It never mattered to us one way or another if he won or not. That night though, walking down Passyunk next to him, with cars honking and people cheering his name, well, *that* is a feeling I'll never forget." Then her hands flew to her cheeks. "Did I say that to the whole internet?"

Tabitha laughed. "Don't worry, this isn't live. I won't add it in if you don't want me to."

"I want you to," Midge said firmly. "Though maybe it has nothing to do with building a park, right?"

Tabitha had dropped to her knees, digging around in a black camera bag. She was doing her best to hide her face. I didn't think anyone else noticed that she'd swiped a tear from under her eye.

I did.

She sniffed. Brushed the hair from her forehead and then stood. Her smile was cranked all the way up. It seemed forced to me.

With a twist, she removed her camera from the tripod and held it up. "If the three of you scoot together, I can take your picture."

My parents hugged me close—Mom on my left, Midge on my right. We'd posed like this for pictures my entire life. A similar image hung in their house from my adoption day, when I was only a few months old.

"*Smile,*" Tabitha sang. Her shutter clicked. She seemed to agree with whatever she saw on the digital screen. "And to answer your question, every person involved in an effort like this *is* the story. Your experiences and memories, your dreams and beliefs, the history of Annie and her holiday flasks...it's all led you here. My favorite part is pulling those messy threads together and showing how they connect. Our lives almost always do, more than we realize."

The next few hours of work passed quickly. Neighbors and friends came and went as we hauled the remaining garbage from the lot and into the dumpster. Tabitha filmed short interviews with everyone there, documenting the process with her camera as she worked alongside us.

We revolved around each other like planets, making frequent eye contact. Sharing smiles that should have felt more forbidden.

I spent most of the time considering her words about messy threads and connected lives. I thought about us walking to school together. Attending those support groups together. Her falling into my lap and moving into Linda's house and the two of us planning this park.

I was an amateur when it came to women and relationships. Tabitha seemed like an expert. Flirtatious, charming. She enjoyed sex and dating probably without hours of pointless worrying.

But even I knew the warmth that spread through me every time our eyes met was a complication.

NINETEEN

DEAN

Later that night, I stood on the sidewalk and stared at a bare space that had been a stinking, trash-filled lot a week ago. The dumpster had been taken. The neighbors had cleared every last bit of debris. All that was left were a few rough-looking bushes and some patches of grass. The street was hushed compared to the noise and activity of today.

Everything ached. I stretched my neck from side to side. I'd been sweating all day and still hadn't showered. I heard the sound of Linda's door opening and shutting. Then Tabitha appeared, scratching the top of her head and yawning. Her hair was still wet. She wore a giant shirt that fell almost to her knees. And nothing else.

"Hey," she said sleepily, holding out a Yuengling. It looked ice cold. "Wanna sip?"

I reached for it. My fingers slid through hers. "Feels like all of your surprises are food and/or drink."

One eyebrow raised. "Is that a complaint?"

I smirked around the bottle as I took a swig and handed it

back to her. It *was* ice fucking cold and exactly what I needed right now. I wondered when Tabitha had started being able to make such accurate predictions of what I wanted, when.

I hoped she had no idea how badly I wanted *her*.

"I highly recommend a long, hot shower and then falling asleep immediately, which is what I plan on doing," she said.

My eyes skated up her outfit. "You're not heading uptown to hit the bars?"

She laughed. "I only have ten days left at Linda's house and way too many shirts with Jon Bon Jovi's face on it to rotate through." She took another sip and passed it to me. Our shoulders brushed together. When I placed my lips where hers had been, I remembered brushing my thumb there. Plump and soft. Her breath on my skin.

"It was a really good day," I said, nodding at the lot.

She gave me a big, toothy smile. "It was the best. Doesn't this look like the site of a future pocket park to you?"

I crossed my arms. "Paint me a picture. I'm not the artist."

"If you *insist*." She took a step forward, reached her hand out to point. "Eric sent me the designs they used for the garden at their school. So you could have raised beds there. And there." She moved her finger along the right side and back wall. "Flower gardens too. If you threw in grass, there could be benches there, like the one you built for Eddie and Alice. I'm sure Aunt Linda would let you hang string lights from her back patio. I talked to Natalia today, and she requested a swing set too. You could place that right in the middle."

Images flooded my brain. Summer beers and fall tailgate parties. Alice hanging her ridiculous Christmas decorations on the back wall. Mom and Midge planting in the garden. Lía and Marco on the swings.

And another one—sitting on that bench with the beautiful woman standing next to me. My arm around her shoulders, my lips in her hair, listening to her tell some funny story in her usual spirited way.

It was a fantasy as pointless as all the others I'd ever had about Tabitha. Made my chest tight for some reason.

"What do you think?" She was looking at me over her shoulder with bright eyes.

"I love it," I said hoarsely. "Now that the initial problem is gone, I can see it now."

She stepped back to my side. "I got a ton of great footage from everyone. Eddie and Alice should probably have their own talk show. And I finally tackled those back weeds and tore them out of the ground. Even have the wounds to prove it."

She extended her right forearm. It was covered in scratches. I acted on instinct, reached for her arm and swiped my finger gently down her skin. She shivered. "You're okay, right?"

"I'm fine. They don't even hurt." Her voice trembled. I reluctantly released her. "I should be able to get a lot of the segments I shot today edited down pretty quick. Get you guys some money before I head to Texas. Especially if some aspects of the park get worked on before I go and I can get footage of it. Though, um…" She tucked a strand of hair behind her ear. "Maybe I'll ask Alexis to take pictures of the finished product, whenever it's done, so I can update my followers on your progress."

I worked on rolling my shoulders back. "I might not be here either when it's finally done. I could be in Vegas."

Her eyes widened as she drank her beer. "That's wild to think about."

Wild was one way to describe it.

"Have you told anyone else yet?" she asked.

Anxiety beat like wings inside my gut. "Rowan's swinging by in a sec. We're heading to family dinner tonight. I'm gonna tell them while we're eating. Not that it's definite or anything. They should still know that I'm considering it."

A beat of silence followed. Tabitha's hand landed on my back, but gently. Her fingers pulsed, just once. "When I told Dad and Alexis I got into UCLA, it was really hard. They were both very excited for me, excited I was following a dream. But you and I don't come from families that leave Philly. Ever. My house growing up was two blocks over from my grandparents' house. Until I moved, the farthest my family had been was up to the Poconos or down the shore."

I huffed out a short laugh. "And I bought a house on the same side of the street as my parents."

She dropped her hand. "If you need a friend—tonight. After." She hooked her thumb over her shoulder. "You can knock on my door. If I'm still awake, I can ply you with food and/or drink until you feel better."

My eyes closed briefly. Sleep-deprived, low on restraint and about to have a tough conversation. I couldn't knock on her door tonight. Not if I wanted to keep avoiding those right hooks.

"Thanks," I said. "I appreciate it. I appreciate—" I waved my hand at the scene in front of us. "All of it." *You.*

She turned, running a hand through her hair. "Please, you'd do the same for me, Mr. Machine. And I'm technically your *lady* so..." Her lips curved into a sexy smile. "It's my pleasure."

She was every dream come true—standing in the middle of the street, bottle dangling from one hand. Shirt falling off her right shoulder, exposing the line of her collarbone.

I was ready to break wide open and knew Tabitha would do the job for me.

"I'm going to head to bed," she said. "You can still knock though. I'm here to listen or...whatever you need."

"Okay." I barely got the word out.

She froze, balanced on the ball of her front foot. She looked ready to take flight. I raised an eyebrow in question.

"This feels like a hug moment to me, but I didn't want to launch myself into your arms if you don't want to."

"It could be scandalous," I said, lips twitching.

She looked unconvinced. "Jesus, what kind of hugs are *you* handing out?"

The look on her face—like the sound of my laughter was some kind of miracle—had me opening my arms without thinking at all.

I thought the next part would be awkward because without my gloves on my whole body always felt clumsy. But Tabitha stepped directly into my space and wrapped her arms around my neck. I felt her body align and press against mine —her breasts, her hips, her face at my neck.

There it was. The breaking.

My hands curled around her ribcage, and then I was hugging her back. The position had my face buried in her wet hair. I nudged my nose through the strands, against the side of her throat. We were pressed too tightly together for either one of us to hide our body's reaction. I heard her quiet gasp. Felt the tremors. I canted my hips back an inch, very aware that my cock had never been harder.

I slowly released the breath I'd been holding. Tabitha arched subtly into me. Her nipples were hard. I could feel them against my chest. I repressed the growl waiting at the back of my throat but gave in to the sweet citrus smell of her skin. I dragged my nose up her neck, through her hair. She made another sound, like a whimper.

Or a plea.

I smoothed my hands down the lovely curve of her spine. They hovered on her lower back. My joints ached with urges I barely managed to ignore. To grab Tabitha's ass with the possessiveness screaming through my limbs. To hoist her up around my waist and simply carry her inside. Right to my bed.

The sound of whistling caught my attention. And then Rowan's fucking voice.

"Hey, big guy, oh—*whoa.* Um...hey?"

We sprang apart, and I only got the briefest glimpse of Tabitha's face, wide-eyed and shocked. Probably matching my own. I forced my face to be impassive as I turned on my heel.

Rowan stood on the sidewalk with a paper bag of groceries in one arm. And a look of total bullshitting amusement on his face.

"Hey, Rowan," Tabitha said, sounding out of breath. She brushed the hair out of her eyes and took two steps away from me. "Long time, no see. Your grandmother's a hoot, by the way."

He nodded, grinning. "Or a menace to society, as Dean has described her."

"I stand by that statement," I said.

"And it's good to see you too," he said. "Looks like the dumpster worked out, yeah? I can't believe how good it looks."

"It's really somethin'," Tabitha said, backpedaling toward Linda's stoop. "*Really* somethin'. Dean's been great. Is great. I mean, all the work he's done, he's good at. He's a good...good friend and worker."

Rowan clapped me on the shoulder with a look that said I was fucking in for it. "I tell him he's a good friend and worker all the time."

She reached behind her, opening the door. Raised her beer bottle at us. "I should let you two get to dinner, then. See you in my dreams. *Have sweet dreams* is what I meant."

The door clicked shut. Rowan hefted his bag of groceries as we walked toward my parents' house. I squinted off into the distance while Rowan kept whistling.

"Looks like Tabitha Tyler wants to make out with your face, dude."

I grunted. Shoved my hands in my back pockets. "She's leaving in a week and a half."

"So?"

I didn't have a real argument or legitimate reason. None of them could withstand what just happened. What finally having Tabitha in my arms did to my ability to care about anything except *more*.

"I'm coming around to the *not overthinking* thing. We're still just friends though."

He made a sound of approval. Then said, "Is that how you hug all of your friends?"

"Yeah. No. Wait, why? Was it...bad?"

"You and me?" he said, pointing between our chests. "We don't hug like that, and I've known your ass for two decades. That was like at the end of a movie when one of the characters saves the planet and the love of their life runs over and hugs them while behind them, an asteroid blows up."

"You're so full of shit."

He pulled his phone out. Turned his screen around and tapped at it. "I'm not the only one who sees it."

It was a text chain between him and his grandmother. The message above was Rowan, asking her if she wanted him to pick up green peppers because there was a sale at the Acme.

The response from Alice, below, read: *YOU COULD CUT THE SEXUAL TENSION BETWEEN DEAN AND TABITHA*

WITH A KNIFE PLEASE GET PEPPERS AND THOSE CRACKERS I LIKE.

I scrubbed a hand down my face with a sigh.

It was looking more likely that I was the one who was so full of shit.

TWENTY
TABITHA

I paced down the narrow hallway. Spun around and paced all the way back. I tapped the edge of my cell phone against my lower lip, staring at the screen and considering my options.

Then I paced all the way back again.

Less than a week ago, I was doing shots with my sister and bragging about my ability to keep my attractions to people *totally in the moment.*

It'd been a day since I'd last seen Dean, and I was wearing a hole in the rug from nerves alone. I'd been undone by a hug. A hug between two friends. Well, Dean's thumb didn't help either. The one he'd used to brush sugar from my lips all while gazing longingly at *me* like I was an ice cream cone *he* desperately wanted to lick. That moment alone had me blushing myself stupid all day long.

Stepping into Dean's open arms and wrapping mine around his neck was somehow even more blush-inducing. He radiated a powerful strength, body warm, smelling like woodsy soap and clean clothes. There was nothing contrived or artificial about Dean Knox-Morelli, and I doubted he'd ever worn cologne. He didn't need it. I already wanted to nip at his skin and taste him.

We'd embraced for ten seconds, maybe less. There was nothing outwardly sexual about the act itself, merely the combination of a dozen tiny movements that left me with a pulse of desire between my legs. There were too many sensations happening at once to focus on—his large hands sliding down my back, his breath caressing my neck, his mouth moving through my hair. We'd been balanced on a tightrope, frozen in motion. Waiting. *Wanting*. If Rowan hadn't shown up I would have fisted my hand in his shirt and kissed him.

Telling Dean that he could knock on my door last night if he needed a friend wasn't some sneaky come-on. I would have gladly stayed up late with him watching movies or dragged him out for cheese fries or, really, *whatever* brought him comfort. He didn't knock though. And I hadn't seen him all day.

Granted, I'd been holed up editing hours of film so I could create the fundraiser for the pocket park. But my craving to see him far outstripped any other fears some very dusty corners of my brain were trying to remind me of.

I dialed his number, chewing on the end of my thumb.

"Are you pacing back and forth over there?" Dean said in greeting.

I stopped, one foot hovering off the ground. "Y-*yes*, I was. Why, can you hear me?"

"Yeah, I can."

I forced myself to stand still. *Cool. Casual.* That was me. "I know it's a little late, but are you free right now to have some fun with me? It doesn't involve food and/or drink this time."

"What does it involve?" The husky edge of his tone gave me goose bumps.

"It's a surprise. But wear your workout clothes and your

running shoes. So, basically, wear what you're always wearing."

"Is it outdoors? Because it's supposed to storm."

I walked to the window and peeked out the curtain. It was just now getting fully dark, but he was right. I could see a scary-looking assortment of clouds on the horizon.

"What's a little rain?" I teased. "Live a little, Mr. Machine."

His laughter was low and rumbling against my ear. "You're scandalous *and* a troublemaker. But it's a deal. Ten minutes?"

"You know where I live," I said, then hung up.

I yanked on running shorts and threw on a tank top over my sports bra, feeling first date jitters. But not the kind I usually went on.

Once downstairs, I went in search of my keys and wallet on the kitchen table and accidentally knocked over the photo album we'd been laughing over at the diner the other night. I dropped to my heels, pressed it to my chest, and noticed one of the pictures lying facedown on the floor. I scooped it up and stood. Anticipating something adorable, I flipped it over with a smile. The gesture froze on my face. Those happy jitters turned sour, all my breath catching in my throat.

It was a picture of my mom.

I fully believed Aunt Linda to be the kind of woman to throw away all the pictures of her brother's horrible ex-wife. I was guessing it'd gotten stuck behind another and accidentally missed.

I held it up in the light. My mom and dad were posing for the camera in their theme party bell-bottoms. Mom was not in our lives anymore on purpose. The last time I'd seen her was maybe my freshman year of college on a random home visit. Seeing her face was shock alone, as was recognizing that we shared the same nose. Something about her posture, the tilt of her chin, reminding me of *me*.

My mother had had a boyfriend, Roger, that she'd been seeing behind my father's back for at least six months before their marriage got *really* bad. All that I understood at the time—all that she'd told me—was she had a friend that was a secret only I knew about. Every time Roger called, her face lit up. And my dad was never to find out about him.

I also knew that she looked similarly happy when my dad was around—tinkling laugh, warm and affectionate. She switched it on and off so skillfully, I remembered feeling legitimately afraid.

I was eleven years old when she decided I could help with her secret.

Dad doesn't know, she'd said, *and I can't tell your sister. But I can trust you, right?*

I'd said yes, of course, even though I was much too young to understand what I was saying *yes* to. Given her hypercritical nature and casual disdain, being asked to keep a secret felt like a burst of maternal love. One that I'd craved with a desperation that still made me cringe, years later.

She was so nonchalant about showing me that true love, for her, was a switch to be turned on or off. It was shallow, fickle, and could be yanked away at any moment.

There was a knock at the door that was probably Dean. I shoved the photo back in the album and scrubbed my hands down my face. I was legitimately excited to see Dean tonight and didn't need mom-memories interfering.

Dean was standing on the stoop in all his dark-and-stormy glory. The shy smile that flared to life when our eyes met sent my heart spinning.

"Am I dressed right?" he asked, looking down at his chest.

I shut the door behind me. "You're perfect. And your muscles look great, by the way. It's almost like you're a professional athlete?"

His brow lifted. "Former."

"Once a pro, always a pro," I said, stepping backward across the sidewalk. "And have you guessed what our activity is this evening?"

I hummed the opening bars to "Gonna Fly Now."

He dropped his head in his hands. "I thought you were joking."

"You and me? We're running the steps at the art museum, just like Rocky Balboa. Or, more importantly, Michael B. Jordan in *Creed*."

"You're really going to make a boxer run the Rocky steps?" he asked mildly.

"I'm going to make you *race* me to—and up—the steps," I clarified.

His gaze lingered on my face, then dropped down to my mouth. "What happens when I win?"

"*If*."

"If," he conceded. "Is there a prize?"

I spread my arms wide with as much confidence as I had. "I don't know, Mr. Machine. And neither will you. Because I shall be victorious."

"And to be clear, you'd like us to *start* running here. And race each other to the museum."

I dropped my hands to my sides. "Yep. About how far is it to run from here to the art museum again?"

I could see him trying not to laugh. "Three miles, give or take."

"Interesting."

After a beat, he said, "Are you much of a runner?"

I frowned. "The last time I was in shape were my blasted cheerleading days."

He slipped his hands into his shorts pockets and removed

a pair of car keys. "What if I drove us there and we only raced the actual steps? My car is parked right here."

I matched his smile and poked him in the chest. "How convenient. Are these competitive mind games? You *do* want to beat me, huh?"

He walked around the side of a large, busted up SUV and opened the passenger door. "Come on. We'll be there in fifteen minutes, and then you'll have even more time to win."

I made a show of *really* considering my options but in the end, flounced on over and hopped inside. "I'll admit that this is one of those *leap before I look* moments. But for the record, I should say that impulsive fun is best served with as little planning as possible."

"That sounds like my nightmare," he said. That happy, amused expression hadn't left his face. "I do know a little bit about running. Being a pro athlete and all."

I laughed as he shut the door, rounded the car. Those definitely-not-first-date jitters rippled under my skin like a frothy, stormy sea. As he buckled in and started the car, I scanned my immediate surroundings for visible clues about Dean. But the car was neat inside, practically pristine, even though from the look—and sound—of it, it was old as shit.

"Let me get this straight," I said. "You're giving up your South Philly parking spot for me?"

He slowed at a stop sign. "Yeah, because of your poor planning. I've been parked there for three fucking months."

That had me laughing again as I stared out the window, watching rows of tidy brick houses fly by. "I think my dad parked his old Buick under the freeway in the early nineties. Hasn't been back to pick it up since. This wouldn't happen to be the truck that Eddie taught you to drive in, would it?"

Dean's focus flicked to the rearview mirror. "Rowan got it when he was sixteen from some friend of an uncle in Jersey.

We've been sharing it since school, but it rarely gets used. Rowan mostly uses it for transporting donations for the center."

We turned right down Broad Street, heading straight toward City Hall, the William Penn statue directly next to it.

"Can I ask how last night went when you told everyone about the Vegas gig?"

His hands flexed on the steering wheel. "It was hard, like you said. And they were surprised. I don't talk about boxing that much anymore. Rowan was pretty quiet, which isn't like him. Mom and Midge were stunned. Sad, I think. But they kept their real opinion to themselves."

I pursed my lips. "And Eddie and Alice?"

"Told me not to take it because I should never, ever leave this city."

"That sounds about right."

He was quiet for a moment, nostrils flaring. "It's not only the leaving-home thing. They all have the same concerns I have about brain injuries."

My stomach churned as I thought about seeing Dean take hits to the temple, the chin, the side of his face.

"It wasn't specifically that concussion that made me retire. It was all the ones I'd had before. All the ones I'd have in the future if I kept competing." He paused here, throat working. "All the injuries I'd be inflicting on other boxers. It wasn't like Bobby's uppercuts were any different from the punches I'd landed on him."

The passing streetlamps and headlights flickered across Dean's face like the shadows of a campfire.

"I'm not saying I'm turning down the job," he said. "I did ask Harry to look into how the channel was talking about this stuff. If they were advocating for any changes or reporting on it differently."

"What did he say?"

His lips twisted into a grimace. "Hasn't gotten back to me yet." He flicked on his turn signal. I dug my nails into the tops of my thighs to keep from hugging him. Which was both inconvenient and unsafe.

"You're good to ask," I said. "You're good to care about your own body. And other bodies. You're a thoughtful person, Dean. I know that whatever decision you make about the job will be the right one."

He didn't answer, but I noticed the color in his cheeks.

"Besides me dropping that Vegas bombshell," he said, "Alice kept trying to get me to spill secrets about you. *Since we're flirting nonstop and all.* That's a direct quote."

I turned to face him in my seat. "And?"

"Told her everything I knew." His smile was almost lazy, limbs relaxing again with the subject change. "She had lemon bars."

"You think there'd be some neighborly loyalty," I said, shaking my head. I twisted around to peek into the back seat. It was similarly clean and roomier than I would have guessed.

"I graduated two years before you, right?" I asked.

"Yep."

I fell back against my seat. "So, I wouldn't have known if Rowan...or *you*...took this baby out to the hookup spot that everyone went to? The whole entire setup in this truck says *steamy windows and heavy petting*."

"Did you just say the words *heavy petting* to me?"

"I don't think that's what the kids call it anymore, but..." I nudged his arm. "The question still stands."

"Rowan did, of course," he said. "I was already training six days a week and competing in amateur bouts. That meant strict diet, strict bedtime. No parties. No..." He paused here. "No girls."

"Is that what you wanted?" I asked.

We curved around the statues on Kelly Drive, the museum rearing up ahead of us, bathed in golden light. There was a solitary parking spot left, and Dean took it with the grit of a lifelong resident, parking like his life depended on it. He killed the engine. It took him a few seconds to look at me.

"Yeah," he said. "Yeah, it was. Even with what I just said, about concussions and injuries, I still felt like I had an identity. A place to be. Training like that, being that young was the most challenging thing I ever did. But I *got* it. I knew how to fight. I knew how to win. There weren't a lot of gray areas or nuance. It was a lot more comfortable at the gym than in high school where I didn't feel like I had a clue how to act."

It made a certain kind of sense. I knew from our support groups what Dean had experienced—homophobia toward his family, bullying at school. He was shy, on the quieter side when we were growing up. I wasn't naïve to the darker elements of having a social life in high school.

"I was happy that my weekends were busy with boxing," he said. "Although I did miss out on things like hooking up in a car at the Phillies stadium parking lot during off-hours."

We got out of the car and walked to the base of the art museum steps, the ones that became famous after *Rocky*. There were a couple of stray tourists taking pictures in front of the statue. But other than that, it was almost peacefully hushed. The air smelled sweetly of rain, storm clouds getting closer.

I gazed up at it like a mountaineer admiring a mythical peak. "I'm feeling *pretty* confident about my victory." I leaned against the stone post and stretched one hamstring. "You gonna warm up?"

"I'm good, thanks."

I shook my head. "Dean the Machine. Undone by his own

hubris."

His dark eyes were playful as they stared down at me. "You never said if you'd had any make-outs at the stadium. I'm assuming you had people lined up to escort you there in their cars."

I scratched the top of my head. "I never did it either."

"You're serious?"

"*Yep.*" I smacked my lips together. "I thought it sounded so glamorous and adult when we were in school. *The stadium parking lot.* Where all the coolest kids had mediocre make-out sessions and then had to sneak back home after curfew." I pulled my other leg into a stretch. "No heavy petting for me until I got to college. I had crushes on people for *days*, but whenever anyone asked me out, I said no. It wasn't the best, being in the front row seat of my parents' divorce. My sister eventually went off to Temple and lived on campus, so she missed a lot of the…" I cleared my throat. "More colorful details of living in a house where there'd been adultery and lies and a lot of hurt feelings. In hindsight, I was doing everything I could to avoid ending up like them."

I clamped my mouth shut before I could spill any other vulnerabilities on this casual hang between two friends. The sincere kindness on his face almost had me spilling more, like tipping over a barrel of apples.

"It sounds like you were protecting your heart," he said.

His words hung between us, charging the air with a seductive weight. There was something daring and dangerous about not being on Tenth Street. We were uptown, with nary a soul around, late at night. A rumble of thunder had the hair standing up on my arms. We both turned toward the sound as a glimmer of lightning appeared in the distance.

"Should we…?" Dean said.

"*Yes,*" I said, with too much cheer. "Absolutely, let's do it."

Center City's skyscrapers glittered behind us, and in front of us were the seventy-two steps leading to the museum's entrance. "Are you going to set the scene for us? Like, what's my motivation?"

I bent down in an approximation of what I'd seen sprinters do on TV. With a raspy laugh, Dean copied me. His body rippled with a confident, intoxicating strength even when still. I was sure he wasn't even aware of it.

"I'm a down-on-his-luck boxer with one shot to make it big," he said, voice low. "An underdog just like the city I'm from. I'm hungry for a win."

There was more thunder, closer this time.

"You better not mess up," I teased. "You've only got this *one shot*."

His lips tipped up. "Don't make me nervous, or I will."

"I'll try not to distract you."

Desire flooded his features. A delicious shiver fluttered in my belly. Dean dipped his head tantalizingly close. When he exhaled, his breath whispered across my cheek. "Your motivation is that you're the boxer's new, mysterious neighbor."

I arched a single eyebrow. "Sounds scandalous."

He nodded. "You're a filmmaker. You see beauty in everything, even if it's hidden or hard to see."

My head spun. His mouth hovered closer.

"Every day, you've been trying to get this boxer to live a little."

Kiss me, I wanted to say. *Kiss me, and I'll show you how to live more than a little.*

His lips brushed mine. *Almost.*

"And it's working," he whispered.

My toes curled in my running shoes. I nudged my nose against his, more than ready.

"*Go,*" he whispered.

TWENTY-ONE

DEAN

Running was a lot more enjoyable with Tabitha.

"*Cheater,*" she sputtered, but she was laughing. Already out of breath. I deliberately slowed until we were shoulder to shoulder on the first landing.

She dropped her hands to her knees. "I'm not giving you the prize when we get to the top."

I nodded up ahead. "My trainers always said the victory's in the movement. Not getting a medal after."

"Your trainers sound like psychopaths."

I tipped my head back on a laugh. "Some days they are. But we've only got sixty more steps, give or take. Come on. No quitters in this friendship."

She shook out her arms. Blew out a breath. And then we ran the next set of stairs together. And the next. If I touched my face, I knew my smile would be huge. It was a reaction to her delighted laughter, the looseness in my limbs, the act of running with no purpose. Not for time. Not for conditioning. Not as a warm-up.

What else had I been missing?

We reached the very top at the exact same time.

"I think," she gasped, "that you might have held back there a little bit."

I shrugged. "Seems like it was a tie, fair and square."

"I call bullshit."

"Maybe..." I hedged. "Maybe, when I was first training, Sly had me run these stairs every day, up and back, ten times."

Her jaw dropped. "You're a *double* cheater."

"How do you think I won all those matches?"

Her laugh turned into a slightly wheezing cough. I tapped her elbow and stacked my hands on top of my head. She copied me. Took a big inhale. Up here, all my fidgety thoughts slowed down. The jagged edges in my mind smoothed over. Since my first day at the boxing gym, I discovered that physical activity had that effect on me. The faster my heart raced, the less I felt the need to hyper-analyze every word I said. Or constantly self-edit. Boxing became a sort of home, the one space where I could think clearly.

Like I was finally myself.

"I always thought it was extra quiet up here," Tabitha said. "Like this immediate hush. But a powerful one. Do you know what I mean?"

I followed her focus. Directly in front of us, the fountain sent sprays of mist into the night sky. The massive stone columns at the entrance always made me think of Rome when I was a kid.

"During matches, the first ten seconds after the gong went off were silent for me," I said. "I couldn't hear the crowd screaming. Or their chants. Or trainers yelling. Only my heartbeat."

Her gaze flicked to mine. "There's a story there. About the precious, quiet seconds before the chaos of a fight." A clap of thunder drew her eyes up to the dark sky. "Like the calm before a summer storm. Maybe I'll make a movie about you one day."

Her tone was sincere. I still scoffed. "That would be a boring fucking movie."

"I disagree."

I pressed my lips together so I wouldn't blurt out how beautiful she was. Instead, I turned to face her fully. "Do you want the authentic *running the Rocky steps* experience for this adventure?"

She cocked her head to the side. "Hell yeah. Do you need to dump a thing of Gatorade all over my head or something?"

I shot her a questioning look. "Tabitha. Do you know what happens in the *Rocky* movies?"

"No," she said, dragging out the word. "I never saw them all the way through, but I don't believe that's a problem."

I ducked my head on a laugh. "We're going a little off script." I held my palms straight out in front of me. "Do you want to do a punching drill?"

"You mean *hit* you?"

"Just my palms," I said. "But you don't have to."

She chewed on her bottom lip. Raised her hands up and mimicked my pose. "Show me first?"

I reached for her wrists and very gently nudged them a few inches higher. I dropped into a fighter's stance. There were times in my life when this pose was as easy as breathing and walking. Easier, usually, than talking to people.

Tabitha made me feel different.

"I won't actually strike your hand, okay?" I threw a few simple straight punches toward her palms. A couple jabs. A cross. Her eyes lit right up as I did. I did half a minute of what would be considered a warm-up for a total beginner. It didn't matter. My body still came to life with every strike.

"That looks *fun*," she said.

I stopped, bouncing back on my feet. I cracked a smile. "It's really fucking fun."

She dropped her hands and made a very sloppy and extremely cute attempt at copying my footwork. "It's like I'm a natural."

I turned so we were standing side-by-side. "I imagine you're very good at everything you try and do."

"You've seen me run so...the answer is *yes*."

I held my palms about a foot apart. "Separate your feet six inches, give or take." I modeled the turn of my hips and shoulders. She studied me closely, rotating the shape of her body to match mine. "Are you right-handed or left-handed?"

"Right."

I showed her how to hold her dominant hand back, weaker hand forward. Walked her through a basic straight punch and a cross. Then I fell back and examined her posture. "Not too bad. How do you feel?"

She scrunched up her nose. "Badass?"

I held up my palms. "Then show me."

Her fist landed against my hand. "Good. Again. Try a cross this time."

Like any beginner, her first few hits were lacking in confidence. But it didn't take long until I could tell she was getting into it, getting into a rhythm that kept us quiet and focused for a few minutes. The air was heavy and humid, and she was clearly out of breath. Yet each time our eyes connected, she was grinning from ear to ear.

"You're a pro already. Rocky Balboa ain't got shit on you."

"Yeah?" Her ponytail swished back and forth. "You're not teasing me, right?"

I shook my head. "I'm being serious. You look real strong."

She hit my palm with a pretty sharp jab. "I feel like a superhero, especially with all of the lightning going on in the background." Her next punch was a decent cross. I pulled my hand away, shook it out. Blew on it.

Tabitha's answering laugh made my stomach flip. I reluctantly tore my attention away, settling it on the famous view in front of us—softly lit statues, the other museums, the international flags, the whole of Center City lit up. Lightning struck in the distance. The air buzzed with it.

"As kids, we must have come here on field trips, what, a dozen times at least?" she said, sounding dreamy. "And my sister and I would go once a month, maybe more. It used to be my favorite place in the whole world. *This* view has never gotten old. It always feels like Philly is the center of the whole universe when you're up here."

I lowered myself to the top step and propped my elbows on my knees. The stone sent a handful of pain signals up my spine, reminding me of past body blows. Tabitha joined me a second later, sitting close. Her knee pressed to mine. Our arms touched. I snuck a glance at her profile, her hair blowing gently around her face.

I knew her parents' divorce had been complicated and devastating for her. Knew, from our support group, that her mother had dismissed Tabitha's bisexuality and never accepted her. Except watching her behind the camera yesterday felt like watching Tabitha rediscover a love she'd lost. I wanted to know why she had to leave.

Why she never allowed herself to stay.

She turned to face me, eyes searching mine. A tentative smile appeared on her face. Those old boxer's instincts told me to press here. That my opponent was wide open for a reason.

"So, uh...last night at your family dinner," she said. "Were my awkward flirting attempts with you the hottest gossip?"

"More like *my* awkward attempts."

Her lips parted. "You've been flirting with me too?"

She was teasing, seemed almost nervous. I kept my expression serious. "You know I've been, Tabitha."

Her throat worked, eyelashes fluttering. The wind caught her hair again. I reached forward and tucked the strands behind her ear. Cupped her face and swept my thumb across her cheek. The world ground to a screeching halt. It was as if the gong had gone off again—there was no sound, no movement, no storm clouds overhead.

"I've been strict about a lot of things since I retired," I said, voice raspy. "It's not only my diet. Or training. I haven't allowed myself to give in to anything that I want. To take what I want."

She swallowed again. Her skin was trembling beneath my fingers. I slowly, slowly dipped my lips until they hung suspended over hers. Our breath mingled. My vision flickered, every muscle taut.

"What do you want to give in to?" she asked on a whisper.

"Pleasure." I gently placed my other hand on her other cheek, until I was gripping her face.

"And what do you want?"

I brushed my lips over hers. Once. Twice. "*You.*"

I kissed Tabitha, and everything changed. I'd been wrong about this moment being like a right hook. That implied pain, when the sensation roaring through my body was lust. The only thought I could form was *finally*.

And then I quit thinking all together. I didn't hold back. Couldn't. Our first kiss grew wild within seconds, Tabitha holding my wrists and opening for me with a throaty moan. The kiss deepened. Became hungrier, almost starved. My tongue met hers as her hands twisted in the collar of my shirt. I wrapped an arm around her waist and pulled her into my lap. Tabitha Tyler was straddling me on the top of the art museum steps, a storm threatening over our heads, in a public place where anyone could see us.

Like I *fucking* cared.

Our lips parted, and we shared a gasping, ragged breath. Until Tabitha kissed me again and I grabbed fistfuls of her hair. Her nails scratched across the back of my neck. My fingers slipped beneath her shirt, hands coasting along the smooth skin of her waist before yanking her more firmly against me.

A soft, warm rain began falling all around us.

We didn't stop. Tabitha's lips roamed away from mine, along my jaw. My right hand held the back of her head as she trailed kisses down my neck. She licked my skin, moaned against it. The sound tore a ragged groan from the back of my throat. I tipped my head back, rain in my hair. I wondered how I'd gotten so goddamn lucky to have Tabitha *savoring me*, to have a combination of her breath, lips, teeth moving up and down my throat.

"You shouldn't be allowed to taste this good, Dean," she panted. She reached down for the end of my shirt and pushed it up and off me. For as long as I lived, I would never forget what she looked like as she stared down at my body. Rain trickled through my chest hair, and Tabitha licked her lips like she had an actual thirst.

My sexual experiences before this moment were mostly in the dark, with pretty strangers who knew my name and my victories in the ring. That was it. And of course, the second I retired, those same women didn't look my way again. Sex was usually fast. Fumbling. More about her orgasm and my orgasm—and nothing else. Each time was mechanical. Impersonal. Some part of me knew I was probably wanted in this way. Even admired, for a short time.

But Tabitha put her lust and attraction to me on full

display. It wasn't a shameful secret. Or dependent on how I performed in a match.

I pressed my forehead to hers as I slid my hand across her belly, then cupped her breast over her sports bra. She hissed in a breath. I swiped my thumb across her nipple and growled as it pebbled. My other hand tangled in her hair, tugging until she exposed her throat. I kissed and nipped the skin there. Nudged the strap of her top down with my nose, kept palming and squeezing her breasts as her body trembled in my arms.

The rain fell harder. My remaining clothing stuck to my skin. Our next kiss was nothing short of sloppy groping, of teeth and groans and a desperate need. Her hands on my chest were pushing. Pushing. I could *feel* what she wanted. There was a steady roar all around us—the rain, the thunder, the wind. I dropped back on my elbows and felt the twinge of an old break there. Tabitha fell with me, hair in thick ropes, water on her eyelashes.

She ground against my cock, and I pictured tearing her shorts off and letting her fuck me here, on the stairs, in the middle of a raging storm. Notions of safety or propriety crumbled in the face of our lust. I didn't care if it was wrong. I didn't care if my body hurt or if I'd have to skip training because my muscles were sore.

What if I said yes to pleasure instead of always saying no?

I pushed back up to a sitting position and pulled her tight against me. I buried my face in her hair just as a crack of lightning had us both jumping.

And then it started to pour. Pour like a flash flood was imminent. We were too stunned to move at first. Tabitha held out her hands and then burst into a peal of laughter. "Your point about it raining earlier is duly noted."

I pushed the hair from her ear. "We need to go. *Now.*"

She shifted off my lap. I gripped her hands, kept her

steady. The sky was terrifyingly dark. Tugging her against my side, we made our way down the slippery steps as carefully as we could. Down below, tourists ran under umbrellas. People shouted for taxis. The skyscrapers looked dull and watery.

Squinting, I wiped the rain from my eyes and fished the keys from my pocket. I reached the back of the car and practically wrenched the side door off.

I shoved Tabitha inside and followed, slamming the door shut.

Seconds ticked by as we caught our ragged breath.

The only sound was the rain hammering against the car and bursts of thunder. Tabitha pressed her hand to the window as the water fell in sheets. I crumpled up my wet shirt and tossed it in the front. Pressed my bare back to the corner, where the door met the seat. The only light coming in was from whatever the streetlamp was throwing off through the rain.

Tabitha ran a hand through her hair, eyes heavy-lidded. I could see her nipples through her wet shirt, all that pale, freckled skin exposed, clothing wrinkled and falling off.

I'd done that.

"To be clear, I thought we'd run the Rocky steps and then get some ice cream. *Not* make out with you in public during a thunderstorm and rip your shirt off like some kind of..." Her lips quirked up. "Sex monster."

It was impossible for my cock to get any harder. Impossible for me to feel any less feral than I already did. Those critics had been wrong about me this entire time—I wasn't some intense robot with circuitry instead of veins. I wasn't cold or precise. I was disheveled. Debauched. Lacking any semblance of control.

I held out my hand. Crooked my finger. "Come here, Tabitha."

Her eyebrow arched elegantly. She slid close. I didn't move. Couldn't, yet.

"Would you look at that," she said softly. "I'm in the back seat of your car, Dean Knox-Morelli. What do you plan on doing with me?"

I stroked the tip of my finger up her throat. Lifted her chin and ghosted my lips over hers. "I plan on taking what I want."

TWENTY-TWO

TABITHA

Dean crashed his mouth down on mine and hauled me into his lap at the same exact time. I straddled him as he reached beneath the seat and lowered it, tilting us backward. If I thought what happened between us on the art museum steps was passionate—and it *was*—this was some next-level need I'd never experienced before.

One big palm of his curved down my back while the other gripped my hair, holding my face still. Dean kissed me like he'd been waiting his entire life to do it. He sank into it, gave me everything he had. We'd part for a few shaky breaths, but then that same perfect, firm mouth would descend to my neck, my shoulder, the hollow in my throat.

I was grinding my body, rolling my hips, desperate for friction. His cock was steel between my legs, his fingers on my skin confident. He shoved his hand under my sports bra, palming my breasts. I licked a single drop of rain from his jaw and tasted salt. The sound of his strangled groans and our heavy breathing filled the small space, steamed the windows as curtains of rain cloaked us in a forbidden darkness.

I realized with a dim astonishment that if the storm hadn't

worsened, I would have gladly ridden Dean on those steps without a care in the world. The chemistry between us was that primal, demanded that much raw, insatiable hunger.

Dean tore my bra off and pressed his face between my breasts with a low growl that sent vibrations through me. He sat up straight in the seat, bending me backward, and then took my breast into his mouth with a look both savage and grateful. His wet tongue swirled around my nipple—feather-light, then gradually increasing in pressure until he was pulling on it with his lips and I was close to sobbing.

The rhythmic pulsing matched the one between my legs, had my head dropping back and keening cries falling from my lips. He'd trapped me still so I couldn't rock back and forth along that thick cock of his, but if I had freedom of movement, I would have come. He wouldn't stop either, kept me pinned down and exposed to his fingers and tongue, lapping at my nipples, stroking each peak with light, teasing circles.

I threaded my fingers through his thick hair and tugged his head back—harder than I intended, but the satisfied curl to his lip made me do it again. His nostrils flared and his next kiss had a bite to it I wanted more of. I managed to work my hand down the flexing ridges of his stomach to his shorts-clad cock. My hand bore down, stroked the impressive length as he used both thumbs to stroke my nipples.

We shared a fraught, open-mouthed moan. He bared his teeth. Hissed out a breath. His hands settled on my hips, but then he spun me around roughly on his lap. One hand wrapped in my hair. The other landed back on my nipple and pinched. Hard. Harder. I cried out, spine arching, and I was treated to Dean groaning my name in my ear.

A bolt of lightning crackled overhead followed by a steady, rolling thunder. Rain continued to fall like sharp stones, bouncing off the windshield, making the back seat feel like a cozy cabin in the middle of a summer storm. The air inside was as steamy as a tropical jungle. Our skin was slick with the combination of sweat and rain, mouths open, panting breath fogging up the windows. Maybe if this spontaneous hookup was happening in a regular old bed with the lights on there would have been time and space for nerves or adjustments.

But it was happening in the back seat of a car—technically in public—and I was positive that was the reason for our desperate, frenzied movements, like we might literally *die* without the other person.

I draped my arms behind Dean's neck, presenting the entirety of my body to him like a gift. His hot mouth dragged down the crook of my neck. His teeth bit down as his hands skated down my waist and gripped my thighs.

He spread my legs wide open and choked out a sound against my hair. I watched his hand slip under my shorts. Felt it slip beneath my underwear. He cupped his hand over my pussy, middle finger nudging my clit for the sweetest second. I would have shot off his lap if his arm wasn't pinning me in place.

His lips caressed the ball of my shoulder. "Tell me what feels good," he whispered hoarsely. "Show me how to make you come."

Heat flamed my cheeks. I joined my hand with his and we touched my clit together. I gasped at the contact. I kissed him again, nipping at his lip and then swiping my tongue against his.

"Like this," I whispered, as we parted. We circled my clit together, large circles getting smaller. Light pressure growing firmer. I let go and tipped my head back. His other hand cupped my throat, holding me there as he kissed my neck over and over.

"Yes," I sighed. "*Yes, that's—*"

He worked faster, skilled fingers moving, those sensual neck kisses turning into filthy bites that sent delicious chills up and down my spine. I writhed on his lap, his firm grip wrapped around my throat.

"Dean," I sobbed. "Please don't stop. *Please, don't.*"

"Never," he growled at my ear.

I was racing toward an orgasm I worried might destroy me. The hand cupping my throat slid higher until he was pressing his palm against my mouth, smothering my cries.

"Is this okay?" he asked.

I nodded and wailed and writhed on the absolute edge of ecstasy. His hand pressed harder and an illicit thrill zipped up my spine. I was half-naked in the back seat of a car with Dean keeping me quiet so people outside wouldn't know what we were doing behind these foggy windows.

"Show me," he urged. "Come for me, Tabitha."

I climaxed on Dean's fingers, moaning into his palm as a breath-stopping euphoria made me feel like I was levitating. Aftershocks still rocked my body as I managed to turn in his lap and kiss him until he was out of breath too. When I pulled back, his lips were swollen. Brow furrowed like he wasn't sure if I'd enjoyed myself.

"That," I said, kissing him, "was *fucking incredible*. You are incredible."

They were the right words—right, as in *accurate*. But after an orgasm that literally melted my brain, the relieved grin that appeared on his face sent a different kind of heat through my limbs. A soft, sweet heat that wanted me to cuddle this tough, strong dreamboat and stroke his hair.

He brushed the hair off my shoulders. Kissed me. Kissed me harder. His arms held me tight as he plundered my mouth until I was dazed and panting again.

"Please let me fuck you," I begged.

"*Yes,*" he growled through clenched teeth.

"Condoms?"

He gave a tight nod and managed to say, "Glove box." I made quick work of getting up there. Yanking it open, I was so happy to see the new box of condoms slide out I could have choreographed an entire dance sequence about it, with outfit changes and everything.

When I turned back around, I caught Dean mid-grimace. Remembering all those videos of him taking blows to his body, I crawled over and lightly touched his cheek again. "Does anything hurt?"

He shifted and let out a sigh. And then he dragged me back onto his lap easily. "I'm okay. I just get stiff and sore from old injuries sometimes. But thank you, for asking."

I brushed a lock of hair from his forehead before I could help it. "Now you have to tell *me* what feels good and won't hurt."

There was that half grin again, awakening butterflies that had less to do with the magic he'd worked with his fingers and more to do with this tender desire to protect Dean. To be the reason behind that smile. To fill his life with joy in the dark corners where it was absent.

I distracted myself by tearing open the condom packet and watching a hedonistic gleam appear in his eyes. I reached for leverage by grabbing the handle near the window and ground my pussy against his cock.

A muscle ticked in his jaw. "Ride me, just like this."

I bent close and brushed the softest kiss against his lips. "Anything for you, Dean."

The rumble of dangerous sound that came from his chest made me shiver with anticipation. Then he settled back against the lowered chair and dragged his hands along the curve of my thighs, the dip of my waist, spanning my rib cage, like he was memorizing my body through touch alone.

His hands finally settled on my hips, the motion drawing attention to the swell of his biceps, his broad chest. I bit my lip, already aching again. I liked him like this—sumptuous, almost lazy, lying back and receiving what he deserved.

I kicked off my shorts, then reached inside his to free his cock. It was as much a work of art as his body was—long and deliciously thick. I wrapped my fingers around the base and gave him the slowest jerk I could manage. Then another and another. His head fell back, exposing the tendons in his throat. His hoarse sound of gratification made me feel like a queen. So did his flexing stomach muscles and wandering hands, dipping beneath my underwear again to squeeze my ass.

I stopped what I was doing only to slip the condom on, my gaze rising to meet Dean's hungry one. I recognized the slight curl in his lip from watching his matches. But there was not an ounce of his trademark cool, refined focus to be found.

Sliding my underwear to the side, I gripped his arms and lowered myself down onto his cock, inch by agonizing inch. Dean helped, holding my hips, but this need to take my time was immediately outweighed by the tortuous satisfaction of being stretched, filled, *claimed* by him.

The second he was fully seated, hitting every nerve ending I had, all pretense of respectable behavior was abandoned. I dropped the handle and planted my hands on that gorgeous chest and rode his cock for the sole purpose of seeing this big, sexy fighter lose his goddamn mind right in front of me.

Lose his mind, he did.

"*Fuck yes,*" he grunted, lifting me up and down in the kind of hot and urgent rhythm that back-seat sex was invented for. He didn't take his eyes off me, watching me bounce on his cock with an expression of untamed lust. A bead of sweat slid down his temple. His chest expanded rapidly on every guttural inhale and growly exhale.

"Christ, Tabitha, you feel so fucking *good*," he spit out. "Get down here so I can kiss you."

I draped my body over his, grinding down, feeling like I might come any second. I wasn't sure I could withstand another orgasm, but in the midst of watching Dean become a damn animal I was suddenly about to come again. His hands landed on my ass, squeezing, rocking me against him while kissing me.

"Oh God," I whimpered into his mouth. I yanked on his hair and buried my face into his neck. I felt his hand slide around the front of my belly and then his thumb, caressing my clit in those same light circles. My muscles gathered tight, *tight*, and an undulating wave of pleasure rippled through me.

Dean caught my mouth with his before I screamed too loudly, but this orgasm *shimmered*. He seized my hips as I was still coming, urging me on, and I rode him as fast as he needed. My thighs slapped against his while I took him deeper. Harder. Dean held the back of my neck, and our eyes never left one another. Not once. Not when those fluttering aftershocks became a swift third orgasm. And not when Dean climaxed at the exact same time, as if he'd been waiting to release with me.

Though hazy and wrung out, I still memorized what he looked like as he finally unraveled beneath me—his flexing abs and shoulders, the fire in his gaze, the way he grunted my name—"*Tabitha*"—as he came. Of everything we'd done tonight, this eye contact was an intimacy that burrowed under my skin and warmed me from the inside, out.

The sound of falling rain crowded into this tight, dark space. I very gently pushed myself up and disengaged, tugging off the condom and disposing of it. When I crawled back to the seat, I didn't even hesitate to climb onto his lap again.

Dean pushed himself up and forward. Wrapped his arms around my back and pressed his face to my chest. I looped my arms around his neck and held him there. Kissed the top of his head, ran my fingers through his curls. Eventually his breathing slowed and he tipped his head up and kissed me. It was unhurried and delicious in a different way—a kiss not as a prelude to sex but a deeper connection.

Buried beneath my perpetual quest for fleeting pleasure was the routine that came after, all the tiny steps that ensured the *fleeting* part of the *pleasure*. I was a storyteller. I knew how this one ended. It was well past time to enact that routine if I wanted this soft heart of mine to stay protected.

But I didn't move.

His eyes opened and locked on mine. Dean shifted me until I was astride him, curled against his chest.

"Well, now you know what it's like to make out with someone in the back seat of your car," I said, voice husky from my triple orgasms. "Steamed-up windows and everything."

He brushed his lips across my cheek. "Was it mediocre?"

The idea was so preposterous that I laughed. "As I've said before, your physical prowess is well-documented. And I have been...*well-documented* as they say."

"Is that so?" He needed to stop nuzzling the shell of my ear or we were going to steam these windows back up.

I indicated our situation—clothing everywhere, snarled hair and bee-stung lips, bodies half-naked and covered in sweat and drying rain. "Talk about scandalous."

He hummed under his breath. "Speaking of. Do I need to get you back, or have you already broken curfew?"

I flashed him a devilish grin. "You better believe I'll be sneaking in. What about you?"

"Sounds about right," he said. "I'll need to get my very beautiful and troublemaking neighbor home first. Have to keep that innocent reputation intact."

I snuggled against his warm chest. "I hate to break it to you, but we just fucked in a car in front of a famous museum during a thunderstorm. I think your innocence is destroyed now."

His smile was just as devilish. "Good."

TWENTY-THREE

DEAN

It took a huge effort to sort the carrots. Twice I had to tip the boxes over and start again.

The potatoes were a goddamn nightmare. I lost half when they rolled under the table. Another few when I fucked up the count. *Five potatoes, one bag of carrots, two cans of soup. Five potatoes, one bag of—*

"Hey, Dean," Rowan said.

My hands stilled. I shook my head and got back to counting. Five potatoes? Six?

His face floated into view. "Yo, what's going on with you?"

I scowled at the onion I was holding. Rowan gripped me by the shoulders. "Oh my God, is that Tabitha Tyler?"

"What?" I said, craning my neck toward the door. "You saw Tabitha?"

Rowan's slightly concerned face sharpened. That concern was replaced with a smirk full of bullshit within seconds. "Nah, I was lying to get your attention. It's so painful to watch you sort those carrots, dude." He took them from me the same way I grabbed tools out of his grandmother's hands. "Wash the strawberries, make yourself useful."

I pinched the bridge of my nose with a wince. "Sorry. I'm... spacey today. Just a little out of it."

He eyed me carefully over the produce but didn't push. I'd offered to help him prep some last-minute food boxes for thirty seniors in the neighborhood who'd requested the extra help. I'd checked the list—Eddie wasn't on it.

We were making decent progress on the boxes. Even if I was doing a shit job.

I walked over to the large sink in the kitchen at the rec center. Flipped on the cold water and splashed my face. It chased away the remaining brain fog that hadn't let up since I'd driven Tabitha home last night.

It had taken me half an hour to find a parking spot after dropping her off. I'd gone to find the truck today, worried that in my shock I'd left my car in the middle of the road with the engine running, keys in the ignition.

I hadn't. It was parked correctly, doors locked and engine off. There was no sign at all of what happened in the back seat.

I filled a large silver bowl with strawberries and focused on washing them. Then I ripped open the final box of carrots. Scooped them out and into my arms. I didn't think about what it was like to have the best sex of my life with the woman I'd been into since high school. Didn't think about her warm lips or her soft skin or the incredible sounds she made when she came on my—

"*Dean.*"

I blinked. Rowan was taking the carrots away again. "Did you see Tabitha again?"

He paused, mid-step. Dropped the produce down and dragged two chairs out from the side table. Kicked one over to me. "Sit down."

"Why?"

"You're being really, *really* fucking weird tonight," he said. "And don't be a dick about me noticing it either."

I dropped into it heavily. "I'm the dick right now?"

He crossed his arms but stayed standing. He pointed at the space above my head. "What's going on up there? Those guys from the bar being assholes to you again?"

"What? No. I haven't seen 'em."

"Then what is it? You've been staring at produce like you're the guy in *Good Will Hunting* tryin' to solve math problems."

I let out an exasperated breath. "I love that movie."

"I've known you since we were four—I know all your favorite movies."

I dropped my elbows to my knees. I wasn't purposefully hiding what had happened between me and Tabitha. Even if it took me a while, I told Rowan everything. I was just in a literal trance. Letting myself think about last night seemed impossible.

Three times. I was somehow the man lucky enough to see Tabitha orgasm three times. How was I supposed to—

"Tabitha and I had sex in the back seat of the truck while parked in front of the art museum," I blurted out.

"*What?*" he yelled. "I spent the first hour tonight bitching to you about the Phillies bullpen, man." He spun around and left me there by myself in the room. His extreme reaction was comforting at least. It matched my own.

I clasped my hands together, right knee shaking. Rowan stormed back into the room with a half-empty bottle of Bulleit bourbon and two mugs. He splashed liquid into both before passing me one. With a sly grin, he knocked his mug against mine. "Sláinte."

"Salute," I grunted.

He settled back into his own chair and poured himself a second shot. "Now what the hell happened?"

I arched my eyebrow. "Last night, Tabitha came by and asked if I'd go with her to run the Rocky steps. For fun."

"For real?"

I nodded.

He slowly rubbed his jaw. "Damn."

"I drove us to the art museum in the truck."

"You gave up that spot?"

I hesitated. "Really wasn't thinking about parking."

"A feeling I know well."

I felt a flush creeping up my neck. Less about what happened later—Tabitha tearing off my shirt and straddling me in the rain—but all the moments leading up to it. Talking in the car, running up the steps while laughing. Watching her shadow box with an expression of eager curiosity.

The only word I knew to describe these moments together was *lightness*. Or maybe *comfortable*. Except both of those words disregarded my physical response to her nearness. Not the dizzying, intense sexual response. The one where I was always...smiling.

I shook my head and snapped out of it. "We got there. Ran the steps. And, uh...made out up there. In the rain."

Rain droplets on her eyelashes. Her nails scraping down my chest. Kissing like we'd never stop.

He reared back. "You made out with Tabitha Tyler in the rain, *in public?*"

"Trust me. I fucking know." A week ago I was so eager to avoid any kind of spotlight I didn't even want to work on the abandoned lot, let alone take the lead. Or risk some angry former fan seeing me do *anything* out in public.

"And then what?" Rowan asked, looking captivated.

Steamed-up windows. Our heavy breathing. Her gorgeous body...soft curves, delicate tattoos, pale skin. I clamped down on the images before I zoned out, lost in memories of a night where I was powerful again, where my body and its needs were admired, returned, yearned for. Where I wasn't a disappointment but a man who'd listened to his instincts and watched, in awe, as Tabitha climaxed over and over.

"That's when we had sex. In the back seat of the truck."

Rowan scrubbed a hand down his face and shook his head. "Holy shit."

"Yeah."

"*Holy shit, dude.* So that's why you can't pack these carrots."

"I'm a little...distracted."

He twisted his mug back and forth on the table. "I'm happy you're having some no-strings-attached fun. You deserve it." He grinned, looking no different than when we were kids. "I guess all of my grandmother's text messages were accurate after all."

Tension rippled between my shoulder blades. The words *no strings* were correct, and Tabitha told me she never got attached. So I unclenched my jaw and said, "Yeah. I guess they were."

"And you two are good with everything?" he asked.

I knew what he meant. "Yeah," I hedged. "Yeah, we're good."

I didn't know what the hell we were. It wasn't like we'd done a lot of talking about it. I was so obviously in over my head, but no part of me could go back now. No part of me wanted to.

My phone buzzed in my back pocket. I pulled it out. Harry was calling. I silenced it and tossed it on the table.

"Was it Harry?"

I nodded, avoided looking directly at him. Of everyone's mixed reactions at family dinner when I told them about becoming a commentator, Rowan's had been cagey. And he wasn't that kind of guy.

"We talked yesterday but he's been calling nonstop. Checking in."

"Trying to convince you," Rowan said.

I exhaled through my nose. "Harry set a meeting with one of the show producers five days from now uptown at a restaurant. He's flying through Philly for work and said he wanted to meet me in person."

"That's a promising sign if you're gonna take it."

I lifted a shoulder. "It could be an honest-to-god comeback for me, Rowan. A way to fix my reputation."

"There's nothing wrong with your reputation," he said firmly. "People's opinions about the decision you made for your own health aren't worth a sack of old shit."

I reluctantly looked back up at him. "I know. But what the hell else am I doing?"

As soon as the words were out, I wanted to snatch them back. They were embarrassing.

But Rowan's reaction was to beam at me like he had life-changing news. "I wanted to wait a few more weeks, especially since you've got a lot going on, but…I've been talking with my director. I think you'd be a good fit here." He tapped the top of one of the boxes filled with produce. "I want to hire you to run the senior food program."

My jaw dropped. "Are you serious?"

"As a heart attack, big guy."

I coughed into my fist. "Sorry, I wasn't expecting you to say that."

Rowan leaned forward in his chair. "I don't need to tell you why getting food to these folks is so important. You and I see it every day. But this program can't be the ugly stepkid of everything we do at the rec center. We need to hire a paid person to run it, smooth out the logistics, expand it. I think it could be you."

I swallowed hard, thinking about Eddie. "What do I know about running a food program? I'm a boxer."

He held out his hand, ticking off fingers. "Would you say sparring with someone in the ring is stressful?"

"Uh...yeah," I said sardonically.

"Have you had to manage your time, going to early practices and traveling and touring and shit?"

I nodded but didn't see his point.

"Can you or can you not think on your feet?"

"That's literally what a boxer does, but why would that—"

"Dean," he said, interrupting me. "You've spent the past three years fixing up leaky pipes for people like Edna Kozlowski. You know our neighbors. You talk to 'em. They trust you enough to let you into their houses. Most importantly, into their *kitchens*."

I jiggled my knee up and down. "Edna didn't have any food in her fridge when I fixed it for her."

His face softened. "That's what I'm saying. She deserves to have a full fridge, yeah? That's the job I think you could do. And do well. Plus, you and I would get to work together at a place that made us who we are. I know its bad timing, coming to you with a chance to work here when you've got your agent coming to you with a huge opportunity." Rowan tore open a bag of carrots and began organizing them into boxes. "But I don't want you to think there isn't a place for you here. Because there is."

I was quiet. It was a lot of information to process. Rowan knew me well enough to let me sit there and figure it out. I shifted my weight in the chair and stretched my right leg out, feeling an ache in my lower back. Apparently having passionate sex in the back seat of a truck wasn't that great for ex-athletes who'd taken one too many shots to the kidneys.

I kept turning one question around and around in my

mind but wasn't sure I wanted to know the answer. "Would you take a commentator gig if it was offered to you now?"

"No," he said.

The uncharacteristic certainty in his voice had me straightening up in the chair.

"I get the impulse," he continued. "And I'll be a baseball fan till the day I die. But my team owners made it clear the only thing that mattered was wins. Our bodies, our health, none of that registered for them. I know that was true for you too."

I stared down at my swollen knuckles. "You're not wrong."

"This job at the rec center has plenty of its own bullshit, like all jobs. But when I show up to work, the priority is people. Our neighbors. No one's making money off whether my arm's having a good day or a bad day. It's about looking out for each other. Like what you and Tabitha are doing with the vacant lot."

Rowan had a point, and it was a smart one. If I sat with the truth that had been bothering me since that first call, I'd pick up the phone and tell Harry to fuck right off. The confidence I'd felt with Tabitha last night hadn't come from tugging on a pair of boxing gloves. It'd come from moving my body for joy and pleasure, without the burden of overanalyzing everything.

Maybe I didn't have to be Dean the Machine anymore. Or have a comeback I didn't want. Around Tabitha, I was starting to feel like myself again.

I just had to figure out how to hold on to that feeling when she packed up her bags and left.

TWENTY-FOUR
TABITHA

I had an extremely adorable niece in my lap, demanding to watch a movie about me.

"*About* me?" I asked Juliet, my chin on top of her head. "Or a movie that I've made? I do have that one I made with all the rescue puppies in St. Louis."

"*About* you," she said.

I tilted my head to look at her, then gave her a kiss on the cheek. "I don't make movies about myself, sweetheart. I make them about other people. For other people."

"Show her the one you posted today," Alexis said. "The one for the pocket park."

By her wiggles alone, it seemed like my niece was highly amenable to that idea.

"You've seen it already?" I asked. Alexis and Eric were curled up together on Aunt Linda's ratty loveseat, wearing pajamas just like me. Juliet had requested a "slumber party at Aunty Tabby's house" tonight, so I'd pulled out all the stops—we'd had pizza delivered and played a rousing game of Twister and spent a pretty intense hour building a castle together out of Play-Doh.

Now we were on the *get Juliet to fall asleep* part of the night.

"Of course we've seen it," my sister said, handing Eric a bowl of popcorn. "We sent it to all of our teacher friends. They were super excited to donate. As were we."

I looked over at the lovebirds on the loveseat. "*You guys.*"

Eric shook his head. "Don't *you guys* me, Aunty Tabby. You send me and your sister school supplies every year for our new students. *And* you very graciously edited that god-awful video I tried to make that one year about my classroom service projects."

"For free," Alexis added.

Juliet was playing with my keyboard, and I was trying to make sure she didn't accidentally delete my hard drive.

"It was an honor and it was *adorable*," I pointed out. "I personally think the world would be a better place if more people got to see how cute it is when third graders decide to make soup and sandwiches for nurses working the night shift at the hospital down the block."

"And it was truly appreciated," Eric said. "You always support our classrooms no matter where you are in the world. It's an honor to support this." He inclined his head toward the window behind him, indicating the now clean empty lot in its pre-park stage.

"Also, that video of Eddie and Alice talking about Annie in her Santa suit is *pretty* convincing," Alexis said. "We showed Juliet before coming over here."

"Mr. Eddie has a cat," Juliet told me. "I want to draw a picture of her for him."

I kissed the top of her head. "He would love that, sweetheart. Mr. Eddie needs a little extra help right now, so I think pictures would bring a smile to his face."

Juliet nodded somberly at this task, in that way children

seemed to so easily accept the concepts of both helping and being helped.

While she was briefly distracted by hitting the space bar on my keyboard one hundred times in a row, I slid my phone out and logged into the GoFundMe page I'd set up for the park. It had been live for only a day but there was already close to a thousand dollars in there. I scrolled down the list, recognized not only Alexis and Eric but a few of their teacher friends. Kathleen and my dad. Members of Kathleen's book club. A couple local businesses and nonprofits. The Buddhist temple on Eleventh Street and the rec center where Rowan worked.

A surge of emotion got trapped in my throat. I was expecting gifts from social media followers and kind internet strangers. But, as usual, this neighborhood stepped up and supported itself. The lot was far from being a park or even an idea of a park. Weeks of work would need to go into pulling it all together, plus constant maintenance and caretaking.

Yet people could already see its potential, this splash of greenery the size of a postage stamp.

I set my phone down. Alexis was watching me closely and smiled as soon as our eyes met. *I love you,* I mouthed.

I love you too, she mouthed back.

I hugged Juliet tight. I was starting to get homesick for Philly, and I hadn't even left yet.

"Aunty Tabby movie?" she said again.

"All right, kid, let's do this," I said, pulling up my Instagram and starting the video. It was short and to the point, with me expanding on the videos and "before" pictures I'd been posting, what the block had in mind and some of the supplies we were raising money for. Juliet's face was sweetly enraptured, eyes starting to get heavy.

Her head lolled against my arm. She was still awake but

starting to fight it, and I inhaled the peace of one of the quiet moments I'd missed so much of. She was only five years old, and I'd been living elsewhere for all of it. Time was flying by—my backpack was getting lighter even as my family continued to change and evolve every day.

Guilt was a strange beast. I carried so much of it for the lies and harm I caused my family. Carried so much of it for feeling like I'd abandoned them ever since I graduated from college. I was forever an outsider, yearning to be let in but wary of the consequences.

"Is she asleep?" Alexis whispered.

"Almost," I said. We were nearing the end of the video, and I was talking about Tenth Street.

"*I don't share a lot about my personal life on my platforms, but I'm enormously proud to call South Philly home. I have known some of the people on Tenth Street undertaking this project for most of my life.*"

Alexis and I shared a grin, both of us sipping lemonade from Linda's collection of funky, bikini-themed glasses.

"*This neighborhood is a special place,*" I said. "*And everyone there means a lot to me.*"

Watching it back now, I heard the note of hesitation in my voice and saw the hint of pink in my cheeks. I couldn't resist stealing a look at the far wall—the one I shared with Dean's house.

The video ended and Juliet had gone dead weight in my lap. Eric swooped in and scooped her up from my lap. "I'm gonna take her up and let her sleep for a bit in your bed, if that's okay?" he whispered.

"Of course, anything she needs," I whispered back, noticing the look of pure affection on his face as he carried her up the stairs with a practiced ease. The second he was gone, Alexis all but launched herself onto the couch next to me.

"Speaking of people who personally mean a lot to you," she said with a sisterly smirk, "we didn't get to finish our conversation about Dean because Juliet wanted to switch from Play-Doh to pretending that the floor was lava."

I grabbed a bag of mini marshmallows from the table—an ideal slumber-party snack and my sister's favorite. Handing them to her, I said, "There isn't much more to say. Dean Knox-Morelli basically"—I cast an uneasy glance at our shared wall, wondering how much he could hear—"*fucked me into the next stratosphere*, and he's probably over there right now, listening through the wall with his ear pressed to a water glass."

Her eyes widened. "Do you really think he's eavesdropping?"

I considered it and shook my head. "No. He's much too nice and respectful to do something like that."

Alexis settled back on the couch and propped her feet on my lap. Twister hadn't seemed like the easiest time to fill in my sister and brother-in-law about what happened between Dean and me at the art museum the night before. So I went with telling them while we were building with Play-Doh instead and proceeded to have a frantic and hilariously whispered conversation using hand gestures and creative euphemisms that made Alexis laugh so hard that she cried. Eric kept putting his hands over Juliet's ears, who was deeply concerned with the structural integrity of our castle and oblivious to the adults at the table.

My sister tapped the inside of my arm with the edge of her foot. "Do you like Dean?"

"Of course I do."

Her brow furrowed, like she didn't like my answer. Eric came back down the stairs, shaking his head. "It's been a while since I've been at Lin's house, so I keep forgetting that Jon Bon Jovi's picture could be sewn into so many different types of fabrics." He dragged one of the dining room chairs over to the couch and sank down into it. He looked at Alexis and said, "She went to sleep easy. No problems." To me, he said, "Are we finally talking about Dean now?"

Alexis passed him the marshmallows. "Tabitha likes him."

His eyebrows shot up.

"What?" I said with a laugh. "He's incredibly likeable. It doesn't mean anything."

My sister sat up and grabbed my hand. She didn't have to say it. I was already struggling to admit it. Dean wasn't some casual hookup, and we weren't discussing this over FaceTime, multiple states and time zones away. It made the truth more glaringly obvious even though my first instinct was to skirt around vulnerability and pretend.

I squeezed her hand back—three times. Her smile widened.

"I like him a lot," I admitted. "More than a lot and more than I should. Last night, our chemistry being so *instant*, only proved a few things that I'd been avoiding. Mostly that you shouldn't have mind-blowing sex with someone who's also a friend. And incredibly kind and humble and charming and slightly broody and very, very cute."

Her eyes softened, and I almost couldn't take it. My gaze wandered over to my pack, still leaning against Lin's bookcase. *I used to dream about packing you girls up and hittin' the road too. Just to escape.*

"Are you worried about hurting Dean if things don't work out?" she asked, drawing my attention back to her and Eric.

I nodded. "Always. And I don't really know how to *do* any of this anyway. Or even if Dean's interested. Besides, I'm moving to Austin in a week. And, just between the three of us, Dean might be moving to Las Vegas for a job opportunity.

There's a lot of complicating factors. Especially if he takes that job."

Eric moved to the couch and squished in next to Alexis. He held the bag of marshmallows open without her needing to ask. And she reached in immediately without looking. They'd had an effortless intimacy for as long as I'd known them together. I didn't believe I'd ever been privy to an intimacy like that.

Though thanks to Dean, I was beginning to understand it.

"I get it, Tab," Alexis said. "It was hard for me to trust when Eric and I started dating and hard for me to be fully honest with him. Dad hadn't met Kathleen yet, and so I only had memories from the Bad Year stuck on loop."

Eric reached between them and entwined their fingers. "We got through it though. It took a lot of patience and a lot of communication." His lips quirked up at the ends. "That wasn't super easy given that we were only twenty-one but it was different between the two of us. I recognized that from the very beginning of our relationship. So fighting through whatever was trying to hold us back was worth it in the end."

I could feel all three of us tense up on the couch. I chewed on the end of my thumbnail. "Does Juliet ever ask about Mom?"

Alexis shook her head fiercely. "She already has two amazing grandmothers. Kathleen and Eric's mom. We'll see when she gets older how we'll talk about it."

"And we're lucky," Eric said. "Juliet already goes to school with a lot of kids who come from interracial families. Families that look like ours. I hate saying that it's likely a lot of those families have had to cut someone out of their lives because of their racism or bigotry. But..." His lips pressed into a thin line. "It is likely. My hope would be that we can all help each other figure out how to have those conversations about race and family together."

I nodded vigorously. "That happened at the Lavender Center for a lot of gay and queer families who went there. They supported each other through a lot of conversations that were difficult to have."

The relationship we had with my mom when Alexis was a senior in college was strained at best. Early on, she'd made it clear that her new family made a lot of demands on her time. And she and my dad weren't amicable anyway.

We rarely saw her and—quite honestly—preferred it that way. After years of being subjected to her criticism—and, for me, her manipulative lying—Alexis and I were much, *much* happier being out from under her thumb.

We weren't even trying to salvage the relationship as much as we were fine keeping it as it was. I still kept trying to convince my mother that my bisexuality was real and valid out of a desperate attempt to make her a better person. Every attempt at that failed, leaving me heartbroken and hurt while my dad and sister were furious.

And then Alexis started dating Eric. He was right—as soon as things got serious between the two of them and she started bringing him over for family dinners and movie nights, their true love was on full display. By that point, our relationship with our mother had dwindled to a passing text or email, but she somehow saw a picture of the two of them on social media.

We never knew exactly what my mom said to my dad when she called him about it, but he distilled it for us to the pertinent points—her daughters had disappointed her often throughout her life, but things had reached a crisis point for her now that one daughter was bisexual and the other was dating a Black man. Honestly, at that point, there wasn't even really a relationship there to cut off.

All of us cut her off anyway.

"It's still confusing to me," Alexis said. "The way that she raised us affected me for years. The fact that she cheated on Dad, broke his heart like it held no value to her, then *left* us." Alexis shuddered. "It fundamentally changed the way I viewed romantic relationships. And parental ones. It's difficult for me to admit that about a person who I've cut out of my life because it gives her too much power."

I felt a frisson of guilt but tried to ignore it. "I hate that her past actions can still steal away a moment of present happiness and affect my decisions. Especially since you and I are surrounded with unconditional love on all sides."

"Yeah, you are, and I know you're both grateful for it," Eric said, "but I think it's like how you talk about filmmaking and storytelling. That your job is searching for the common threads that unite us. As awful and stressful as it is, she's still a thread in all of our lives, even if it's only an echo at this point."

I passed my hand across the top of my head. "Two things I didn't anticipate happening when I came home for a visit. Getting romantically involved with a friend and not a sexy stranger." I bit my bottom lip. "And feeling like all that stuff with Mom happened yesterday and not years ago. I thought I'd locked it all away."

I'd never been more tempted to blurt out every last remaining secret that I had. The only thing holding me back was fear—fear that when my family found out I'd known about my mom's affair all along, had gone along with her lies, they'd stop trusting me too. Some part of me knew that emotionally keeping myself at arm's length was *why* I felt like an outsider in my own family, even as they so clearly loved the hell out of me. But they weren't the problem. I was.

At least now as I traveled across the country, far from them for long periods of time, I could feel their love—in their calls and text messages and emails. Their silly care packages and cat videos. I'd made the decision to cut my mother out of my life when I was an adult. She'd, however, up and left me when I was just a kid. My darkest, middle-of-the-night worry was that I'd unburden myself of secrets only to find all that unconditional love changed to *conditional*.

"I feel that way too, and I live here," Alexis said. "Sometimes it doesn't feel close or that it matters. Other days, it's like you and I are teens again, watching Mom and Dad fight. It's not something I can control." She smiled. "The only silver lining to all of this is that when Eric and I got married, we saw it as an opportunity to love each other and parent the way we wanted. And we love Juliet *so much*. We support and lift her up no matter what she wants to do. And we both work with kids every day and encourage their imagination. Their creativity, their wishes. And we don't care about their mistakes."

"The opposite of how Mom raised us," I said grimly.

"Exactly."

I pulled my knees into my chest and gazed at two of my most favorite people in the whole world. "Your story is the real deal. It's a happily ever after."

Alexis cocked her head. "Yours is too. Whether it was a story you'd written or one you'd shot on that old camera we had, Mom went out of her way to ignore it or pass judgment on it. And now look at you. All of your stories are about love."

I hummed a little, considered that description. "I always describe them as being about the power of a community, coming together."

"Isn't that love too?" she said.

Juliet called down for her parents, who both rose off the couch and made their way to the stairs.

"This is random," I said, "but do you guys want to actually stay the night? I can take Linda's guest bedroom to sleep in, and she has so much garbage reality television to watch, I'd hate to binge *Real Housewives* on my own. I'd rather open a bottle of red wine and hang with the two of you."

I couldn't say the last time the temporary place I was staying in felt like a home. In my aunt's house, with Juliet running around and Eric and Alexis's laughter, there was a contentment and safety curling around my heart that I didn't realize I was missing. I knew this attachment feeling could be dangerous but felt much too vulnerable to turn away from it.

Eric looked down at his outfit and shrugged. "I'm already in my pajamas and am seriously behind on those housewives."

Alexis gave me a knowing look. "We've only got you for a little while longer anyway before you leave again. I need to soak up as much time as I can get."

I patted the spot next to me on the couch. "All aboard the cuddle express."

Eric laughed. "I'm going to soothe our daughter, and then someone better have opened that bottle of wine."

He jogged up the steps, and Alexis watched him go. She drummed her fingers on the banister for a second. "I don't know if this helps with the Dean situation or not," she said, "but when we were at Benny's the other night, you said you were able to keep your relationships casual by always staying in the present moment and not getting hung up on the future."

I smirked. "I fell into Dean's lap like an hour after saying that, and a week later I was actively disregarding every single thing I said."

Alexis grinned. "You were tempting fate, that's for sure. But maybe you were onto something. I think you can stay in the present moment and fully enjoy this time with Dean while also opening up your heart." She held up her thumb and index finger. "Maybe just a *little* bit?"

I chewed on my lip and shot a glance at the wall Dean and I shared. "I'm willing to experiment with that."

She skipped up the steps looking so much like her younger self I had to breathe through a sharp pinch of bittersweet nostalgia. That was the curious thing about living in row homes. Linda's house looked both nothing like the house we grew up in and *exactly* like it at the same time.

I took my phone out and dialed Dean's number, thinking about Alexis's advice. Every time that man smiled at me, my heart spun and toppled like a clumsy ballerina. I could probably open it...just a little. Right?

He picked up in the middle of the first ring. "You don't have to call me, you know. You can just knock on my door."

"I like to switch it up. Keep things interesting," I said. "How did you...sleep last night?"

"Very well," he said. "It helped that I had a pretty tough workout right before I went to bed."

Heat flooded my body at the rough scrape in his voice. The same voice that had commanded me to come as he'd groaned raggedly against my ear.

I *tsked* into the phone. "I've heard running those Rocky steps can get you into all kinds of trouble."

"I can confirm that's true," he said. "I missed you today. Guess I've gotten used to you showing up at random times to try and get me to eat a hoagie or whatever."

I laughed and twirled a strand of hair around my finger. I stopped when I realized that I probably looked like a teen girl on the phone with her crush. Although this situation wasn't far from that.

"I missed seeing you too," I said. "Can I come over tomorrow?"

"Yes," he said quickly. "I'd like that."

"I have a couple of ideas. I'll text them to you, and you can choose what we do this time."

"That's a lot of responsibility."

"I believe in you, Mr. Machine," I said. "Good night. Check your phone."

I leaned past the couch and peered up the staircase. I could hear Alexis and Eric talking to Juliet still. Sinking back into the cushion, I fired off a message, thinking about pleasure and giving in and taking what you wanted.

Can I make one of your sexual fantasies come true? I texted. Pressed my phone to my chest nervously until he texted back.

You're already a fantasy, Tabitha.

I glanced at the wall and imagined him standing right there, hand touching it, with a smile on his face.

What about another one? I texted. Based on what he'd said last night, Dean Knox-Morelli was a man with unmet needs.

I was eager to meet them.

His response had me grinning. This fantasy was so like him—a timeless classic, no frills, to the point. Just like Dean himself.

When I knock on your door tomorrow night, you're going to want to open it, I sent.

Now I needed to get myself a sexy trench coat and some lingerie.

TWENTY-FIVE

DEAN

The boxers on the screen opened their mouths to show the ref their mouthpiece. They touched gloves. The ref said, "Fair fight, clean fight," while the two glared at each other. Behind them, an audience jostled and applauded.

The trip gong sounded, and three years later I still got a massive head rush of adrenaline. Still had synapses firing off an attack response though I was only on the couch in my living room.

They were light heavy-weight boxers, like I had been. In fact, I knew them both, and if I did this commentator job, I'd be analyzing bouts like this one.

The boxer on the left took a jab that opened a gash on his cheek. The crowd roared with bloodlust. There was no other way to describe it. Sometimes in the ring I felt like a Roman gladiator and wasn't sure if that was good or bad.

They danced around each other, occasionally getting a hit in. The upbeat commentators talked about every move they made carelessly and critically. I thought about what Rowan said: *No one's making money off whether my arm's having a good day or a bad day.*

There was money to be had in every hit these guys took to the temple. Money for me to make. I glanced around the first floor of my house. I kept it neat. Tidy. But it was still shabby and a little run down. I was frugal, had managed to live off my winnings and the meager income I made as a handyman. But I'd peeked at my bank account yesterday morning and gone queasy.

If things didn't change, I was about to be in more than just a rut.

I took in the first round by maintaining a kind of impassive interest. It was just bodies. Just fists and gloves.

By the third round I had to close my eyes.

By the fourth, I turned it off.

With a muttered curse, I tossed the remote onto the coffee table. I'd only turned on the match because of Harry's urging. I'd felt a little less confused after talking about it with Rowan the other night, while packing those food boxes. But Harry had been hounding me all day—said the in-person meeting scheduled with the producer was basically an *in*. They only needed to hear me say yes.

He wants to talk to you about concussions, Dean, Harry had claimed over the phone a few hours ago. *Says he's interested in hearing your concerns. This could be a sea of change for your sport, and you could be at the forefront.*

I'd once made the mistake of watching my match with Bobby McKee. Had seen the vicious upper cut to my chin that sent me to the ground, unconscious. I didn't remember any of it. Not the minutes before. And obviously not the shocked silence of the crowd. The medical crew, rushing under the ropes. Or Rowan, who'd had the bad luck of being in the audience that night, running to my side with fear in his eyes.

I scrubbed a hand down my face, exhausted and amped up at the exact same time. There was a soft knock at the door.

My heart stopped. *Tabitha.*

Last night, when she'd asked if she could make a fantasy of mine come true, I'd dropped my phone so fast I almost cracked the goddamn screen.

I could have filled a phone book with the fantasies I'd had about her since she moved in next door. The entire day had been one long, tortuous wait for the sound of that knock. I'd gritted my teeth through a dawn training session with Sly. Had worked a few jobs off Ninth Street around lunch. Then I'd driven the truck over to Home Depot and filled it with a first run of gardening supplies for the park.

I did it all in a daze. Stunned, as usual, by Tabitha Tyler.

I stood and walked to the front, moving the curtain back a half inch. Blinked in disbelief at what I saw there, even though I'd been told to expect it.

I opened the door and leaned one arm against the side. Tabitha's hair was piled in a high bun. Her lips were stained a dark red. The trench coat was tied in the middle, and she wore high heels.

My gaze rose to meet hers. A dark lust was taking hold of me. I reached for the knot in her belt and dragged her inside. Then I pressed her back against the door.

I stroked my finger up and down the buttons of the jacket. "What is this?"

"Your fantasy, come true."

"Is that so?" I asked, voice already sounding like a growl. The adrenaline from the sound of the bell still coursed through me, combining with a frantic urge to taste every inch of this woman.

"It's a present," she purred. "Why don't you open it?"

This was probably a dream, but I didn't stop to pinch

myself. Eyes locked on hers, I worked open the knot. Didn't drop my gaze as I slowly undid every button on that jacket. There was the tension and the release, bit by bit. A gradual reveal of hidden skin I didn't allow myself to see yet. Her berry lips parted on a shaky exhale. Her pulse fluttered in the hollow of her throat.

I leaned in and stole a desperate kiss. Tabitha moaned and opened for me. My tongue swept into her mouth, her fingers threading into my hair.

The last button opened.

I planted my hands on either side of her face and looked down.

"For *fuck's sake*, Tabitha," I swore. I shoved the now-open jacket off her shoulders. It pooled at her high-heeled feet. A lacy, red bra cupped the pale skin of her breasts, and she wore matching underwear that made my mouth water for a taste of her. She was all curved hips and dark ink and freckles.

"I was lucky that Target carried lingerie in the *femme fatale* vibe I was going for tonight," she said.

I didn't respond. Only stared at her in sheer, honest wonder. I fell to my knees in front of her and skated my palms up her smooth thighs. Caressed her belly with my lips. She shivered.

"Is your..." She paused. I heard the tremble. "Is your fantasy to your liking?"

I gave in and pressed my face between her legs, mouth open against the lace. "I don't deserve you."

She hooked her fingers under my chin. Lifted. "Yes, you do."

The look we shared threatened to stop my heart again. Or send it into overdrive. There was temporary fun, and then there was *this*—Tabitha staring down at me like I was the only thing that mattered.

My hands moved up the back of her thighs, gripping her round ass. I could have fucking *wept*. I pulled her ass cheeks apart, hefting them in my hands.

Her eyelids fluttered. "What's next in this fantasy of yours?"

I nuzzled against all that red lace, already slick with her arousal. "I want to make you come right here. With my mouth."

I waited for her permission. She granted it by hooking her leg over my shoulder with a nod and flushed cheeks. I used my other shoulder to pin her leg in place. Spread one hand across her belly to steady her. With my other, I grabbed the edge of those lace panties and pulled them to the side.

At the sight of Tabitha's pussy, an all-consuming lust guided me forward. She was slick. Wet. I inhaled the smell of her naked skin, felt my cock harden to the point of physical pain. This close, in this position, it wasn't possible for me to second-guess what I wanted. She was right there, open for me. Legs wrapped around my head. I tasted her with my tongue, diving into her folds. She was earthy and lush. Sweet. A strangled groan ripped from my chest. Her fingers twisted in my hair. I gave her the laziest lick I could manage, savoring her. Committing this act, this moment, to memory. When I reached her clit, she gasped.

Spreading her, I dipped my mouth lower and wiggled my tongue inside of her, licking as deeply as I could. I felt her reaction—a tremor in her legs. Fingers, scratching at my skin. I slid in and out, an easy rhythm. Realized I could do this for the rest of my goddamn life—fucking Tabitha with my tongue against a door—and die happy.

"How do you...do that?" she sighed, hips rocking into my mouth. I let my gaze travel up the length of her body. Watched her writhe above me, head tipped back. I groaned against her skin. Replaced my tongue with two fingers—gently, working them inside, eying her closely for signs of what she liked. What she craved. I hooked the pads of my fingers against her inner walls. A smile bloomed on her face—fast, euphoric.

"Like this?" I asked, pressing a kiss to her inner thigh.

"Yes…" She nodded. "Oh yes, like that."

I didn't stop moving my fingers. I lowered my tongue to her clit. Curled around it. Circled it. Lapped at it as a bead of sweat ran down her chest. She looked out of her fucking mind. I was there too, mindless and nothing but need.

I pulled the cup of her bra down and rolled her nipple back and forth against my palm. Tabitha let out a garbled cry, ending on a moan, hips punching forward.

"How about this?" I sucked her clit between my lips.

"Fuck," she whispered harshly. Her hands slapped against my shoulders. I grinned—couldn't help it. Then I doubled everything in intensity—fucked her faster. Lapped at her clit. Pinched her nipple as her cries grew louder and more nonsensical. When she began chanting my name, I knew she was close. Wanted to roar out a primal scream with the power surging through me—that I could bury my tongue in Tabitha's pussy and get her off, fast, like this. Hot and eager and urgent, like this. That Tabitha Tyler was gripping my hair and riding my face and then coming, coming, *coming*.

"Oh my God, oh my…oh my…" she panted.

I watched her, greedy for her release. Her flushed chest, exposed throat, hard nipples. The way she shivered all over and I had to hold her up. The way I was lucky to do this for her.

She stared down at me, catching her breath. Her dark eyes were wide. Her bun had come undone, red strands everywhere.

I stood and gave her a fast, brutal kiss. Then I bent at the knees and scooped Tabitha into my arms like she was my blushing bride.

"Wait," she said quickly, "this doesn't hurt right?"

I muttered, "If it did, I wouldn't care," against her lips and then proceeded to carry the woman of my dreams up the stairs and into my bedroom. I kicked the door open and nudged the light on. No more mechanical, impersonal sex. I needed to see all of her. I wanted her to see all of *me*.

I tossed her back onto the bed with more force than intended. I shed my clothing. Liked having her watch, liked the goose bumps it gave me. The strength. When I wrapped my fingers around my cock, stroking upward, her breathing got faster again.

Her knees dropped open. Her teeth sank into her bottom lip like I was something delicious she planned on devouring.

I lifted my chin at her, and she tossed her bra at me with a cheeky grin. The lace panties followed. Tabitha lay naked on my bed with swollen lips and disheveled hair. Every victory I'd ever had paled in comparison.

I had no clue what the hell I'd done in this life—or any other—to deserve this.

But I was ready to take it.

I reached for the condom on the wardrobe behind me. Rolled it on while watching Tabitha writhe naked on my bed. I prowled up her body and settled my hips between her legs. Then I captured her mouth with my own, drank her in. Our kissing grew frantic. My lips roamed down her throat. My tongue swirled around her nipples as she cried out again and again.

"Dean, please, *please*, fuck me," she begged.

Grabbing her wrists, I pinned them over her head and thrust my cock inside of her. Like last time, our attempts to move slowly failed within seconds. Her knees rose high on my waist as I rocked back and forth inside of her—a steady, driving rhythm that set my body on fire with pleasure.

It felt so damn good to move like this, to fuck like this. For the two of us to moan and sigh as we kissed. I released her wrists. Her hands gripped my cheeks, tongue stroked into my mouth. I hitched her leg higher and ground my pelvis against her clit.

"More," she demanded, mouth at my ear. "I want more of you."

Those words wrenched a snarl from my lips. I sat back on my heels and turned Tabitha onto her hands and knees. She looked at me from over her shoulder—a temptress to the very end. I curled over her body and kissed a slow path up the column of her spine, grinding my cock between her legs as I did so. By the time I smoothed the hair from her face, her breathing was unsteady. Eyes unfocused. I opened my mouth to suck on the crook of her neck. I slid my hands under her, cupped her breasts as my lips found her ear.

"I meant what I said," I whispered. *"You're* the fantasy, Tabitha."

Her fingers twisted in the bedsheets. "Then take me, please. *Please.* You can have me." She turned her head for a sloppy, fevered kiss. And I knew she wanted to give me something hot and erotic, a night of pure bliss just because. But there was a fierce emotion in those words that made my head spin with possibilities I didn't need to hope for.

I sat back on my heels again, gripped her hips. I gave her a quick, shallow thrust, and she moaned my name. My next was deeper, then deeper still. She pushed her hips back against mine until I gave in and fucked her faster. Harder. I worked my cock between her legs with everything I had. The front of my thighs slapped against her legs. She tilted her hips again, adjusting the angle. I slid deep enough to have us both crying out. The only word on her lips was my name, urging me on, taking everything I wanted to give.

Her knees slipped wider. She pressed her face to the mattress. I curled my fingers between her legs to rub her clit, the way she showed me the other night.

"Oh *yes*, right there...right *there*..." She moaned. I could feel her internal walls fluttering. I increased the pressure on her clit. Tabitha screamed with pleasure and bucked against me, squeezing me so tight that an intense orgasm crashed over me without warning. My head fell back on a grateful, satisfied groan. It took me a few seconds before I could move again, gently pulling away from Tabitha, who immediately flopped onto her stomach with an extremely satisfied smile on her face. I carefully removed the condom but stopped on my way to dispose of it to smooth the hair from her face.

I dipped my head and kissed her cheek. "I liked my fantasy."

She giggled, opened her eyes. "Oh, you did? I couldn't tell. Your reaction was pretty subdued."

I nipped at the shell of her ear. "Don't you dare move."

I walked to the bathroom, tossed the condom. It took me all of five seconds, but when I came back, Tabitha was already curled on her side with her eyes closed. I tried not to linger too long on how right this felt, to have a sleepy and satisfied Tabitha dozing in my bed.

But I guessed she probably had rules for this sort of thing.

I smoothed my hand down her back. "Tabitha? Are you asleep?"

"I didn't move." Her voice was muffled. Happy-sounding.

I hesitated, unsure of what to say.

But then she peered at me with dreamy eyes through her snarled hair. "Can I stay?"

I nodded. Flipped off the light with trembling fingers and

climbed into bed. I opened my arms as if we'd always done this. In the dark, I felt the bed tilt and then her warm, naked body curling into my chest.

Turns out, there were many different kinds of fantasies to long for.

I stroked her hair and kissed the crown of her head. "You can always stay," I whispered.

"I want to," she murmured, so soft I almost didn't catch it.

TWENTY-SIX
TABITHA

The next morning, I woke to the sound of a steady, comforting *thump*.

I nuzzled closer and was rewarded with Dean's hand, caressing my hair, and his arm banding more tightly around my waist. I splayed my palm over the center of his chest. His muscles twitched beneath my touch.

Thump...thump.

I opened my eyes as I realized I'd fallen asleep to the sound of Dean's heart beating, our limbs entwined and peaceful like we'd been lovers for decades.

My brain fired off a flurry of SOS messages. It wasn't that I'd stayed the night—I didn't usually have a problem falling asleep in other people's beds, even if I'd carved clear boundaries and limits into our relationship. It was that we *hadn't* done that. I hadn't subjected him to my usual speech filled with terms and conditions, all the little ways I could control the situation so no one got hurt.

Instead, I'd let this foolishly soft heart of mine open a *fraction* of an inch, and the first thing I did was cling to Dean all night long like he was a raft and I was a shipwrecked sailor.

I attempted a subtle morning stretch while still trapped against Dean's delicious body. My own was eager to remind me of all we'd done last night. I touched my swollen lips, the tender skin of my throat. Felt a burn between my legs and an ache in my hips. On the floor were the discarded remnants of Dean's fantasy—the stiletto heels and lingerie set I'd bought in a hurry to make his dreams come true.

The man had fallen to his knees in front of me with a look of true astonishment, had used those strong shoulders to hold me up as he licked me like he'd never, ever get enough.

My ear vibrated, slightly, at the sound of the contented rumble coming from his chest. Then he turned onto his side, toppling me slightly. His dark eyes blinked open, focusing on me for a second of confusion. And then recognition.

And then that same expression of astonishment rose on his face, sending a burst of affectionate pleasure through me.

"You're still here," he said.

I brushed a lock of hair from his forehead. "I had to see for myself how adorable you are first thing in the morning."

One side of his mouth lifted in a sleepy grin. "What's the verdict?"

I pulled back an inch to peruse him—mussed curls, gravelly voice, stubble on that strong jaw of his. The bed sheet twisted around his waist, displaying the breadth of his shoulders; the rugged planes of his chest; those strong, confident hands currently sliding up my thigh.

"If there was a *Sports Illustrated* magazine dedicated solely to being cute, you'd grace every cover, Mr. Machine."

His reply was to pin me with his dark gaze and thread his fingers through the mess of my hair, moving it from my face until he was cupping my cheeks. Holding me still as he set his mouth to mine for a firm, commanding kiss that turned me liquid in seconds. His lips moved against mine leisurely, tasting me, with seemingly no destination in mind. I grabbed his wrists, needing to anchor myself as I let him control every breathless second.

It brought back every single minute of last night, the way he'd handled my body with a confidence that was never cocky but *reverent*. His teeth on the back of my neck and his deep, deliberate strokes.

The way he'd growled *You're the fantasy, Tabitha* like I meant so much more to him than just a hot fling. Eric's words from the other day barreled through my hazy, lust-drunk thoughts. *It was different between the two of us. I recognized that from the very beginning.*

Those frantic SOS messages cranked up louder, even as I arched into Dean's touch like I'd never, ever get enough.

When he finally released me from the kiss, I was dazed while he appeared composed.

"Someone's in a good mood," I said.

His grin was as mischievous as I'd ever seen on him. "I've got a thing for trench coats. And gorgeous troublemakers."

I smiled, humming under my breath. We turned more fully onto our sides, facing each other. He reached for my leg and hooked it over his waist, pulling me flush against him. "I know it was technically your fantasy, but there was a point last night where it felt like my body had ascended onto like an astral plane. And I was levitating and orgasming all at once."

He laughed, low and teasing. "I don't know what an astral plane is, but I think I was there too."

I thought he might lean in for another sexy kiss. But he merely pressed his lips to my forehead, held them there for a few seconds. The sweet, tender gesture did surprising things to my heart rate, had me yearning for a closeness I often ran from.

"My cuteness research not withstanding...it was okay with

you that I stayed last night?" I asked quietly—the *barest* tiptoe up to those rules and boundaries.

His eyes dropped away from mine. The glimpse of vulnerability there had me nervous until he refocused. "It was very much okay with me." He paused. "And...you were okay too?"

"Totally," I said, with way too much excitement given the early hour. "Cuddling is a fun activity, right? And it was certainly spontaneous. Fits our work hard/play hard plan to a *T* now that I think about it."

"It does," he said slowly. "And I had fun too. A lot of it."

I moved even closer to Dean, feeling weird about my cowardly response. This was not a conversation I usually balked at. Or had *ever* balked at. This brief, vague exchange wasn't even close to a boundaries-and-rules conversation.

"You, uh, did snore. Loudly."

I froze. "I did not."

"Took all of the blankets. Left me to shiver for hours."

I poked him in the chest until he looked back up again with barely repressed mirth. "You got jokes all the time now, huh? I bet I was the perfect specimen of sleep loveliness."

His throat worked. "You were. You could be on your own magazine."

I preened. "For being lovely?"

"For snoring."

I burst out laughing. "*Dean Knox-Morelli.*"

He gathered me back against his chest, and I could feel the wicked shape of his lips as he kissed down my face. "If there was a magazine dedicated to being *too beautiful for words*," he said against my skin, "you'd grace every cover, Tabitha."

I buried my face in the crook of his neck to hide my tomato-red blush. My heart opened another fraction of an inch. I couldn't have stopped it even if I wanted to.

I settled back against the pillow and brushed a few more

wayward curls from his forehead, fingers grazing down his cheekbone. Up close, in the morning light, the toll that boxing had taken on his body was evident. My fingers traced the criss-crossed scars under his left eye, which looked like white, jagged hash marks. I trailed down the rough bump on the bridge of his nose as a flicker of a smile appeared on his face. I touched the indent in his lip.

"I'm sure there are a lot of these I can't see too," I said softly. Under the blanket, his palm was heavy on my knee, thumb stroking along my skin.

"Torn rotator cuff, both sides," he said. "Dislocated right shoulder. Broken collarbone, three times." I smoothed my hand down the right side of his body. "My ribs have been bruised, fractured, broken. Dozens of times." His tongue poked in the side of his cheek. "Two missing teeth in the back. Broken off."

"Eh, you don't need 'em," I shrugged. "The teeth you have are perfect."

Dean kissed me. I played with an especially charming curl while his eyes lingered on my face. I didn't want to rush him. Speaking up in our support group at the Lavender Center was always a little intimidating, but whenever Dean opened up I felt seen. He didn't share often, but his words carried a weight that I respected. *It's not having two moms that makes me feel lonely,* he'd once said, *it's when the rest of the world judges us that makes me feel that way.*

"Sometimes..." he started. I went still. "Sometimes I wonder if people would have accepted my decision to retire if they could *see* my concussion. I've heard other boxers with brain injuries say something similar. Feels like an invisible injury when it's not. But people don't believe you if they can't see it for themselves."

I stroked my thumb across his forehead and along his temple.

"I got lucky in a lot of ways," he said. "My concussion was classified as minor, but I still had symptoms for half a year after I got knocked out. My short-term memory felt off and didn't really feel like it came back until a year had passed. I had these horrific migraines that would incapacitate me for a whole day. Still get them. They come on suddenly, without a warning."

I pressed my lips to the top of his head.

He smiled. "The first few weeks I was supposed to rest with the lights off. No TV or anything with flashing lights. The whole block..." His smile widened. "The whole block took turns coming by to talk to me so I'd have something to do. Rowan was there every night. He'd do a super detailed, minute-by-minute description of the Phillies game. Crowd reactions and everything."

I laughed because I could see this so clearly.

"I recovered," Dean said. "But I was grateful to my doctor. She made it clear about her long-term concerns. Every athlete knows there's a point where the price is too high to pay. I was twenty-two, still young, with a long career ahead of me. About to compete in a world championship that was already getting heavily televised even when I was set to fight Bobby beforehand. Commercials advertised it. There were already bets taken out that I would win." He shifted on the bed, tugging me closer. "My doctor talked to me about the reality of sustaining that many concussions over a lifetime."

My gut twisted. I'd read about this online, curious after Dean talked about brain injuries being a reason why he might not take the commentator job.

"It's..." He cleared his throat. "It wasn't a risk I was willing to take. Subjecting my brain and body to something that could lead to early dementia. Depression and mood swings. The doctor said it could even cause me to get aggressive. Angry and paranoid." He made a sound in the back of his throat. "All these fans, all these analysts... In their minds, it was like I gave up more than they could understand. But it wasn't for them to understand. It wasn't their health and memory. Wasn't their relationships. Like I could keep competing, knowing what it might do to my family?"

I shook my head, no longer shocked at the depth of protectiveness I felt toward Dean. No wonder the whole block showed up to take care of him.

"Thank you for telling me," I said. "I can't imagine it's easy to talk about. And you're absolutely right. It's *your* body to make decisions about. Not theirs. It sounds like you made the right one for you. At the end of the day, you're a human being, not a literal machine."

He gave me a tiny smile that felt like a gift. "It's been nice to start feeling like a human again, with your help. I'm not ashamed of my injuries. Or that I left. But it's harder to talk about than I thought it would be."

I brushed my mouth across his forehead, unable to resist. "I'm proud of you." His fingers flexed against my skin. "I know I wasn't home at the time. I know I'm..." I swallowed. "Leaving. Soon. But I'm proud to know you, Dean Knox-Morelli. If you ever wanted someone to plan a parade down Passyunk Ave in your honor *just because*, I'm your girl."

A lightness came over his expression. "What would you be honoring?"

"Oh, I don't know. Astral planes?"

He kissed the spot right below my ear. I shivered.

"Dean."

"Mm-hmm?"

I pulled back before I got too distracted by lips and teeth. "You're not going to take that job in Vegas, are you?"

I didn't see how he could. Not with everything he'd just shared.

For the first time this morning he avoided my gaze, staring at a spot past my shoulder. "Rowan offered me a job at the rec center."

My eyebrows shot up. It wasn't a direct answer to my question, but it was certainly new information. "He did? Doing what?"

He worked his fingers through my hair, rubbed a strand between his thumb and forefinger. "He wants to start a formal food program for seniors in our neighborhood."

"Like Eddie," I said.

He nodded tightly. "Yeah. Like Eddie. He wants to hire a program manager to get it off the ground. Give it legs, get it funded. He wants it to be me."

"I personally think you'd be great at that job."

"Oh yeah? Why's that?"

"I've worked with a lot of nonprofits doing hunger relief work," I said. "And conducted a lot of interviews with staff speaking frankly about the challenges of getting people to open up about their needs. Asking for help filling their pantries. Especially people Eddie's age. There's a lot of pressure to be self-sufficient, and people think they can't ask for help. Or shouldn't." I shot him a wry look. "It's not like we make asking for help easy. But a lot of seniors we know would relate to your personal experiences." I touched his chin, held his focus. "You know what it's like to have eyes on you all the time. To have people whispering things about you. You grew up with two gay moms *and* you were a professional athlete. If anyone can sympathize with not wanting all this unwelcome attention on your personal life, it's you, Mr. Machine."

For a moment, I thought I'd overstepped or said something horribly wrong. He didn't speak, merely stared at me. Until he claimed my mouth with a kiss that sent that clumsy ballerina in my chest spinning away.

"Do you want to garden with me today?" he asked, completely out of the blue.

I tilted my chin. "*Garden?*"

He looked ever-so-briefly bashful. "Yeah. For the lot. I took some of the money you raised to get a few flower beds down. Natalia and my parents gave me a pretty specific list. It could be, you know, a type of spontaneous fun."

A grin exploded across my face. "Let me check my schedule."

I rolled across the bed and glanced at my phone. My heart sank when I saw all the email inbox alerts from the Austin marketing team. Task reminders that I had to check my flight and finally book a hotel room. Technically, this should have been a day spent working my new Texas contacts, checking out potential clients with fascinating stories to film once I finished my time with the eco-hotel.

Technically wasn't *definitely* though.

I dropped my phone facedown and crawled back to Dean. He opened his arms and I swung my legs around his waist, straddling him easily. With a groan, his palms landed on my ass, rocking me softly against his already-hardening cock.

"Looks like I'm all yours today," I said. "Are we in a rush?"

His mouth trailed lazily down my neck, hands curving up my body. "Does it feel like I'm in a rush?"

I reached between us, sighing with pleasure as I stroked his thick length. He hissed, the pressure of his hands tightening on my rib cage.

"No," I purred. "That's not what this feels like at all."

His teeth nipped at my lower lip. "Then don't stop."

I pressed our foreheads together so we could watch my fingers moving up and down his cock in a slow, teasing speed. Dean captured my mouth on a strangled groan. I sank into the kiss, into the sensuality of our bodies still warm from sleep, the intimacy of sharing a bed the way we had last night. I kept my hand moving at a leisurely pace, enjoying his reaction, which was to grip my face and kiss me through every grunt and sigh and curse.

His skin was slick, cock thick and heavy in my palm, and already I needed him. Dean tore his mouth from mine and slid his fingers between my legs as his tongue landed on my breast, circling my nipple. My lips parted on a moan, head tilting back as he flattened his tongue and circled my opening with shallow thrusts of his finger.

I began jerking him faster, and he penetrated me, adding a second finger and stroking my inner walls.

"Don't stop what you're doing either," I sighed, holding his head as he pulled on my nipple with his lips. He kept the speed of his fingers frustratingly slow. I whined, snapping my hips, urging him to do what I wanted.

With one hand, he grabbed my wrist and stopped me from touching him. With the other, he curled his fingers deeper until he caressed a bundle of nerves that made my entire body shake.

"Oh my God, *Dean*," I panted. I was gently, but firmly, flat on my back not a second later, with Dean holding my knees open with an expression so ravenous I almost came from the force of it. He sat back on his heels, his powerful body naked and thrumming with a quiet intensity. Eyes locked on mine, he curled his hands around my ass and lifted me up so he could drop his mouth to my sex.

He replaced his fingers with his tongue, licking deep inside my pussy and sending me arching on the bed, hands gripping the edge of the mattress. I whined. I whimpered. At one point, I begged as he refused to speed up or intensify his movements. His tongue curled through my folds, *close* to my clit but always avoiding it. I was boneless *and* mindless, hair stuck to my forehead as I thrashed beneath the wonder of Dean's mouth.

"We're not in a rush, are we?" he asked, eyes glittering.

I laughed raggedly, the sound ending on a desperate moan. "Please, Dean. *Please*, let me come. Let me...*let me*..."

I was released, but one hand splayed on my stomach, holding me still. Dean reached for the condom on the bedside table, and I could tell he was hanging by a thread—sweat on his brow, muscle ticking in his jaw, throat working as he rolled the condom down his cock. He roamed up my body, hips settling between my thighs. With a bruising kiss, he thrust all the way in, and I flew off the precipice he'd kept me on all morning. I came with a cry, filled with ecstasy, but Dean didn't stop. He entwined our fingers in the iron of the headboard and fucked me fast and thoroughly through every aftershock until I was moments from orgasm again.

His talented mouth hovered at my ear. "When I was a pro, do you know what I was known for, Tabitha?" He tilted his hips, grinding against my clit.

"Oh, *fuck*," I moaned, my own body rising to meet his. Urging him faster. "I don't know...multiple orgasms?"

His laughter was a dangerous vibration. "Patience."

I was close. So close.

"Focus."

His name fell freely from my lips now, my second climax beckoning.

"Dedication."

He crashed his mouth over mine, and I came again, brilliant and dazzling in the morning light as Dean shuddered and released with me.

I held him against my body as our breathing eventually slowed and the sweat dried on our skin, wishing I could freeze this moment in time and enjoy it forever.

"I still think you *should* be known as a purveyor of multiple orgasms," I said sleepily. I felt him smile against my skin. "But patience, focus, and dedication are all pretty cool too, I guess."

He propped himself up on his elbow with a crooked grin, his curls in disarray. It was funny that Dean called *me* a troublemaker. I'd never been more in trouble than when I was around him.

"Are you doubting my professional reputation?" he asked.

"Surely only time will tell." I winked at him. Color rose in his cheeks, even after what we'd done.

So much trouble.

He dipped his head and brushed our lips together. "Then it's a good thing you're all mine today."

TWENTY-SEVEN

DEAN

Five Days Later

I sat sprawled on the couch, head tipped back against the wall. I was covered in sweat. Dirt stained the tips of my fingers. My shoulders ached and there was a twinge in my right knee that would need an ice pack later.

I'd never been happier.

Tabitha and I had spent most of the morning and early afternoon in the pocket park, working in one of the raised beds we'd built. We planted seeds, hands brushing in the dirt, shoulders pressed together as we knelt. She'd opened Linda's side window and turned a big speaker out, playing a Motown record my parents used to dance to when I was a kid. Like every day this week, neighbors stopped by to chat and help, to organize or get supplies. Eddie and Alice sat with Pam on the bench under the umbrella, calling out encouragement.

Tabitha had looked so pretty, singing along to the music. Flirting with me beneath the sunshine.

liant and dazzling in the morning light as Dean shuddered and released with me.

I held him against my body as our breathing eventually slowed and the sweat dried on our skin, wishing I could freeze this moment in time and enjoy it forever.

"I still think you *should* be known as a purveyor of multiple orgasms," I said sleepily. I felt him smile against my skin. "But patience, focus, and dedication are all pretty cool too, I guess."

He propped himself up on his elbow with a crooked grin, his curls in disarray. It was funny that Dean called *me* a troublemaker. I'd never been more in trouble than when I was around him.

"Are you doubting my professional reputation?" he asked.

"Surely only time will tell." I winked at him. Color rose in his cheeks, even after what we'd done.

So much trouble.

He dipped his head and brushed our lips together. "Then it's a good thing you're all mine today."

TWENTY-SEVEN
DEAN

Five Days Later

I sat sprawled on the couch, head tipped back against the wall. I was covered in sweat. Dirt stained the tips of my fingers. My shoulders ached and there was a twinge in my right knee that would need an ice pack later.

I'd never been happier.

Tabitha and I had spent most of the morning and early afternoon in the pocket park, working in one of the raised beds we'd built. We planted seeds, hands brushing in the dirt, shoulders pressed together as we knelt. She'd opened Linda's side window and turned a big speaker out, playing a Motown record my parents used to dance to when I was a kid. Like every day this week, neighbors stopped by to chat and help, to organize or get supplies. Eddie and Alice sat with Pam on the bench under the umbrella, calling out encouragement.

Tabitha had looked so pretty, singing along to the music. Flirting with me beneath the sunshine.

I had to keep reminding myself to breathe.

Now she walked back into the living room holding two giant glasses of lemonade. Setting them on the coffee table, she laughed as I tugged her down on top of me.

"Of all the laps in South Philly," she said, stretching her legs long.

I reached up to pinch a leaf still tangled in her hair. "What kind of neighbor did you promise to be that night? Quiet and respectful?"

She arched one lovely eyebrow. "Are you implying I am neither of those things?"

I held her gaze until her lips twitched. "I don't think the things we did in the shower this morning were very respectful. Or quiet."

She looped her arms around my neck. "It would have been easier to be quiet and respectful if my neighbor didn't constantly walk around in a towel, looking like a calendar model."

I slid my hands around her waist and pulled her closer. "It happened *one* time."

"I still stand by what we did in the shower."

I grazed my lips through her hair. "You were very focused and dedicated."

"And you were very *impatient*, Mr. Machine."

I'd been in the middle of lathering this morning when Tabitha had drawn back the shower curtain and dropped to her knees beneath the spray. She'd teased my cock with her lips and tongue, cheeks hollow as she took the length of me into her mouth. She was right about my lack of patience. I'd hauled her up to stand and taken her from behind, hot water turning to steam. And my hand between her legs as she begged.

It was impossible to hide the constant smile on my

face now.

Five days had passed since I'd woken up to the real-life fantasy of Tabitha in my bed. She'd been busy since then spending time with her family. Raising money and making videos. In between, we worked in the park, chatting with the neighbors. We drank cold beer on the stoop at night, lingering late to keep talking. Then we'd have the kind of passionate, astral-plane-level sex I never thought possible for me.

Tabitha always stayed. And I discovered the intimacy of sharing a bed, of sleeping and waking together. The feel of her soft, warm skin and the scent of her hair. Her breath synced with mine as she dozed off with her head on my chest.

Tabitha's laptop pinged. I steadied her on my lap as she leaned forward to scoop it up.

She hummed happily. "It's an alert from the donation site. The Tenth Street pocket park now officially has $2,275 to spend on renovations."

Warmth flooded my veins. "I still can't believe total strangers are giving us that much cash."

"It's not strangers," she said lightly. "It's a lot of people from around here. People you know. Is your trainer named Sly Sorrentino?"

"*Sly* donated?"

"Yep. Kind of a lot too."

I had seen the appeal of Tabitha leading a fundraising charge for us. But deep down, I didn't think anyone would donate to some random, trash-filled lot in the middle of Philly. But Rowan had seen it when he'd convinced me that day at the rec center. *Every day is your chance to make this city better.* The park's transformation would be slow. It would take time and working together. But I was starting to see what Tabitha saw from behind her camera.

"Most of the gifts are less than $25, so it's a lot of people," she added. "If you need something heartwarming, read the comments on the fundraising page. There are tons from donors who built parks on the abandoned lots on their street too."

"Are there any comments about the videos you've been making?" I asked.

She set her laptop down carefully. "There are. It's been unexpected but nice to see people respond to what I talked about in the fundraising ask. That understanding of home and the neighbors you love there. What you would do to make their lives better."

"I would expect it," I said, voice rough at the edges. "You have an impact on people, Tabitha. A very real one."

Her lips curved shyly. "I appreciate that."

She wiggled off my lap and settled back against the cushion. She kicked her legs up and draped them across mine. My eyes landed on her camera gear, spread across the table. It looked high end and well-loved at the same time.

"What made you first pick up a camera?" I asked.

She paused in the act of fixing her ponytail. "My mom."

"Seriously?"

"I wish it wasn't," she said wryly. "But I first picked up my dad's digital camera as an act of defiance. She was such a critical person and the beauty of self-expression was utterly lost on her. Alexis and I were only kids at the time—dancing, coloring, reading out loud." Her nostrils flared. "She always pointed out every mistake and error. Every place where we'd made our own decision but she would have done it differently. It wasn't like my sister and I were applying to fucking *Juilliard*. I'm talking about the simple joy of making things when you're a kid."

"Before you're an adult and the world judges it," I said.

"Yeah, or makes you feel like an imposter. I picked up my

dad's camera because I wanted to enjoy my own creativity without her influence. To follow a story idea or a voice or some random inspiration that popped up while walking home from school. To stretch out past the bounds of her control and her criticism."

We could hear Alice and Eddie laughing outside, through the storm door. The sound turned Tabitha's head. "Being behind a camera makes you pay attention to all the details that pass us by. Stories that need to be listened to. Nature that's being stomped on. Love letters tucked into the flaps of old books. Street art the size of a quarter hidden in city alleys. It's all there for us to see if we take the time to see it."

I reached for her hand and held it. "I'm starting to see it now too."

Her smile was dazzling.

I squeezed her fingers. "You talked about your mom in our support group, said she didn't accept your identity. Did she ever change?"

Sadness quickly replaced the smile on her face. She didn't hide it or cover it up with a joke. "No, she never did."

"I'm so sorry," I said. I wrapped my arm across her legs and held her tight.

Her eyes softened. "I know you understand. In the end, my bisexuality was another way she tried to control and criticize me. She didn't *want* a queer daughter, so her first step was to try and show me where I was mistaken or had poor judgment. My bisexuality was only confusion at first. And then a hormonal phase. And then plain not real." Tabitha's lips quirked up at the ends. "Our support group taught me a lot about ownership of my identity. My bisexuality doesn't exist or not exist based on her belief or approval. It's mine, all mine. And I'm so proud of it."

I brought her hand up to brush my lips against her knuckles. "I'm proud of you too."

She bit her lip. Then crawled across the couch to kiss me sweetly. When we parted, the way she stared at me wasn't temporary. Used to be when I was in the ring, I thought if you anticipated a hit, it hurt less. It became one more thing to analyze. Pain avoidance as a topic of study. My gut told me I wasn't some meaningless hookup for her, though we were only having fun. Yet every morning together felt less temporary. More permanent. She didn't talk about Texas and I didn't bring it up. I wasn't thinking about my two job offers. And she didn't pry.

I wasn't so sure I could avoid what I already saw coming. And still couldn't dredge up enough willpower to stop it.

A knock on the door startled us both. I could just make out Alice's white hair.

"Tabitha? Are you decent?"

She smirked and swung her legs around, walking to the door. She pushed it open and said, "Have I ever been?"

"My favorite types of women rarely are," Alice replied. "And I wanted you to know that I've just put my face on and Eddie's telling Annie stories if you'd like to make a movie about us again."

Tabitha's face brightened. "You look gorgeous. I wasn't planning on filming today, but..." She tossed me an amused grin over her shoulder. "What the hell? Let's make a movie."

A few minutes later and we were back in front of the bench. It didn't take Tabitha long to get set up, positioning Eddie and Alice the way she had the other day. I leaned against the fence behind them. Rowan came round the corner with his usual bag of groceries for his grandmother.

"Are we doin' a photo shoot?" he asked.

I nudged his shoulder with mine. "We're making Alice and Eddie internet famous again."

"Tabitha, you can put my grandson in the video too if you need additional charisma," Alice said.

Tabitha raised playful eyes at the two of us. "Hi, Rowan. Did you bring some extra charisma for me?"

"Always," he said. "Are you having fun with my good friend and worker, Dean?"

She reached down and tossed a fistful of fresh dirt at his feet.

He jumped back with a laugh. "Hey, don't start shit with a pitcher."

Tabitha smirked behind the camera. "Okay, we're rolling. Dean and Rowan, are you two comfortable with being in the background of this shot?"

I nodded and settled back against the fence, arms crossed, without my usual fear of the spotlight or jumble of nerves. Probably had something to do with Tabitha falling asleep in my arms five nights in a row. Or the fact that I was happy fucking around with Rowan and my neighbors with dirt under my fingernails. It had been a long time since my home had felt like home to me.

"So where do you want to start?" she asked.

"Ah, we were just shootin' the shit," Eddie said. "Remembering how Annie used to sit out here on her stoop every night and every morning, long as it wasn't too hot or too cold, and read for hours. She'd take breaks to talk to neighbors or watch the kids running around for a little bit. But I swear to God it was a stack"—Eddie held his palm out about three feet from the ground—"just like that. Paperbacks. Would pick one off the top like she was taking a chip from the bag."

"And she would lend her books out to the whole street," Alice said. "Especially her romance novels, which she ordered from her Harlequin catalog. She was a woman who preferred the allure of the cowboy."

"Gave me a book with so much sex in it once, I thought I was having some kind of heart attack," Eddie said.

"I still have many of them," Alice said regally.

Next to me, Rowan scoffed. "Where have you been keeping this box of illicit romance in the house?"

"A woman should always have her secrets," she replied.

Tabitha was pressing her lips together, trying not to laugh. "What if the park had one of those little free libraries installed? Especially for kid's books. Might be a nice way to honor her legacy of book lending."

Eddie rubbed the top of his head. "Yeah, I like that idea."

"Annie would love it," Alice said.

"Back in the day, who had the best stoop on Tenth Street?" Tabitha asked.

"*Eddie,*" Rowan and I said in unison.

"Wow," Tabitha laughed. "No hesitation at all."

Eddie looked smug. "When you're the best, everyone knows you're the best."

I watched Tabitha angle the camera toward the two of us. Rowan elbowed my arm. "Until we started going to the rec center, Dean and I had too much energy to be inside those tiny houses. Every other minute some adult was like—"

"Get the hell out of here," I said. "And Midge meant it, you know, affectionately."

Rowan started laughing. "Aw, man, we *terrorized* this street when we were, what, nine? Ten? If Dean and I hadn't gotten into boxing and baseball a few years later, we would have ended up being those kids who set trash cans on fire."

Eddie shrugged with a twinkle in his eye. "I was on day shift at the plant, so I wasn't around that much. I told the kids on the block they were welcome to sit on the steps or hang out long as they were respectful."

I rubbed my hand across my jaw. "It was a capture the flag headquarters. A freeze tag neutral zone. A general hang to eat ice cream or water ice."

"Or to sneakily play video games if, say, you were grounded and not allowed to play video games."

"*Rowan O'Callaghan,*" Alice said with a shocked look.

Eddie raised his hands. "I didn't know, I swear."

Tabitha arched an eyebrow at me. *I knew,* I mouthed with a wink.

I thought about summer days that seemed to last longer than humanly possible. And running a five-block radius with Rowan knowing that, in some way, we were safe. Someone had their eye on us. Someone had snacks or Gatorade already prepared. Someone had left sunscreen on the bottom step in case we needed it.

"Things really changed for us once we were on the professional sports track," I admitted. "We were young, but our days were more intense with training and matches."

"Away games, traveling, spring training," Rowan said. "It wasn't kid stuff anymore. Dean was the only one who got it. When I blew out my arm in the majors, he didn't pity me or tell me a bunch of bullshit about silver linings. He knew I was in a lot of physical pain and that I needed a friend that knew what it was like to have all that pressure on you. To be perfect all the time."

I squeezed Rowan's shoulder.

"I don't know exactly how kids are gonna use this park," I said. "But Rowan and I got to just *be* here. Felt free and happy. It would be nice for other kids to feel that way too."

My gaze slid to Tabitha's, and her smile was a sweet reveal that felt just for me. A few seconds went by and then Rowan cleared his throat and Eddie coughed. Tabitha blinked and turned her camera off.

"You know, that was a lot of good stuff," she said quickly. "I'm going to shoot a bit of the gardens and take a couple of pictures. The internet is hooked on this pocket park transformation now. I've got to feed them some juicy updates."

Tabitha wandered off with her camera while Rowan dug around in the grocery bag he'd placed on the ground.

"I'm still furious about the video game betrayal," Alice said primly.

Eddie shot me a sly grin while lighting his cigarette. "Hell, it was a decade ago. And you've been holding out on me. Didn't know you had a stash of Annie's romance novels."

"Yeah," Rowan said, voice muffled. "And they're apparently hidden behind a secret bookcase because I've never found 'em and I was a teenage boy living in that house. I know how to hide shit."

"Yes, video games apparently," she replied.

Rowan cracked a sheepish smile before pulling out two white boxes. "Are you gonna be mad, or are you gonna eat the cannoli I brought you?"

I followed Tabitha as Alice and Eddie cheered and grumbled, respectively. She bit the tip of her thumb and grinned when she saw me.

"You know, before I met you in school, I had no idea you were such a little hellion," she said. "Freeze tag. Sprinklers. Illicit *video games.*"

"I hide my inner bad boy pretty well," I said.

"I don't think it's that hidden." She pressed up onto her tiptoes and kissed me. "All the footage I've taken about this street and its history represents the best of what I love about living here. Of what I miss. And..." She paused, tucking a strand of hair behind her ear. "I know how easy it is to focus on the worst that was said about you, after you retired. I do the same thing. But I only see pride and respect. This block loves you." She held up her camera. "That's what I see. Whether you take that job in Vegas and move or decide to stay here, that's a constant that won't change."

I lifted her chin with one finger and kissed her. There was nothing I could say. *Thank you* didn't feel like enough. *Please don't go to Texas* felt like too much.

"What are you doing tonight?" I asked.

"I'll probably take a look at what I filmed and then shower off all this gardening. Get some real work done. And I have to start packing."

I shoved my hands into my pockets. Loosened my jaw. "Do you want company?"

"Desperately."

I bent down and kissed her temple. "I'll come see you."

I stood on the sidewalk until the door shut behind her. When I finally turned around, Rowan was there.

"Not eavesdropping, I promise," he said. "Eddie asked me to get more napkins."

"You're all good," I said, slapping a hand on his back. "I'll come with you."

Rowan peeked over his shoulder. "Okay, I'm *really* happy we didn't accidentally spill how many girls I made out with on Eddie's stoop. Or that he made it way too easy to find his beer."

"The video game thing was a smart distraction."

"Is everything okay with you and Tabitha?"

I weighed my answer. Everything was great. But that wasn't what he was asking. "Yeah, we're okay. Why?"

"I don't know," he said. "The way you two were looking at each other seemed kinda…intense."

I ran a hand through my hair. "We've been hanging out pretty much constantly. And having sex. A lot of sex."

"Yeah, I know, dude. As my grandmother would say, you could cut the sexual tension with a knife."

"It's that obvious?"

His voice grew serious. "It's not the only thing that's obvious."

I looked at him and grimaced. "She leaves in a couple days, and I feel weird about it. This no-strings-attached stuff is all new to me."

I held Eddie's door open while Rowan ducked inside and grabbed napkins from the kitchen. "Have you guys talked about it?"

My gut churned. "Yeah, we have. I know the deal. We're good."

All of that was true. I knew the deal. Things between us were good. My late-night fear was that I'd misread everything—Tabitha didn't care about me the way I cared about her. And packing up and leaving in two days wasn't an issue because she did it all the time.

Rowan returned with napkins but eyed me curiously. "I'm sure you two will figure it out."

I heard the question in his tone but didn't know how to answer.

"Yeah, we will."

He nodded once but didn't say anything else. Again, his caginess had me wary.

We reached the edge of the lot, and he stopped me. "So I finally got to talk to my director yesterday about bringing you on board at the center. She's very interested."

"In hiring an ex-boxer who barely finished high school?" I asked.

A clever smile slid up his face. "She hired an injured baseball player who also barely finished high school. And you and I know finishing—or not finishing—has nothin' to do with whether you can work a good job. The center hires folks from the neighborhood. Always. Long as you don't, you know, move to Vegas, then she thinks you're a perfect fit."

Nerves twisted in the pit of my stomach. I still couldn't tell if they were real or just fear-based, like everything else. Speaking into that camera about childhood memories and my hopes for a park had made the Vegas option seem like the cold, impersonal choice.

"I am interested," I said. "But Harry's still calling every day and giving me the tough sell. It's confusing. Even though I tried to watch a match the other day and I couldn't get through it. So I don't know why I'm dragging my feet."

Rowan frowned. "It's his job to make you feel like boxing is the only thing you'll ever be able to do. He makes money off you, and he's gonna make money off this deal if it goes through. I'd be saying this even if I *didn't* want you to come help me out. I've had my own skeevy agents too, dude. They're paid to talk you into shit."

I exhaled through my nose. Pressed my lips together. "Maybe I need to stop taking his damn calls for a few days. And come spend some time with you at the center."

Rowan shrugged. "It's not a bad idea. I've got plenty of work you can help me with. But I don't want to be the Harry of South Philly. You gotta decide on your own."

I resisted staring at Tabitha's door as we walked past it. I appreciated Rowan's faith in me. And Tabitha's own confidence that the rec center was where I belonged.

They weren't the problem. It was me.

"I didn't..." I dropped my eyes to the ground. "Didn't think the identity thing was gonna bother me so much. I spent the last three years wanting people to leave me the hell alone. But

I've also been powerless and bored. It made me want that high again, of knowing I was Dean the Machine and that it *meant* something. I've wanted it and hated wanting it at the same time. I thought I'd be so ready to finally be someone else. Not stuck, unsure of which decision to make."

I held my tongue, not wanting to say the rest. About Tabitha tumbling back into my life. Her presence was distraction enough. Seeing her pack her bags for her next destination with a carefree smile had me wanting to follow her. Even if Las Vegas and Austin weren't exactly *close*. I could sense it though, a mental tug at the back of my mind. Hopping on a plane the way Tabitha did seemed like the answer when rationally I knew it wasn't.

Understanding dawned on Rowan's face. "That first year after I quit, I woke up every morning hoping my shoulder was magically healed."

I swallowed. "I remember."

"Well, it never did heal," he said. "I told myself I didn't want to go back to playing ball, but that was a whole lot of fucking lies. I did want to go back. Even pissed off and over it, I did. We've been athletes since we were basically kids, Dean. If you want my opinion—"

My lips quirked. "I do this time."

He brightened. "Being stuck makes a lot of sense, and that's comin' from someone whose been exactly where you were. It's not like flipping some switch."

"No," I admitted. "It's not. I wish it was. But you're right. I do need to decide what's best for me on my own."

I just didn't want my rush of recent confidence to be as temporary as Tabitha's time here. Because right now, it felt flimsy enough to fall apart at the slightest pressure.

TWENTY-EIGHT
TABITHA

I dragged my pack out from against the wall and set it on its side. I'd been avoiding starting this task all week. But now I only had forty-eight hours left before my flight to Austin.

I couldn't delay any longer.

I focused on the task at hand—folding every single bit of laundry I had and shoving it into this pack where it would immediately get wrinkled again. My hand landed on the pile of new things I'd be bringing with me—a sweatshirt from the Broad Street Diner. Drawings that Juliet had done for me. The novel being read next month in Kathleen's book club.

So much for packing light.

I tried to swallow around a lump in my throat that wouldn't go away. I'd spent a lot of time with my family over these past five days. I cooked brunch for Alexis and Eric while Juliet ran around the kitchen. I had a hilarious spa day with Kathleen. Last night I'd sat at the counter in the diner, chatting with my dad during the slow periods and editing videos about the park on my laptop during the rush.

I had stepped back into their lives—back into *my* life—so

seamlessly I'd gone and gotten attached again. But I also spent those moments with them embroiled in a slowly twisting guilt, tightening like a screw. It was a reminder of what I was missing. And a reminder of everything I could lose if I spilled my secrets. So I kept my smile cheery and hoped my mental tap dancing wasn't noticeable.

My laptop pinged twice with incoming emails. It was open on the coffee table next to where I knelt in front of a pile of laundry that had somehow gotten bigger since I arrived. I leaned over and checked it.

One was from Meghan, summarizing our meeting yesterday and checking in on my first few working days in Austin. *The team's loving your ideas,* the message said. *Can't wait to get started!*

The second email was a confirmation from the hotel I'd be staying in for the first week. As soon as I arrived, I needed to find a place to stay, figure out my *next* contract, and learn a brand-new city where I knew no one and no one knew me.

The realization that my time home was essentially over hit me like a literal ton of bricks. I'd taken my own relationship advice—*stay in the present, don't think about the future*—to such an extreme that I was boarding a flight to Texas in two days and had done nothing but dodge it like it was a monster under the bed.

I only had myself to blame for my lack of preparedness. I'd been suspended in a state of Dean bliss. Spending time with him had become seamless too. Every moment together felt as intoxicating as it did normal—the way he blushed every time our fingers touched in the dirt when we planted seeds. The careful attention he paid to his neighbors when they wanted to add something to the park. The stack of cat food he left on Eddie's stoop one morning when he thought I wasn't looking.

I had no boundaries or limits that could suitably encompass a man like Dean. Every night we had sex so hot it melted my brain. Every morning I woke to the sound of Dean's heartbeat. And the contentment melted my brain in a different kind of way.

Crunch-crunch-crunch.

Butterflies sprang to life inside my rib cage. I'd become finely attuned to the sounds of Dean. Biting my lip, I stood and stepped around the leaning piles of clothing.

Crunch-crunch-crunch.

I peeked out through the curtain and saw him pacing on the sidewalk with a rigid posture. He wore jeans, boots, and a black T-shirt, which was about as fancy as he got. With a smile already forming on my face, I pushed the door open and hung out the side of it.

"You know you're very cute when you're pacing," I said.

That lopsided grin appeared on his face, but I could sense his nerves from here. I hooked my finger into the collar of his shirt and dragged his face close so I could kiss him.

"I know I promised you company," he said.

"You did."

"Do you have plans for dinner?"

"My plan was laundry and takeout," I admitted.

He rocked back on his heels. "I'm on my way to family dinner. Would you like to come with me?"

Now I knew why he was nervous. I'd spent the past two weeks casually spending time with the whole of Dean's extended family on this block. I'd accidentally gotten *drunk* with Midge and Maria my second night here.

This was different. His outfit, his nerves. The way he said *would you like to come with me* like he was asking me on a date. I knew, this close to leaving, the more emotionally attached I got the more painful it would be. If I'd truly wanted to hold

Dean at arm's length though, I shouldn't have begun opening my heart in the first place.

Those dark-and-stormy eyes locked with mine, and a "Yes, of course," tumbled from my lips before I could even think to protect myself. Not once, since moving in next door, had I been able to resist this man.

He raised a brow. "Are you sure?"

I looked down at the pajamas I was wearing. "Abundantly sure, but I should probably change, right? You look so handsome."

"I know it's not the calendar-model look you usually go for."

I laughed as he followed me into Linda's front room. "I like what I like, Dean," I called over my shoulder, running up the stairs. "And I happen to like you shirtless."

I opened the hallway closet and quickly pulled through the few sundresses I owned. One was magically unwrinkled so I tossed it on before *I* got nervous. Grabbing a pair of earrings and slashing on lip gloss, I ran back down the stairs and twirled for approval.

"Now I look like a calendar model," I said with a cheer.

Dean yanked me against his chest and gave me a firm, commanding kiss. He pinched my chin, kissed me again. "You look too beautiful for words. Like always."

"Th-thanks," I said, stumbling a little. "Should I bring anything?"

"Both of my mothers would never forgive me if I let you do that," he said, starting to tug me outside.

"Oh, wait," I said, running back to the dining room table. I opened the photo album and snatched the one of his parents in their bell-bottoms. "I've been meaning to give this to them all week. Is this an appropriate gift for a Knox-Morelli Sunday-night dinner?"

Warm affection flashed in his eyes. "I've never seen this before." He held it closer. "Is that *Eddie*?"

"And Alice too."

"Shit, someone has to show Rowan." He handed it back to me, and I followed him outside, our hands still entwined.

"Apparently Linda's house has always been the party house," I said. "Most of her photo albums are from theme parties through the decades. That probably makes her, ultimately, a superior neighbor over me."

He dropped his head to kiss the top of my hair. "That's not possible," he murmured.

The vibrations sent a shiver up my spine. The moonlight lit up his rugged profile, highlighting those scars. My fingers ached for my camera, all the dazzling threads of this story, of *Dean's* story, coming together in my mind in a way that was as exciting as it was terrifying. Telling Dean what I saw every day —*this block loves you*—was about as dangerously close to real vulnerability as I'd allowed.

He squeezed my hand one more time, and then we were walking into Midge and Maria's house—the house he'd grown up in. Inside it was brightly lit and smelled amazing. The walls were covered in pictures of their family. A song by the Temptations played on a stereo balanced on a dusty bookcase filled with pictures of Dean and recipe books.

From the kitchen, I could hear his parents speaking Italian, pots clattering in a sink.

"Is that Tabitha?" Maria asked. She poked her head out, drying her hands on a towel. "Oh, what a surprise, dear. Dean, you should have told us."

I glanced at him. He shrugged. "If I told you I was bringing her, it would have turned into a seven-course meal."

"Which I'm not opposed to," I said as Maria hugged me.

She barely came up to my shoulder, but she'd been a fierce hugger when I used to see her after our support groups.

"Do you like spaghetti and meatballs? Midge has been cooking her sauce all day."

"Do I?" I said. "I'm Drew Tyler's daughter, and he raised me up right."

"Good, good," Maria said. She pulled out a chair at their small dining room table and pushed me down by my shoulders. "Sit next to Dean. We'll be out in a second."

Midge ducked her head out. "Oh, Tabitha, I didn't hear you come in. You don't happen to have that whole family of yours with you, do you? I've made enough for seventy people."

Dean sat in the chair next to me. "As usual," he said with a wink. Under the table, he dropped his palm onto my knee.

"I wish," I said. "You'll have to start inviting Dad and Kathleen to kiddie pool nights after I leave. She'll bring the right energy. Some people even claim she's *more fun* than I am."

Maria pressed a glass of red wine into my hand and a glass of ice water into Dean's. I took a long sip of wine while grabbing Dean's hand under the table and squeezing. Thinking about life on Tenth Street continuing without me, of my family visiting had knocked me for a sudden loop.

Dean's brow furrowed until I smiled at him. "I don't think I was ever at your house when we were in school, was I?"

"Trust me, I would have remembered," he said. His cheeks got pink. "Um, so no."

I reached for a framed, faded picture in the center of the table. I stroked my thumb across it—Midge, Maria, and a baby with a mat of dark, curly hair.

"Is this you?" I asked.

His lips tipped up. "You finally got those baby photos you've been after."

I grinned at him. "But for real, you are the world's cutest baby."

He peeked at it. "My adoption day."

His parents came in a second later carrying dish after dish of sauce and pasta, bread, and salad. "Thank you for acknowledging our son as the world's cutest baby," Midge said, a twinkle in her eye as she began dishing up our food.

"The picture is all the proof the world needs," I said.

"It's why, when I was boxing, I was always worried some reporter would interview Mom or Midge," Dean said. "It's tough to cultivate an image as a ferocious fighter with your baby pictures floating around."

I twirled pasta around on my fork and admired the looseness of his body language here. That two weeks ago he'd been strung tight, muscles taut, quick to scowl. Today, when Rowan and Dean had laughed through their childhood stories, I didn't think he noticed the way Alice and Eddie shared a look of relief.

"And now that you don't have that damn lot to glare to death, you'll have even less people to try and scare away," Midge said.

I nudged his calf with my toe. *Scaring away* had been the opposite of what he'd done to me.

"It's looking so good already," Maria said. "Do we need more money?"

I swallowed a bite of pasta and checked the donation page on my phone. "Right now, the amount is over $3,600, and Rowan worked on a budget with Dean to help estimate what's remaining."

"If we break $5,000, we'll take it," Dean said. "We can hold the rest in savings for maintenance and to buy plants and seeds every year. Tabitha basically got the park fully funded."

Midge and Maria cheered, but I waved my hand and shook

my head. "No way. I take no credit for this one. All I did was put a few videos up about your neighborhood. All the Philly supporters did the rest."

Maria touched my hand. "It's your neighborhood too, dear. If we all played a part, then yours was just as important."

Dean swiped his thumb over my pulse. I swallowed a couple of times. This was my neighborhood. Of course it was. I recognized I was doing the switch, putting one city in the rearview mirror and focusing on the next. Austin, not Philly.

It wasn't until I'd gotten on that plane to fly to UCLA—with a manipulative mother newly cut off two years earlier—that my lungs were fully able to expand. That I'd taken in full, sweet breaths and known it was going to be okay.

I'd held everything I loved at arm's length to maintain that momentum, staying one step ahead of guilt and memories. But maybe cutting off my love for this place too was the mistake. Because I'd been home for all of two weeks and I was feeling ready to reclaim it as mine just as it was time to go.

"It's been an honor," I said, feeling unsettled. "Next time I'm back the park will look so different."

"When do you think that will be?" Maria asked.

"I...have no idea," I said with a nervous laugh. "I'm sure I won't be gone as long as last time."

Dean let go of my hand.

I reached into my purse, needing the distraction. I handed them the picture from Aunt Linda's photo album and watched them reel with laughter.

"Found this the other day at Lin's place and thought you might appreciate it," I said.

Maria was laughing against Midge's shoulder. "Oh my God, *our hair*."

I leaned forward in my chair. "My dad told me the other day about coming to see you both after I came out. He told me you gave him really good advice. About listening and not passing judgment. And loving me for who I am."

Midge set the picture down, reached across the table and squeezed my hand. "It was years ago, but I still remember how nervous he was. He told us everything about your mom and the cheating. All the fights. He never said the exact words, but I think he felt guilty about all of it. He wanted to do this one thing right for you."

I couldn't speak for a second, so I twirled my spaghetti until my throat opened. "He did it right. More than right," I said, voice thick. "Thank you for being so open and vulnerable with him. I'm sure it wasn't easy, but coming out and having him as my dad made the difference for me. Especially since my mom—"

"Is a real piece of work?" Midge said harshly.

"*Midge,*" Dean whispered.

"It's okay, really," I said, starting to laugh into my glass of wine. "Those are nicer words than Kathleen uses. And it's true."

Maria looked thoughtful as she folded her hands over her plate. "Midge and I were lucky in so many ways. Her father had passed years earlier, but her mother and my mother and father were supportive when we came out and when we got together, in a way we never imagined."

Midge leaned in. "When her parents were still alive, they threw one of the best Pride parties in Philly. Your father, he reminds me of them. But of course..." She cleared her throat. "Of course, Maria and I lost people. When we got married. When we adopted Dean and started our family. My only brother doesn't speak to me. Two of Maria's four sisters refuse to acknowledge that I exist in her life at all. Cousins, aunts and uncles, friends. People at work."

My heart grew heavy. "I remember those stories the most from our support group."

"Me too," Maria said softly. "It's one of the commonalities in all of our experiences."

Under the table, Dean's hand found my own again. "The counselors would always tell us that you find the people who love you more loudly than the ones who don't," he said. "That's your real family, your found family, in the end. To me, it's what the park represents."

He caught my eye and held it. The sweetly tender look on his face only amplified how fiercely I'd been denying what was really going on between us. What had I bragged to my sister that first night?

I just sleep with people I already know I won't fall in love with.

Clearly, I'd become quite the expert in lying to myself.

TWENTY-NINE

DEAN

My parents were trying to teach Tabitha how to do the twist.

I leaned against the wall, hand in my pocket, and tried to figure out if they were successful or unsuccessful. What I did know was that Tabitha was flushed and sweating. At one point she was laughing so hard she had tears in her eyes.

I hadn't stopped grinning once. Tabitha had caught me pacing outside her house tonight because I knew inviting her here was possibly a really stupid idea. Judging by my reactions to her all evening, I'd been right about that. But all I knew was that I couldn't picture showing up to family dinner without her.

Except I'd have to next week and the weeks after.

"You can ask Dean," Tabitha panted, swiveling her hips in a circle, "but I'm kind of a natural when it comes to physical activity."

"You should see her run the Rocky steps," I said.

My parents were twisting their hearts out, singing along to the music. Mom twirled around in a circle. "The two of us like to cut a rug when we can. And are pretty damn good at it, if I say so myself."

The three of them danced in our tiny front room—furniture shoved back, the rug rolled up. Dinner had been finished an hour ago. Tabitha and I had tackled the dishes while my parents told her a mix of slightly embarrassing stories about me and incredibly embarrassing stories about their relatives back home in Italy.

Watching them dance and laugh made me realize how affected they'd been by the past couple years. Not just the initial symptoms of my concussion but everything that had come with losing my identity.

It was nice to see them having some spontaneous fun too.

Tabitha crooked her finger at me as her hair flew around her face. "And I've been trying to get *you* to dance with me since I bumped into you at Benny's."

I raised an eyebrow. "Who says I can dance like that?"

My parents shot me matching smirks. But then Mom slowed down and tugged Midge toward the kitchen. "Come on, dear. Let's put the decaf on and pack up a few plates of leftovers for Eddie and Alice."

Those matching smirks only grew as they walked past me. Mom muttered something to Midge in Italian. I barely caught it but thought I heard *such a cute couple*.

Tabitha was still moving in the center of the room. I slowly walked toward her.

"You know," she said, "this dance move was considered quite *scandalous* back in the day. Too much provocative hip action."

"You would know, troublemaker," I said.

Her double middle fingers had me laughing. The song started again. I grabbed her hand and began mimicking her dance moves as her eyes widened. She went still. I kept dancing, smile playing on my lips.

"Holy shit. Dean Knox-Morelli *can do the twist*?" she asked, shocked.

I turned her gently around and kept dancing. "I was a boxer, Tabitha," I said softly. "I know how to move my body."

She looked over her shoulder, dazed. "Physical prowess. Well-documented. I remember."

My smile grew. "It was impossible to grow up in this house and not know how to do a lot of different types of dancing. You should see Rowan. He's even better than me."

Tabitha spun back around looking adorably pleased. "And we could have been dancing in swanky uptown clubs all this time."

"I prefer dancing with only you."

Her throat worked. "You're amazing. An amazing...dancer."

I made sure my parents were still in the kitchen, distracted. Then I looped an arm around her waist and tugged Tabitha against my chest. I bent her backward and kissed her. I didn't know what came next for us. Didn't know how many kisses we had left.

She sighed against my mouth. I was back to acting on pure instinct again, giving into pleasure like I was supposed to. This was certainly a pleasure—seeing Tabitha make my parents laugh and dance with flushed cheeks and move to music for no reason other than joy.

I ended the kiss reluctantly. "You're amazing too," I whispered.

We broke apart at the sound of my parents coming back into the room with decaf coffee.

"I, uh...think I'm an expert now," Tabitha said, running a hand through her untamed hair. "Thank you for teaching me.

I'm going to torment Dean with my sweet moves for the rest of the night."

"Speaking of," I said. "I should get this dancing queen home."

"Please, stay for another few hours. I'll whip up some desserts," Midge said.

I kissed her cheek. "You've already done so much. Thank you."

She gave me a maternal look that didn't need interpreted. It was happiness with a healthy dose of concern. I hadn't bothered to hide that Tabitha and I were *something*. Midge also knew she had a flight to catch in two days. I nodded at her—a recognition that both were true and I didn't have a solution to it yet, *cute couple* or not.

"Thank you for coming along with Dean," Mom was saying. "You are always welcome in our house, my dear. Whenever you're home, for however long. I mean that. Your family is our family."

I doubted my parents picked up on the way those words affected Tabitha. But I did. She wrapped them both in a long hug that pulled on pieces of me I rarely acknowledged.

Then my parents turned the music back on and got back to their dancing.

As we walked down the sidewalk, I squeezed the back of my neck to soothe an ache there, probably from dancing. I could feel Tabitha watching me. Tonight felt different than all the others for a hundred different reasons. Outside the warmth of that dinner, reality was rushing back in.

"Thank you for inviting me," she said as I unlocked my front door. A brief wave of dizziness came over me. I blinked, gripped the doorknob. "It was really meaningful to talk to your parents about their experiences. And to thank them for what they did for my dad. It almost felt like we were all back in our support group again. But with less stale cookies and more delicious pasta."

I couldn't read her body language—hesitancy or nerves? "You'll always mean a lot to them. Here or traveling, it doesn't matter. You know what it's like with a found family."

Her eyes shone in the light from the streetlamp. "You never let them go."

I shook my head. "Never."

A sour taste rose in my throat. Tabitha reached for my wrist. "Hey, are you okay?"

"Yeah." My tongue was thick in my mouth. I blinked again, and the whole street pitched forward. And then the migraine struck me between the eyes like an icepick.

"*Fuck,*" I hissed, grabbing my forehead. Pain radiated from my skull, down my neck. My stomach roiled. A cold sweat broke out over my skin.

"Oh my God, Dean?" Tabitha's arms held me up as I swayed for real this time. I would have fallen if she hadn't propped me up. "What's wrong?"

"Migraine," I bit out. "They come on...fast."

Goddammit. I must have had warning signs over dinner that I didn't notice. It was easy to do whenever I was in Tabitha's tempting orbit.

She whispered a curse. "I'm going to get you inside and walk you to the couch. Does that sound okay?"

"Mm-hmm," was all I could manage.

The door gave way. She helped me walk, the nausea like a sharp knife. But she turned me until the backs of my knees touched the couch. Gently sat me down. As soon as I touched a soft surface I crawled until I could stretch out my body. The room got darker, but I still wanted to puke.

Her fingers landed on the back of my neck. "Does ice help?"

"Yeah."

A minute later and the first real relief appeared—an ice pack Tabitha placed gently on my forehead and a soft, cool sheet she draped over my waist. The cushions dipped. I could feel her body heat but still couldn't open my eyes. She picked up my hand and held it.

"Tabitha," I whispered. "I have...medicine that I take. In the bathroom. Orange bottle."

She kissed my cheek lightly. "Be right back."

I was mildly aware of doors opening and closing. The slightest movement brought an onslaught of pain. I focused on my breathing. That Tabitha was here when I was usually alone when this happened.

Water ran in the kitchen. Her fingers caressed my face again.

"Sweetheart," she said. Beneath the pain, my skin warmed slightly at the endearment. "I have pills, but I think you should double-check they're the right ones."

"Okay." She moved the curtain behind me back an inch and pressed the pills into my hand. I squinted one eye open, read the label, and my head screamed violently.

"It's them." I fell back, mouth sour and throat hot. "Two with water."

She gave me two and a glass of ice-cold water. I sloshed them down with a grimace. I sensed the room get even darker. She added a second ice pack, to the back of my neck, and I could have cried my gratitude.

"Tabitha." I exhaled through my nose. "Can you...my clothes?"

"They're probably super uncomfortable, huh?"

I winced but didn't respond. Lightly, very lightly, Tabitha undressed me. My boots and socks, slowly tugged off. Then her fingers at my belt, the zipper.

"Can you lift a little?" she asked.

I tilted my hips up. She worked fast and then my jeans were off too. I sighed.

"Better?" I heard the smile in her voice.

"Thank you."

The sheet was pulled up to my chest again.

"What else can I do to help?" she whispered.

"Stay down here with me?" I said, each word like a boulder. Like this, awash in pain, I had nothing to protect my feelings for Tabitha. But nothing to censor them either.

"That's not even a question," she said. She was gone for a minute but returned with pillows and more blankets. Her body stretched long next to mine. She arranged herself so that I could lay with my head on her chest and her arms wrapped around my back. She hummed a sound of contentment.

"Am I too heavy?" I asked.

"You're the perfect blanket," she replied. A comfort I'd never experienced before moved through me, being held like this. "What else feels good?"

What else felt good? I knew half this block would come running to help if I asked for it. But I usually crawled into bed for a day and didn't come out.

"I...I don't know," I said thickly.

Tabitha stroked her fingers through my hair. Then she very gently rubbed my scalp. I began to relax into her touch, the cool ice, the very beginning of the medicine starting to work.

"Can you keep doing that?" I asked.

"Always, sweetheart," she whispered. It was too dark. I was in too much fucking pain. My heart shouldn't have responded to the emotion I swore I heard there.

We lay like that as I grit my teeth through the first worst of it. Her other hand stroked my back in large, soothing circles.

She rubbed between my shoulder blades, caressed my temples. My breathing started to sync with hers, the pain ebbing to something sharp but less vomit-inducing.

"Are they always this bad?" she asked.

There was no reason to lie. "Yes. I don't know how long I'll have them for. But I've had them for three years now. Since the last concussion."

"And always that fast?"

I nodded.

I felt Tabitha's lips in my hair. "I was so worried about you. I'll stay with you all night, if you want?"

"I want," I whispered.

There were so many different ways to *give in*, and this was one of them. To give in to Tabitha's arms around me all night. Her fingers moving through my scalp as I dozed fitfully through the pain. She was up frequently—replacing ice packs, helping me drink water, massaging my neck when my muscles seized up.

Sometime around midnight, the pull of deep sleep was stronger than the migraine. The last thing I remembered was Tabitha tugging a heavy blanket up us both. She resettled her body, holding me close, skin warm and soft. A continual comfort.

In a lot of ways, it wasn't the best time to realize I was in love with her—head throbbing, passed out on a couch, two days before she left.

But I did realize it. Because I was desperately in love with Tabitha Tyler.

Talk about a sucker punch.

THIRTY
TABITHA

A noise woke me from a deep sleep. I sat up on the couch and reached for my phone. It read 4:32 a.m.

With a groan, I fell back against the makeshift bed I'd made for Dean and me to sleep together here in his living room.

Only he wasn't there.

Heart racing, I threw the covers off and turned on the lamp by the coffee table.

"Dean?" I called. "Dean, where are you?"

I walked to the bottom of the staircase and listened for movement. His migraine had scared me absolutely shitless last night—watching him go from dancing with a slightly cocky grin to curled up on this couch, ashen-faced and trembling in less than half an hour. His agony was obvious in his hissed breathing, his strong fingers twisting in the sheet, the way his words came slowly when they came at all.

Being allowed to care for him last night was a lucky privilege. I would have done it for a straight week if he asked me.

"I'm okay." I turned at the hushed, raspy voice. It was Dean, grimacing as he stepped, shirtless, out of the kitchen with a glass of water. "I'm up. Head's a lot better, thanks to you."

I crawled back onto the couch but studied him for signs he was still in the grips of it. There were dark thumbprints under his eyes, and he was moving extra carefully. His fleeting smile, though, had him looking like himself again.

"Are you sure?" I asked, opening my arms. He slid on top of me, head pressed to my chest. I nuzzled my nose in his hair.

Holding him like this all night had also been a privilege.

He kissed the side of my neck. "Sometimes they knock me out for two days. And sometimes, if I take those pills at the right time, it'll break like a fever a few hours later. Each one's different. Makes it hard to know how bad it will be."

"That one seemed pretty bad," I murmured.

"It was," he said simply. "I'm wiped. And I wouldn't get up and do a bunch of jumping jacks or anything like that. But no more pain."

Shifting against the cushions, I wrapped my arms more tightly around Dean's back. With my flight looming, this was usually the time when I was eager to pull up stakes, not plant them deeper. It must have been the time—that witching-hour stillness from the street. The two of us being awake right now was a gift. A few hours without consequences before reality rose with the sun.

"I'm so sorry," I said. "So sorry that happens to you. That it's unpredictable and strikes like lightning."

"You helped," he said. "I'm usually alone. Holding me. Keeping the ice packs on my head. Keeping me company. It meant a lot, Tabitha."

"You...you mean a lot to me, Dean," I whispered. I'd barely slept and was already emotional. The quiet all around us made me want to give in a little too. Not to pleasure. But to wanting what I thought I had to deny myself.

An affectionate rumbling sound came from Dean's chest. He dragged his nose up and down my neck. A shiver danced its way down my body.

"Can I tell you a secret?" he asked. Goose bumps broke out down my arms.

"Of course," I said. "You know a lot of mine now."

That wasn't even remotely true.

He propped himself up on one elbow, making direct eye contact. I could see he was nervous. "My sophomore year of high school, when we were going to group all the time and walking to school together, I had the biggest crush on you, Tabitha. If it wasn't painfully obvious."

My eyebrows shot up to my hairline. "You did? And, well, no, it wasn't obvious. Like, at all."

A petal-soft glow suffused my limbs as his words fully sunk in. It made me feel like I was back in high school right now.

"I thought you were unbelievably beautiful. And charming. And kind at a time when I needed a friend." His brow furrowed. "I always had Rowan. And other kids from the neighborhood too. But boxing, it's solitary. It's a team of one. My coaches, my trainers, they were in the corner with me during a match but they weren't putting their body on the line the way I was." His gaze moved to a spot just over my shoulder, jaw muscle flexing. "When people said shit about my family or I felt too awkward in every social situation, knowing you understood made me feel less alone. And I feel that way about you now."

That poor, clumsy heart of mine. It kept opening whether I wanted it to or not, racing like a cheetah with every word out of Dean's mouth. I brushed his sleep-mussed curls from his forehead. Tipped my head up and kissed him.

"I was always, *always* happy to see you and talk to you,

Dean," I said. "In fact, the first time you gave me a real smile that night at Benny's, I remembered that making you smile had been a favorite task of mine."

The one that appeared on his face—shadowed in amber lamplight—had my toes curling against the back of his calves.

"When I saw you at Benny's that first night, I remembered thinking the word *wowza*," I added.

"Wowza?" he drawled, eyebrow raised.

"Yeah, well, I might not have had a crush on you in school, but I'm sure my immediate and very awkward crush on you recently has been hysterical for you to witness."

"You mean like the time you called me a *Sports Illustrated* cover model?"

I covered my eyes. "Yes. And all my other babbling attempts at flirting that have failed miserably."

His lips ghosted across my jaw. "You're wearing my shirt and naked underneath. Wouldn't call that failed. And I like you flirting with me. A lot."

His rough palm skated down my thigh, dipping under that shirt to grip my hip. His mouth was doing that leisurely neck-kissing thing that never ceased to turn me on.

"You liked it?" I asked, back arching as his hand roamed up my belly. The pads of his fingers circled lazily around my nipple. I bit down on my lip, as if making a sound would shatter a morning that felt removed from real life.

"You made me feel like my body was mine again," he murmured. "Made me feel confident. Powerful. I liked you looking at me like you wanted me as badly as I wanted you."

I trailed my nails down his back until I could grab his ass. He nipped at the crook of my neck with a harsh-sounding breath. "I did want you," I whispered. "I do want you. If I'd had it my way, I would have dragged you to bed that first night."

He made a noise that was part dark laughter, part low

growl. Then he dropped his mouth to my shirt-clad breasts. With a hunger that sent waves of heat to my core, he sucked on my nipples through the fabric until I was boneless and writhing beneath him.

"Dean," I gasped, pushing my breasts into his lips. "Your migraine. You're not... Do you feel... Are you okay?"

With his other hand, he grabbed both of my wrists and gently held them over my head, pressed into the arm rest behind us. The action set my entire body on fire. His hips pinned me to the couch, face hovering a few inches over mine. When he kissed me, it was with a slow savor. A savor that turned commanding and possessive as he began rocking his cock against my bare sex. Grinding into me, swallowing every sound I made with a sweep of his tongue.

"How do I feel, Tabitha?" he asked, thrusting against my clit.

"Good," I panted. He bit my ear. "Perfect, I mean. Hard. So hard, so...oh God."

"Better than okay, then?" His grin was half-wicked, half-sweet.

I matched it, capturing his bottom lip between my teeth and tugging. "So now we're cocky, huh?"

His quiet laughter sent me into that full-body shiver. As did his next kiss, the pressure of his fingers on my wrists, the deliberate movement of his hips between my thighs. With every slide of his cock through my folds I was climbing closer and closer to orgasm, splayed out on this couch with the morning sky still dark outside. He dragged his mouth down my cheek to my ear and began tonguing the shell, up and down. Sensation spiked through me. I nuzzled against him, urging on those lips, the scrape of his teeth offering a pinch of pain just when I needed it. His hand slid back under my shirt to thumb my nipple in strokes that matched his cock, that matched his tongue, and suddenly I was poised to explode.

"Yes...yes...," I started to cry, eyes closed, head tipped back, needing all of it from him. But then he stopped all of his movements, and I groaned in protest. Dean gripped my chin and gave me a rough kiss.

"Not like this," he growled. "In my mouth."

Dazed and out of breath, I could only watch as he dropped down my body, shoved the shirt over my hips and propped my legs open wide. I was already shaking, so fucking close the slightest touch was going to set me off. I thread my hands through his hair, and his eyes found mine as he curled two fingers inside of me. My back curved off the cushions so dramatically Dean had to hold me in place. And then he pressed his palm over my mouth and firmly licked my clit, and I broke completely apart. I screamed against his hand as pleasure detonated outward from his tongue and his fingers, licking and fucking me through peak after peak of my orgasm.

He eased me through the aftershocks with an understanding born from the past five days of learning my body's needs inside and out. The intimacy of that knowledge had me staring at him, wide-eyed, as he crawled back up with a look on his face filled with affection and lust and desire—an endless wanting that would have scared me if I wasn't wearing the same expression. I shifted off the couch before he could settle on top of me. His lips quirked as I pressed him back and tore off his shorts. His cock rose, thick and veined, and I knew exactly what I wanted.

I took a second to admire him, his scars and chest hair, rippling stomach and powerful shoulders. With a pleased smirk, I straddled him so he could watch me tug my shirt off and send it flying across the living room. Through a tiny gap in the curtain, I caught the first glimpse of the sky over the row homes, beginning to lighten.

"Tabitha," he groaned, gripping my hips and starting to move me. But I shook my head and kissed him instead, then took a long, long time kissing down his throat. His head tipped back, a strangled breath escaping when I reached his chest. Dean was so strong, and his body had endured so much, and he deserved to be worshiped the same way he'd so eagerly done. I let my lips and my mouth taste his skin, caress every flexing muscle as his fingers sifted through my hair. When I finally reached his cock, I nuzzled my cheek against it. It was like velvet over steel, and nothing made me happier than flattening my tongue at the base and dragging it to the tip while Dean's lips curled into a primal snarl. He speared his hands into my hair, twisting it back. I waited, teasing him, stroking him gently with my mouth poised over the tip.

"Do it," he commanded.

I took Dean's cock into my mouth and let it sink as deep as I could to the back of my throat. I would never, for as long as I lived, forget the sounds he made—a husky, grateful moaning of my name that had me aching to come. I moved my lips as slowly as I could manage, enjoying myself, enjoying the view —flexing abs, his throat exposed, the way his teeth bit his bottom lip.

Dean had other ideas. Gripping my face gently, he sped up my motions, starting to fuck my mouth and rock his hips. I moaned around his skin, almost unbearably turned on.

"Your mouth is so hot," he gasped. "So wet." I hollowed out my cheeks and sucked even harder. "Fuck, Tabitha, what the fuck," he spat out through bared teeth, and I'd never felt so needy and hungry. His hand slipped between us to palm my breast. My nails bit into the side of his ribcage. Maybe I was going to come like this without even being touched, just the pure erotic power of reducing Dean Knox-Morelli to these primal urges. But I shouldn't have worried. Not a second later and his hands were locked around mine, tugging me up.

"I need to fuck you. Now," he said, dark eyes glittering. I released his cock and nodded, speechless. I still wanted to take care of him, so I straddled his hips again as he settled back against the cushions.

"Condom?" I asked, hovering over him.

He swallowed, eyes closing. "Upstairs."

"Or..."

His eyes flew open. I draped my body over his and kissed him deeply. "I'm protected and clean," I said quietly. "So if you are too and you want me to fuck you bare, say the word."

He dug his fingers into my hips, jaw clenched tight. "I'm clean."

I held his gaze. "Yes?"

"Yes." He reared up and claimed my mouth. "Please."

I lowered myself down the length of Dean's cock, marveling at the perfect fullness. I kept my chest on his, my mouth on his as I rode him in a steady, delicious grind that had us gasping. He grabbed my ass and helped me move, circling and rocking, taking my time with an angle that curled my toes and kept us face-to-face. Like that night in the car, Dean didn't break eye contact as the pleasure mounted, as my movements became less sensual and more frantic.

His hands skated up my ribcage and then cupped my breasts, thumbs tweaking and pinching. "More," he whispered, eyes searching mine with pure astonishment. "Give me everything, Tabitha."

I didn't hold back. I was too close, too on edge. I sat up, propped my hands on his chest for leverage, and rode him fast and dirty. The changed position had us both tipping our heads back, and the very second Dean's fingers grazed my clit I came instantly. The orgasm was glorious—shook my entire body, had a smile blooming on my face as Dean thrust his hips up and up and up with sweat on his brow. I bent over again for purely selfish reasons, wanting to kiss him as he climaxed. And I did, feeling him growl out barely coherent words as he came inside of me with a soft roar of satisfaction.

THIRTY-ONE
TABITHA

A few minutes later and I was still collapsed on Dean's chest, content to listen to the sound of his heart as my own finally slowed. He gently rolled onto his side and tucked me against him so we were facing each other on the narrow couch, in his living room starting to fill with dim morning light. That hushed witching hour had come and gone, and I now had a flight to catch tomorrow.

I stroked the soft skin at his temples. "How's your head?"

He kissed the inside of my wrist. "Much, much better thanks to you."

My cheeks got hot. He chuckled. "Not because of the sex. Though I'm sure levitating during an orgasm is good for your overall health."

I hummed. "That good?"

He brushed my hair back and kissed my forehead. We inhaled together. Exhaled. "Yes. Always. But mostly I feel better because you took care of me. Thank you."

"No thanking necessary," I said firmly. "You would have done the same thing for me. Will you feel any leftover effects today?"

He paused. "Hard to say. That migraine broke fast. I'll still be foggy today though. Exhausted by tonight. When they last longer, if they last for days, I feel tired and shaky for a long time after. Like my brain gets replaced with cotton balls."

I scratched his scalp in gentle circles. I'd done this last night right before he'd drifted off to sleep, and he'd seemed to like it through the haze of pain. His eyes closed with a grateful-sounding sigh. "Does this help?"

"So much."

We lay there together without speaking as I tended to him, so comfortable I was tempted to drift off asleep again. But then Dean murmured words I didn't catch.

"What's that, sweetheart?"

His eyes opened, lips rounding up. "You called me that last night."

My face heated with another blush. "Well, you're very... very sweet. I was merely stating a fact."

Dean smirked. "Mm-hmm."

I laughed. "Was that your question?"

"I asked if you had any more secrets. Now that you know how I felt about you in school."

Curled into Dean's body, soothed by his solid weight, it was harder to indulge my duck-and-weave style of answering vulnerable questions. Life, for me, had always been about moving forward. Dean talked about his tendency to overthink, but maybe my lightly packed way of life was a sneaky way not to think at all. My preference for leaping without looking didn't end at silly dates or travel adventures. It also included never confronting my fears and guilt so I could jam my wrinkled clothing into a pack and board a plane.

"Yeah, I do," I said, and his expression shifted at the tremble in my voice. "Can I tell you something I've never told anyone else before?"

He nodded, passing his hand over my hair. "Of course."

"When I was eleven years old, I came home early from school without calling first. My dad was at the diner. Alexis was staying late for some extracurricular thing. When I walked in, my mom was standing in our kitchen with a man I didn't know."

Dean's entire body went tense against mine.

"His name was Roger. Now he's my stepfather but my family doesn't have a relationship with them at all. And if my mom was always dismissive of my bisexuality, Roger was—and is—worse."

Dean kissed my palm.

"At the time I was only a kid. I didn't know this was the man my mom was having an affair with. She told me he was a friend, but a secret one. She asked me not to tell Dad or Alexis or any of my friends. I didn't. Sometimes I covered for her, though I wasn't sure what that meant. When she was fighting with my dad or being awful to Alexis, I protected her. During the Bad Year, when she and my dad fought nonstop, I never spilled my secret. And when they announced their divorce, I already knew the reason was Roger."

He lifted his head and stared at me intently. "Tabitha. You were just a little kid."

I blinked rapidly so I wouldn't cry. "She didn't show us a lot of love. You know that. She was—is—very critical. And controlling. Then suddenly I was sharing this secret with her and I got all this special attention. Like she loved me, you know?"

The real devastating secret buried within my mother's story was the one Alexis and I often danced around, too scared to really touch it. Did our mother love us at all?

"That would be confusing for anyone, at any age," Dean said gently.

"I protected..." I swallowed past a throat tightening like a vise. "I protected someone who only became more awful as time went on. A homophobic racist who told her daughters she was too busy with her new family to spend time with them. That's whose side I took as my dad was pretending not to cry while packing our lunch in the morning."

Dean's hand, cupping my cheek, was a steady, comforting pressure. "Tabitha, look at me."

I reluctantly dragged my eyes back to his and was stunned at the compassion there.

"Your mother was an adult who should never have involved her child in her affair," he said. "She forced you to share her guilt. You were eleven years old. And could never have known how bad your mom was going to get."

"Her actions have affected all of our lives, Dean," I said. "I'm not saying I was responsible for her cheating. I do feel responsible for all the rest of it. Because if I'd at least told my dad that very first day, I really believe so much of the worst parts of their divorce and her leaving would have been avoided. Not that she would have stayed. But...but mitigated, for sure. Alexis just told me how deeply our mother's behavior has affected so many of her choices and reactions to things, even to this day, and the whole time she was telling me that I kept thinking I could have put a stop to this. And I didn't."

I didn't realize I'd been crying until his fingers came away wet from my face. "You've never told them?"

I shook my head. "No, and I don't...I'm not sure how to or if I will. Telling them now exposes me as a liar, like she was. The more I don't tell them, the worse I feel. But I love my family more than anything in this world. I think, deep, deep down, I'm terrified they'll never look at me the same way again. At least now I'm on the road a lot and we talk over video all the time and I stop home for quick visits. What if I lost all of their affection and trust?"

Hearing those words out loud dialed up my anxiety to an almost unbearable level. Since graduating from UCLA five years ago, I'd breezed past these fears by staying on the go and rarely entertained considering what I'd done. Whispering all of this to Dean was a confusing mix of lessening the weight while strengthening my worries.

"Tabitha." Dean touched my chin lightly until I looked at him. "Do you... Are you punishing yourself for this?"

"What?" I asked. "No. Of course not."

His face said otherwise. "You always leave this place you love. The people you love."

"It's distressing," I managed. "I've only been home for two weeks, and it's like I can hear her in my thoughts again. Making me feel bad for things that happened years ago. Every moment with my family is precious to me but, you know..." I trailed off, emotion constricting my chest. "It's better, for me and for them, if I leave."

Dean's nostrils flared, a line forming between his eyebrows. "Is it better though?"

The unsaid sentiment hung in the air between us, mingling with the now bright morning light. *Could you stay?* If he wasn't thinking it, I clearly was. But I must have taken too long to answer because the very real, very un-temporary hurt that flooded his features for one harsh second felt like taking a hit to the solar plexus. I fully understood, in that moment, how far I'd fucked this up—that avoiding our tricky reality while giving in solely to pleasure had been a surefire way to hurt us both.

And hadn't that been my mother's preferred method all along?

"Dean," I said nervously, "we should probably—"

His body went rigid again, pulling away from me on the couch even as I wasn't entirely sure how I planned on finishing that sentence. But I already wanted to snatch him back, snatch back the past two weeks. His phone started ringing, and I flinched at the piercing sound. Dean sat up with a ragged breath and grabbed his phone, scowling at whatever he saw on the screen. Then he stilled and swore under his breath.

"What is it?" I asked.

"Is today Thursday?"

I scratched my head. "Yeah, because tomorrow is Friday and that's when I leave."

His eyes darted up to mine, then dropped back to his phone. He silenced the ringer and dragged a hand down his face. "My agent scheduled a meeting this morning with the Game Time producer who wants to hire me. It's...fuck, in thirty minutes, and I totally forgot about it."

The sound of a truck parking on the street snagged my attention. But I shook my head and refocused on Dean, tugging on his underwear and raking a hand through his curls. "Wait, you mean for the boxing job in Vegas?"

He nodded as he tugged on his jeans and peeked out the curtains. I could hear voices now and the beep of a truck backing up.

"I thought, well, I guess I assumed you weren't taking that," I said cautiously. Why I felt that was safe to assume I had no idea—we'd only spoken about it that one morning in bed.

Dean cleared his throat. "I haven't given Harry an answer yet."

"Oh. I didn't know that." I tucked my feet beneath me. It wasn't like I had any claim to where Dean ended up or what job I thought was the best fit for him. This still hurt though.

His gaze slid to mine then behind me, and his jaw tightened. "I think there's a developer looking at the vacant lot."

"What?"

I joined him at the curtain, ducking under his arm. A few guys wearing construction gear were milling about on the sidewalk in front of a large black truck that read *Oswald Properties*. My stomach pitched.

"Do you know who they are?" I asked, dread filling me.

"Yeah."

His phone started ringing again, and I thought he might break it between his fingers.

"Are they good news or bad news?"

He stepped back, away from me. "They're bad fucking news."

THIRTY-TWO

DEAN

At the height of my training with Sly, the warning he repeated the most was to never let myself get cocky when I ducked under those ropes. A quiet confidence was one thing. Feeling like you deserved every victory just by being there wasn't.

His warnings were true. The few times as an amateur when I stepped into the ring cocky, I took a surprise hit below the belt every time. Couple of those and you straighten up, real quick.

How do I feel, Tabitha?

I'd been boasting, hadn't I? Woken up on that couch flush with the kind of head rush I always got when I was no longer in pain. As if our secret sharing, that *sex*, this entire morning could exist without consequences.

As if I ever thought falling in love with Tabitha Tyler would have a happy ending. But now I had Harry calling me nonstop, developers on the block, and Tabitha shyly admitting it was better for her to leave.

"New plan," she said, pulling her hair up into a ponytail. "You take your call or...get ready for your meeting, I guess, and

I'll go talk to Mr. Bad Fucking News. See if I can't shake out what's going on."

She changed quickly, mouth tight, and I caught her peeking at my prescription bottle open on the coffee table. She'd looked shocked that I hadn't turned down the commentator gig. A good part of me was shocked too. But now that feeling was competing with an uneasy guilt. I'd bared my soul, had told her all of my complicated issues about the industry and my own injuries. She'd seen the effects last night, feeding me pills because I was in too much agony to take them myself.

With a polite smile, Tabitha slid on her shoes and walked outside. I couldn't worry about Oswald Properties and the terrible fucking things they'd been known to do across this city. Yet. Instead, I answered my ringing phone with a weary sigh.

"Yeah, Harry? Sorry, I'm here."

I walked up the stairs and yanked a clean shirt from the dresser. Set Harry to speaker phone so I could splash cold water on my face.

"I should hope so," he said, tone clipped. "Rex is meeting me at the coffee shop down the block from you in ten minutes. Can I ask where the hell you are?"

I paused in the middle of drying my face off with a towel. "The meeting's here, in South Philly? I thought we were meeting uptown?"

"Dean." Harry's frustration was obvious. "The biggest sports network in the entire world wants you, so yeah, he's willing to come wherever you are to sign this deal."

I tenderly rolled my neck from side to side and considered telling my agent how I'd spent my night—in searing pain that knocked me out better than any uppercut ever did. But he'd never been the kind of agent who cared about that.

"I know this is shitty fucking timing, but I still don't even know...don't think I want this job. I don't want to waste his time." I leaned my shoulder against my bathroom wall and glanced in the mirror. The post-migraine dark circles under my eyes and five o'clock shadow weren't a real professional look.

Harry coughed into the phone. I heard him giving directions to what was probably a cab driver. "You don't know if you want to pass on one of the best opportunities in the entire industry? To meet with the guy who runs the programming that paid you all those purses you won?"

I flexed my fist open and shut. "Like I said, I'm grateful."

"Can you give him twenty minutes?" Harry's tone had softened an iota. "I know you're nervous. I know you think you're out. But I'm not talking a regular old comeback. I'm talking about you being the newest wave of young analysts. Maybe even changing the way things are done."

I walked to the bathroom window and peeked out. Tabitha was speaking with the two guys wandering around the park. The very real concern etched into her face had my stomach twisting.

Goddammit.

"Dean? You there?"

"Fine," I bit out. "I'll see you in a few."

Shoving my phone into my pocket, I went back downstairs as Tabitha was coming inside. "So what is it?" I asked.

She crossed her arms and peeked out the window. "It's the scenario you and I talked about in the very beginning of all of this. Not just that a developer would come buy it from the city. But that they were the bad-fucking-news kind. The guy out there told me if the purchase goes through, they'll be building the three-story condos they've put up all over the city. I got the impression these were very expensive condos."

I grimaced, rubbing a hand over my mouth. "In this neighborhood, when they go up, they've been selling for three times what our houses are worth. And we've got a lot of renters getting priced out and having to leave. Landlords kicking out their tenants."

Tabitha took her phone out and started tapping away. "I'm going to put the word out on social media and see what other people have done to prevent this kind of thing from happening. Then, before I pack, I'll go round up the neighbors, fill them in on the situation. We'll send out a bat signal, and I'm sure we'll find a way to save this place for Annie." She stopped typing and glanced up at me with a dazzling smile that took me back two weeks ago, when she was pointing me toward this park transformation I was too in my head to see.

I walked past her to push open the door, chest tight with nerves. "I have to go meet with this producer."

Her smile dimmed.

"If you're talking to the neighbors, I'll come find you. But..." I hesitated, thoughts a mess. "I don't know if there's a way to save that park. We can't buy it. We can't stop them from buying it. I always...always knew this could happen." I blew out a breath full of irritation. "We'll need to figure out how to return everyone's donations from that website, right?"

I understood what was happening here. It felt just like the past few years, being stripped of power by a force bigger than me. Like a city full of disappointed fans. Or a city full of rich developers who didn't give a shit about the neighborhoods they built in. I'd put myself out there, had gotten people I cared about to give time and money they didn't have a lot of.

And was going to disappoint them. Again.

But Tabitha was shaking her head with a determined look on her face. "I sincerely hope we don't. Because we can save it. I know it."

"Aren't you leaving Philly tomorrow anyway?" I asked with

an edge I didn't mean. There was a spark of hurt in her eyes, but she didn't respond at first. I watched her hide her vulnerability with a pasted-on smile and a straightening of her shoulders.

It was worse than if she'd gotten pissed or frustrated. She hadn't run from opening up to me this morning, and every cell in my body ached with wanting to fix things for her. To go back in time and tell her mother to fuck the hell off. To convince Tabitha that what had happened wasn't her burden to carry alone.

I wanted to show her that she could stay. Be honest. Not be afraid.

"I am leaving tomorrow," she said with a false cheeriness. "But I've been known to work a few miracles." She scooped up her purse and quickly neatened the pillows on the couch where we'd slept. Where she'd taken care of me. Where we'd had sex so intense I'd almost said something stupid after like *I'm in love with you*. The sight of her removing any trace of *us* out of politeness ratcheted up those nerves. "Good luck at your meeting. If you can't find me, I'm sure I'll be around a kiddie pool trying to convince Alice not to commit an act of violence against that truck parked there."

She crossed over to her stoop and slipped inside her house with a wave. With a curse, I yanked my own door behind me and strode down the sidewalk. To my left was the pocket park, being measured by a couple contractors to determine its value. It hadn't looked like much two weeks ago. And yeah, it didn't look like much now—a couple benches. A few garden beds. Supplies stored in the corner. There wasn't any grass yet so parts of it still resembled a jagged scar. But because of Tabitha, I knew what it could have been for the people on this street. Maybe something like this wasn't gonna change the world, but Tabitha had shown me that stuff didn't always have to be on some dramatic scale as long as what you did was helping a little.

I glared at the lot as I walked past, no different now than the night Tabitha had fallen into my lap. The reality was settling in as I turned the corner toward the coffee shop. The disappointment. The loss. The embarrassment. If I'd been walking to this meeting with Rowan, I know what he would have said—to bail, big time. That I was too angry and much too distracted to put myself back into a professional athlete's mindset.

But he wasn't here. By the time I was shoving open the door to the shop a minute later, I didn't want to talk about boxing at all. I wanted to tug on my gloves and punch the ever-loving-shit out of whatever surface was closest. It must have showed too. I rolled my shoulders back as I approached Harry's table, and I swore I saw him gulp.

He tapped the arm of the suited-up man next to him. The Game Time producer, Rex Carter, had a fake orange tan and a watch that probably cost twice my mortgage. The obvious look of awe on his face when he saw me activated a darker fight-night power in my chest that I had never felt comfortable with. He was a man who knew this sport inside out, who'd met a lot of the greats and respected their talent. He wasn't mad. Or full of frustrating sympathy. He stood to shake my hand and gazed up at me like he understood I used to win every night of the week.

"Dean the Machine," he drawled, gripping my hand tightly. "It's an honor to meet you in person, and I'm not only saying that. I was telling your agent here that I've always been a die-hard fan."

I inclined my head and sat down. "Nice to meet you, sir. Welcome to Philly."

"Rex was just talking about the job and what it entails,"

Harry said, sliding a cup of coffee my way. "Being on TV. Moving to Vegas. He knows you have a lot of concerns."

Rex flashed me a smile. "We're very serious about investing in this as your next career, Dean. Almost as serious as we are about the health and safety of our boxers. If you need some persuading, I've got the time today to do that."

I twisted my coffee between my hands. I was hyperaware that the instincts coursing through my body were not the right ones or even the ethical ones. That the old power I was searching for at this table was flashy and unsustainable. It wasn't helping people like Eddie or seeing my parents dance in their living room or accepting that transformations take time. It had nothing to do with the confidence that came from Tabitha Tyler kissing me like I was the air she needed to breathe and then holding me when I was in pain.

But that was the thing about instincts, I guess. Sometimes they led you astray.

"I've got the time today," I said. "And I'm open to persuasion."

THIRTY-THREE
TABITHA

The vulnerability hangover was very real.

As the neighbors milled about on the sidewalk, anxiously discussing the fate of the park, I was chewing on my thumbnail and wondering if I might throw up. I hadn't expected to feel so achy and exposed after telling Dean about my knowledge of my mother's affair. It was deeply uncomfortable for me. As was watching him leave for that meeting with body language that was the opposite of last night's family dinner: shoulders up to his ears, lips pressed together, forehead creased. Having our night and early morning be so tender and emotional only made this sudden awkwardness that much more unsettling.

And I knew why. The whole pattern—strong emotion followed by covering it up followed by walking away—directly mimicked the way my parents argued during the Bad Year. Mom would say something harsh and hurtful, setting off a quick, mean-spirited argument that would tie my stomach into knots. There would be no reconciliation, but at some point, Mom would be wearing a serene smile and Dad would brightly offer to take Alexis and me out to eat and we'd leave. Putting on a happy face became the norm, especially for me.

I just couldn't shake this dreadful feeling that I'd behaved more like my mother in this situation toward Dean than I ever thought possible.

A light pressure on my wrist shook me from my reverie. It was Maria, looking much too kind for my current emotional state. "You're not too sore from dancing, are you, dear?"

Thinking of twisting the night away with Dean's parents last night almost wrenched a sob from my throat. "Oh my goodness, not at all," I said, placing my hand over hers. "I can't thank you enough for making me always feel so welcome. I've looked up to you and Midge for my entire life."

She stared at me quizzically before giving me a hug. She patted me on the back and said softly, "Whatever is wrong, I know you can fix it. Have faith, dear."

I swallowed past a lump in my throat bigger than the Oswald Properties truck parked ominously in front of the vacant lot. "I appreciate that," I said, although I wasn't sure if I could fix the mess I'd made. Over Maria's shoulder, my gaze slid to the garden Dean and I had started planting, and my heart sped up at the sight of it. Even if things were a mess in my personal life, that didn't mean we couldn't save the park. I hadn't been lying when I told Dean about miracles. You couldn't have the privilege of getting to know as many community activists as I'd done during my career and not witness your fair share of last-minute marvels.

Maria released me and I turned to the neighbors and clapped my hands to get their attention. Natalia and Martín, Eddie and Alice, Midge and Maria went quiet. I cocked my thumb at the truck. "This fucking sucks."

"You could say that again," Eddie grumbled with a scowl.

"What are we gonna do to stop it?" I asked, hands on my

hips. "I put out some feelers on the fundraising page for the park and on social media, so I can follow up on any leads that come my way."

Natalia and Martín shared a look. "Our friends—the Santos family, who started their own park—we're heading there now to go talk to them," Martín said. "I'm hopeful they'll have a solution."

"That's perfect," I said.

"We can talk to some of the community coordinators at the Lavender Center," Midge said. "They don't do garden projects there, but they've had to do plenty of work with the city, gettin' around red tape and a whole bunch of other bullshit."

"And I'll call my grandson," Alice said.

Eddie coughed into his fist but stayed quiet.

"All of these ideas are brilliant and top-notch. There's no way in hell they're taking Annie's lot from us." I shook my head. "From all of *you*, I mean. I've got a flight to catch tomorrow, but I know we can pull this off." I avoided six sets of sympathetic faces by peering over at the park.

"Oh, we are going to *miss you*, Tabitha Tyler," Alice said. "Don't you dare sneak off to that airport without coming to see me."

"I would never," I said with the kind of false cheer I'd seen my dad express at the diner, every time the conversation turned to my next job. Dean rounded the corner at that same moment, sending my stomach flying like a flock of sparrows.

Knowing you understood made me feel less alone. And I feel that way about you now.

Everyone turned to both greet him and then immediately vent about the possibility of having Annie's old lot being turned into a "three-story monstrosity that'll block out the fucking sun," according to Midge. He listened with his usual respect for his elders but didn't make eye contact with me once. His hands were shoved into his pockets, body vibrating an energy I couldn't decipher.

Maria studied him closely, her gaze darting back and forth between the two of us. I winced, guessing our awkwardness was in the process of being discovered. When I tuned back in, everyone was starting to head off for their tasks. Dean greeted his parents, one hand on his stoop railing, and said, "I'm going to come by and see you both later today."

"Of course," Maria said. "We'll be home. Is everything okay? I mean, besides all of this." She indicated the park, and Midge muttered a few unkind words toward Oswald himself.

He nodded. "Yeah. Everything's okay."

When he didn't expand further, his parents said a fluttery goodbye to us both, and I watched them walk down the sidewalk, hand in hand, with a pang in my chest.

"You don't really think we're gonna get to keep it, do ya?" Eddie asked, lighting a cigarette with narrowed eyes.

"I'm not gettin' my hopes up," Dean said. The pang intensified.

Eddie blew out smoke with a look of resignation. "City does this shit to people all the time. Don't know why I got myself all excited."

"We'll save it," I blurted out, too upset at Eddie's hunched shoulders and the hurt in Dean's eyes. "I get being realistic and I get the frustration, but I think we have to fight for it and not give in because this guy has money to throw around."

Eddie ran a hand through his hair, then gave me a slightly mischievous grin. "I can't help being the grumpy old man in this scenario. I've just seen more things that make me pessimistic than optimistic. Things get tough around here. But hell. Guess I could call some Army buddies and run it by them. Even if we just make this Oswald asshole squirm for a bit it'll be worth it." He reached into his back pocket. "Your sister and niece saw me at the diner, and Juliet drew me this."

I took it with a smile. "She told me the other night she wanted to draw you a picture."

"Yeah, well, I appreciated it. Really did. Don't know why Pam has three heads, but what do I know about art?"

Eyebrows raised, I glanced down at the sheet of paper and confirmed that, yes, Juliet had drawn what looked like a stick figure of Eddie and a messy swirl of colors that was Pam. The swirl had three floating circles—each with a set of whiskers—and the house she drew over them had flowers and trees growing out of the roof.

"Oh, Eddie, it's beautiful," I said, showing it to Dean. A genuine smile pulled at the ends of his lips, and I went warm all over at the sight of it. "What are you going to do with it?"

"Frame it," he said seriously. "Juliet said she'd draw me another one, so I might get a couple frames at the store just in case."

I handed it back to him. "I'm taking quite a few pictures with me to Texas too. No three-headed cats, but a lot of drawings of our family eating at the diner."

He folded it carefully and placed it in his pocket. "She's a good kid. That whole family of yours are all keepers."

Eddie shuffled off toward his house, and I couldn't help but wonder about his story and what came next. The block seemed to be taking care of him just fine, but would he ever allow himself to be helped by a program like the one Rowan wanted Dean to run?

With a sigh, I pulled the door open behind me, and Dean held it open but stayed planted outside. His hesitation was obvious in the way he couldn't keep eye contact. I did spot his focus land on my backpack.

"Do you want to..." I indicated the living room. I sank onto the couch and dragged my laptop across the coffee table to give my nervous hands something to do. When the door finally closed and Dean was inside, I was torn between relief and that same dread. "It sounds like the neighbors got you pretty caught up on the pocket park situation, but I think our combined efforts—plus I sent a ton of emails to past nonprofit clients asking their advice—should lead us in the right direction, don't you think? We can't let anything happen to it. We have to fight."

He rubbed the back of his head. "Everyone's ideas are good ones, and I...I trust you. It's just, if that developer is going to buy it from the city, what can we actually do to fight back? I'm not trying to sound like some asshole here. Just think our hands are tied."

A wave of dismay threatened to knock me over, but I managed to beat it back—just barely. "You're not wrong," I admitted. "Maybe I'm the naïve one. We knew this was likely but didn't ever—" *Take it seriously* is what I wanted to say, but the sentiment wasn't sitting right. "Never really talked about it openly. I feel bad, raising that money and getting people invested with all of the videos, but that's also why I'm not willing to accept defeat even if it appears as though our hands are tied. This community wants to see this pocket park happen, and I think we owe it to them to try our hardest to make it work."

A muscle ticked in his jaw—he was all coiled, restrained movement. Like that night we met at Benny's, and it was so obvious to me Dean Knox-Morelli was holding himself back in ways I didn't understand yet.

"You shouldn't feel bad," he said. "I started all of this without a plan of action. Got everyone involved and excited. Getting Eddie and Alice talking about Annie again. This is why I don't... This is why I shouldn't..." He raked a hand through his hair, trailing off when I suspected he wouldn't have this morning. Before things changed.

"Why you shouldn't what?" I asked, tucking my feet under me. "Dean, you did the right thing here. I've been filming you for a week now, and if you could only see how much everyone loves and respects you regardless—"

"I'm going to take the Vegas job."

I paused, mouth still open. "You...are?"

He nodded, eyes on the floor.

"The meeting went well, then, I'm assuming?" I said, through a burst of jittery laughter covering up my shock and disappointment. Two emotions I didn't have a right to express with my own bags packed for a contract I was feeling lukewarm about myself.

"I know it's a lot to take in. And a surprise. But looks like I need to pack a bag too."

"For Las Vegas," I said slowly, trying to picture Dean in a place so different from where we'd grown up was distorting my brain. That and the elephant in the room—that I'd held this man last night as he endured the lingering side effects of his many concussions from the sport he just agreed to represent on television.

"It'll be an adjustment, like you said. And I'd rather run the steps at the art museum a thousand fucking times than go tell everyone I'm leaving." His voice was flat and free of emotion. "But after they get used to it, I think they'll be proud to see me on TV."

"Of course they'll be proud," I said. "Your parents are proud of everything you do. I guess I'm just..." I bit my bottom lip, fingers tapping against my knee. "Maybe I shouldn't say this, but did you tell them what happened to you last night? Does it seem like they care about injuries like you've been saying?"

Dean cut his eyes back to the floor, the motion spiking through my complicated emotions. "Harry doesn't care about shit like that."

I bit my tongue to keep from saying *He doesn't care about your health?*

"The producer made some promises about change I think he'll keep," he finished. I caught the dip and sway of his tone, and it concerned me more than anything else.

"So I'm leaving. And you're leaving," he said, that dark-and-stormy gaze rising back to mine and pinning me in place. "Looks like we might meet at an airport sometime after all."

"Yeah, looks like," I chirped. "Wow. I'm, well, I thought you were going to work with Rowan and run the food program."

Dean swallowed. "He'll find someone more suited for that job."

I'd never seen him stand so still, like he was receding into himself. The past two weeks, I'd witnessed the careful unfurling of this man's confidence—his smiles coming easily, his limbs loosened, his dry humor and warm affection for the ones he loved. Now he stood straight as a soldier, and I wondered why this meeting had the opposite effect of what working on the park had done.

It was like Dean had an on/off switch like my mother, an observation that had me wanting to retreat like I had so many times as a kid.

"It's a once-in-a-lifetime opportunity, Tabitha," he added. "Most athletes can only dream of retiring and ending up making better money by sitting behind a desk."

"That's true," I admitted. And it was. Yet that first morning we'd spent in bed together came back in a rush I couldn't ignore, how my heart had ached as he'd categorized his injuries one by one. *All these fans, all these analysts...In their minds, it was like I gave up more than they could understand. But it wasn't for them to understand. It wasn't their health and memory to lose.* "I imagine it wasn't an easy decision to make."

"No," he said softly. "And leaving won't be either."

For the first time since Harry's phone call interrupted us, his words held the same level of yearning currently coursing through my own veins.

"It's certainly harder this time for me," I said, surprised when the words came out in barely a whisper. "I feel completely at fault here, Dean."

He re-squared his shoulders.

"Usually"—*I'm not, you know, falling in love with my temporary fling*—"I'm very serious about being honest with the person I'm having sex with. Setting clear boundaries is important to me. Especially with a friend. A friend like you. Now I'm leaving tomorrow, and we've had zero conversations about being on the same page."

He hesitated, eyes searching mine until he seemed satisfied by whatever he found there. "Why would you be at fault? I knew what your deal was. You told me. No attachments, only fun." A heavy, fractured pause followed. "And that's what the two of us had. Worked hard, played hard. Right?"

I studied him, assessing the cracks in his armor. I, again, had no right to feel frustrated in this moment—I had my own protections guarding my heart. They just appeared in the form of silly flirting and funny jokes. His face was so impassive though. I would have said his nonchalance was a lie, but he wasn't the lying type.

"Right," I said, drawing out the word.

"So we're good, then?" he asked.

All of those badminton-playing butterflies, hammering around in my chest, up and died. This whole thing was like some karmic retribution for the dozens of times I'd been the Dean in the situation. The person maintaining their cool while ending a relationship meant to be casual that was so clearly not casual to the other party.

Except I had seen the pain and hurt on his face this morning when I was talking about going to Austin, hadn't I? It had been so naked and raw my sternum throbbed like I'd taken a combat boot to it.

That wasn't nonchalance.

My usual boasting about casual sex and hot summer flings seemed so pointless when I'd gone ahead and done exactly what my mother did every time. I'd been *pretending* to my family for so long, I must have gotten too comfortable with it. I'd clearly just pretended my way out of a friendship and relationship that meant more to me than I'd ever known was possible. I'd hit my own switch out of cowardice and had hurt a kind man with the biggest heart.

"We're good," I forced out. "I did have a lot of fun, and I'm glad we spent the past couple weeks together. Your friendship will always mean a lot to me, Dean."

His fingers fluttered by his sides for all of a second before going still. "I feel the same way. Have always felt that way." Then he cleared his throat and opened the door. "What time is your flight tomorrow?"

"Late," I said. "After dinner. I'm heading over to Alexis's house tonight for a big Tyler family sleepover. But in between that and tomorrow, I'll be here, working on pocket park stuff." A rising swell of emotion threatened to bring tears when I was desperate to stay in control during this conversation. No matter what happened, I'd never be able to think about this tiny lot without thinking of the two of us doing it together. Every single step—from that first morning picking up trash to planting flowers with our fingers embracing in the dirt.

A line formed between his brows. "Okay. I'm sure I'll see you before you leave, then."

"Absolutely," I said cheerfully, even as tears wanted to spill.

His lips twitched at the end. "Or maybe I'll even see you out in Vegas sometime." Then he left and shut the door behind him.

I wrapped my arms around a pillow covered in the logos of every Philly sports team, pressing the edge of my palm under my eyes as I cried for the first time in years. My heart had known all along—the newly opened one with a clumsy ballerina's penchant for falling. I'd been in love with Dean this entire time.

I'd only hurt him in the end.

THIRTY-FOUR

DEAN

Later that night, I rounded the corner onto Tenth Street going much too fast for the end of a six-mile run. Though the six miles had been fueled by feelings more powerful than adrenaline.

I reluctantly slowed to a stop, breath labored, head pounding with the beginnings of a tension headache. Those didn't affect me as badly as my migraines did, but working my body too hard less than a day after getting one was the reason why my temples throbbed now. Dropping my hands onto my head, I took giant breaths as I walked past the park on tired legs. The feeling that had fueled my run—regret—ripped through me at the sight of it, chased by a hollow sadness that had me scrubbing a hand down my face.

I was a bastard, telling Eddie and Tabitha this morning that I didn't have hope we could win this fight when I'd dragged us into it in the first place. When I'd told Rowan that if no one was coming to help us out here, we needed to do it ourselves. Now a *kind* of help was coming, but it wasn't the kind this street needed. I was too in my head earlier to offer real ideas, but I'd let my brain churn through every possible solution on my run and I'd still come up with nothing.

As the sun started to set on this shitty day, I was gripped by memories of this place—Tabitha singing in the sunshine next to my neighbors as they cleared the trash. Her cheeky smile every time she brought me food. The way she'd looked behind the camera, telling me I was part of the story too.

Tabitha standing in the street beneath the moonlight with wet hair, pressing her cheek to my chest and holding me tight.

I hadn't been this low, this *angry* since that first week after my concussion, when I realized how pissed off my fans and the industry had been at my retirement. Like that same week, I felt backed into a corner now, on the defensive and unable to think clearly. Somewhere around mile three I realized that Tabitha's advice to me about the Game Time job had been eerily on point. She'd said my tendency to overthink was probably the best way to decide given how dramatically it would change my life.

I'd done the exact fucking opposite. Had shown up to the meeting hot under the collar and impulsive. I hadn't even stopped by to give Mom and Midge the news in the afternoon. I was too twisted up in knots, too aware of the voice in my head telling me the choice I'd made was a mistake.

Hands on my hips, I walked to my house, casting a sideways glance at Linda's door the way I had every day since Tabitha had moved in. The lights were off. The house was quiet.

So we're good, then, right? Tabitha Tyler had me on the ropes, as always, and I'd fought back by throwing up every wall I had.

"Yo, Dean, how ya doin'?" Eddie said, shuffling up the sidewalk with a glass container I recognized. "Just the man I was looking for."

"What's up?" I said, still out of breath. "You all right?"

"Me? I'm swell. I'm on my way to Edna's house, bringing some of the leftovers Midge dropped off last night."

"Edna Kozlowski?" I asked.

"The one and only." He indicated I should follow him down the block. I did, too out of it to ask where we were going. "I saw her sister at the Acme, and she mentioned Edna was feeling a little under the weather. So thought I'd share some of this delicious spaghetti and meatballs with her."

"Do you want me to carry it for you?" I asked.

He waved his hand. "Nah, I got it."

I shoved my hands into my pockets and studied the profile of a man I had known my entire life. He and Alice had always been my family, not only my neighbors. One of the mornings when I was still in the hospital, I'd woken up to Eddie scowling at the paper he was reading while slurping coffee from a Styrofoam cup. He didn't say anything, just let me rest while patting my hand every few minutes as if he knew I needed the reassurance. He didn't have much—if any—to share, but the little he did went to feed a feral cat and other neighbors who needed cheering up.

"That's nice of you to stop by," I said. "Do you know if there are other times she needs help?"

He frowned. "Things probably get tight for her at the end of the month like it does for most of us, I'm guessing. I hear about it from her sister 'cause she works the deli at the Acme. And I hear about if her sister needs help from seeing Edna at church. Now, if they were *both* not at church, you'd know somethin's up with the Kozlowski sisters. But they're about as tough as your parents are, so they ain't going nowhere."

I smiled down at my feet. "Folks keep an eye on each other around here."

He scoffed. "Growing up, wasn't like we had—what is it

that Tabitha did, a GoFundMe page? You just had to go around and ask people if they needed help and then believe their answer."

"Like when you helped me," I said. "When I was kicking around after retirement, not sure who I was, you let me take over your handyman clients."

"Of course I did," he said, like being that generous wasn't negotiable. "Hell, when you love a person, you do anything for them to be happy. I always wanted you to know that I never cared one bit what those assholes in the paper said about you quittin'. Having a parade is nice every once in a while, and I'll never forget that night you won the Golden Gloves for as long as I live. But I think all of this"—he waved his hand at the city around us—"is about more than just winning or losing things. Your life is more than that, Dean."

I let out a breath I didn't realize I was holding.

"Look, we're almost where I'm supposed to take you," Eddie said. "Rowan called Alice about an hour ago. Said you weren't picking up your phone and he needed to see ya at the center."

I saw the lights of the basketball court and a few offices still occupied. My stomach rolled with anxiety. But then I dragged my gaze back to Eddie, bobbing his head as we got closer, and I knew what I had to ask. We had reached the short pathway that led up to the rec center, but I touched Eddie on the shoulder, stilling him.

"Has, uh...has Rowan told you about the new program he's working on in there?" I asked, inclining my head to the front door.

Eddie fidgeted. "No. Why?"

You just had to go around and ask people if they needed help and then believe their answer.

"He's starting a program that provides boxes of food once a

week for a lot of seniors around here. People like you said, who don't have a lot of extra money lying around. Food's expensive. Least we can do is help out a few older folks."

"Like the Kozlowski sisters, maybe?"

I lifted a shoulder. "Yeah, sure." I made sure he was still looking at me. "You could get one of those boxes too. If you needed a little extra. Doesn't mean Mom and Midge wouldn't still bring you lasagna every time they made it. But it could help you worry less, if you got one. I know this shit sucks to talk about," I lowered my voice. "I hope you know you can talk about it with me. Because I love you too, Eddie."

He looked out to the street, jaw clenching. I let him think it through. When he finally answered, it took me a second to realize he was speaking in Italian. He hadn't done that since I was a kid. "Sometimes...sometimes it's easier to help other people than yourself, yeah?"

I answered in Italian. "I've got some experience with that myself."

He sighed. "I always worked real hard. Always had a job. Never, *ever* thought..."

I waited. He sniffed. "You don't think toward the end of your life that you might not have enough money when all you've ever done is what's been asked of you."

I squeezed his shoulder. "We ask a lot of people. Then we expect them to do more with less."

He squinted, handing me the leftovers and shaking out a cigarette. "Edna gets a little embarrassed when I bring her food, but she doesn't have to be. What are we gonna do, let her fucking *starve*?"

I shifted the food as he smoked, the smell of tobacco and worn leather taking me back to sitting on his stoop in the summer with Rowan. "Do you remember when I was in fifth grade and Mom was out of work for, like, six months?"

He nodded. "Yeah, she had some shit boss at the time."

I pressed my lips together. "You and Alice brought us food all the time. 'Cause we needed it. Having extra made it so that we didn't have to worry."

He grinned. "When did you get to be such a clever smart-ass?"

"Takes one," I said, matching his expression.

He chuckled, stubbing out his cigarette and taking back the leftovers. "If Rowan has a box I can have, weekly, I'll take it. But I don't need all of it, so I'll share with a few folks on Tenth Street who might want some."

Relief washed over me. "I think that sounds good."

Rowan poked his head out the front door, and Eddie raised a hand in greeting. "I delivered him to your doorstep," he said, back to speaking English.

I jammed my hands into my pockets and spun on my heels, walking toward Rowan. "Say hi to Edna for me."

"Yeah sure," he said. "I'll see you tomorrow anyway. I know we're gonna find a way to get that park back."

I went still. "So you're optimistic, now?"

"Tabitha convinced me," he said. "She's real smart about these things."

A host of complicated emotions jammed at the back of my throat, making it hard to swallow. The way she'd said *Absolutely* in her usual singsong voice as I was leaving, but her eyes shone with tears. And I'd walked out like an asshole.

"She's very smart," I said. "The rest of us are just trying to keep up."

Eddie left, and Rowan held the door open to the rec center for me. His smile was as cocky as ever. But I didn't miss the concern in his eyes.

"You wanted me delivered here?" I asked.

He closed the door behind us, and we walked down the

hall toward his office. "I did. I heard some rumblings about a fancy developer and Tabitha leaving tomorrow and one sighting of Dean Knox-Morelli at Al's coffee shop, sittin' with two dudes in suits."

I rolled my already tightening shoulders back. "I need to talk to you."

"I bet you do." He kicked out a chair for me next to his desk. I sank down into it. When he set his gaze on me, the concern there had doubled. "There's no other way to say this. You look like shit warmed over, dude."

THIRTY-FIVE

DEAN

Rowan swung his office chair around and sat in it backward. "Did you get a migraine last night?"

I rubbed my temples. "Yeah, how'd you know?"

"The looking-like-shit-warmed-over part. Do you still have it?"

He was already standing up and walking to the kitchen. I took the brief moment to scan his office, filled with food donations. But then he appeared next to me with an ice pack in his hand.

"Thank you." I placed it on the back of my neck. "I went for a hard run just now. Gave myself a tension headache." At Rowan's arched eyebrow I said, "I know it was a mistake. One of many today."

He placed a glass of ice water and a bottle of Tylenol next to it. I swallowed two and finished the glass.

"Easy, big guy," he said. "The only perfect person in this room is me, so you don't gotta go all hard on yourself."

I flipped him a middle finger, which made him laugh. He swung his leg back over the chair. "Seriously though. What the hell is going on? Is Eddie okay?"

"Eddie's good," I said. "I talked to him about the food boxes, and he wants to sign up. But only if he can give half to the neighbors."

A real smile flew across Rowan's face. "You did it."

I lifted one shoulder. "It was no big deal. Think he just had to feel comfortable." I glanced back around at the boxes, the pictures of kids and families on the wall. I listened to the sounds of people working late, someone playing the radio softly. I was feigning being casual about Eddie. Talking to him about what he needed help with had felt important. Knowing this place could help, even a little bit, had warmed my chest. Made me proud. Throughout the meeting with Rex and Harry, they'd kept emphasizing the lifestyle I'd have out there—makeup, lights, being on camera, always having a hot take on some boxer's skill or lack of.

I'd felt only a hollow, shallow interest that became a spiky panic by the time I'd shaken Rex's hand and said, "Yeah. I'll do it." Maybe it was the greed in Harry's eyes. Or the fact that it was clear Rex did not, at all, care about the health and well-being of any athlete unless it was giving Game Time bad press.

On Rowan's computer, he'd stuck a Post-it note that said *Every day is your chance to make this city better*.

"I fucked up," I said.

His eyebrows knit together. "With Tabitha?"

I hesitated. "Yes, with Tabitha. But not only that. I took her to family dinner last night. It meant a lot to me, seeing her with my parents like that. Seeing the way they light up around her. When I got the migraine, she stayed and took care of me, and we talked all morning. Like it wasn't temporary at all. Like Tabitha and I were two people in love, sharing a life together."

Those eyebrows shot up to his hairline. I knew why.

"But then..." I dropped the ice pack onto the desk, right knee shaking. "Then an investor showed up. Oswald."

"Fucking asshole," Rowan muttered.

"He wants to buy Annie's lot. And it was a mess. And I could feel Tabitha pulling away from me, getting ready to leave. I got angry and overwhelmed. I'd forgotten the meeting Harry had set up with the Game Time producer, but by the time I walked in there I was pissed and powerless, and when he talked about tons of money and having this giant comeback I..."

"Retreated," Rowan said.

"I was going to go with *was a total bastard*. I said yes and didn't tell you. Even though..."

Rowan let me trail off and collect my jumbled thoughts. I rubbed my forehead, rubbed my eyes. When I finally looked up, I couldn't avoid what I wanted.

"Dean," he said. "It doesn't matter what I want or what some slimy producer wants. I'll miss you like hell, but I'm not gonna be mad if you want that job." He paused. "Do you want it?"

I pushed the empty water glass away with one finger. "Harry's been blowing a bunch of smoke up my ass, telling me the network had a plan in addressing head injuries during matches. I was skeptical. The only way to prevent those injuries is for boxers to stop taking hits above their chest. It would mean no blood. No broken teeth. No knockouts."

"No drama," Rowan said grimly.

"It wouldn't be boxing," I said. "I threw this out to Rex while we were meeting. He gave me a spiel so full of bullshit you could see it from space. Said they'd do more to honor boxers who had passed away from their injuries, make some donations to research institutions. Small donations. I could tell he thought I'd be impressed. That my interest in this was surface level—because he gave me a bunch of surface-level solutions."

"Did you sign a contract or anything?"

I shook my head. "No, and thank God. Two hours after I left them I knew I'd made a mistake. But I knew Tabitha was leaving and the park wasn't going to work out, so I don't know. I thought it was my best option, going back to an identity that doesn't fit the same anymore." I glanced back over at the food boxes. "I'm not Dean the Machine, and I don't want to be."

"I know," Rowan said. "You don't think a ton of retired athletes would have contemplated taking that offer? It's a tempting one. What I do now, the satisfaction's all internal. There's no flash. No crowds of cheering fans. It's less of an adrenaline rush, for sure. Lately though? It's hard to see the appeal of that old life."

I raised an eyebrow. "You mean you don't miss sitting in an ice bath after every game?"

His response was a wolfish grin. "About as much as you miss getting your teeth knocked out on a Saturday night."

I snorted, tapping my fingers on the table. "How's the pay here?"

"Terrible."

"And the hours?"

"Long. Plus I've heard there's another, possibly more attractive ex-athlete that already works here. Could make you jealous."

I shook my head with a smile. "Something tells me your director is going to regret putting the two of us together."

He waved that off. "No way. Something tells me that the two of us working together could bring some great programs to this neighborhood."

I swallowed hard, overcome by his generosity. "I want this job, Rowan."

He nodded. "Good. It's all yours. And you've already got Eddie signed up."

I released another tightly held breath. "Harry's gonna have my head when I tell him the news. But also I've been wanting to fire him for years so maybe this call won't be that bad after all."

Rowan whistled low under his breath. "I let go of mine a couple years ago. Best decision I ever made."

A space was shifting and opening around the center of my chest. "It sounds like that'll be the next one I make."

I glanced over at the note stuck on Rowan's computer. It was impossible not to remember Tabitha that first night, telling me about her passion in life: *I like to tell stories about wildflowers growing through sidewalks, basically. All the things that take up space, demanding attention and justice in the face of larger forces trying to make them silent or invisible.*

"What really happened with Tabitha?" Rowan asked.

I leaned back in the chair. "Exactly what I knew would happen. And what she told me would happen from the beginning. We had a lot of sex. Had a lot of fun. She obviously didn't get attached, a promise that she kept." An uneasy sadness filled that newly open space in my chest. I'd done what I was supposed to do—gotten laid, didn't stress about it. I'd still known the ending this whole time, so why was I so upset? "This morning, she seemed to feel bad about us not talking about, you know, ending things when she went to Texas. Because we weren't on the same page. I made sure she knew I was fine with it."

I knew from the tears in her eyes as I left there was something she wasn't telling me. She'd projected that bubbly cheer my way, and I knew she was faking it. I just didn't know what she was keeping to herself, which hurt more than all the rest.

Rowan muttered a curse under his breath, snagging my

attention. There were two spots of color in his cheeks. "Now it's time for me to admit that I fucked up."

"What are you talking about?"

"I pushed you into this," he said. "Pushed you to hook up with Tabitha when you told me you didn't think it'd work out the way you wanted. I knew..." Rowan blew out a breath. "I knew from the moment you started talking to her again that she wasn't just some old crush from when we were kids. Tabitha is—always was—different for you. I feel like I gave you the kind of advice you'd want for some one-night stand with a stranger. Not the woman you're in love with."

My eyes darted to the ground. "It's not your fault. Not one bit. Once I kissed her, that night at the art museum, there was no other option for me. Falling in love with her was my mistake to make."

The words ripped through my throat, but I felt better, saying them out loud.

Rowan was quiet for a while. So quiet I wondered if I'd pissed him off. But he was looking at something on his computer, lines creasing his forehead. "Dean."

"Yeah?"

He cleared his throat. "You, uh...you know I love you, yeah?"

I clapped him on the arm. "Of course. I love you too."

"You made the right call, quitting boxing when you did," he said in a tentative voice. "But it's been hard, seeing you kinda lost. Seeing you feel worthless when you're not. I pushed you with Tabitha because all of a sudden you were happy again. Not happy like when you were pros. Happy like what we were telling Tabitha the other night, before we were athletes and we were only kids."

I swallowed thickly. I knew what he meant. "Carefree."

"Am I wrong?"

I raked a hand through my hair. "That's the way she made me feel."

His eyes darted back to the computer screen. "And you're sure Tabitha didn't want a relationship with you or had feelings for you the way you did?"

I didn't answer right away. I watched her pull back from me this morning. That was real. So was everything else that was good between us the past two weeks—the bright light of her tempting me to open, to soften, to trust again. Every secret, every teasing joke, the sound of her laughter, muffled against my chest in the morning. The desperate, urgent way she clung to me every time we had sex. The tender way she'd stroked my hair when I was sick, promising to stay all night.

And, most of all, her stubborn belief that people coming together could always make a difference. Tabitha had shown me her heart, time and time again. That was as real as anything I'd ever experienced.

"I'm not sure," I said slowly. "I don't know if she's scared. Or running away for some other reason. But what's been going on between us isn't temporary."

He turned his computer around. It was a website with Tabitha's videos, linked to the pocket park donation page. I cringed when I saw all those names again. People we'd probably have to return money to. "Did you ever watch any of the videos Tabitha made about Tenth Street?"

I shook my head. "Not yet."

Rowan hit Play on the most recent one. "She uploaded this a day ago. She said it was a bunch of random segments and some behind-the-scenes shots."

Curious, I leaned in to read the caption: *There are a lot of things to love about the neighbors working together on Tenth Street's pocket park. It's almost impossible to capture. So I present to you a short compilation of random moments that never made it into any of the videos I posted. I'm even in the background of a few of these from the day I set up my camera to record a long before/after piece. After watching this, you'll see why this place means so very much to me.*

I couldn't help but smile at the images appearing on the screen, many I recognized from days Tabitha had jumped around with her camera. But there were some I hadn't seen: Rowan and me laughing, telling stories about Eddie's stoop. Me, helping my mothers plant tomato plants, Midge clearly teasing me as I grinned. Alice patting my cheek as I brought her a cup of coffee on the bench.

Tabitha and me playing a game of hopscotch with Lía and Marco. The two of us, gardening together. Cleaning together. There was a quick shot of me, leaning against the wall as Tabitha told me some grandiose story, her hands moving around her face. The expression I wore was amused and affectionate.

Focused. Only on her.

"It was that obvious then?" I asked, face hot.

"What was obvious?"

I indicated the screen. "I was in love with her this whole time."

Rowan stopped the video with a wry laugh. "That wasn't what I was showing you." He clicked back, waved the mouse over the handful of posts about the park. "If you watch all of these, there's one thing they all have in common."

"Everyone can see I'm a fool for her?"

"Nope." He pointed at the screen. "Every single one of these videos is about *you*."

I froze. Replayed what I'd just seen until I understood what Rowan was trying to show me.

"Maybe she is running scared," he said. "And I can't blame her. This fallin'-in-love stuff sure seems scary to me. When I watch these? It's clear to me you weren't the only one acting like an obsessed fool."

I dragged my attention back to the screen and shivered with goose bumps. The paused image was a shot of me and Rowan, talking with Eddie as I hauled a bag of trash over my shoulder. My body language was relaxed and I looked happy and content.

Tabitha stood off to the side, clearly enjoying whatever it was we were saying. She was biting the tip of her thumb with a wide grin, brown eyes shining up at me, and only me, like I was...like I was...

"See what I'm sayin'?" Rowan asked.

I huffed out a surprised breath. "Yeah," I said, stunned. Talk about a hit I hadn't seen coming: Tabitha Tyler, looking at me like I was the love of her life.

THIRTY-SIX
TABITHA

I was quickly learning that chalk drawings of tiny rainbow hearts didn't smudge that much when you cried on them.

Juliet pointed at the heart I'd finished coloring in. "Aunty Tabby, you messed that one up."

I peeked over her shoulder and pressed my lips together at the tear tracks. "You're right, kiddo. I sure did. How about I fix it with some more green?"

She nodded and went back to her own drawing, which appeared to be another portrait of Pam but with more heads. I cast my eyes up to Alexis, who was sitting on the stoop, hands clasped in her lap, chewing on her bottom lip like she was about to cry with me. "Do you want me to get you some tissues?" she asked.

"Nope," I said firmly. "I'll cry if you bring them out, and besides, I'm not going to cry again. Besides, I'm basically at the end of my story, which is that he said something like, maybe I'll see you in Vegas sometime, and then he left. And I bawled my eyes out all over Aunt Linda's sports-themed couch pillows."

I sat back on my heels and brushed the hair from my face, holding a stick of green chalk in one hand. As requested, I wore pajamas and was prepared to crash on the floor in Alexis and Eric's living room, with Juliet sleeping in a tiny tent and Dad and Kathleen claiming the big couch. Juliet had come up with the idea after the success of our previous sleepover, and I couldn't have imagined a better way to spend my last night in Philly.

Well, there was one better way—having a giant family slumber party in a world where I hadn't hurt the man I'd fallen in love with.

Alexis leaned over and grabbed my hand, squeezing it three times. "Oh, Tab. I'm so sorry."

I looked away and released her. "It's okay. Really. It's...it's my fault. I mishandled the whole thing from the start, so I'm not sure what other outcome I expected."

I refocused on shading in the green I'd smudged, breathing through the heavy knot in my chest. I couldn't stop the morning's events in my head, like some kind of shitty time loop I couldn't escape. How over the course of a couple hours, we'd retreated to separate corners with only awkwardness hanging between us. *So we're good, then, right?*

How many times had I parroted that same phrase to a person I'd been casually involved with?

Alexis left her perch on the stoop to crouch next to me. She reached forward, stilling my coloring. "Obviously I'm always biased when it comes to you, but I also genuinely believe that this situation cannot possibly be *all* your fault."

"I disregarded every opportunity for open communication," I said. "Instead of being honest, I pretended I didn't want more, pretended that my heart was still closed instead of being fully open. Dean said I didn't need to apologize. That I'd been clear about never getting attached and he got it. But I still did exactly what I never wanted to do. Got involved in something messy and unclear and left the other person hurt and confused."

"Why do you think it's all your fault, then?" she asked. "It sounds like you must have had some communication about your situation if Dean knew what you were about."

I glanced over at Juliet, who was distracted with her cat drawings. I lowered my voice. "You remember what we talked about the other day, the way Mom's behavior still impacts our lives? Seeing how formal and polite Dean became, how stoic, it was as if the past two magical weeks together hadn't happened. Like we were perfect strangers and not friends who cared about one another. I *know* Dean." I cleared my throat through rising emotion. "Seeing his warmth and humor and affection disappear...it was like watching Dad walk around after an argument with Mom, pretending things were okay after she'd done one more thing to devastate him. Those weekends when we'd take Dad to John's to get water ice are burned into my memory. How small and defeated he looked. I always knew I'd never be like her, never stomp all over people's hearts the way she did. Relationships are easier if you can control every step of the way. Just flirting, just sex, no emotions. If I'd stuck to that formula with Dean from the start..."

Alexis saw through that lie immediately. "Be honest. Do you really believe you two were destined for some casual fling? Because you can be a good, thoughtful person and try your hardest to avoid hurting the person you're with." She ducked her head to catch my gaze and held it. "But we cannot control relationships in that way. Certainly not the kind you had with Dean. Real passion, real *love* doesn't adhere to those rules. The more you try to contain it the more it resists being contained."

I closed my eyes to better imagine the scenario I'd painted for my sister. One where I bumped into Dean at Benny's and we then pursued a purely sexual relationship comprised of impersonal trysts and shallow conversation. Instead, I could only remember Dean's boyish grin, his body moving confidently as we danced in his parents' living room. His eyes on me last night had seared like a brand, and every smile we shared was the sweetest victory.

How deliriously happy I'd been, as if we were always meant to have that dance, have that dinner, have that life.

At some point, Alexis had wrapped me in her arms.

"Oh God, am I crying again?" I said, sniffing against her shoulder.

"Yeah, but it's no biggie. You think people in this neighborhood haven't seen someone sobbing on the sidewalk before? It's a regular occurrence during football season."

I snorted, but it ended on a croaking half sob.

Juliet patted me softly on the back. "Do you miss Mr. Dean?"

"Yeah," I managed to say. "I miss Mr. Dean."

The counselors would always say that you find the people who love you more loudly than the ones who don't. That's your real family, in the end.

Dean's words from last night only caused more tears to roll down my cheeks. This level of connection had happened often in our support group—he would share one or two sentences, or I would share via my usual excited rambling. After finishing, our eyes would find each other from across the room, both of us seeking the comfort of a friend.

That safe space was often the only place where I was ever truly honest. It required a bravery and vulnerability that terrified me more than my current lightly packed way of life. And it was growing clear to me now that the moments between us when I'd pushed past the fear, been truly free with my emotions had created an intimacy more poignant than my worries.

"Alexis?"

"Mm-hmm?"

"I'm in love with Dean. I can't believe I told you that having a crush on someone was the best feeling in the world when this *sensation* makes me feel like I could fly to the moon. I never, not once, had legitimate control over it."

She nodded, laughing softly. "That's true love right there."

"I want to tell him. Need to tell him." I pulled back from her to wipe my wet cheeks. "Nothing else matters—where he's living or where I'm living or if our jobs take us all over or root us back home. Even if he doesn't feel the same way"—a hole cracked open in my chest at the thought—"he deserves to know. Dean Knox-Morelli deserves to know how deeply he is loved. I want to find a way to apologize for turning away when I should have leapt into his arms. To apologize and make things right."

Alexis arched one blond eyebrow. "Take it from someone who knows the privilege of being married to their soul mate. Dean looks at you the way Eric has always looked at me. And I think you already know that."

I broke out in a full body blush as I replayed all the ways in which Dean had looked at me since the night I fell into his lap: shy and sweet, cute and charming, ravenous, hungry, passionate, devoted. Our time together really had been as intoxicating as it was normal. Perhaps that was the shape of true love formed by friendship. A heightened, electric desire bursting forth from a foundation of kindness and trust.

How beautiful it would be to live a life where giving in to pleasure also meant giving in to love.

"There have been, um...many moments between us where, yes, you would be correct," I said nervously.

She smirked. "When can I take you out for shots and give you a bunch of advice on committed relationships?"

I laughed, dropping my head into my hands. "I'm hopeless, aren't I?"

"Hopelessly in love, Tab. There's a difference."

Juliet stopped drawing and suddenly wrapped her arms around my side. I pulled her into a hug, kissed her hair, rocked her gently back and forth. Every type of undefinable love forced its way past any residual resistance to it. And not just romantic love, all of it: my niece, hugging me when she sensed I was sad. My sister, making me laugh as I cried. Dad, Kathleen, and Eric cooking us dinner in the kitchen with music in the background.

It was impossible to fully describe the depth of my family's loud and bright love. But one thing was clear: it had never been conditional. That had been my mother's style, not theirs. I had to trust that this unconditional love wouldn't waver when I was finally honest with them. I'd avoided fully accepting it—had even, literally, run from it—because with this kind of love there could be no shameful secrets. No hiding of what had happened between me and Mom and the guilt I carried.

I was going to have to tell them everything. Which meant I'd get to stay, a realization that sent a jolt of pure joy through me.

Alexis touched the top of my hand. "Are you okay? You seem stunned."

The world was tilting around me, a myriad of missing pieces sliding into place. "I'm wonderful," I said softly. "I was simply trying to figure out how to respectfully break a contract without burning every professional bridge I had in the great city of Austin, Texas."

Her eyes went wide. "Tabitha. Don't joke."

"I'm not, I swear."

Eric pushed the storm door open and hung from the side. "Raise your hand if you're ready for the best homemade pizza you've ever had in your life."

Alexis and I raised our hands, eyes still locked together with matching smiles we'd inherited from our Dad. "We'll be right in," my sister said.

"I'm ready," Juliet squealed, leaving my side and running up the steps.

"Way to show enthusiasm sweetheart," Eric called after her. Then he turned back to us. "And I don't know what's happening right now, but it sure looks like good news."

I squeezed Alexis's hand three times. It wasn't necessarily good news or bad news but the beginning of a story I'd been seeking all along.

THIRTY-SEVEN
TABITHA

The difference was unmistakable as soon as we gathered round to eat. Kathleen had opened up a bottle of wine and Dad kept the music on, though at a lower volume, and for a while we were rapt listeners as Juliet spun us a tale about a giraffe with wings she swore she'd seen at the park the other day.

For once, watching my dad ask Juliet a lot of adorable questions—*What do you think her wings were made of? You say her neck was how long?*—didn't evoke such a bittersweet sting. I wasn't looking forward to what I was about to tell them. But the knowledge that I wasn't moving to Austin grounded me fully in the moment. I didn't have to side-eye the door, one foot already out as I pretended that zipping into and out of their lives was easy for me.

Licking tomato sauce from my thumb, I reached forward and nudged my laptop open where it rested on the coffee table. I'd started working on this surprise a few days into my visit, after discovering the gold mine of family photos residing in Aunt Linda's many bookshelves. At the time I considered it to be a going-away gift, to say thank you for making my trip home so special.

Now I understood what it was all along: A love letter to Philly. My own plea to stay.

"What's the update on the park, hon?" Kathleen asked, setting down her wine glass. "And I want you to know I have fully activated my book club members and their impressive networks."

I flashed her a grateful smile. "You're a legend and always will be. We need the help. The good news is that the emails I've sent out to past clients and the SOS call I put out on social media is generating a lot of interest and attention. People have even donated more money, which is extraordinary. Everyone on Tenth Street is using their own connections too. We need a huge amount of funds to buy the lot from the city. Or a miracle."

"Or a book club member," Kathleen said wisely.

I laughed. "Yes, ma'am. On the one hand, it's demoralizing to see how quickly the park's been put at risk, especially since it's not even finished yet. The best is definitely yet to come for Tenth Street. And on the other hand, it's so inspiring to see the response from our community, wanting to help in any way they can. There have even been a few people nearby offering to collaborate to create parks using the abandoned lots on their block. I guess I'm both super anxious and panicking and really optimistic and hopeful, all at the same time."

Eric grinned. "The two elementary school teachers in the room can certainly identify with that confusing mix of emotions."

My sister laughed and kissed him on the cheek. "Something has me feeling extra, extra hopeful today."

I smiled down at my plate. Seeing Alexis be excited for me staying was giving me the courage I needed for whatever happened next—all of it would require making scary changes, canceling contracts, even disappointing some people. But I could sense the reward waiting for me on the other side of authenticity, a reward that looked like the people sitting around me now.

And maybe, if I was really, *really* lucky, I'd get to be with Dean.

"I'm feeling hopeful too," I said. "Also a little nervous because I made a movie for you."

Dad's eyes lit up. "Aw, Tab, you didn't have to do that. We're just happy to see ya one more night before you go."

I shook my head, unable to stop the happy smile from spreading across my face. "Dad. I'm not going. I'm moving back home."

There was a charged pause, and then half the room shouted "*What?*" all at the same time. I started laughing, and Alexis clapped her hands together.

"It's last minute—and even more impulsive than my usual very impulsive decision-making—but I've decided I'd like to move back home, to be here with all of you. It's going to mean an awkward phone call to the hotel I was going to do work for in Austin, plus getting a place to stay and finding new clients." *And confessing my love to Dean.* "I want to be here, though, with all of you. Desperately. These past two weeks..." I swallowed a few times, and my dad wrapped his arm around my shoulders. "Being with all of you has essentially made it impossible for me to leave. You're too fucking charming."

I slapped my hand over my mouth and stared at Juliet, who appeared to be enthralled by her coloring book. Eric covered her ears with a smirk.

"It's fine," he whispered. "She hears worse when we walk to the Acme. Also, I'm so fucking happy you're staying, Tab. Juliet misses you all of the time."

My dad cleared his throat with eyes as watery as mine. "I wasn't going to say anything because you know that Kathleen and I would still talk to you every day even if your next job was on the moon. You seem different here than when we call you when you're traveling. I was never sure what it was. Now that you've been home, I don't know. You're still happy but also more relaxed. Comfortable."

I would have replied, *Because I'm not pretending as much*, but Kathleen was squeezing me in a hug and patting my hair. "There were times we'd get off the phone with you, in some new, beautiful location, and I thought you sounded lonely."

The harsh truth of that was like taking a glass of ice water to the face. "I've always loved my job, and spending five years traveling and working and living in different places was a privilege I don't regret at all. But I do think, underneath all of that, I was lonely and never knew how to talk about it."

I wasn't surprised that my family had noticed a difference in me here. I had too, and it wasn't only because of Dean. I'd run myself ragged since college, fleeing emotions and memories. Never letting anyone get too close. It was hard to acknowledge that I was carrying a loneliness with me from town to town, city to city.

It was even harder to acknowledge the role my own guilt and secrets contributed to that loneliness, but silence was only giving my mother more power. And it was time to reclaim every piece she'd stolen.

Juliet turned to her parents and asked if she could play in the kitchen. As she ran off—not before giving me a sloppy kiss on the cheek—I took it as a sign to have a more serious conversation.

Alexis must have seen my expression change because she cocked her head and said, "Tabitha, what is it?"

My stomach roiled, nerves on high alert. "This is really

hard for me to do, but I need to talk to you guys about Mom," I said. I was squashed between Dad and Kathleen on the couch and felt them react to my words. "I knew...I knew about Mom's affair six months before Dad and Alexis knew. I came home from school early one day, and she was in the kitchen with Roger. He was a stranger and I was young, but I could tell he was pissed at me. I had no idea what for. Mom though..." I dropped my gaze to the carpet. "She convinced me that Roger was an extra-special friend and that keeping him a secret from the rest of the family made me special too. It was ours to keep together, and I liked getting her attention. When you and Mom were arguing or she was lashing out at me and Alexis in some way, it still made me feel like I had to protect her. So I did. When Dad was sad or Alexis asked me what I thought was really going on with our parents, I pretended not to know. She'd take phone calls with Roger sometimes when I was around, and I could tell by the way she talked to him that he wasn't a friend. That he was kind of like a boyfriend, which was confusing to me because she already had a husband."

I blinked and realized that Alexis was crouching in front of me, holding both of my hands with tears in her eyes. "I'm so sorry that happened to you" she whispered.

"Sorry?" I shook my head. "No, you don't understand. We talked about this the other night. How awful she is. The imprint she left on us. I chose her, Alexis. I *protected* her. If I'd said something sooner, I know things would have been better for our family. Dad would have at least known what was happening, and you wouldn't have felt so abandoned. We could have avoided so much heartache and emotional pain, I just know it. She's always been a horrible liar, and she made me one too."

Alexis brushed the hair from my face and smoothed it over my shoulders. The gesture was so sisterly and soothing, I wondered how I'd so freely lived apart from her all these years.

"Is this why you always leave?" she asked quietly.

"It's easier," I admitted. The pressure in my chest was shifting like tectonic plates. "Especially once we cut Mom off. It was the right thing to do, but I knew then I had to keep what I'd done a secret. What if you stopped trusting me too? I already blamed myself enough for what happened to us. If you felt the same way, if I compromised the most important relationships in my life..." I shuddered. "I made a choice to lock it all away, and the guilt and the shame has kept me from opening up. I hide it instead."

Kathleen was unusually quiet next to me, although she never once stopped holding me by the shoulders. Eric perched on the edge of the coffee table, one hand holding Alexis's and the other on my knee. Dad shifted next to me and cleared his throat.

"Tabitha, look at me," he said. I did and was bowled over at the love in his eyes. "If you are punishing yourself for the actions of your mother, you can stop now."

My breath caught in my throat. Dean had said the same thing this morning.

"There is nothing that you can do or say that would make me love you less," he said with a kind smile. "And I wanna make this clear, okay? Your mother should not have done that to you. You were a child. She was an adult making adult decisions to end our marriage. Her lies were not your responsibility to tell. And this guilt is not yours to carry either. Your mom did not want some cordial ending. If I'd known earlier, filed for divorce earlier, it wouldn't have changed her behavior one bit. I can't imagine how lonely you must have felt, keeping that to yourself."

Lonely. There was that word again. For the first time in

years, I allowed myself to ache for the girl I'd been at eleven, confused and in the middle of complex dynamics I had no ability to understand.

"Mom was really good at making the people around her feel guilty," Alexis said. "I always, always saw her being more critical of you than she was of me, Tabitha. And I still beat myself up over it, like I didn't do enough to stand up for my little sister. Like I went away to college, escaped, and left you here by yourself."

I grabbed her wrists. "I never felt abandoned by you. Ever. And my memory is that she was harder on you."

Her eyes searched mine. "It's so normal to do what you did, to keep a secret instead of hurting the ones you love. I don't think there's a family that doesn't have secrets like that. Or tells a lot of little white lies to cover up the past. And we always view ourselves differently too. I'm devastated, knowing the way Mom manipulated you, the way she put you in the middle and you didn't feel like you could ever talk about it. And, meanwhile, I've been over here thinking I was always the worst sister ever—"

"Nothing, and I mean nothing, is further from the truth," I said firmly. I pulled her into a long hug. "You've always been my hero, and I mean that."

I released her, both of us laughing at our matching tear-streaked faces. It was more than sadness. It was acceptance and relief and welcoming the beginning of forgiveness. Without my usual armor, I was just a Philly girl who missed her family and wanted to come home.

Dad touched us lightly, drawing our attention his way. "I carry a lot of guilt about exposing the two of you to a person like your mother. She wasn't like that when we met, wasn't like that when we first got married. I swear to God if I'd known..." He coughed into his fist. "The stuff she used to say to you two wasn't how I wanted us to parent our daughters. Not at all. But sometimes after pulling a double shift at the diner, I'd come home, exhausted to my bones, and whatever she was doing I'd just leave it. I wouldn't engage. I wouldn't step in. I'd head to bed and swear I'd fix it in the morning. Half the time I didn't. I'd be lying if I said I didn't still feel bad about it. I'm sorry about that and will always be sorry."

"Oh, Dad, you don't have to be sorry," Alexis said. "We were all doing our best in a horrible situation."

"And you're the best dad, the coolest dad, and our favorite dad," I said, watching the regret on his face transform into a tentative smile. "Nothing will ever change that."

The knowledge that Dad and Alexis had carried their own confusion and remorse was as heartbreaking as it was affirming. Though I couldn't be that shocked—we'd all lived in that house together. Escaping our mother's manipulations wasn't an option.

Kathleen made a frustrated harrumph sound that had the four of us turning toward her. The fierce protectiveness etched into her face settled over me like a warm blanket. "My feelings about Theresa are well known so I won't repeat them again. It's even clearer to me now that everything that she's done has been about her choices. She chose to hurt. She chose to lie. She chose hatred and close-mindedness. I believe every one of these things is unforgivable. Being more honest with your family is a good thing, a healthy thing. But continuing to blame yourselves for the past helps no one."

The intense, unspoken emotion shared between Dad and Kathleen broadened the relieved smile on his face. "You're right. As always."

"Of course I am," she said, lifting her chin.

"And I like what you said about being more honest. Tabitha's back home; we'll be seeing each other even more. I don't want to hide from the tough stuff when it happens," he said. He directed his next words at me. "I don't want you to feel like you have to protect us anymore."

I closed my eyes, unable to stop a hot rush of tears. Dad hugged me through the worst of it, and I resisted the urge to fake a smile or a joke or twirl around until I'd convinced myself it didn't bother me. I allowed the beautiful threads of this story—the one I'd been telling myself from the second I stepped out of that cab—to root me here, with my family, my community, my home.

"I love you more than words can say, Tabitha," he said. "I always have. I always will, okay?"

"I love you too, Dad," I said, laughing as I sat back and accepted a handful of tissues from Alexis. "Now you'll never be able to get rid of me at the diner."

"Good," he said. "I prefer it that way." Then he cleared his throat, gaze darting around the room.

"What is it?" I asked, slightly nervous at the scattered gleam in his eyes.

He drummed his fingers on the coffee table. "I'm not trying to pry or get into your personal business, but, uh —"

"Are you and Dean going to get married and have babies, or what?" Kathleen asked, pointing at her phone. "The book club needs to know."

I raised an eyebrow, still wiping my cheeks. "I thought the book club was 'activating their networks' to save the pocket park?"

"What, they can't multitask?"

I blew out a long breath. "I don't know what's going to happen with Dean. Whatever *was* happening between us is over, although I did tell Alexis while chalk drawing that I'm desperately in love with him. As I'm sure everyone already knows because I've been so freaking obvious about it this whole time."

A warm smile spread across Eric's face. "It's different between the two of you, isn't it?"

I nodded, my heart spinning and spinning. "I knew it from the beginning too."

He chuckled, shaking his head. "Congratulations. Now you know what the fuss is all about." He bent over to kiss the top of my sister's head.

"I'd like the record to show that I still believe Dean to be one of the good ones," Dad said. "But if it doesn't work out with you two...?"

"I'm staying here regardless of what happens with Dean," I said. "I'm choosing home, choosing Philly. I'm ready."

"Good," Kathleen said firmly. "You deserve to start this next chapter based on what you want, honey. Not anyone else."

"I completely agree," I said, laying my head against her arm. A future without Dean was impossible to fathom, but even flush with optimism I had to accept there was a chance he wouldn't want me. I could only entertain that notion for a split second before wanting to cry my eyes out. But beneath that despair I still only yearned for one thing. Home.

Eric called for Juliet over his shoulder. "Do you want to hear something amazing about Aunty Tabby?"

We laughed as she sprinted back into the living room. "What is it?" she asked shyly.

"I'm not leaving tomorrow, sweetheart," I said. "I'm going to stay here and be around all the time."

The sweetest expression rose on her face. My niece tiptoed over before collapsing into my arms for a hug. "We can have sleepovers?"

"Totally."

"And color with chalk?"

"We can fill a whole museum."

She stared up at me with wonder, and I knew I'd never made a better decision than this one. "It's because you miss me all the time?"

"That's exactly why," I said. "Hey, do you want to see a movie I made about your mom and dad? And Grandma and Pop-Pop?"

Her eyes went wide before she scrambled up to sit between us on the couch. I leaned in to my laptop, much less nervous now. "This was going to be a going-away gift, but it's even more enjoyable now that I'm not going anywhere."

I opened the file and hit Play. I'd compiled Linda's pictures and a bunch of my own, plus a handful of family videos I'd shot as a teenager. They were randomly arranged, set to music, and while our mom wasn't in them, Eric, Kathleen, and Juliet featured prominently.

"Would you look at that," Dad said in awe. "You made a movie about us."

"It's my favorite one yet," I said. I didn't need to see what was on the screen—I had each image and video memorized at this point. They covered a giant span of years, from Dad and Linda as kids to Dad and Kathleen on their wedding day. Our first-day-of-school portraits and random family barbecues and summer trips to Linda's shore house. Alexis and Eric at Temple, the day Juliet was born, slightly blurry pictures from move-in day at UCLA. I mostly watched my family's reactions, listened to their inside jokes and laughter.

How I ever thought I was going to leave them again was beyond understanding.

About ten minutes in, Kathleen nudged my arm. "I might have a lead on helping out the park," she whispered.

"Wait, really?"

She nodded, indicating I should follow her. Everyone else was focused on the screen and didn't notice us slipping into the kitchen.

"Can you make popcorn while you're in there?" Dad said, sounding distracted.

I popped my head out. "It's a real blockbuster, huh?"

"Oscar worthy," he said.

I found a bag of popcorn in the pantry and tossed it into the microwave. Kathleen was scrolling through her phone, shaking her head.

"What is it? Show me," I said.

She was squinting at her screen. "Paulette, one of my book club members, her nephew works at some nonprofit called the...let's see here...the Community Land Bank. She already spoke to her nephew and said to call him tomorrow morning because he's pretty sure they can help."

I leaned in and read over her shoulder, afraid to hope too much. This Land Bank place purchased abandoned lots for neighborhoods to do what they wanted with them—playgrounds, gardens, parks. *We keep land in the hands of residents, not investors.*

"Oh my God." I took out my own phone so I could send Paulette's nephew a late email. "Kathleen, this might actually work."

She crossed her arms with a sly grin. "I told you the book club would save the day."

Pure gratitude and elation had me grabbing her in a hug. She patted me on the back like what she'd done was insignificant. I'd never known her to be anything *but* significant.

"In case I don't make it known enough," I said softly, "you'll always be my mom, Kathleen. My real mom."

Her arms tightened around me. "You make it very known,

dear. Having you as a daughter has changed everything for me."

I pulled back, and she wiped the tears from my cheeks with her thumbs. "You're nothing like her, Tabitha. You never have been. You forget how long I've known you, how long I've watched you choose *love* over anything else. That's the only way to make it through this world."

My smile was a little watery, but there was a sense of purpose and optimism coursing through my veins. "Some would say I learned how to love from the best."

"I have read a *lot* of romance novels in my book club."

I reached behind me to grab the newly popped popcorn from the microwave. "Do you know Alice O'Callaghan? I believe she'd make a fabulous new member."

She waved her hand through the air. "Let's get to the juicy stuff. What are you going to do about that hunky friend of yours?"

I sputtered out a laugh. "I thought you wanted to make sure I was making the choice for me and not the hunky friend I'm super-duper in love with."

"I do. And it's clear that you are, and I'm glad that you're staying for you." She grabbed my shoulders. "But, honey, you can tell that man loves you from space."

My hands flew to my cheeks, as nervous as I was giddy. "Everything is a little messed up between us right now, but I want to show him how much I love him. How much this neighborhood adores him. I want to show him that he's been the hero of this story all along."

More than that, even. He was part of my story now, and I never wanted that to change.

I began tapping out an email to the land bank as a shower of sparkling ideas went off in my brain. "What should I go with as a subject line?" I asked. "Something like *Please respond—the fate of a tiny park and also true love is on the line*?"

"It'll certainly get his attention," she mused.

I set the phone down, tapping my fingers against my lips. I couldn't stop thinking about the first morning Dean and I had spent together, when I told him I'd throw him a parade in his honor just because. The thought of a parade certainly fit my desperate urge to demonstrate my feelings for him. But Dean never wanted flashy and he despised being the center of attention.

My phone pinged with a message. It was Paulette's nephew, with a quick response: *I know it's late, but I've already been briefed on what needs to happen with the property on Tenth and Emily Streets, and we're prepared to help. Can you talk now?*

"Kathleen."

"Yeah, hon?" She was pouring popcorn into tiny bowls, big hoop earrings jangling.

"I have an idea that is probably impossible to pull off in a day, but if we pull it off, I think we can save the pocket park from getting bought by Oswald."

She gave me a knowing look.

"And show Dean how much I love him."

She seemed pleased with that answer, picking up her own phone and typing furiously. "Then it's a good thing I've got a book club already mobilized and ready to help. And you know they just *adore* a happily ever after."

THIRTY-EIGHT
DEAN

I knocked on Tabitha's door, then shoved my hands into my pockets to keep them still. There was some bit of commotion in the lot to my right. I could hear music and people laughing. I ignored it the way I'd ignored every other distraction today—Rowan's calls, my parents stopping by, Harry's pissed-off emails. I'd woken up this morning without the sweet warmth of Tabitha's body draped over mine, and everything disappeared except my one goal. It was as if I'd stepped back into the ring the first few seconds after the gong went off, when every sound went silent and every person vanished except the one across from me.

I'd been much less of a machine since Tabitha had tumbled into my lap. But I didn't mind harnessing some of that old focus so I could do what she did all the time. Leap without looking. To give in to what I wanted, without holding back.

The door opened. Tabitha stood there, barefoot, in a short white summer dress. Her brown eyes landed on mine, pink lips curving into a pretty smile.

She was everything that I ever wanted.

Those eyes widened. "Dean."

"Hi."

"What are you..." She glanced nervously over at the lot. "Sorry, I thought you'd be with Rowan today?"

I arched an eyebrow. "He called me a few times, but I didn't pick up. I was busy. Working on things to show you." I looked down at the ground. Took a step closer and let my gaze rise to hers again. "Can I come in?"

She blinked at me, looking stunned. Until she stepped back inside and said, "Of course" in a shaky voice.

I stepped past her, much too aware of her body heat. The freckles on her bare shoulders. I carefully slid two pieces of paper from my pocket and sat on the edge of her couch. I saw her peek out the front curtains before refocusing on me.

"Is everything okay?" I asked.

"Yeah, I just wasn't expecting you." She ran a hand through her red hair. My fingers ached to touch her there. She sat down next to me, our bodies apart, eyes glued together. A flush rose up her neck. I wondered if she was replaying us here yesterday. The casual way I'd shrugged everything off. As if she'd been a temporary fascination, when nothing could have been further from the truth.

I dropped my elbows to my knees. I smoothed open the first sheet of paper and handed it to her. "This is a list of ideas I've been working on to save the park and keep Oswald Properties from buying it. I have no idea if they'll work. But while I was researching, I saw so much evidence of what you always talked about. People doing the right thing without being asked. Neighbors helping neighbors. Communities fighting for their rights. No wonder you love what you do, Tabitha. And I'm sorry about being so pessimistic and unhelpful yesterday. I'm sure I came off as an asshole."

Tabitha's lips quirked. "You're not an asshole, Mr. Machine. No matter how hard you scowl."

I rubbed a hand down my jaw, grateful for her teasing after a day without it. "It still wasn't fair to you to leave you hanging. To walk off, pissed, while you rallied the block." I tapped the edge of the sheet. "I'd like to talk to you about some of the ideas. See what we can do, even if you're in Austin. If a condo gets built there, I know we'll all be disappointed. We could go back to the drawing board and start a new community project though. Long as we don't give up."

She laughed, sounding delighted. "Actually, you don't have —"

I gently touched her knee. "If it's okay, I'll lose my nerve if I don't say the next part. I've been practicing all morning."

Her eyes searched mine as I swallowed past a knot of fear in my throat. Tabitha clasped my hand in hers, shifting until we were pressed together. The knot loosened. "Go ahead," she said.

It was time to leap.

"I don't really have words for how sorry I am about yesterday and everything I said before rushing off to that meeting. Especially since you'd shared so much. About your mom, what she did to you. I know being open about stuff like that is like your worst nightmare."

Her eyes shone, but one corner of her mouth lifted. "Like the Lavender Center all over again."

I squeezed her hand. "Exactly. And right after you told me, I took that call from Harry, angry and out of it. Everything happened so fast then. With the park. With the Vegas job. I never got to say thank you for allowing me to know something so private and painful. You're incredibly brave, Tabitha, and strong in a way I don't think you see."

This had bothered me all damn day—a nagging feeling

that one of the many things I'd done yesterday morning was be a shitty friend and listener. There were rules in our support group to acknowledge how raw people felt after sharing. Raw and usually scared.

I'd stormed off and left her there.

"You deserve true happiness. Not the shallow kind you have to fake so everyone around you is comfortable." I was holding her hand, so I felt a tremor go through her.

"I felt safe with you yesterday morning," she said. "You were the first person I'd ever told. I know everything kind of... imploded after that, but there's a reason why I chose you, Dean. You always made me feel like I could be myself around you. You still do."

My nerves were being chased away by a tenuous hope. I lifted her hand and pressed my lips to the inside of her wrist. My eyes rose to meet hers. There was no mistaking the emotion glittering there.

"Tabitha," I said roughly, "I was dishonest with you from the beginning. I never...it was impossible for me to consider spending time with you in a way that was casual. You know how I felt about you when we were in school. How much I admired you. The second I saw you at Benny's I started falling in love with you."

She was trembling now, tears on her cheeks. But her smile was dazzling.

"I let you believe I was fine with our arrangement. I wasn't," I said firmly. "I wasn't *ever* fine with it. Even if you getting me to have fun again was exactly what I needed. It's not a secret that I've been wandering around lost and frustrated since retiring. Wound tight and letting the opinions of an entire industry make me feel guilty for a decision I'm proud of. But I was still worried that I'd never be good at anything else but fighting. You made me remember that I was a human being again. Not a machine. You made me remember that my life was mine, my body was mine, my choices were mine. I didn't think I'd ever experience the way I felt as a kid ever again. Carefree. Enjoying things without rules behind them. Leaping without looking."

Tabitha was still quiet, sensing that I needed to reach the end of the speech I'd practiced. Her body language was anything but—I thought she might levitate straight off the couch. Every time I saw her smile, I was helpless not to return it. Reaching into my pocket, I slid the second item across the table. Her eyes went wide when she realized what it was.

"Dean," she started.

"I officially turned down the commentator job in Vegas," I said.

Her mouth dropped open. "You did?"

I nodded. "I don't want to be Dean the Machine again. I'm not a person who wants to make money off a sport I love but that isn't my home anymore. That isn't a place I can trust anymore. Being a pro gave me a feeling of power and identity and purpose that was really addicting. I think I've been chasing that feeling ever since. Sometimes in wrong places, like taking a job I didn't want so I could feel like a big deal." I smiled, the next words making a whole lot of sense to me. "I'm staying here, and I'm gonna run the senior food program at the rec center. I convinced Eddie to sign up, so I'm off to an okay start."

She laughed, sounding relieved, wiping the tears from her eyes. "That's better than an okay start. That's brilliant. You're going to do so much good for our neighborhood, Dean."

I couldn't ignore my heart's reaction to the words *our neighborhood*. Or how passionately Tabitha spoke them.

I tapped the ticket. "I already asked Rowan if I could have some time off, maybe in a few months. To come see you." I gathered my remaining courage from a source I knew came from my family. "Tabitha, I couldn't care less where you live if you still want to be together. If you still want to be with me. I know none of this is ideal. But I can't turn my back on fighting for you. Fighting to love you. My parents—" My voice cracked. "My parents have had to fight for their love, their family, their right to be here for their entire lives. Alexis and Eric have had to fight. All those people in our support groups having to demand their right to exist. I walked out the door yesterday out of fear and my own self-doubt. I don't ever want to let that get between us again."

Tabitha launched herself into my arms. I barely had a second to realize I was holding her warm, soft body—barely a second to understand that just twenty-four hours apart had wrecked me. Then her mouth was on mine, hands holding my face, and she was kissing me. I speared my fingers into her hair and drank her in, pouring all of my hope and yearning into the space between our breaths. She pulled back just a few inches, still straddling me. Still cradling my face in her palms.

"I'm not going to Texas," she said breathlessly. "I officially, well, broke that contract in Austin, though I was able to hook them up with a videographer friend who's on her way out there now to take my spot. But I'm staying in South Philly, Dean."

Gratitude had me kissing her again for a long, sweet minute. Until we both trembled. "You're coming home for good?"

She nodded, eyes bright. "Last night, I realized a couple things all at once. That I had been punishing myself for the role I thought I played in the worst years of my family's life. Always leaving so I could stay one step ahead of my own guilt and regret. Never letting myself be truly vulnerable with anyone." She touched my lips. "Until you. It gave me the courage to tell my family everything."

I curled my hands up her back and pulled her closer.

"They'd been holding on to their own secrets from that time. Their own guilt. We were all trying to protect each other from the worst of what our mother did. But all those secrets, all those white lies, they weren't allowing us to heal together. Hiding those parts of myself also meant I hid them from you. Pretended I wanted a sexy summer fling when the truth is..."

I held her face. Swiped her tears away with my thumbs. There was no sound, no distractions. I was only focused on the woman of my dreams.

"The truth is I knew from the very beginning that what I felt for you was different," she whispered, voice thick. "That it was precious and rare and deserving of my honesty and true feelings. Instead, I pushed you away and told you I wasn't interested in anything real over and over. I am so sorry, Dean. I'm desperately, head over heels in love with you, and I had no idea it could be this beautiful—"

I had Tabitha on her back on the couch a second later. We reached for each other at the same time, mouths crashing together in a possessive kiss. I broke us apart to hold her face, our gazes locked. "I'm desperately in love with you, Tabitha Tyler. You're everything that I was missing in my life."

Her smile became laughter, filled with relief. And that sound became a muffled, pleased moan as I kissed her in earnest. Those luscious, tattooed thighs hooked around my waist. I licked down her throat as her nails bit into my back. I slid my hand down her leg until I could palm her pussy, already hot and wet against my fingers. Her back arched at the contact.

"Why are we always having sex on couches?" she sighed. "And why are we always wearing *clothes*?"

I nipped at her ear. Circled her clit with my fingers. "Do you want me to stop so we can move?"

"No, no," she laughed. "Please...God, I need you."

I hooked my fingers into her underwear and slid it down her legs, tossing it to the ground. Our mouths on each other were relentless. The kiss deepened. I returned my hand to her folds, teasing her clit, circling her opening. Tabitha moaned and whimpered against my lips, tongue stroking against mine. She fisted my shirt, clinging to my shoulders, writhing beneath me. Raw power coursed through my veins. It was the confident knowledge that the woman I loved also loved me. It was a deep gratitude for the connections that brought us back together. It was her vulnerability. Her openness. That charming smile and goofy humor coaxing me back to a life filled with color.

It made every other type of power I'd felt in my life pale in comparison.

Her hands landed on the zipper of my shorts, fingers clumsy. "Now, Dean," she begged. "I want you, here. Just like this."

We made quick but awkward work of kicking off my shoes and tearing off my shorts. We were laughing by the end, my lips traveling over her hair, across her face. "The next time we do this," I said, dragging my cock against her. "We will be naked. We will be in a bed. We will not be on a couch or against a door or in a shower or the back seat of a fucking truck."

"I completely agree," she said, still giggling until I hooked her knee high and thrust my cock deep in one fluid motion. I groaned raggedly, overwhelmed with too many sensations. I pulled back a few inches. Gave her a few slow, shallow strokes that became fast and deliberate. I drove between her legs with our lips close, kisses messy, teeth nipping at skin. She grabbed my ass, urging me faster.

"So close...so close," she cried. Her internal walls were squeezing tight, pushing me to the brink. I reached between us to caress her clit, and she gasped.

"I love you," I whispered.

"I love you too. I love... Yes, oh God." Tabitha came, taking me with her, and my climax was earth-shattering and satisfying in a new and different way. We lay together, panting and sprawled on the couch. When I finally had the strength to lift my head, Tabitha was flushed and gazing at me like I was the love of her life.

"How was that astral plane?" she asked, brow raised.

Once I started laughing, I couldn't stop. She held me like the other night, when I wasn't happy but in agonizing pain. Both times I was in love with her. This time, we had a future to look forward to.

"You're really staying here?" I asked.

"I really am," she said, brushing a curl from my forehead. "I'm staying because I miss my family and I've wandered long enough. Because I love this place all the way in my soul and leaving it again seemed impossible. But even if you were going to Vegas, I would have done the same thing you did. Buy a ticket. Commit to this no matter what. Fight for our love."

I cleared my throat. "In that case, can I take you on a date?"

She blushed adorably. "You can take me on a hundred dates." Her eyes slid to the plane ticket I'd bought. "Eric and Alexis told me they've always wanted to go to Austin for a family vacation. We could donate that ticket to them, and I could buy the other one. They deserve it."

"Perfect." I ghosted my lips across her temple. "And I'll come up with some first date ideas."

A blast of music from the street had her pushing up to peek over the couch and out the window. "Oh shit. It's already time." She started wiggling out from under me, the exact opposite of what I wanted. "We gotta get going, Mr. Machine." She paused as she was sliding her underwear back on. "Is that still an appropriate nickname, or would you like another one?"

I stroked my knuckle up her throat. "I like that one."

"Good. And from now on I will formally be known as Dean's Lady."

I grinned and tried to drag her down to the couch. "Where are we going? And can it be back to bed?"

She pursed her lips. "We will definitely be spending a lot of time in bed. Later. Much later. Because first I've got a spontaneous-and-fun activity lined up for us."

She tossed me my shorts, waggled her eyebrows. I stood slowly, getting redressed. Enjoyed the way her eyes trailed up and down my semi-naked body. "Does it involve a dessert?"

"It's way more adventurous than that." She opened the door and peered out. Whatever she saw there had her looking ecstatic.

"Are we running up something? Or doing something touristy?"

"We're stealing the Liberty Bell. Are you in, or are you out?"

I shook my head, laughing against my hand. "I'm never getting that innocent reputation back, am I?"

She paused, hand on the doorknob. "Do you still want it?"

"Hell no."

She crooked her finger. "Then follow me."

Intrigued, I followed Tabitha into the hot summer sunshine. Now that the haze of telling Tabitha I loved her had lifted, I was aware that the pocket park was filling with people. And food. And music.

"What..." I started, dazed. She held my hand and tugged me down the sidewalk until we stood in front of what had been an abandoned, trash-filled lot.

And before that, the lifelong home of a cherished neighbor.

"What's going on?" I asked. There was a grill heating up. My parents were dancing. Kids were running through the gardens. It was still unfinished, would need time and work. But there were string lights hanging from the wall down to the fence. Paper lanterns on the tables. Flowers blooming. A sign, in the front, that read *Welcome to Annie's Pocket Park*.

"Tabitha?" I glanced over and was swept away by the joy on her face.

"Surprise," she sang softly. "Late last night, a member of Kathleen's book club got me connected with a land bank here in the city. They do the opposite of what Oswald Properties does. They purchase abandoned lots from the city but then give full control of their care and maintenance to the neighborhood. For things like parks and community gardens. We were lucky because Oswald hadn't purchased it yet, so the land bank swept in with the paperwork to purchase it at auction. It'll take a few weeks for everything to finalize, but at the end, this lot will be yours. Ours." She turned to me, cupping my cheek. "Kathleen's book club and all the neighbors were happy to plan a classic Tenth Street block party totally last minute. Rowan and your parents were supposed to be distracting you all day so that you wouldn't notice."

I arched an eyebrow. "So that's why they wouldn't leave me alone. But it wouldn't have mattered. I was too focused on figuring out how to show you how much I loved you."

Her lips curved. "You definitely showed me."

I rubbed a hand across my mouth, stunned at the joy surrounding us.

"The neighbors wanted to celebrate the good news that the park was saved. And I was very happy to celebrate *you*, Dean Knox-Morelli. As was this group of people, our found family, who adore you so very much."

Eddie and Alice sat on their bench with Pam. Kathleen was serving punch with Tabitha's dad. Tabitha's sister and brother-in law were showing the garden to her niece. Rowan held a beer while dancing with my parents, a goofy grin on his face. Neighbors spread out, eating, laughing. Music filled the street. The skyline rose in the distance as people walked by, joining in the festivities.

Weeks ago, I would have stood off to the side, guarded. Ready for stares and whispers. Unsure of my place. Now I stood hand in hand with Tabitha, prepared to face the world together.

I looked down at the woman who'd been part of that transformation. The woman I'd admired even as a teenager, when I had no clue how we'd come back together. She caught me staring and winked. Then she cleared her throat loudly. Everyone around us stilled, then cheered. Tabitha pointed at my chest. *They're cheering for you,* she mouthed. I didn't miss the tears in my parents' eyes. I didn't miss Rowan, raising his beer to me with a wide smile.

I decided to leap without looking, hooking an arm around Tabitha's waist for a kiss that dissolved into laughter. Another cheer went up, with a few wolf whistles mixed in.

"They're cheering for you too," I whispered.

She held my cheeks, still grinning. "They'll be talking about us around the kiddie pool for years."

"Let 'em," I said, pressing a kiss to her forehead. Then she was tugging me toward the dancing. And Rowan was cranking up the music. Tabitha twirled ahead of me, opening her arms to her sister as she ran toward her. I couldn't help but smile as we were welcomed by our neighbors, our found family. Our home.

Tabitha spun around, searching for me. When she caught my eye, stars exploded across my vision. So did the planets, the moon, the sun.

She'd made me a believer. And was everything I'd been missing all along.

EPILOGUE

TABITHA

One Year Later

I stood in front of the steps at the art museum and waited for my dark-and-stormy boyfriend to arrive. He'd sent me a text message while I was filming that said: *Up for a spontaneous activity?*

I said yes, of course. One year in and I was still helpless to resist that man. He'd told me to wait for him here, although I was disappointed not to see his old truck pulling up. It'd been a while since we'd put the back seat to better, sexier use.

Not ten seconds later, Dean Knox-Morelli was strolling toward me down the sidewalk with those broad shoulders and that shy half grin. My stomach dipped, filling with butterflies—a physical reaction to his presence that only heightened the longer we were together.

I propped my hands on my hips. "I'm here for my activity, Mr. Machine. Will you tell me what it is?"

Dean reached me, lifting my chin for a sweet kiss. "I can't. That'll ruin the surprise."

I hummed under my breath, eyebrow raised. He simply took my hand as he walked toward the middle of the steps we'd run together before getting drenched in a storm while hardcore making out.

"They're not predicting bad weather, are they?" I asked innocently.

His eyes burned. "You wish, troublemaker."

"A girl can dream." I waved my hand up the steps. "You're finally going to race me again, huh? My only request is that you don't double cheat like last time."

His lips twitched. "I thought I'd give you a chance to defend your good name."

I held on to his arm for balance as I reached behind to slide off my sandals. "While barefoot, at that." I tilted my head. "So before I race you and win, are you gonna tell me if you guys got the grant today?"

"We did."

"You *did*?"

A smile flew across his face. I hugged him, holding him tight. "That's fucking incredible news. The center deserves that funding."

He kissed my cheek before gently releasing me. "I have a theory that the video you made that we submitted about the senior food program, along with the grant, might have given us the boost we needed."

I shrugged. "Hey, I'm just the lady who holds the camera. Eddie and Alice are the real charmers."

"Rowan's worried that any day now his grandmother's gonna ask him to get her an agent."

I laughed. "I would pay actual money to see those two on the big screen."

Dean's journey toward a new identity, away from boxing and toward community work, was a long one and not without its bumps in the road. But over the past year, I'd witnessed even more of his confidence returning. And even more of his joy. Like all things, Dean approached his new job at the rec center with a dedication and focus that had the fledgling program growing faster than ever. Rowan arranged for Eddie to be paid as a consultant, and Dean brought him to the office frequently to pick his brain on the most helpful ways to approach our neighbors. Eddie helped Dean build trust in the community and gave him updates from the web of communication that kept South Philly folks in the know.

Dean did a damn good job of trust-building too. It was a regular occurrence for me to be walking home to Tenth Street from the subway stop and do a double take as I spotted my hunky boyfriend sitting in a lawn chair, casually chatting with a person who Rowan or Eddie had identified as needing extra food. Some folks were comfortable right away. Others were resistant, but Dean had always been known for his patience.

He was still recognized as Dean the Machine when we were out together, with the usual mixed bag of sympathy or judgment. More and more though, it was clients and neighbors saying hi, updating him on their grandchildren and how their gardens were doing in this heat.

While Dean was growing programs, I was busy rooting my business in Philadelphia, making contacts and focusing on stories about activism. The land bank had hired me almost right away. And working on Annie's pocket park had inspired me so much I started studying other urban green spaces in the city and the neighborhoods that had fought to build them. I had enough footage that I was toying with the idea of making a documentary. Although it was currently on the back burner for my newest project: making a movie to celebrate forty years of the Lavender Center helping people like me and Dean.

I hitched my thumb over my shoulder. "You're not nervous to lose to me, are you?"

He dropped down into a runner's lunge. "Win or lose, I still get nervous around you, Tabitha."

I mimicked him, fingers grazing the ground. "You did this last time, you know. Flirted with me until I was distracted."

He seemed to ponder that statement. But then he whispered, "Go" and went sprinting up the steps.

I briefly enjoyed the sight of Dean running and flirting with me on a warm night. Then I followed behind him, racing up the steps shoulder to shoulder, out of breath and trying not to laugh.

I'd spent my first six months back home living with Alexis and Eric and getting to be a full-time aunt to Juliet. It gave my family and me even more time to connect with each other without the burdensome weight of secrets or guilt. My sister and I had more conversations about our childhood, about the things in our past that still impacted our present. We were slowly but surely untangling the worst of it.

I spent every Tuesday night keeping my dad company at the diner, and every Saturday morning we rotated who cooked a big, Tyler family breakfast. The first time Dean cooked for all of us—wearing an apron and everything—I was teased mercilessly for my inability to stop staring at him. But I couldn't be blamed for the way Dean looked in the kitchen—forearms flexing as he flipped pancakes, a streak of powdered sugar on his cheek, the look of adorable apprehension as he waited to see if my dad liked the food.

He'd loved it, of course. Drew Tyler hadn't stopped being a fan just because Dean stopped boxing.

I'd moved in with Dean after I left my sister's house, and though I didn't have many things he made me feel at home. It helped that everything we did together was still as thrilling as it was comfortable. We spent a lot of weekends with our hands in the dirt, growing flowers in the gardens of the pocket park while that tiny space flourished all around us. The miracle of green things continued, as trees and grass and vegetables became a permanent fixture. Annie's Park became the place for block parties and barbecues, for cups of coffee and mindless gossip on summer nights.

It was a beautiful thing to behold.

Through it all, we took turns surprising each other with fun activities – some wild and adventurous, and others as sweet as sitting on our stoop, limbs entwined, and watching the city pass us by. One year in and making Dean smile was still my favorite thing to do. I'd never known that being in love had its own rush—of passion and tenderness, desire and intimacy. It was hot sex and quiet nights and teasing seduction and cozy mornings in bed.

Forget temporary. I wanted Dean *forever.*

We reached the top at the same time. He pulled me in for a kiss to celebrate, hands sliding up my spine as his firm lips made me dizzy with butterflies.

"I think we should call that a tie," he murmured. "Don't you?"

"I think we should go find a back seat."

He laughed against my hair, the vibrations sending goose bumps across my skin. He turned me gently until I was facing the famous view. His arms wrapped around me, his chest a solid wall of warmth.

"Before I met you tonight, I went to go see your family," he said. "I wanted to let them know what I was going to ask you. And to thank them—for loving you as much as I do. For supporting us this first year. I'm not sure what to do with the cat videos that Kathleen sends me, but Mom and Midge seem to like them."

I laughed, my body filling with a tingling awareness.

"They wanted me to let you know that depending on how things go, your dad's gonna shut down the diner for a big party tonight. Alexis and Eric are making the playlist. Kathleen's got cocktails. All of Tenth Street will likely show up, so you should prepare to do the twist with my parents."

I turned my head. "A party? For what?"

Dean wasn't standing there.

He was down on one knee, holding a very pretty ring.

For as long as I lived, I would never forget this moment. Would never forget the look of true love on Dean's face.

"This ring belonged to my grandmother," he said, voice trembling at the end. "When I told my parents I was going to ask you to marry me, Midge got this ring out immediately. She told me she was saving it for me. Apparently, they'd been waiting for me to ask for it since the day you moved back home."

I laughed, wiping my eyes. "They must have strategized around the kiddie pool."

His smile was adorable. "This is the grandmother who used to throw huge Pride parties for my parents, to celebrate them and their love. She was a lot like you. Bold and big-hearted. When I imagined slipping a ring on your finger, it was a ring worn by someone who would have celebrated who you are, Tabitha."

Tears fell down my cheeks without me even realizing. Which was wild because I was smiling so much my face hurt.

"I want to spend the rest of my life with you," he said. "I want to tell stories with you and go on spontaneous adventures and build parks together and sit on our stoop eating water ice. I want to give in to pleasure with you, give in to a love that is loud and takes up space. No holding back. No hesitating. I love you—" He paused, swallowed. "Tabitha, I love you more than I ever thought was possible." He raised the ring. My heart spun, nerves sparkling. "Will you marry me?"

I dropped to my knees in front of Dean, too emotional to stand. *"Yes,"* I said. "Yes. Yes. Nothing would make me happier, Dean Knox-Morelli, than marrying you and loving you forever."

The ring would have slid on easily if not for the fact that we were both shaking too much. But the instant it was on, I fisted my hands in his shirt and kissed him for what felt like hours. Dean was laughing, kissing me back, and when I gripped his face his cheeks were wet.

There were too many threads in this love story to count. But they'd brought us here, to this moment, holding each other on steps high above the city as the world spun and dazzled.

We were finally home.

BONUS EPILOGUE

DEAN

I tugged off the tie I was attempting to fix and tossed it on the ground.

"What the hell do you wear on a first date with a woman you're already in love with?" I grumbled to Rowan, who was leaning against the door to my bedroom with a barely hidden smirk.

"I don't really know, big guy," he said. "But you're missing the point. You don't have to impress Tabitha tonight. You already got the girl."

I re-buttoned my white shirt and eyed my own reflection in the mirror. "She still deserves to be impressed, though."

Rowan was quiet, watching me. Then he said, "I see the student has become the teacher."

"You still know more about this stuff than I do."

He shook his head. "Not this. Not love and commitment and a real relationship. You're way past my experience. You're the expert, now."

I stopped fidgeting and faced him. "Do I look somewhat normal?"

I'd gone with a short-sleeved shirt with buttons and the darkest jeans and nicest non-running shoes I owned.

He grinned. "Yeah, dude. And you're gonna do great. You know Tabitha's probably getting dressed at her sister's house, just as nervous. Watching you two is like watching a Hallmark movie come to life, I swear to God."

"And what do you know about those movies?"

"I like a little romance at Christmas sometimes," he said behind me. "*Only* in my movies."

I ran my hand through my hair and snatched up my phone. "When you do fall in love and start doing a lot of stupid shit like I did, I promise not to be too much of an asshole about it."

He laughed, but I was only kinda joking. Maybe it was because I was now, as Rowan had pointed out, a walking advertisement for romance, but I didn't think it'd be long before he found himself where I was. Which was walking around dazed and with a permanent smile on my face, apparently like some kind of guy out of a Hallmark movie. All thanks to the red-haired ray of sunshine I was about to take on a first date.

I wouldn't have it any other way.

I glanced at my phone and froze with my hand on the door. "Your grandmother texted."

Rowan peered over my shoulder and whistled low under his breath. "If Alice O'Callaghan is dropping f-bombs then you better take the advice."

I'd received a string of messages from her while getting ready – HAVE FUN WITH TABITHA TONIGHT SHE'S A LOVELY GIRL and also SHE REALLY LIKES YOU DEAN WE ALL CAN TELL AND HAVE BEEN

TALKING ABOUT IT and finally DON'T FUCK THIS UP.

Once we started laughing, we couldn't stop.

"If you think this is bad, Mom and Midge stopped by this morning with the same advice," I said.

He shrugged. "She threw a block party for you, dude. In this neighborhood, that means she gets to stick around."

My stomach went hollow with excitement. Until a few days ago, I'd had to get used to the idea that Tabitha would be leaving on the next flight out of here. Not sticking around...*for good*. And even better...*with me*.

I slid my phone into my pocket and pulled open the door with a grin. "No one needs to worry about my intentions towards Tabitha."

He clapped me on the back as we walked down the front stoop. "Yeah, you've made that obvious."

Eddie walked by with Pam in his arms, just as I was locking the door behind me. He grunted a greeting and gave us a wave. "You getting ready to take Tabitha out?"

I nodded, looked down at my chest. "I look all right?"

He shrugged. "Sure." He glanced over his shoulder then took a step closer to us on the sidewalk. "Listen. Do you need any advice for tonight?"

"Advice?" I asked, brow arched.

"Yeah, like..." He dropped his voice. "Advice about women. I'm not some Lothario or nothing, but if you're nervous about going on a date, I might be able to help you out."

Rowan cracked a bemused smile.

I touched Eddie on the shoulder. "Thanks, but I feel okay. This isn't our first time...hanging out together."

In fact, I'd spent the morning with a sleepy and adorable Tabitha in my bed for the tenth day in a row.

"Ah," Eddie said, blushing a little. "Then you'll do great.

BONUS EPILOGUE

Also, just passing along a general message but, uh...don't fuck it up, okay?"

I shook my head and chuckled. "I promise I won't."

Rowan squeezed Eddie's shoulder and began walking with him, back towards his house. "Come on, Eddie. The sooner we let Dean go on his date, the sooner Tabitha will come by and give us all the details."

I shot them a look they both cheerfully ignored. Rowan pointed at me. "Remember. You're the expert now, big guy."

I nodded my thanks and then I set off toward Tabitha's sister's house, where she was staying while getting resettled in Philly. A few neighbors were sitting on the benches in Annie's Park, and Natalia waved to me from her spot watering the new tomato plants hanging from the fence. The block party had gone past midnight, the crowd ebbing and flowing as the evening wore on, with a constant stream of food and music. Tabitha and I had laughed and danced with the neighbors for hours, my body loose and happy as I realized she wasn't leaving. And I wasn't leaving. Because the two of us were together.

Feeling comfortable enough to actually dance in front of people hadn't been a reality for me since I was a kid. But that was the Tabitha Effect, opening parts of myself I'd closed off out of fear.

I moved through the busiest section of the Italian Market, past the vendors closing up their shops for the night and people wandering toward bars and restaurants. At the corner of Seventh Street, I headed toward Alexis and Eric's house, feeling that hum of nerves I always got before seeing her. The anticipation wasn't the same as stepping under the ropes before a match, or even the same as the two weeks we'd just spent together. This moment felt different—the beginning of something new and unknown.

Eric opened the door as I arrived, leaning against the wall

BONUS EPILOGUE

with an easy smile. He shook my hand and then indicated the staircase behind him. "The Tyler sisters have sent me to keep you occupied while Tabitha finishes getting ready. You all right? You a little nervous?"

I rubbed the back of my neck. "More than I thought I'd be."

"I felt that way on my first couple dates with Alexis," he said. "It was a different kind of nerves. Probably because I knew she was going to be the last first date I ever went on."

I released a breath I didn't realize I'd been holding. Flashed Eric a grateful smile. "I needed to hear that."

Tabitha appeared behind him then, ducking under his arm and flying down the steps. "I'm here, I'm here, late as usual, but in my defense, I think I look amazing. And *wowza*, so do you, Mr. Machine."

I blinked in awe as she grabbed my hand, registered her polka-dot dress and red, curving lips and high heels.

My last first date.

Alexis came around next to Eric in the doorway. He looped an arm around her shoulders.

"Wowza, indeed," Alexis said. "Dean, you should know that Eric and I had to mount a pretty serious defense to protect you from Dad and Kathleen being here with their video cameras."

"Like two proud parents sending their daughter and her boyfriend off to prom," Tabitha said, wrinkling her nose. "It's only because they might be more obsessed with Dean than I am."

I squeezed her hand in mine. "All of Tenth Street kindly requested that I don't—" My lips twitched. "Fuck this up. You've got a lot of fans on that block."

Tabitha touched her ear. "I can just hear the gossip now."

We shared a smile until Eric coughed and broke our focus.

BONUS EPILOGUE

"We'll, uh, see you in the morning, Tab. Try not to get into too much trouble."

Alexis winked at us, blew a kiss to her sister, and then pulled Eric inside. Finally alone, I stepped back to admire my date. She did a little twirl for me, skirt floating in a circle, dark eyes sparkling.

"What do you think?" she asked.

I dipped my head to her cheek. "Too beautiful for words. As always."

Her hands slid up my chest. "And I stand by my *wowza*."

Laughing, I tucked her against my side and wrapped an arm around her shoulders, walking us toward our destination.

"I hope it's okay that I told Eric and Alexis I'd be staying the night," she said. "Maybe it's a bit presumptuous following our first real date, but I did wake up in *your* bed this morning, so I thought the odds were in my favor."

I ducked into an empty side alley and gently pushed Tabitha up against the brick wall. Gripping her waist, I bent down and stole a sweet, lingering kiss. We parted with a sigh.

"Hi," I said.

"Hi back," she replied.

I nuzzled the shell of her ear. "You'll definitely be waking up in my bed tomorrow morning," I murmured. "After I have you in the shower. And maybe the couch for old time's sake."

Her husky laughter sent chills along my skin. "So *cocky*, Mr. Machine."

Our next kiss was harder, tripling my heart rate and quieting every other sound around us. I held her chin, kept her still, and we didn't stop until we were breathless. Her long lashes fluttered, eyes pinned to mine.

"I was a little nervous," she whispered.

"Me too," I said. "I don't go on a lot of dates."

"Well, you're doing great so far." She reached up and

brushed a strand of hair from my forehead. "Tonight is *more* than a first date. That would imply we were strangers instead of the truth."

"Which is?"

Those red lips curved into a pretty smile. "We're already in love."

I captured her hand and held it against my chest, throat tight with emotion. "I love you, Tabitha."

She ghosted her lips over mine. "I love you, Mr. Machine. Consider this date *one* out of the one hundred we're planning."

I tugged her back into the busy street and tossed her a grin. "Gladly. And I hope you like Ralph's."

Her eyes widened as we stopped in front of one of the Italian Market's most famous—and oldest—restaurants. She clapped her hands together and sighed.

"Dean. This used to be my favorite place to eat when I was a kid. Next to the diner, of course."

I lifted a shoulder. "Alexis might have helped a little."

She bit her lip, smile growing. "I'm so happy to hear that."

The hostess showed us to a private table inside—dark mahogany walls, candles on the table, a bottle of wine already opened. We didn't break eye contact once as napkins were set and the wine was poured and the menu specials were rattled off by a server. Our hands stayed linked under the table, the candlelight reflected on her face, as beautiful as ever.

I blinked, seeing stars again.

"When we were in school together," I said, "I used to dream about asking you on a date. I was scared as hell so never did it. But I think tonight, this date, is the one we were meant to go on."

Her eyes shone, fingers tightening in mine. "This was our destiny all along. Thank you for bringing me home, Dean."

Leaning across the table, I kissed her, not caring who saw. "Thank you for making South Philly my home again."

A blush rose in her cheeks. "If this is what all of our dates are going to be like, I'll be real-life swooning in no time."

I lifted her hand and pressed a kiss to her palm. "Making you swoon sounds like the kind of spontaneous fun I can get behind."

"And you're already surprising me with food and/or drink," she said, pointing at the table.

I laughed. "I had this gorgeous, trouble-making neighbor who spent the past couple weeks helping me live again. So I learned from the best."

She grinned. "I had to work hard to earn my title as Dean's Lady."

I held her gaze. "The title was always yours, Tabitha."

"Good," she said. "I intend to keep it."

Hours later, Tabitha and I closed down the restaurant without realizing it, talking and flirting until the other tables emptied and we were the only ones left.

As first dates went, it was the very best.

A NOTE FROM THE AUTHOR

Dear reader,

Go birds, baby! Thank you *so much* for reading this cute South Philly romance. Dean and Tabitha's adorable love swooped in and *totally* stole my heart while writing them.

I have a lot of favorite scenes from this friends-to-lovers romance: Tabitha falling into Dean's lap at the bar, their water ice date, their – *ahem* – date at the art museum, when she's doing the twist with Dean's parents, when Dean and Eddie talk about his food needs at the end, *Pam!!*, all of the neighbors on Tenth Street, Alice's all-caps text messages, Rowan being charming, Tabitha's entire family, Kathleen's boozy book club saving the day, the – *ahem, again* – lingerie scene, their sweet memories of growing up together and going to the Lavender Center...and on and on.

If it wasn't obvious, I started writing this book in March 2021 – one year into the pandemic – and it was the soft, warm hug that I needed at the time. I was so grateful to be able to escape into the happy, cozy world of one single block in South

Philly...and to write about neighbors coming together to help each other out.

It is often said – correctly – that no one loves Philadelphia as much as Philadelphians do. As a born-and-raised resident of Delaware County (Delco, for those in the know), and having lived in South Philly for more than three years, I can confirm that those from this underdog city *love it* with a ferocity that's hard to explain. Even as they criticize it or are disappointed by it, Philly is a city of deep roots, family connections and close-knit neighborhoods that will fight to protect one another when they need to.

I have loved this city for my entire life – even when I lived far from it, like Tabitha does in this story, I was always overjoyed to step off a plane at the airport and breathe in that sense of *home*.

On the Ropes is meaningful to me for a number of reasons – and not just that it's set in my hometown and in my current neighborhood. As a bisexual lady, I was thrilled to write my very first bisexual main character. The second that Tabitha appeared on the page – with her goofy humor and loveable charm – I felt called to tell her story through the lens of being a queer woman and the many unique ways that her sexuality shaped her life, her struggles and triumphs, her reactions and her relationships to those around her. I'm always overjoyed to see bisexual folks get their own happily-ever-after...and for Tabitha to find that love with Dean was extra special. Dean's own experiences being raised by gay parents also shaped who he was and his world view, and he was, in so many ways, the perfect person for Tabitha – kind, compassionate, thoughtful, and understanding of the things they experienced and shared in their support group.

As a bisexual person in a straight-passing marriage, it was a privilege to write a love story that looked like my own and to

A NOTE FROM THE AUTHOR

celebrate love, identity and relationships in *all* of their many beautiful and unique forms. For those who have been made to feel invisible, who have had their identities questioned or been told they are simply "confused" or going through a phase – I see you.

And I based The Lavender Center on two groups here in Philly serving the LGBTQ+ community: The William Way Center and the Attic Youth Center.

Throughout the pandemic in Philly, there have been incredible acts of mutual aid and community care that shaped and informed many aspects of this book. Our city does have many abandoned lots for a variety of (often complicated) reasons, but there are also many, many people who have done exactly what Dean and Tabitha have – created a green space that serves their neighborhood. It has also been an honor to volunteer with South Philly's network of community fridges and pantries, which operate with a "take what you need, leave what you can" mentality and have helped so many of our food-insecure neighbors keep food on their table during this tumultuous time.

On the Ropes mentions several beloved Philly landmarks – John's Water Ice on Seventh and Christian Streets is a must, as are all of the Italian Market and the Philadelphia Museum of Art (including those Rocky steps!) The Broad Street Diner (where Tabitha's dad works) is indeed open 24 hours a day, seven days a week.

I imagined Dean and Tabitha's block to be located in a part of South Philly between Passyunk Square and Little Saigon – a beautiful and culturally diverse neighborhood, where many different languages are spoken (Italian, Spanish, Vietnamese, Mandarin and more), and there are as many churches as there are Buddhist temples. There are also two neighborhood-based nonprofits doing amazing work: SEAMAAC (which supports

A NOTE FROM THE AUTHOR

and serves immigrants and refugees *and* has turned a lot of abandoned lots into community gardens!) and Juntos (a community-led, Latinx human rights organization in South Philly).

The nonprofit in Sacramento that Tabitha refers to in the beginning of the story – the one that helps kids become published authors – is 100% based on 916 Ink, one of my favorite organizations!

Thank you for spending time with Dean the Machine and Tabitha Tyler as they fell in love during a hot summer in South Philly. If you're near Tenth Street, swing by for a beer and some gossip. And don't forget to visit Annie's Park while you're there. The neighbors would *love* to see ya.

Love,
Kathryn

ACKNOWLEDGMENTS

I wrote, re-wrote and revised *On the Ropes* with the help and support of many incredible people. All of my gratitude goes to:

Faith, my best friend and developmental editor, who knew through the power of sisterhood *exactly* when I needed her to call me and give me the writerly pep talk I needed to type The End. I will never forget how loved, understood and supported I felt in that moment.

Jessica Snyder, my story and line editor, who very patiently listened to my (many) sleep-deprived voicemails as the *real* ending of this story came to me in a fit of inspiration – Leslie Knope-style – after I finally slept for more than twenty minutes. Her flexibility, knack for plot and eye for detail continues to impress me.

Korrie and Kalie, my sensitivity readers, who were kind and generous enough to offer feedback around Alexis and Eric's interracial relationship and biracial daughter and the ways in which racism and bigotry can cause the loss of family members you once trusted. I am immensely grateful for their time, wisdom, and sensitivity.

Jodi, Julia and Bronwyn, my beta readers, who continue to amaze me with their ability to spot the gaps, the pacing issues, the character nuances and all the missing pieces that make a book whole. This was a tough one, for a lot of different reasons, and I am so grateful for their patience and support.

The *giant* support system that gets me through every book: the Hippie Chicks (who are the *literal best*), Joyce and Tammy (also the literal best), Lucy, Claire, Pippa, LJ and Stephanie, who continue to be some of the best people in our romance community, and Tim, Rick and Dan who are directly responsible for the beautiful book you hold in your hand. When I say I couldn't do this without you all, I absolutely mean it.

My parents and brother, who are truly devoted to Philly and always have been. So many of our best family memories have taken place there – from strolling South Street, to going to concerts at WXPN, to our Christmas traditions in Center City. And it should be mentioned that they've *always* celebrated me for being who I am.

And finally for Rob, my husband, soulmate, and very favorite person to share a cold beer with on our stoop on a hot South Philly night. We've been very lucky to live in so many different places together but being with you makes every place a home. Of every love story, ours is my favorite one.

HANG OUT WITH KATHRYN!

Sign up for my newsletter and receive exclusive content, bonus scenes and more!
I've got a reader group on Facebook called **Kathryn Nolan's Hippie Chicks**. We're all about motivation, girl power, sexy short stories and empowerment! Come join us.

Let's be friends on
Website: authorkathrynnolan.com
Instagram at: kathrynnolanromance
Facebook at: KatNolanRomance
Follow me on BookBub
Follow me on Amazon

ABOUT KATHRYN

I'm an adventurous hippie chick that loves to write steamy romance. My specialty is slow-burn sexual tension with plenty of witty dialogue and tons of heart.

I started my writing career in elementary school, writing about *Star Wars* and *Harry Potter* and inventing love stories in my journals. And I blame my obsession with slow-burn on my similar obsession for The *X-Files*.

I'm a born-and-raised Philly girl, but left for Northern California right after college, where I met my adorably-bearded husband. After living there for eight years, we decided to embark on an epic, six-month road trip, traveling across the country with our little van, Van Morrison. Eighteen states and 17,000 miles later, we're back in my hometown of Philadelphia for a bit... but I know the next adventure is just around the corner.

When I'm not spending the (early) mornings writing steamy love scenes with a strong cup of coffee, you can find me outdoors -- hiking, camping, traveling, yoga-ing.

BOOKS BY KATHRYN

BOHEMIAN

LANDSLIDE

RIPTIDE

STRICTLY PROFESSIONAL

NOT THE MARRYING KIND

SEXY SHORTS

BEHIND THE VEIL

UNDER THE ROSE

IN THE CLEAR

WILD OPEN HEARTS

ON THE ROPES

Made in the USA
Columbia, SC
25 September 2024